Y0-DKB-976

River Stories

Tales from Bo Rockerville

River Stories

Tales from Bo Rockerville

Monte Smith

Pahsimeroi Press
P.O. Box 190442
Boise, ID 83709

ISBN 1-886694-01-X

River Stories

Eugene (Bo) Rocker, the "*River Master*," is one of the best whitewater paddlers in the world. But whitewater greatness isn't enough for Bo Rocker. He wants a movie career, and he'll do anything to get it. He's convinced that with the right break, he can parlay his paddlesport notoriety into a starring role in a major motion picture.

Bo's relentless quest for cinematic exposure takes him to the far corners of the globe, into the realm of Hollywood producers, Tibetan potentates, zany poets, exotic lovers, and two ill-tempered Yetis. No location is too remote, no river too forbidding, from the frigid headwaters of the Salween in Tibet, to tiny Cataract Creek in North Carolina . . . until it ends in an awesome canyon in the wilderness of central Idaho.

Get ready for a boat load of river adventure, in the company of such unforgettable characters as "Wild" Bill Barkley, the irrepressible poet and screenwriter; Claudette Remey, the queen of bondage; Hank Menzel, the gentle giant; Jennifer Lemke, the multimillionaire restauranteur; the outrageous Swami Akalananda, practitioner of levitation and the art of walking on water; Frieda Thompkins, wild woman of the Cumberland Plateau; Jacques Povlsen, Hollywood producer; and lovely Amy "Cascade" Reynolds, whose main interest was looking out for Bo – until that fateful day on the upper Deadwood.

So climb on board the Bo Rocker Express for a whirlwind tour of wild rivers, exotic movie sets, tumultuous romance, grandiose dreams, and a first-ever look into the private lives of Yetis. It's all part of . . .

River Stories

River Stories

The pilot rolled the helicopter onto its side, giving his passengers an unimpeded look straight down into the canyon of the upper Deadwood River. Thousands of feet below, water was alternately crashing through mile-long rapids and disappearing into horrendous logjams. Shortly upstream of the biggest rapid on the river, several rafts could be seen tediously making their way through the obstructions.

"Holy of holies," Amy was saying, as she took her eyes from the sight below and quickly flipped through the thick river guidebook she was holding open on her lap. She found the right page and scanned the text. "They rate the river Class V in here, and that's when it's free of logjams." She looked again at the swirling, sucking water. "What kind of place is that? And who are those people down there?"

Bo said, "It's a film crew. Old friends of mine. I figure they might need a helping hand about now."

River Stories

River Stories

Hank Menzel stepped up on the porch of The Down Yonder Saloon, and heard the planking creak beneath his weight. It was a dilapidated old building; not a place he visited often. But it had always been one of Bo Rocker's favorite watering holes, and Hank missed his drinking buddy. He hadn't seen him in almost a year. He would have one drink for old times' sake, and then roll on down the road.

As he pushed open the door of the saloon, Hank heard the unmistakable sound of a chair splintering over somebody's head, followed by a cascade of shattering glass, and a cacophony of voices calling encouragement to the crowd favorite.

Big Hank Menzel, the gentle giant, edged open the door and stepped inside. He took one look around and muttered, "Oh, my goodness. Tell me it ain't so."

But it was so. Bo Rocker was back in town. The "River Master" was at it again, holding forth in his inimitable fashion.

Hank Menzel's life would never be the same.

And neither will yours, once you launch into . . .

River Stories

Other Books by Monte Smith

Southeastern Whitewater
(50 of the Best River Trips
from Alabama to West Virginia)

*A Paddler's Guide
to the Obed/Emory Watershed*

Rating Rapids and Rivers
(Development of the TRIP Scale)

Smokescreen
(A Novel)

Acknowledgements

With special thanks to Les Bechdel, Don Ellis, Mike Glasgow, Ed Grove, and Bobbi Smith for reading earlier drafts of this volume and offering helpful comments and recommendations.

Contents

On the Cover of Rolling Stone

Shortly after Doctor Walt Blackadar drowned on the South Fork of the Payette River, the *Idaho Statesman* published an editorial on river safety. The editorial concluded with this pithy observation:

> "He was the undisputed master of Idaho kayaking. If a man like Blackadar – a man who was first to run rivers that other experts considered impossible, a man whose kayaking skills were almost legendary – can die on an Idaho river, what are the odds for other kayakers?"

"Other kayakers? What about open boaters?"

Those were my thoughts as I hugged a makeshift eddy at the top of the biggest runnable drop in a canyon that Idaho paddlers now call Blackadars. They call it that because in the heart of the enormous chasm, between Lowman and Banks, lurks the rapid that took the legendary big-water paddler's life.

It wasn't Walt's rapid that I was sitting at the top of, though. I had already run Walt's drop. This one was even bigger, and all I knew about it was its name: Surprise.

1

After three months of living in Idaho, spring snow melt had finally arrived and this was my first trip down Blackadar Canyon. I'll admit I was tense – this river *did* kill the premier boater of an era. And the water underneath me was undeniably running high. We were riding the crest of spring snow melt, when rising temperatures finally penetrate Idaho's lofty Sawtooth Mountains, transforming tons of ice and snow to liquid, sending thousands of cubic feet of runoff every second flushing down the steep drainage of the Payette's South Fork.

But it wasn't just high water and the ghost of Blackadar on my mind. Something else was making me uncomfortable. Over the years I've developed my own way of running rivers. When faced with an unknown stretch of water, my modus operandi is to head on downstream, take the initiative, and outmaneuver whatever obstacles I encounter.

Yet in Blackadar Canyon, with its walls towering hundreds of feet on either side, with a rapid downstream chanting, "Come on down, the water's fine," with the stream pulsing by at six hundred miles an hour – well, it *looked* that fast – I found myself hugging a micro eddy at the top of an unknown rapid in order to let others run first.

Let others run first? What's going on here? Nobody in my paddling group had ever run this stretch either. For me, sitting in an eddy and waiting for somebody else to run a rapid first was a new experience – and I didn't like it.

The Most Precious Commodity in Paddlesport

On this trip, however, I had promised to let Willie Buckner run each rapid first whenever possible, in order to set up with his new toy, a miniature-format video camera, and thereby capture that most precious commodity in paddlesport: *Video.* Buckner had flown more than two thousand miles from

Nashville to paddle western rivers with me, and I felt obligated to assist him in his relentless video quest. And a *quest* is exactly what it was. Buckner, you see, is an editor – and editors are all basically alike. They're always after that elusive big story. A scoop, as Clark Kent and Lois Lane used to call it at the Daily Planet. The exclusive that will make them famous. The story they'll always be remembered for.

A friend of Buckner's works for *Sports Illustrated*. And while the national media guys can always get photographs of professional athletes, what they lack (and what the public increasingly demands) are genuine action shots of intrepid weekend quasi-athletes (people like you and me) doing stupid things like running outrageous rapids.

"They want shots of ordinary people doing exotic things," Buckner had explained. "Things way out there on the cutting edge. Things like running Niagara Falls on an inner tube, or throwing shyster lawyers off the New River Bridge. The kind of stuff Eugene (Bo) Rocker used to do all the time. If we can video something like that, my buddy will publish stills from it, and I'll write the text. Or better yet, we'll get Wild Bill Barkley to write it. You remember him, don't you? He used to pal around a lot with Bo Rocker. Just think, your picture could be on the cover of *Sports Illustrated*."

Uh, oh. Did he say on the cover? Why'd he have to say that?

Eugene (Bo) Who?

And why did he have to mention the notorious Eugene (Bo) Rocker? In all the years I paddled with Bo Rocker, as his photographs appeared in every outdoor and paddling magazine across the land, I never once got my picture in anything. And now, in retrospect, I know why. It was my river-running modus operandi: I was always out front, first to put on the river, first to challenge every rapid, and first, once the trip ended, to take off the river and head pell-mell for the nearest cultural oasis – some place like The Down Yonder Saloon.

And while I was at The Down Yonder, striving assiduously to improve my mind, Bo Rocker would lollygag around the takeout, telling outrageous lies, flirting with any woman who'd as much as look at him, cornering every editor and writer he spotted, and smiling like a hyena at anything resembling a camera lens. I'll never forget one trip with Bo on Chattooga Section IV. It was way back when we first started running that stretch. The water had run unusually high all spring – high enough to attract Walt Blackadar's attention in Idaho. When Walt arrived, it was running six feet on the US 76 bridge gauge, which was higher than most anybody had ever seen it. Undeterred, Walt put on the river and ran every rapid straight down the gut. When he came to the biggest drops, he'd pivot around and run them backwards, just to show off.

When Bo Rocker learned that he'd been upstaged by a sawbones from the Idaho hinterlands, he was outraged. He decided that one-upmanship was the proper revenge. If Walt could run the Chattooga in a *kayak* at high water, then Bo Rocker would run the Chattooga in a *canoe* at flood stage.

Back then, Bo thought of himself as a paddling purist; he paddled C1s, and nothing but C1s. He had little experience with canoes. But that didn't seem to concern him.

After contacting every writer and photographer and television reporter he knew, Bo practically dragged Kathleen Westenbroek and me to the Chattooga and harangued us into running the river with him.

Kathleen worked for one of the local rafting companies, and spent her free time training for the racing circuit. She could make the run if anybody could. She was tough. (She had to be; she had even dated Bo a couple of times.) As for me, I was still paddling a kayak at that time. It was several years later that major lumbar trauma sent me to an open canoe. I wasn't a top paddler like Bo or Kathleen, but I had the advantage of a bullet-proof roll.

And at the putin, I realized I'd be using my roll a lot that day. The water was even higher than when Blackadar made his descent a few days earlier. We couldn't tell exactly how much higher, because the flood had ripped the gauge off the US 76 bridge abutment and deposited it in some undisclosed downstream location.

Whatever the water level, everybody agreed there was plenty. The river was definitely on fast-forward; it was boogy-ing on downstream, producing swirlerdown eddies with four-foot walls. Kathleen and I were doing okay in our kayaks, although we were both getting knocked over regularly. Our rolls were our salvation. Some rapids would knock us over two or even three times, but we were strong little puppies; we'd been doing our sit-ups, and we were popping rolls almost before we'd go over. It was one of those magical days when everything was working. Upside-down was almost as much fun as right-side-up. We were zoned, and we were loving it.

By the time we approached the Five Falls region of Section IV, however, it was obvious that even Bo Rocker had bit off more than he could handle in a canoe. He had rolled that big barge more times than anybody had a right to expect, and we could tell from the look on his face that he'd already decided to abandon trip. He was standing up in his canoe, scanning the canyon walls, looking for some foot trail out of the Chattooga Trough, when he hit a big reaction wave, lost his balance, and pitched head-first out of his boat at the top of Entrance Rapid. He washed into Corkscrew, the second big drop in Five Falls, flailing and bellowing incoherently. He was flushed through the rest of Five Falls – the whole kit and caboodle – before we could catch up.

We finally caught him at Sock-em-Dog, where he was stuck in the hole at the base of the drop. After getting a rope to him, both Kathleen and I had to strain like mad to break him loose from the grip of the hydraulic.

You know how morose and sullen most people become after they take a bad swim? Not Bo Rocker. After we fished him out, the first thing he wanted to know was how many rolls of film had we snapped of his epic swim? He was incensed to learn that we'd been too busy saving him to shoot any pictures. When he finally settled down, he had the unmitigated temerity to tell lies about his swim all the way to the takeout. Floating the river in a canoe at flood stage hadn't been exciting enough for Bo Rocker, or so he said. He had *deliberately* jumped out of his boat to swim the Five Falls, just to prove it could be done, to show what a coward Walt Blackadar had been to stay in his boat through those drops. Bo had enjoyed Sock-em-Dog hydraulic so much that he didn't want to come out of it; that's why we had such a hard time hauling him from it. He bragged about how he had called his good friend Dr. Hunter S. Thompson, in Aspen, and told him how much *Rolling Stone* readers would enjoy an article about whitewater sports. When we reached the takeout, he assured us, Thompson would undoubtedly be waiting to conduct an interview, and he would give the good doctor an earful. Bo confidently predicted that Thompson's story would land on the front cover of *Rolling Stone*.

Bo's braggadocio was running deeper than Yonah Lake. The air was thick with hubris.

When we reached the takeout, some ol' Carolina boy had parked a '49 Desoto right down by the lake. He had that old jalopy shined up until you could see your reflection in it, especially in the bulbous, convex hubcaps. Bo had lost his contact lenses during his long swim, and for all practical purposes was blind as a bat. Just for meanness, Kathleen and I told him the good ol' boy standing there was the famous writer, Dr. Hunter S. Thompson, and the Desoto was a *Rolling Stone* press bus hauling a load of photographers.

"Great scott," Kathleen said to Bo. "I thought you were kidding about knowing people at *Rolling Stone*. But here they are, all right, convened for the express purpose of immortalizing the only man in the world with nerve enough to one-up Walt Blackadar. The only man alive with the balls to run Section IV in a canoe at flood stage."

Kathleen was so convincing, she practically had me believing the ol' boy standing there, chain-smoking unfiltered Camels, was Hunter S. Thompson. Any second, I expected to see him whip out his pen and notebook and start taking notes.

And Bo?

Well, Bo went bonkers. He could barely see two feet in front of his face, but somehow he spotted the protruding hubcaps on that old Desoto and convinced himself they were fish-eye camera lenses, the ultra-wide angle kind that professional photographers use. Back-and-forth, from one hubcap to the other, he pranced – brandishing a smile that threatened to split both his ears – strutting and prancing, telling one lie after another about how the trip had fallen apart upstream, and only his personal heroics had averted a catastrophe.

Bo was not a happy camper when he learned how we had tricked him. When he finally cooled down, he forgave Kathleen for her complicity. All she had to do was smile at him a couple of times. But I don't think Bo ever forgave me.

Sometimes that worries me, knowing that ol' Bo is still carrying a grudge like that, just waiting for an opportunity to get back at me. But . . .

That Was Yesterday

. . . and today is a whole new ball game, a ball game without the meddling interference of Eugene (Bo) Rocker.

"Things will be different today," I had smugly told myself earlier, when I started downstream into the canyon section of the South Fork of the Payette. Bo Rocker's image won't clog the lenses today. Today it's *my* turn for pictures. And tonight, back in the comfort of Boise, we'll roll the video and watch the screen glow with *my* name. We'll watch enthralled as the high-resolution screen shimmers with the full-color image of *my* daring feats.

My game plan was to hold back and let Willie run every rapid first, to give him plenty of time to set up the camera. Time to check his light meter and get his lens focused. Time to catch his breath and steady his hand. All the better to hold that camera perfectly still. To capture my image, in brilliant living color.

Yeah, it was a good plan. The more I thought about it, the more I liked it. Just wait until ol' Bo looks at the cover of *Sprots Illustrated* and sees . . . *Me!*

Truckin' on Down Blackadar Canyon

Despite my intentions, however, a couple of hours after putin I discovered myself out ahead of the rest of the group, running first through unknown rapids, eager to see what was downstream. Realizing that I had deviated from the game plan, I slowed my pace through a couple of rapids and then flushed over a low, horseshoe-shaped waterfall with a big hydraulic in its middle. I surfed several waves as long as I could hold them, then dove into a small hole, waiting for the others to catch up. Ordinarily I'd hang an eddy and wait, but today this river had precious few eddies, and the stream was trucking downstream fast.

Without warning, the river suddenly doubled in velocity as vertical canyon walls squeezed uncomfortably into the stream-flow. Ahead of me, the river dropped out of sight through a mine field of exploding frenzy. I caught the last and only eddy, an "Idaho Special," tucked tight against the overhanging river right cliff. From that vantage point I saw clearly that if action footage was what Buckner and his editor friends were after, then I definitely should wait for him to run this rapid first and set up the camera.

From the eddy, I looked around at the awesome canyon of the South Fork Payette, with its walls rising for what must have been a thousand feet above the water, and remembered that a popular guidebook describes this as a small stream. It is – if you consider 5,000 cfs "small." And many veteran Idaho paddlers do.

All I knew for sure about this part of Blackadars Canyon was that it harbored the biggest rapid of all, a monstrosity called Surprise, easily the most bodacious rapid on the river. And it was in the micro eddy on the edge of Surprise's entrance that I sat, waiting for the estimable Willie Buckner to appear from upstream.

Come on down, Willie boy. The water's fine.

Bits and Bytes

Willie Buckner didn't come on down, but one-by-one, decked boaters in our group did: they swept around the bend, eyes blaring oversized like Maserati headlights, staring into the random exploding violence downstream that big-volume freaks call a rapid, back-paddling wildly and glancing covetously at the only eddy in sight: the one I was in, the one barely big enough to accommodate my boat, the one I wasn't about to relinquish under any circumstances because all I had to do was hang in the eddy until Buckner ran the rapid and set up the camera and then: *I'd be a media star!*

Realizing the futility of overcoming the current through frantic back paddling, Fritz, the first decked boater, reluctantly selected a line and flushed into the right side of the heaving energy field. "He's going to die," I said aloud, matter-of-factly, surprising myself with the calm finality of my announcement. "The right side is no way to run this rapid."

But in all honesty, how could I know which side was better? I'd never run the rapid before.

As Fritz dropped into the frenzy, the river reached up and seized him, literally picked him up and slammed him down thirty feet to river right. Into the first hole he tumbled, where he received an epic thrashing – and then he disappeared. He reappeared a hundred feet downstream, popped to the surface on the upstream side of a humongous standing wave.

I made a mental note: avoid river right. As I was entering the note into my computer, another kayaker, Gwen, swept around the bend and screamed at me, "Which way?"

"Try river left!" I suggested, "River right's in a bad mood today."

Into the left side she tumbled, and disappeared. Where'd she go? There she is, way over there. No, she's gone. Where is she? There! Near the bottom of the rapid.

But it wasn't the bottom, as I was to discover. It was merely as far downstream as I could see from my vantage point, where a huge hump-like wave announced that the river had decided to hook abruptly left and race toward jagged, basalt canyon walls.

I keyed in a reminder to avoid river left and lost sight of her during a random surge. On a variable-interval schedule the river underneath me surged upward, sending me crashing into the overhanging canyon wall. "Crunch, crunch." My helmet took the brunt of the thrust on each heave. Now I understood the true function of helmets: Idaho eddy-hugging head protectors. Surge absorbers.

I heard a voice. Could it be Buckner! Or the after effects of a concussion? Where is he! I wheeled around and discovered yet another decked boater, Bill from Virginia, backpaddling madly, face contorted in wild emotion. "Let me in!" he screamed.

"There's no room in here for . . ." Another variable-interval surge interrupted my pronouncement, sending me crashing upward into the canyon wall. "Crunch. Crunch." That ominous sound. Head against cliff. Bill saw my predicament and decided he wanted no part of the canyon eddy-hugging experience. He pivoted around to face the inevitable, shouting over his shoulder: "Which way?"

"Down the middle!" I suggested, "or perhaps . . ."

"What?"

Too late. He careened into the middle of the South Fork Payette's hysteria, bracing furiously. An exploding wave sent him tumbling into an ugly hole, then careening off something the size of a Greyhound Bus, but somehow he managed to stay upright, disappearing around the hump into the downstream unknown.

I made another entry: avoid river center. Many more entries like this and I'll have to write a macro.

Two other decked boaters, semi-locals from Utah, backpaddling on the lip of Surprise's entry, watched Bill's fate and exchanged puzzled glances. They shrugged and plummeted into the bowels of the maelstrom, bobbing and bracing against the fury, flipping and rolling with choreographed regularity. Chaos theory at work. Synchronicity amidst random craziness.

Watching their plight, I made another entry: avoid the whole rapid.

"Where's Buckner?" I asked myself. "I'll never get on the cover of *Sports Illustrated* at this rate."

"Crunch. Crunch." Another surge, followed by a quick ebb and yet another *"crunch, crunch!"* It was the biggest surge yet.

I couldn't take the pounding much longer. I peered around the canyon wall, looking upstream – but still no Willie Buckner. "I can't wait in here any longer," I concluded. "I'm going for it."

I wedged my paddle against the canyon wall and prepared to shove, tensing my body for the required crossover peel out stroke and reminding my vestibular center to prepare for the forthcoming neck-jolting about-face, when Buckner swept around the bend.

"Wait!" he shouted, spotting the incredible turbulence downstream. "Let me run first; I'll make you a star."

Trapped in a Micro Eddy

And there I was: trapped in a micro eddy on the South Fork of the Payette, jammed by pulsing water into a minuscule indentation in a towering cliff, waiting at the top of a crazed rapid, with the water surging madly, periodically slamming me into the overhanging canyon wall. Trapped by Buckner's command. Trapped by the surging water. But most of all, trapped by my ego.

That's when I took a deep breath and assured myself that the glory of the eventual outcome would more than justify the agony of the wait. We're talking about the cover of *Sports Illustrated!* The cover photograph, not some small shot buried in the back pages.

And besides, these Idaho rivers aren't half as tough as they're cracked up to be.

Just think, *Sports Illustrated!* I punched a reminder into my computer console: be sure to send a copy to my mother.

* * * * *

Now, Willie Buckner is not perfect. He has some faults (as you and I will discuss later), but when it comes to reading complex whitewater in a microsecond, Willie Buckner is about as good as they get. Not only can he glance at a complex rapid he's never seen before and flash-read the best route through it, but he'll then smile ear-to-ear as he runs it flawlessly. That big smile is Buckner' trademark, and he was wearing it boldly when he first flushed around the bend into my line of sight. That confident smile, however, instantly faded to a frown as he approached close enough to stare into the sledgehammer that Idaho paddlers call Surprise.

"How did everybody run this thing?" he called over his shoulder.

"They didn't," I yelled back. "It ran them."

He deftly sideslipped an entry hole and then drove into the heart of the cataclysm, slashing diagonally from river center toward river right, his boat bucking and torquing in the heavy water. He looked indefatigable until he rode up a mighty wave, dropped into the trough downstream, and disappeared.

"Oh, no, Buckner's in trouble!" A massive adrenalin rush jolted me into action. "Got to help the ol' boy," I told myself.

With my paddle poised inches from the flushing current, ready for the peel-out, I stole a last furtive glance downstream in a vain effort to interpret the craziest hydro action I'd seen since my last ride through the upper Gauley's Pillow Rapid, and there I saw Buckner, still upright and in his boat. He hadn't gone over, after all – or if he had, he'd rolled back up in a flash – but he *was* backwards in the heaving current, riding it like a bronc-buster from hell. I last saw him as he rode up the left side of the immense hump and disappeared, still backwards, his bow tilted toward the narrow slit of sky above the canyon, his stern headed toward the looming basalt canyon walls downstream.

I punched in another note: avoid slashing diagonally from river center toward river right.

* * * * *

Despite witnessing the trials and tribulations of all the paddlers preceding me, I was calm. Although I could only guess at what surprise awaited me downstream of where that ignominious hump disappeared around the canyon bend, I was confident I could handle it with aplomb if only I could success-fully negotiate the mad turbulence at the top of the rapid.

I pulled up my file labeled 'South Fork Payette River: Surprise Rapid' and reviewed it. It advised me to: "avoid river right, avoid river left, avoid river center, avoid a left-to-right diagonal path, avoid the rapid."

Oh, well. I had to run it somewhere. A canyon with vertical walls permits neither scouting nor portaging. I loaded the virtual reality simulation CD labeled: "Preview: Probable View at the Bottom of Surprise," called up my proprietary multimedia command language, and scanned the output. On the display monitor, I could see Buckner at the bottom of the rapid, perched on a river-left ledge, catching his breath, his camera at the ready, throw bag near-at-hand . . . smiling. That trademark smile. Sunlight glinting off his blue paddling helmet, wet from the spray. Red and yellow spectra rope spilling from his throw bag across the dark basaltic rock.

Across the river, Gwen and Fritz and Bill and the other decked boaters are hugging a strip eddy, their boats slamming into the canyon wall with each surge.

I punched in an upstream scan command in order to inspect the bottom of the rapid, from Willie's viewpoint, but my display monitor choked with visual noise. The last readable message from the CD file said: "Data incomplete on Surprise Rapid; nature of surprise not known; simulation aborted; viewer advised to exercise circumspection."

Exercise what?

I Did It My Way

Computers! Nothing but a hassle when it comes to important stuff – stuff like running rapids and visualizing what's at the bottom, and getting my picture on the cover of *Sports Illustrated*. The mere thought of a cover spread sent my confidence soaring like an eagle. The rapid was mine; I could feel it! Confidence and calmness coursed through my veins.

I powered down the machine. To hell with computer guidance. I didn't need it. I would run the rapid by the seat of my drysuit. Like Luke Skywalker, the fighter pilot in *Star Wars*. I would *feel* the power.

I took a deep breath and held it. "Now!" I reached across and caught the current. The boat whipsawed around and I headed into the storm. I had about four or five seconds to read and react, and I lost no time, marshaling every iota of experience gleaned from every river I'd ever run.

I spotted a line. There, right there! I'll skirt that boulder, thread between the two biggest holes, and . . . No! Not there, that leads into the biggest breaking wave outside the Grand Canyon.

Where then? Where? There has to be a way. But where? Where!

Then I saw it, and when I did I could only marvel that I had overlooked it until now. A line as clean and easy as a cake walk lay amidst the hydrologic bedlam.

"No wonder I feel calm," I thought to myself, "I knew there'd be a clean line through this pretentious little riffle, and I knew I'd find it."

All I had to do was run diagonally right to left, stay out of the whirling suck hole at the top, and follow the obvious line. "As long as I clean the top of the rapid, it can't get any worse downstream around the bend. Right?"

With plenty of time left – a second or two – I maneuvered into position. One draw stroke, with a quick fade to the stern, and another, and another, and one more. There! An on-side reverse quarter sweep, and I'm in perfect position. I'm going to ace this one. I'll send a copy to my brother, too.

On the cover of *Sports Illustrated!*

Attack of the Howling Banshees

And then it happened. I heard it before I saw it. It came howling up the stark corridor like attacking Banshees. It picked up spray from the exploding waves and slammed into me with the impact of a fist of steel, halting my forward momentum and moving me several miles too far to the left.

Wind!

Wind as it can blow only in austerely beautiful western canyons.

I compensated with a crossover high brace. Hold the brace! Draw. Hold the brace. Draw. Another draw. There, I made it back to my line. But I wasn't moving! I was sitting stationarily on the lip of the drop, the forward speed of the current completely negated by the howling wind from downstream. When will it stop? Will it stop?

At last it ebbed – a good thing – because my calm had departed for parts unknown, my heart was pounding out of control, destined to plunge into tachycardia any second. I dug in with a forward stroke. Then the gale struck again, stronger than before. I skittered thirty feet across the lip of the rapid and dropped sideways into the churning chaos.

Brace, brace! Now you're in it. Surf it. Surf it. Surf out!

I squirted out the side of the hydraulic and caromed off the canyon wall, pitching into an abysmal trough. As I rode toward the bottom of the depression, I assessed damages. One glance brought glorious news: my boat was still dry. My spirits soared!

I was nowhere near my planned clean line, but I was upright, in control, and destined to be on the cover of *Sports Illustrated*. Nothing can stop me now!

Nearing the top of the next wave I angled right and read the water downstream. Merciful heavens! I shouldn't have looked. I was moving twenty miles an hour and tearing over, into, and around a violent wave train. Up the next wave, paddle, angle, down the other side, brace, stroke, angle.

I looked downstream again. Where's the hump? There it is! What's downstream of it? Can't see. Maybe after this next wave.

Holy hydraulics! The next wave is enormous. Up, up, I soar toward the sky, finally reaching its crest. Now, read the water downstream! Too late. A blast of wind and water stings into my face.

Turn on the windshield wipers.

In the trough I shake off the water and start up the next wave. I can sense that the river has begun its hook to the left. Got to see which way to go at the bottom of the rapid. They don't call this one Surprise for nothing. What's down there?

Now I can see the hump. Oh, it's gigantic! Looks like a hole on river right – don't go over there. No problem though, I'm riding down river center. I'm in control.

Below the rapid, strung along the river-right canyon wall, I can see several decked boaters. Just where I thought they'd be. Huddled in the eddy, sheltered from the river's storm, like serfs cowering in their hut to escape the wrath of the manor lord. But where's Buckner? And then I see him too, but not with the decked boaters. Over on river left. He's found an eddy and climbed from his boat, up on an outcropping about ten feet above river level. I knew it, with the camera! They're gonna put me on the cover, on the cover of . . . !!!

Oh, the heck with *Sports Illustrated.* I wanna be on the cover of . . . *Rolling Stone! Rolling Stone!!!* With accompanying text by Dr. Hunter S. Thompson himself. No, no, Thompson's not right. Text by Tom Wolfe. Yes, yes: Tom Wolfe!!! This story'll put *Bonfire of the Vanities* and *The Right Stuff* to shame. We'll call it: *Slam Dunk of the Humilities!* I'll help Wolfe write it. No, no! He can help *me* write it. Yeah, that way we'll get it right!

I'll send two copies to my mother! *Rolling Stone!* Four copies for my brother! *Rolling Stone!*

If only Eugene (Bo) Rocker could see me now! (Seventeen copies to Bo.) Tape it Willie boy! Get it all down. Capture this glorious moment.

I glance at the decked boaters. They're agog. (A copy to each of them! And to their mothers. It'll be the biggest selling issue in *Rolling Stone* history.)

I suck in my gut and puff out my chest, exaggerating every movement for photographic effect. Swivel the hips. Rock the boat! Remember to smile. "Hi, Mom!"

I still can't make out what's on river left. Probably another hole. Where does the huge hump go? It probably forms a clean tongue. With all this volume, it has to. What a dramatic cover picture this will make. It must be a ten-foot drop down there. What if the hump pours into a hole? Who cares? With the momentum I have, nothing can stop me now. I must be moving forty miles an hour! I plot a line straight for the hump and stroke hard. *Rolling Stone!* Stroke! *Rolling Stone!* Stroke!

Nothing can stop me now!

I'll have two hundred copies delivered to Bo Rocker's penthouse! No, make that a thousand! To hell with it . . . a truck load!!!

I'll be on the cover – on the cover of *Rolling Stone!* And *Sports Illustrated!*

One more stroke and I'll be on top of the hump.

Hah!

These Idaho rivers aren't so tough!

Rolling Stone!

I look at Buckner and behind the camera he's smiling. If he's let that camera battery run low on power, I'll . . . never mind. I have to concentrate on the river. On the river and on . . . *Rolling Stone!*

In my mind's eye I can see Bo Rocker lounging in his Atlanta penthouse, stretching out on a plush recliner after a hard day at the office. He's balancing a dry double Martini in one hand and with his free hand he's reaching over to pluck a magazine from a reading table. Now he's staring at the cover enviously as he takes the first sip from his drink, and grimacing as the first swallow goes down sour because he's made out the identity of the stalwart paddler on the front cover, in full color: *Me!* Me, defiantly running down the middle of the big hump at the bottom of Surprise Rapid. Tough luck, Bo; now I'm the star!

And Then, Back in the Jungle

But back on the river, my sixth sense tells me something's not quite right in the realm of my newfound video stardom.

What is it?

I look at the decked boaters, cloistered in the narrow, pulsating strip eddy, and now they're smiling too. Why're they smiling? Suddenly they commence to howl, gleefully. What's going on over there?

The rapscallions.

Why're they howling? What's at the bottom of the hump anyway?

I top the hump and look down . . . and down, and down, and then down some more, and I understand why they're howling.

The reprobates.

Not to be outdone by the clowns in the strip eddy, I commence howling too, at the top of my lungs, arcing my head toward the heavens.

But somehow, my howls aren't gleeful; they're doleful.

As I plunge inexorably into the bottomless chasm, I glimpse a swimmer in the froth, alongside my right gunwale. Oh, no! A hand reaches out. Grabs my boat. Who is it?

Nobody; just my imagination!

I peer into the hole and feel a twinge of panic, realizing I've never seen anything quite like this. Not on any river. But before the panic can build, I feel the force coming back. To me. The force is with me. And I know it. And I know the unfathomable depth of the hole doesn't matter. Because no obstacle on earth is powerful enough to stop me now!

Right? The force is with me. I'm moving too fast. I've got momentum!

Someday I'll Learn Big Words Too, Like . . . Circumspection!

I've paddled a lot of rivers, up and down the Appalachians, from Alabama's Little River Canyon to the West River in Vermont, and much of what lies in between. Last year I paddled in Colorado, and this year I moved to Idaho. Although I'm irremediably a steep creek freak, I've made a point to sample big water also: the upper Gauley, the New River Gorge at high water, the Lochsa during spring flush, the Tygart Gorge at flood, and so on.

In those trips I've run through some pretty good holes, including Woodall Shoals on the Chattooga and the monstrosity at the bottom of Hydro Rapid in the Watauga Gorge. Only once did I hit a hole I couldn't surf out of: the big one at the top of Koontz Flume on the upper Gauley, and that was because Bo Rocker talked me into lackadaisically dropping into it sideways.

Open canoes – even most of the solo variety – are long enough and heavy enough to bridge virtually any hole, *if* you hit it with a full head of steam. Momentum's the key.

And if anybody was ever moving through a rapid with momentum to spare, it was me when I topped the hump in Surprise. I was confident nothing could stop me. I could have rammed into Stone Mountain and knocked it aside. I felt like Luke Skywalker. The force was with me, in the hip pocket of my dry suit, or so I thought.

Bo Rocker Revisited

The ugly truth is: I hit the hole in Surprise rapid, and *stopped*. All forward motion ceased instantly. All my momentum was to no avail. Also to no avail was every tactic I knew about surfing and playing holes. This wasn't a hole I was in; this was Idaho's best kept Surprise!

I know all this because Buckner gave me a copy of the video. (Oh, what friends we have in editors.) In various states of sullen humiliation I've watched his disgusting video in a futile effort to discover what I could've done differently to overpower the hole. Over-and-over I watch my perfect run deteriorate as I plummet into the hole, stop dead, surf for a while, and then relentlessly sink into the anti-momentum monster-machine known as Surprise.

The baleful rapid ripped the helmet from my head (breaking the chin strap), snapped the shaft of my paddle like a match stick, sucked me out of my boat in a split second, and blew enough water up my nose to impact my sinuses for weeks. (The doctor said to me, "What'd you do, boy, try to French-kiss a high-pressure fire hose?")

Why do I share this bad news with you? Because you're going to learn about it soon enough anyway. In case you haven't already seen the video (Buckner made a good-faith effort to show it to every paddler on the east coast) you'll see it soon in the national media. Remember when I said editors stick together? Well, they do. And Willie Buckner is an editor of his word. Just like he promised, he sent the video off to one of his friends. No, he didn't send it to the editor of *Sports Illustrated*. Instead, he sent it to Eugene (Bo) Rocker and asked his advice. (See, I told you Buckner had faults.)

What did Bo suggest? Yes, you guessed it. After making a few edits of his own, Bo forwarded the video to one of his old cronies in New York – the executive producer of that disgusting television show: *World's Most Pathetic Home Video Bloopers*.

In Many Ways It Was a Perfect Run

So take it from the only person who really knows what happened. After you laugh your guts out looking at the miserable video that Buckner wouldn't sell me for any price, just remember what really happened. Don't believe a thing you see on your television screen. (Bo Rocker extensively doctored the video with special effects – just to make me look bad.) The truth is, my run was perfect in every way until I encountered that malevolent Surprise lurking at the bottom.

The way I see it, I ran the first hundred yards of Surprise flawlessly. The last thirty feet don't count, right? We're all in agreement on this, right?

Right.

Oh, and by the way. When you plan your next western excursion, keep this in mind: Idaho rivers aren't all that tough.

Come on out, the water's fine.

The Story of Winkin'
Blinkin' and Nod

Deep in the heart of West Virginia, there's a river called the Gauley that every river rat aspires to paddle. It's commonly regarded as one of the top ten whitewater trips in the world, and one thing is certain: run it once and you'll never forget the experience. It's a big, bad, intoxicating treat that hardcore paddlers love.

Unfortunately, the Gauley is dry most of the year, due to a massive blockage known as Summersville Dam, which steals water that ordinarily would flow downstream, diverting it into an immense reservoir.

Once a year, however, the reservoir is drawn down. During these annual releases – normally in September and October – thousands of cubic feet of water every second spew from the base of Summersville Dam through enormous "release tubes." The released water sluices into the river's natural streambed and rampages through the downstream canyon, creating a whitewater cornucopia. Paddlers launch their boats at the base of the dam, eager to challenge the unsurpassed rapids. Hardcore paddlers have been known to set up a base camp in the vicinity of the dam, and to run the river every day that water is available.

The reservoir holds so much water that releases commonly last for weeks at a stretch. For paddlers, it's almost like a fifth season. In fact, veteran paddlers often refer to the autumn releases as . . .

Gauley Season

It was during one of these resplendent release occasions that Eugene (Bo) Rocker, paddling the river in a C1 with a slew of his kayak buddies, witnessed something that changed his life. Somewhere between Insignificant and Pillow Rock (two of the stream's biggest rapids), he saw a canoe paddler laboriously making his way down river.

Bo and his friends were astonished.

It was the first canoe they had seen on the Gauley. After all, conventional wisdom dictates that some rivers are too difficult for canoes to negotiate, and the upper Gauley was supposedly one of them. Canoes are open vessels. In turbulent water (with which the upper Gauley is copiously endowed), canoes inevitably take on water, and the more water they ship, the less maneuverable they become. With enough water, they eventually lose all maneuverability, and swamp.

Yet, here it was, happening before Bo's very eyes, the impossible: a canoe bobbing and weaving through the big water intensity of the upper Gauley River. Bo was so intrigued by what he saw that he fell in behind the open boater and watched his progress down the river, observing that his descent wasn't without mishap. In numerous rapids, his boat took on so much water that he was out of control. And several big waves knocked him over, pitching him into the river for long, bruising swims. And he even portaged a couple of the tougher rapids. Nonetheless, with a lot of exertion and a boat load of determination, he finally managed to negotiate most of the river — in a canoe.

It reminded Bo of the time he tried to run the Chattooga River in an open boat. He did all right until somewhere in the vicinity of the Five Falls, when he discovered how bruising a swim could be. He sold his canoe after that experience, and decided to stay with his trusty C1.

The more he thought about the canoe bobbing and weaving along the Gauley River, however, the more it intrigued him. He had noticed that boat manufacturers were coming out with a lot of new whitewater canoes. Every year they seemed to have a new model, built expressly for solo whitewater paddling. He was thinking that with a little practice, he could probably run a canoe down the Gauley himself. He was also thinking that with some additional effort – and a moderate-sized bribe – he could probably talk a television producer into doing a docu-drama about a stalwart paddler running the upper Gauley River in a canoe. With a little luck, a show like that could be his big break, his stepping-stone to the big time, to a role in a major motion picture.

After the river trip ended, and Bo was back in the campground, he talked it over with his kayaking buddies, including Hank Menzel, whose opinion he respected. All his friends, however, assured him that paddling the upper Gauley in a canoe was about the dumbest stunt they had ever witnessed, and certainly not something that any of them would attempt. Nonetheless, Bo was still intrigued. He was wondering why the ol' boy had been out there today in a canoe. Was it possible the open boater was planning a movie of his own? Planning to steal Bo Rocker's thunder?

Bo couldn't let that happen. The movie was *his* idea, *his* vehicle to stardom. He couldn't stand by idly and let a lowly open boater steal his brilliant movie idea. Following dinner, Bo and Hank decided to seek out the open boater and ask him why he had floated the river in a canoe. A half dozen of Hank and Bo's paddling friends tagged along with them, to ridicule whatever lame-brain excuse the canoeist offered.

They located the open boater in an out-of-the-way corner of the campground. He was hunkering over a backpacking stove, one of the noisy little brass versions from Sweden, trying to cook dinner, and didn't hear them approaching. They appointed Wild Bill Barkley, who was never without words and an acknowledged prince of tact, to initiate the conversation. Wild Bill strutted up, tapped the lone ranger on the shoulder and said, "Okay, Bozo, where'd you put it?"

"Excuse me?" the open boater replied. He was still squatting over the miniature stove, and was startled to look over his shoulder and discover his campsite overrun with decked boaters.

"You hiding it around here some place?" Wild Bill continued, looking around the campsite accusingly.

"Hiding what?" the open boater said, defensively.

"Your brain, Bozo," Wild Bill replied, his voice dripping with derision. "You must keep it around here some place, because you sure didn't have it with you on the river today."

The open boater came to his feet. He was about normal height, so he towered over Wild Bill. "What the hell are you talking about, squirt?" he growled defiantly.

Hank Menzel's big hand reached out and found Wild Bill's shirt collar, clinched tight, and yanked him out of harm's way. Then Hank stepped up into his place. Hank towered over the open boater. He said, "My little buddy wants to know why you paddled the river today in a canoe."

The open boater, craning his neck to make eye contact with Hank, replied, in a decidedly more civil tone, "It's more challenging, that's why."

Several of the congregated decked boaters nodded solemnly, agreeing that it had to be a challenge.

"Oh, sure," Wild Bill Barkley said, peering out from behind Hank Menzel. "A twenty-six-mile swim's gotta be challenging, all right."

The lone ranger made a move toward Bill, but Hank's big hand on his chest brought him up short. "No offense, Mister," Hank said.

Wild Bill, from the shelter of Hank Menzel's bulk, said, "You know, I didn't watch your whole run today, fella. But I did see a good portion of it. Tell me, in those times I wasn't looking, were you ever *in* your boat?"

"Anybody can float a watertight compartment down the river," the open boater retorted. "But it takes a *River Master* to paddle a canoe down the Gauley."

"It takes a damn fool, in my opinion," Hank Menzel said, in that Ajax and sandpaper voice of his. He turned to Bo. "Ain't that right, Bo?"

But Bo, lost in thought, didn't answer.

* * * * *

When they were leaving the lone ranger's campsite, it occurred to Hank that they'd been too rough on the stranger. Hank stopped and called back to him, "By the way, fella. I got a stove over in my camp that works. You're welcome to come over and use it."

And Wild Bill Barkley added, "It's a Coleman. Made in America. I'll show you how to light it."

"Thanks," replied the open boater, sarcastically. "I'll be right over."

"Great," said Hank, taking him at his word.

"Oh, can you do me one small favor?" the loner said to Wild Bill.

"Sure," Wild Bill replied.

The lone ranger said, "Hold your breath 'til I get there, okay?"

While Hank and Bo and the others were walking back to their campsite, Bo was mumbling something under his breath, but all Hank could make out, over the din of Wild Bill's fusillade of threats directed in the general direction of the open boater, were the words: ". . . *River Master*, huh?"

The Experiment Begins

Bo Rocker disappeared from camp that night and wasn't seen until next day, when he showed up at the putin with a canoe, which, against the vehement protestations of all his friends, he promptly launched on the river.

His inaugural trip wasn't without incident. He took a few swims. And, much to the annoyance of his companions, he was stopping constantly to bail and dump water.

But next day he was back, with the canoe, and this time making the run without a swim – and with only a single portage (Iron Ring). And with significantly fewer dump stops.

By his fourth canoe trip down the Gauley, Bo was running every rapid, high and dry, no longer needing to dump water, and stopping only occasionally to bail, at which times he always made a point of tossing his bail water on any nearby decked boaters, while ridiculing them for lacking the courage to challenge the river in a "real" boat. Whenever he approached a rapid and saw kayak paddlers out on the bank scouting, he'd run straight into the rapid, yelling at the top of his lungs as he swept past, "Get a boat!"

By the end of Gauley season, the ranks of Bo's decked boat friends had dwindled appallingly. Unconcerned, Bo threatened to return the following Gauley season and paddle the entire river while standing up in his canoe, running the bigger drops backwards, and whistling "Dixie" the whole way.

"I hope he tries it," Wild Bill Barkley said.

"I don't," Hank Menzel replied.

"You're right," Bill admitted, after giving it some thought. "It'd be a disaster. Bo's rendition of "Dixie" is abominable."

The Experiment Continues

Next Gauley season, Bo showed up not only with a canoe, but also with it loaded atop a shiny new motor home. And sharing the motor home with him was a slender young dark-haired woman named Amy who caused a lot more comment than either the motor home or Bo's choice of boats.

"He can't pick boats worth a hoot," Wild Bill Barkley declared. "And that motor home is reprehensible. But I got to hand it to him, he sure has taste in women."

"She's about the prettiest woman I ever saw," Hank Menzel admitted. "How is it Bo always attracts such good-looking women?"

"That young lady has more going for her than looks," Doctor F. Katz said. "There's class *and* talent in that package. Have you seen her canvasses? Some of those creations are spectacular. The big one she did yesterday of the Summersville Dam release tubes is astonishing. I offered five hundred for it, and she just smiled and said, 'No thank you, Doctor.' Like five hundred dollars was nothing to her. Who is this Amy, anyway? What's her last name?"

"Never seen her before," Hank replied, backing up to the campfire. The late September days were warm, but at night, especially near the river, a fire felt good. Hank continued: "Bo says he met her on a trip to New York. But she told Wild Bill

The Story of Winkin' Blinkin' and Nod

she lives down in North Carolina some place. Where was it she said, Bill?"

Wild Bill frowned. "North Carolina? Did I say North Carolina?" He shook his head. "Naw, I must have been confused. A woman like that's gotta be from some place like . . . Venus. Yeah, that's it. That woman's from Venus."

Doctor Katz said, "What was she wearing when she told you where she was from?"

"A string bikini," Bill replied.

The doctor looked at him like he was a canker sore. "Uh huh, you were confused, all right. All your little pea brain could think about was getting your lecherous hands on her tight buns."

Hank said to Doctor Katz, "Why don't you just ask her yourself where she's from, if you're so curious?"

"I did," Doctor Katz replied. "But when I inquired, she just smiled at me, and somehow after that I . . . well, I kind of lost my train of thought."

"And you a doctor," Wild Bill sneered. "That's disgusting. Have you no professional standards?"

Doctor Katz ignored Wild Bill.

"Doesn't it strike you as a bit odd?" Katz asked Hank.

"What?" Wild Bill said. "Doctors without standards? Not really. In fact, it's pretty much the norm, I'd say."

"Still your tongue, dolt!" Doctor Katz said to Wild Bill. Then the doctor turned back to Hank: "I mean, doesn't it seem odd that Bo shows up here at the river with a gorgeous young woman who's a talented artist, and nobody even knows her last name or where she's from?"

The dozen or so paddlers gathered around the communal fire mulled over the doctor's question for a while. They liked to think of themselves as educated people, able to think and act right up there on the same intellectual plane as doctors and other professionals. At the moment, however – nobody wishing to be the first to make a fool of themselves – reflective silence seemed to be the intelligent response. There were lots of furrowed brows and thoughtful expressions.

Wild Bill Barkley, using the silence to full advantage, made a big show of sticking out his tongue, clamping it tightly between his thumb and index finger, and staggering around the campfire, emitting horrendous gagging sounds, but nevertheless complying fully with the doctor's order to keep his tongue still. Finally tiring of the childish game, he stumbled over to his ice chest, fished out another beer, popped the tab and guzzled the whole thing, making repulsive slurping noises as he sucked down the last ounce or two. Then he belched loud enough to wake the dead. For a man of modest stature, Wild Bill could absorb vast quantities of beer. Or alcohol in any other form, for that matter. He crumpled the can and tossed it into the fire, a practice which he knew enraged Doctor Katz's ecological sensibilities.

Hank said to Katz, "You don't know Bo very well, do you doctor?"

Wild Bill said, "One time Bo showed up with a Russian circus acrobat. You remember her, Hank? Had a haircut that looked like they'd put a bowl on her head and cut off every-thing that wasn't covered. She was cute though, and that's saying something, given her haircut. But she didn't know the first word of English, did she?"

"That ain't so," Hank replied. "She knew two words: "Zounds, Bo!"

"That's right," Bill said, laughing. "I'd forgotten that wonderful phrase. Even though I must have heard it a million times. But we didn't know her name either, did we?"

"Sure we did," Hank reminded him. "It was Olga."

"That's right," Bill confessed, fishing around in his ice chest for another beer. I'd forgotten that."

Hank said to Bill, "You remember the girl from California? The classic beach bunny? Fantastic tan, long blond hair? The one that could talk a blue streak?"

"I remember her *and* her name," Bill said triumphantly. "Celeste. A certified space cadet. But a decent paddler, I have to admit."

"Yes, she was," Hank agreed. "But after the first day, she wouldn't paddle again, because paddling a river was something everybody in camp could do."

Bill added, "And she started blabbering about sky-diving."

"And skiing at Tahoe, and scuba diving in Baja, and trekking in Nepal and . . ."

"But it always came back to sky diving," Bill said. "It was sky diving this, and sky diving that, and sky diving in the morning, and sky diving in the afternoon, and sky diving in the buff, and if you weren't a sky diver you weren't anybody, and if you weren't a sky diver you hadn't lived, and finally we were all just sick and tired of it, and Bo said to her, 'Why don't you just rent a plane and sky dive right into the river?' "

"And she did," Hank said.

Doctor Katz said, "She sky dove into the Gauley River?"

"Yes," Hank replied.

"Why?"

"To impress Bo, I guess."

"You guess? Didn't anybody ask her why she did it?"

"Well, actually," Hank said. "I don't think anybody ever saw her again."

"Egad!" said the doctor. "You mean she killed herself?"

"Heck no," Hank replied. "It was better'n that. Her plan was to surprise Bo. She was planning to land on the bank at the takeout, just as he was arriving. But her plane was a few minutes late and she missed the target a little way and landed in the river. We were already out on the bank, with our boats loaded, when she splashes down. So she starts yelling, 'Help me, Bo! Save me! I can't swim!' And Bo says, 'Yeah, sure. The world class scuba diver can't swim.' But before he could untie his boat and get it down off his van, this kayaker who had just floated down to the takeout hears her screaming and paddles out to save her, and she says to him, 'Oh, no thank you, I can be rescued only by Eugene (Bo) Rocker. Otherwise, I will be swept to my death in the horrendous rapid downstream.' "

"You're kidding?" Doctor Katz said. "So what did Bo do?"

Bill Barkley answered: "When Bo heard what she told the kayaker, he said, 'To hell with her; let her drown.' He got in his van and drove off."

Doctor Katz, drawing the inevitable conclusion, said, "Then Bo shows up with all types? Acrobats, space cadets, whomever. In that context, a fabulously talented but unknown artist doesn't really seem so odd, does it?"

"Bo Rocker might show up with anybody," Wild Bill said.

There was general agreement around the campfire.

Hank Menzel agreed, too. Then added, "But I'll let you in on something that is odd: Bo told me he's not sleeping with her. Can you believe that? He's not sleeping with a woman that looks like that? But that's what he says. He says they're just good friends, and they enjoy traveling together."

"I saw them hugging," Wild Bill said with a leer.

"They do that," Hank agreed. "But apparently that's all part of being good friends, and that's as far as it goes, Bo says. That's one reason why he leased that motor home. So they'd have separate beds. And of course, more room for her canvasses, of which there must be a couple dozen by now, at least. Have you been in it? Smells just like paint in there."

"Actually, it smells like an artist's studio," Doctor Katz said.

"Except when they brew up that new tea," Wild Bill added. "Then it smells heavenly in there. That stuff is yummy." Bill rubbed his stomach, gave Katz a foolish grin, and belched loudly.

Hank said, "You mean that stuff I've seen them brewing in Bo's old coffee pot?"

"It's tea of some kind," Wild Bill advised him. "She told me so. She called it sabadilla, or something like that. Didn't she, Doctor? You were there," he said to Katz. "What was it she called it? It was some witch doctor term that an old quack like you should remember."

"That *is* what she calls it," the doctor confirmed, looking down his professional nose at Wild Bill. "But that's not what it is."

"What is it then?" Hank demanded to know.

"Drugs, that's what!" Wild Bill declared. "Good drugs, I'll testify to that. She gave me a cup." He commenced rubbing his stomach again, with more vigor this time, and licking his lips. "*Really* good drugs," he added, for emphasis.

"Bo don't do drugs," Hank declared. "I know that for a fact." He turned to Katz. "You sampled that tea stuff? Then tell me what it is they're drinking?"

"Drugs," Wild Bill declared again. "Good drugs."

"It's a herb," the doctor announced. "South American in origin, nothing more than folk medicine, really. You can buy it in all the high priced New York natural food boutiques. It's the latest rage among the avant-garde artists in the big city. That's probably where she discovered it. You know what they say: anything that money can buy can be bought in Manhattan. But that particular herb is certainly nothing new. Been around for ages. Literally."

36   River Stories by Monte Smith

"Then it's not a narcotic?" Hank asked.

"Not at all," the doctor replied.

"Drat!" Wild Bill said.

"Any side effects?" Hank inquired, remembering Bo's threat to run the river this year standing up in his canoe. "Does it cause impaired balance, or anything like that?"

"Euphoria!" Wild Bill said. "That's what I felt after only one cup. And Bo, think how he must feel! He pours it down a potful at a time. No wonder he ain't sleeping with her. A man don't need sex that pours that stuff down a potful at a time."

The doctor looked at Wild Bill disdainfully. "Some people claim to experience a mild sense of elevated well-being following ingestion of the substance. But that's merely the power of suggestion: weak intellects in search of chemical guidance. I've tried it on several occasions with no discernable mood alteration. Believe me, I have vastly more effective agents in my little black bag."

"I know you do," Wild Bill said, looking around the camp-site, his gaze finally settling on Doctor Katz's tent. "And just where is that nifty little black bag of yours, anyway," he inquired of the doctor.

"Locked safely away from your vile clutches," the good doctor assured him.

"Drat!" said Wild Bill.

"But, to continue my pharmacognosy," Katz said, "the only medically established side effects of the substance under question are perceived muscle relaxation and, in rare instances of long-term ingestion, pronounced ocular reactivity."

"What?" Wild Bill said. " 'Pronouns or cue radioactivity?' What kind of medical claptrap is that?"

"You liberal arts buffoon!" the learned doctor replied contemptuously. "Have you no comprehension of scientifically precise language? I'm referring, of course, to hypersensitivity of the orbs when exposed to air, wind, or water."

With that, the doctor turned on his heel and strode away.

Wild Bill staggered backward, in exaggerated shock. He finally gained his balance and turned to Hank, "What'd he say?"

Hank replied, "I'm not sure, Bill, but I think it was something to do with your mother's pedigree."

Bill was making growling noises, clenching his fists. He said, "I don't know which one to kill first, that disgusting old malpractice artist or the uppity open boater in the corner campsite."

Pronounced Ocular Reactivity

Next day on the Gauley, Bo was convinced the Summersville Dam engineers were releasing an unusually large volume of water. What else could explain how the waves kept rising up and slapping him in the face? Causing his eyes to burn like fire. With his eyes burning so painfully, he forgot all about his promise to run the river standing up in his canoe.

By the time Bo got off the river, he was blinking and squinting incessantly. Retiring to the motor home, he discovered that the only relief was in closing his eyes, and keeping them closed. As long as he remained at rest, with his eyes closed, the burning discomfort was minimal.

But the moment he ventured out of the motor home to sit around the campfire and swap war stories, his condition flared up again. His constant squinting made it hard to see where he was walking. Occasionally he'd misstep and stumble. Other paddlers in the campground, witnessing his squinting, blinking, and staggering behavior, began whispering and conjecturing about what it was that he brewed up in that battered old coffee pot of his.

Several paddlers, perhaps still smarting from Bo's scornful ridicule the previous season, and perhaps envious of his uncanny ability to run a canoe through all the big rapids on the upper Gauley, were soon circulating a rumor that he brewed peyotl juice in that coffee pot every morning and slugged down a quart of the vile concoction before putting on the river! It was a brutal and outrageous rumor, of course. Which probably explains why it spread like a wildfire through the Gauley campgrounds. Stories about his abject state of drug addiction eventually grew so vicious that only a handful of degenerates would paddle with him.

After a while the burning, squinting, staggering, and rumor mongering (not to mention incessant badgering by Wild Bill Barkley for his tea recipe) became so irksome that Bo had to do something about it. He experimented with scuba masks and exotic goggles, but they distorted his vision, altered his sense of balance, and were forever getting smacked off his head by big waves. Finally, he stumbled onto a unique solution. To avoid the eye sting, he commenced tightly closing his eyes whenever he suspected a big wave was about to well up and explode in his face.

It worked!

In fact, the tactic worked so well that the following day Bo commenced closing his eyes at the top of each major rapid and holding them tightly shut until he reached bottom.

Somehow he made it through the trip alive.

* * * * *

By this time he was truly the talk of the river, and some of his fair weather friends took him aside to tell him they were afraid to paddle with him anymore. They were convinced he was going to flush into an undercut with his eyes closed, and that would be the end of him. And they wanted no part of it.

Even his staunch friends became concerned, thinking he was apt to kill himself. Hank Menzel, de facto leader of the small group that would still deign to paddle with Bo, assured his companions that Bo had things under control.

But then, after a few more river trips, Bo surprised even Hank, and started running not just individual rapids, but entire stretches of the upper Gauley with his eyes closed.

One evening, Bo retired early, with severely burning eyes. Around the campfire, which was located only a few yards from Bo's motor home, Wild Bill Barkley swilled more alcohol than usual and became quite intoxicated. As was Bill's habit when he was in his cups, he commenced lecturing his unfortunate companions. Bill's topic this evening was Bo Rocker's behavior on the river. Bill declared that Bo's floating the Gauley River in a canoe with his eyes closed was such a phenomenal accomplishment that it should be on television. And then he began, quite shrilly, conjecturing about how much fun it would be if an NBC News crew showed up the next day, with the assignment of immortalizing Bo Rocker as he challenged the upper Gauley in a canoe, with his eyes closed.

Inside the motor home, Bo was wrapped in slumber. Wrapped, also, in dreams of countless television cameras, every single one of them aimed straight at him.

Personal Adjustments

Next morning, Amy Reynolds, the mystery woman, the delicate-featured beauty from North Carolina who was sharing Bo's motor home, never understanding that it was her herbal tea that had caused Bo's ocular distress in the first place, and hoping to put an end to his seemingly irrational behavior, made an appeal. She asked Bo to stay off the river that day.

Bo, almost out the door to join Hank and the others on another river trip, was stunned. He came back inside and closed the door, and blurted: "But, but, but . . . the cameras! The helicopters! The news anchors. They're all here today. All to film me on the river. They're gonna make a television special. I'll be the star."

Amy glared at him, with her hands on her hips, her expression set, determined. Bo could tell she was dead serious. She had just crawled out of bed and was wearing one of his long-sleeved shirts, which she used for a nightgown. He kept looking at her legs, thinking they were the nicest he'd ever seen, wondering if she had anything on under the shirt. He was pretty sure she didn't. He was thinking how great it would be to know for sure what was under there, when she said, "Are you listening to me, Bo?"

"Of course I am, but . . ." He turned, and looked out the window, longingly, toward the river.

"I want you to stay here with me today," she said. "I want you to forget about that river for a while. Stay here with me. There's something we need to do. We've waited long enough."

Bo, still looking toward the river, expecting to see a television helicopter buzz over the canyon wall at any second, said, "What is it we need to do, sweetheart?"

"We need to get better acquainted."

That brought his head around.

She was slowly unbuttoning her shirt, starting at the top, working her way down, from button to button, slow and easy. Taking her time, watching him. She was on the next-to-last button when Bo started making little moaning sounds and edging toward the door.

"Something wrong with you?"

Bo kept on moaning.

Amy said, "You've been really sweet to wait the way you have. I just wasn't sure at first, but now I am. I want you to stay here with me today. All day."

Bo was looking from her to the river, and then back again. She unfastened the last button on the shirt and then slowly, enticingly, pulled it open and let it slide off her shoulders and down her arms and let it drop onto the floor at her feet. Bo's heart was in his throat. It was the first time he had seen her like this. In a string bikini, yes. In ultra short-shorts, yes. Topless, yes. Even a glimpse of her bottomless, once. But not like this. She was lovely. Tall and firm and shapely and with the most luscious tan lines he had ever beheld. And with that long black hair cascading down over her shoulders.

"Bo! Are you coming?"

It was Hank Menzel's voice, outside the motor home. Hank's big fist thumped against the door. "We're leaving Bo. We can't wait no longer."

Bo looked at Amy, at the door, at Amy. He swallowed hard. "Tonight," he said. "All night."

She raised her chin, and said calmly, "You leave, and I won't be here tonight."

"Hey, Bo!"

It was Wild Bill Barkley, outside the door.

"Hey, Bo," he said again. "I saw a van-load of camera equipment wheel by here a few minutes ago. It had NBC scrawled across the side panel. I think they're heading for the big overlook at Koontz Bend. What're you waiting for in there? This could be your shot at the big time."

Bo was backed up against the door, leaning on it. Without taking his eyes from Amy, he reached around and twisted the knob and felt the door give way and his weight hurtle him through the opening and down the steps and onto Hank and

Wild Bill and the ground. Amy stepped up to the door opening and looked down at the three of them writhing on the ground and struggling to their feet. She shook her head, frowned sadly, and shut the door.

* * * * *

It was a confused river trip for Bo. He was trying to keep his eyes closed, in case NBC had cameras positioned on the canyon cliffs. He wanted the cameras to clearly record that his eyes were tightly closed as he careened through the river's immense turbulence. But he couldn't resist occasionally opening his eyes to scan the cliff sides. If the cameras were up there, he wanted to know where, so he could put a little extra into his performance. At one point, he was convinced that he saw a camera crew on the boulders along river right, not far downstream of Carnifax Ferry, so he quickly shut his eyes and stood up in his canoe. While still standing, he caromed down the quarter-mile length of Lost Paddle and Tumblehome Rapids with his eyes tightly closed.

And he had to watch for helicopters, too. So he was constantly sneaking peeks of the sky. They'd most likely come in low, to get close-ups, with cameras dangling out the side of the choppers, like they did with .50 caliber machine guns in Nam. Probably with Oliver Stone at the chopper's controls, lining it up for that exquisitely perfect camera angle that would make him instantly famous. He'd be a celebrity overnight. Shot up one side and down the other – with cameras, not with machine guns. With him standing up in his sleek new canoe, eyes clinched tightly, smiling confidently.

All down the river he sneaked, and peeked, and squinted, his eyes burning unmercifully. Once, back in the trees, he thought sure he spotted Jane Fonda and Ted Turner and a film crew numbering in the hundreds. But it was only a couple of tourists with a video cam and a gaggle of kids. And soon, he was forced to face the sad truth: There were no cameras, no helicopters, and no film crews.

And then he started thinking about Amy.

When he returned to the campground, she was gone.

That opened his eyes.

* * * * *

She left behind only a scribbled note asking Bo to give the big canvas, the one depicting the thundering release tubes, to Doctor Katz.

Bo heard that she had packed up and caught a ride out from Summersville Dam with a power plant operator named Daniel. It turned out she had. And Daniel had never seen such pulchritude in jeans and a flannel shirt. "Oh, I remember her, all right," he told Bo next day. "I ain't about to forget her. My ol' truck, it don't have air conditioning, and it was hot yesterday, so we had to have the windows down and the wind was blowing her long hair all over the place. So she pulled this ol' bandanna out of her hip pocket and tied it around her head, and rolled up the sleeves on her shirt, and said with a smile, 'There, that fixes that.' It was yeller. The bandanna was, I mean. Or a cross between yeller and orange. I'm not too good at tellin' one color from another, but man, I'll never forget how good that bandanna looked on that woman, tied back against her dark hair like that."

He had driven her to Summersville, to the bus station, and let her out. She tried to pay him twenty dollars for his trouble but he refused to take her money.

"No offense to you, Mister," he said to Bo, "but you have a woman looks like that, you oughta take better care of her so she don't run off and leave you. It was obvious she was a lady, and out of her element down here with all this river riffraff."

Bo told Daniel she was his friend and not his lover and she had a strong will and a mind of her own and made her own decisions. And she was an artist, too, Bo told him, as if that might help to explain things.

Daniel listened to what Bo had to say and replied, "Well, I reckon I can believe she's strong-willed and makes up her own mind." Daniel gave Bo a hard up-and-down look, and chose his words carefully. "But, do you reckon maybe you oughta go get her?" he said. "Or at least make sure she's all right? She was mighty delicate looking. Bad things can happen to a gal like that out on her own, in this rough country."

Bo broke eye contact with the mountain man and stared down at the ground between them. "She'll be fine," he said finally. "She's not the kind of woman you can give orders to."

Daniel nodded. "Yeah," he said. "I reckon I could see that."

More Adjustments

The departure of his friend and not his lover threw Bo into a veritable funk. While it was true he and Amy had not become lovers, it was also true that they had become the closest of friends. They had been touring around together for over a month before coming to the Gauley. The relationship had been awkward at first, but it had grown into a gratifyingly comfortable arrangement. At first Bo had been intent on seducing her, but as the days and nights passed and they settled into a pleasant asexual domesticity, he had lost sight of his visions of romantic entanglement. Until this morning, that is, when she was standing there with his old shirt around her ankles, asking him to stay with her. And he had foolishly gone off to the river instead. And now he kept seeing her, standing there, without so much as a stitch of clothing, with that look of bedroom urgency in her eyes. Saying, "Stay here with me, Bo, there's something we need to do. We've waited long enough."

He missed her terribly, and spent long hours staring at her paintings. To get a better view of her work, he would prop the paintings against the interior walls of the motor home. Soon, he had hauled out enough canvasses, from where she had been storing them in the back room, to completely line the walls, door-to-door, floor-to-ceiling, creating a 360-degree panorama.

Her productivity during the time they were together had been phenomenal. She had continuously worked on at least two, and sometimes three or four canvasses simultaneously. He had once asked what was behind her incredible outpouring. She gave his question a lot of thought, while wearing that serenely wistful expression that only Amy, of all the women he had ever known, had mastered. The answer he wanted to hear, that her creative outburst was attributable to the wonderful new friend she had met, wasn't forthcoming. She said, instead, "The home milieu is not supportive."

Bo had replied, "The home what? ain't supportive?"

And she had smiled, and kissed him on top of his head.

He still didn't know what that word meant. Must have had something to do with landscapes. She painted a lot of them. Painted a lot of portraits, too, for that matter. Several of him. And a disgusting representation of Wild Bill Barkley, slopping down a cup of tea, that captured the very essence of his volatile temperament. She painted a load of still lifes, too, and a lot of stuff that he couldn't make much sense of. Abstracts, he supposed. They were abstract to him, anyway.

Hauling out all her paintings and turning the motor home into an art gallery was hard work. He worked up quite a thirst. Which he whetted with tequila. And not a small quantity of Bass Ale, along with the cactus juice. And always brewing that concoction in that beat-up old coffee pot. Partly because it reminded him of her. Reminded him of that grumpy-friendly morning smile that he had come to like so much, of the way she would hug him when he returned safe from the river, and stroke his hair and tell him that although they weren't lovers she loved him nevertheless. He brewed pot after pot, slugging it down, thinking about her. Rarely sleeping. Staying up night after night, watching for the first light of day. Some mornings, when missing her was worst, brewing up two potfuls and swilling both before hitting the river.

And using his new shut-eye paddling technique with a vengeance now. To show her, maybe, that he could close his eyes on the river if he damn well wanted to. But almost, too, as if he believed that by shutting his eyes tightly enough, and keeping them closed long enough, he would open them to find her back with him again, standing there in front of the easel the way she would do, staring intently at the canvas, feet apart and one hip cocked out at an angle, cradling the palette in the bend of one arm, her other hand working the brush, occasionally looking over her shoulder to catch him watching her work, smiling at him. Smiling also with those marvelous brown eyes.

Incipient River Tragedy

But Bo still had the river. And in its own way, it was as absorbing as his erstwhile artist friend. And he still had – for whatever they were worth – his hardcore, ne'er-do-well paddling companions.

As Bo would slowly drift blindly through the long pools, his eyes tightly closed, his companions would paddle furiously on downstream to the next big rapid, where first-time rafters who had never heard of Bo Rocker or his burning eyes or his inexplicable attraction to canoes, would be out on the bank scouting. His friends would pull over to the bank also and get out of their boats, ostensibly to scout the rapid, pretending they too were on the river for the first time. After a cursory glance at the rapid, however, they'd commence to scoff loudly at the timidity of anybody who'd hesitate to run such puny water.

"Why, it ain't even a rapid!" Hank Menzel would exclaim, after taking a quick glance at one of the Gauley's big Class V rapids. "It's just a little riffle!"

"Yeah," Wild Bill Barkley would add, casting a scornful glance at the anxious rafters gathered nearby. "Only a coward would consider portaging this dinky little drop."

Doctor Katz would then suggest, loud enough for all the rafters to hear: "I'll bet this insipid little declivity could be run in a canoe."

To which statement some irritated rafter would invariably respond, "No way, man. Nobody in a canoe could run this rapid. Maybe you kayakers can run it, but nobody in a canoe could make it through alive."

And Hank Menzel would reply, "A hundred dollars says it could be run in a canoe."

Hank and Wild Bill would make several bets with the rafters, and then, to kick the process into overdrive, Doctor Katz would proclaim: "Hell's bells, I got five hundred bucks says a canoe paddler could run this little rapid with his eyes closed!"

Not surprisingly, this reckless statement would precipitate a renewed flurry of betting. And minutes thereafter, Bo Rocker would drift around the bend with his eyes closed, and flush right through the rapid.

Toward the end of Gauley season, Bo's friends were making out like bandits. Bo would close his eyes just after putting in at Summersville Dam, open them briefly above Insignificant to spot the entrance, then sneak fast peeks just before Pillow Rapid, Lost Paddle, Iron Ring, and Sweets Falls, the biggest cataracts on the river. Otherwise, his trip would be totally closed-eyed.

They were making more money than they knew how to spend.

Until, one day – unbeknownst to his companions – Bo slugged down two extra pots of brew before putting on the river.

The Room of Doom

Everything went according to schedule at Insignificant, the first big rapid on the river. After running it, Hank and the crew sped on downstream ahead of Bo, to Pillow Rock Rapid, the river's second big rapid, where Hank quickly became embroiled in a heated argument with a crew of rafters who insisted that *no* canoe, no matter who was in it, could successfully negotiate the Class V maelstrom around which they had elected to portage. Not only were these rafters highly opinionated, they were also willing to put a lot of money where their mouths were.

After making sizeable bets with several of the rafters, Hank and Wild Bill glanced up and noticed Bo in the pool above Pillow, slumped forward more than usual. "Something's not right with Bo," Wild Bill Barkley whispered in Hank's ear. "For some reason, he hasn't taken his customary sneak peek at the rapid's entrance."

Hank took a long, hard look at the lone figure upstream, slumped forward in his boat, drifting precariously close to the huge rapid's point of no return. He knew Amy's departure had taken a heavy toll on his friend. But he also knew that if there had ever been a *River Master*, it was the man in the canoe, drifting toward the enormous rapid.

Wild Bill said, "I don't think he's gonna make it this time, Hank. Just look at him!"

"Ah," replied Hank, "of course he's gonna make it. He ain't nothin' but the best there's ever been. Bo's okay. He's a smart businessman, that's all. Somehow or other he's got wind of just how much money's on the line, and he's determined to help us pull in one or two last minute bets."

Hank turned around to the rafters, "Look yonder, y'all. Ain't that some ol' fool asleep in his canoe?"

The rafters took one look at the boater, who by now had drifted beyond the point of no return, and clamored to raise their bets. Naturally, Hank and his companions quickly accommodated their demands. As the final bet was settled, Bo bobbed into the gargantuan maelstrom, flushed into the hideous Room of Doom (the dreaded recirculating hydraulic that dumps into the shadow of Pillow Rock), washed around for a while like a match stick in a toilet bowl, and then spurted out into the whirlpool at the tip of Pillow Rock, with his boat still upright and his eyes still closed.

Pandemonium ensued on river right, as the rafters first protested loudly, but eventually capitulated and paid off their bets, albeit grudgingly.

After the rafters put back on the river, Hank and his companions gathered on the rocks alongside the big rapid, counting their money and gleefully recalling the rafter's consternation when Bo, caught in the dreadful Room of Doom, never bothered opening his eyes. "What discipline!" Hank Menzel declared. "I've never seen anything like it. He just bobbed around in there, his boat pulsing and gyrating and occasionally banging off Pillow Rock, and Bo slumped over the whole time, never bothering to lift his paddle, until the current finally squirted him out into that whirlpool over yonder, at the edge of Pillow Rock."

Doctor F. Katz was sitting cross-legged at the base of a big rock, giggling ecstatically as he stuffed a fist-sized wad of fifty dollar bills into his dry bag. "My staff at the clinic can't understand why I enjoy paddling so much," he said between giggles. He reached back inside the dry bag, retrieving the gob of bills he had just stowed away. He had to have one more look, one more caress. He planted a big kiss on the wad of bills before shoving it back home. "What fools are my staff! What utter lack of comprehension they chronically manifest!" He started giggling again. "And just think, before Bo learned to paddle with his eyes closed, I thought I was making a lot of money from my nut cases at the psychiatric clinic. Hell boys, that Bo's more profitable than Prozac. A couple more trips like today and I can retire to Sun Valley!"

Plugging an Undercut at Tumblehome

When Doctor Katz finally got his glee under control, and the group was about ready to put back on the river, somebody noticed that Bo wasn't around.

"Oh no!" Wild Bill Barkley said, springing to his feet and looking frantically up and down the length of Pillow Rapid. "Don't tell me Bo's drowned. And without leaving me his peyotl recipe!" Bill was distraught. He added, "And I must've asked him for that recipe at least a thousand times."

Hank, also rising to his feet, said sternly: "Bo doesn't have a peyotl recipe, Wild Bill. That's tea he brews in his pot every morning. Doctor Katz said so. South American tea. Right Doctor? That tea don't have nothing to do with drugs. Bo don't like drugs. Won't put up with them, or the people who use them. Ain't that right, doctor?"

Katz was sitting on the rocks, clutching his bulging dry bag like he suspected a purse snatcher might dash out of an alley any second and rip it from his grasp. He relaxed his death grip on the bag for a moment and said, "What he brews every morning is from South America. That much is correct." Whereupon he started giggling again.

Hank Menzel shot Katz a look that could kill. "You said yourself it was harmless folk medicine, something from South America."

Katz was laughing so hard he was beginning to cry. "That's right, Hank," he managed to say. "That's all it is: a harmless folk remedy."

"I'm afraid Bo's drowned," Wild Bill lamented, still scanning the rapid from top to bottom. "I don't see him anywhere."

Two boaters who had been taking lunch beside Pillow Rock, and who had watched Bo make his run through the rapid, came over to where Hank's group was assembled. One of them, named Maurice, said that Bo definitely hadn't drowned, but was squirted out of the whirlpool while still in his boat, and had drifted on through the downstream pool, without ever once looking up.

"Incredible feat," Maurice said. "I know it's a trick because I saw him do it yesterday – but not without first taking a quick peek before heading into the rapid. Today, though, he didn't even look up when he washed into the Room of Doom over there." Maurice gestured toward the far bank, to the hideous recirculating hole. He added, "I've never known anybody who could paddle like him. Or maybe I should say float like him, since he never once took a paddle stroke. That Bo Rocker definitely has ice water in his veins."

Doctor Katz started giggling again. "That ain't all he's got in his veins."

"Now wait a minute," Hank said to Katz. "Loose talk like that only feeds the rumor mills. You know as well as I do that Bo brews tea in that pot every morning."

"Yeah," Doctor Katz said. "He brews tea: high octane tea." And with that he was off again, hugging his dry bag and giggling.

"I knew it!" Wild Bill said excitedly. "He puts something else in there with the tea, don't he? I've seen him sprinkle it in. Some kind of powder. What is it? Tell me, you worthless old sawbones! What kind of powder is it? I need to know."

Katz shrugged. "You wouldn't believe it if I told you."

"Try us," Hank Menzel said, scowling. "I'd like to know, once and for all."

Katz looked up at Menzel, who was towering over him. Hank was a big guy. Something on the order of six foot six. And all of it sinewy lean.

"You really want to know?" Doctor Katz said, looking infinitesimally small, sitting at the giant's bootie-clad feet.

"Tell me," Menzel said, staring down at him.

"It's a complex alkaloid, with a molecular structure somewhere between nicotine and cocaine."

"You're saying Bo takes narcotics?" Hank said.

"I knew it!" Wild Bill screeched.

"No, it's definitely not a narcotic," Doctor Katz assured them. "It's more like a naturally occurring tranquilizer. It originated as a privileged recipe of the Inca aristocracy."

"A tranquilizer?" Hank said incredulously. "The Incas?"

Wild Bill jerked out his recipe and poetry notebook. He dabbed the end of a stubby pencil against his tongue and strutted up beside Hank. "Where's he get that stuff from?" he said to the doctor. "What's in it? How do I make it?" He gritted his teeth. "Don't hold out on me, Katz. This is important. I need that stuff. Just exactly what is it, anyway?"

"That's the part you won't believe," Katz said. "It comes from desiccated and triturated arachnitidus magnoliophyta."

Wild Bill was scribbling furiously. "Wait a minute," he commanded. "Slow down. Iraq night magnolia fight us what? How do you spell that?"

Hank said, "What is . . . whatever that was you just said?"

"It's poisonous spiders that live only in the high Andes," Katz said. "The Indians pick them off coca plants, kill them with a long needle, and dry them in the sun. When they're good and dry, they grind them up with stone mortars and pestles. Then they sprinkle the powder in coffee and drink it. It works just as well with tea. It's basically harmless. Folk medicine. The Indians claim it has a calming effect."

Maurice butted in: "I'm pretty sure it works. Bo Rocker was definitely calm out there." He nodded toward the river.

"Could you overdose on that stuff?" Hank asked Doctor Katz.

"Naw," Katz said confidently. "Your eyes'd burn out first." He started giggling again, uncontrollably.

"What'n hell's wrong with you, man?" Hank yelled at him.

"Inappropriate affect," Wild Bill announced solemnly. "I'm making a note of it right here." He paused momentarily to show Hank his lengthy notations, then commenced scribbling furiously again, talking the whole time. "It's a common behavioral manifestation among burnt-out old shrinks. Especially among morally degenerate old shrinks like this one." His pencil stilled for a moment, and he said to Hank, "By the way, what rhymes with shrink?"

"Jesus Christ!" Hank bellowed, raising his eyes to heaven.

"I don't think so," Wild Bill said, jotting something down on his pad. "Shrink - Christ. Christ - shrink. No, I don't think so."

"I'm surrounded by imbeciles!" Hank screamed at the heavens.

Wild Bill put down his pencil and looked at the crowd of river runners gathering around them, everybody curious about the yelling and giggling they had been hearing. "Yeah," Wild Bill said, looking at the crowd. "There're some really dumb looking people around here, that's for sure. Wouldn't surprise me none if they're open boaters."

That precipitated another round of giggling from Doctor Katz.

Hank Menzel let out an angry howl and effortlessly yanked Doctor Katz to his feet. "Now listen to me, you old nitwit, I'm going to ask you one more time, and this time I better get a straight answer to . . ."

". . . to the question of where can we buy the stuff!" Wild Bill interjected. "That powdered spider stuff."

"Shut up!" Hank screamed, shaking Katz vigorously.

"That means you," Wild Bill said to Katz.

"That means *you,* Wild Bill," Hank said between clenched teeth.

"Mums the word, sir," Wild Bill replied, meekly.

"Now give me a straight answer," Hank said, shaking Katz once again. "Is it possible to overdose on this spider juice, or whatever it is?"

"I don't think so," Katz gasped. "I've never heard of it happening."

"What if you drank a whole lot of it?" Hank growled.

"Yeah," Wild Bill added, "What if you slugged it down by the potful? What if you became so despondent because the girlfriend you weren't sleeping with ran off with a dam engineer she didn't sleep with back to her old boyfriend who she also probably didn't sleep with that you couldn't sleep yourself from thinking about all the sleep everybody was missing – not to mention all the sex – so you stayed up night after night belting down one potful after another, wishing you could fall asleep? Or maybe have some sex? Huh! What would happen to you then? Huh!"

Wild Bill, suddenly realizing he had spoken against Hank's command, audibly gulped, and quickly added, "Right, Hank?"

Hank scowled at him, and then looked back at Katz. "Yeah, what if all that happened, and you drank way too much of the stuff?"

Doctor Katz said, "Other than transitory ocular discomfort?"

Hank and Bill exchanged puzzled glances. Wild Bill shrugged. "Yeah," Hank said, "other than that."

"Yeah, other than that!" Wild Bill echoed, looking up at Hank for approval. "Right, Hank?"

Hank nodded. "Yeah, what else would happen?"

Katz said, "In my considered professional opinion, you could drink a ton of the stuff and nothing else could possibly happen except, well, perhaps if you drank a vast amount for days on end, you might possibly nod off and . . ."

It seemed to hit everybody at once, the realization that Bo must have slugged down so much of the stuff, and missed so much sleep from walking the floor over Amy's departure, that he actually nodded off after he put on the river, while in his canoe. And if it was true, he had washed through Class V Pillow Rock Rapid not only with his eyes closed, but also while sound asleep!

"Holy crapatoly," Wild Bill said solemnly, slapping shut his notebook. His voice rose as he spoke: "I can see it now. An epic poem: Rhyme of the Somnambulist Mariner. I'll be famous, I tell you. My name up in lights. Book contracts out the wazoo. Speaking engagements coast to coast. There'll be a National Book Award in this before it's over, just wait and see. Maybe a National Poetry Prize. A Pulitzer Prize, too. Who knows, maybe even the Nobel Prize!"

"Nobels are awarded in recognition of sustained contributions," Katz said. "They aren't handed out for individual poems."

"In that case, I'll refuse to accept it," Wild Bill declared, with an expansive gesture. "Remember when Marlon Brando turned down the Oscar for best actor? Well, Wild Bill Barkley will be the first to turn down the Nobel Prize for poetry! It'll be an act of defiance so brilliant that it'll stun the world. I'll be the talk of the ages. They'll write books about me. I'll be on all the talk shows. There'll be statues of me in the nation's Capitol. There'll be . . ."

Hank released Katz and slowly turned downstream. In fact, all eyes turned downstream, as finally even Wild Bill got the picture and shut his trap, and all the paddlers stood speechless, the numbing realization slowly sinking in of the prodigious task before them. There was no alternative. They had to catch up to Bo before he flushed into Lost Paddle, which wasn't far downstream. Lost Paddle was quite possibly the most hazardous rapid on the river.

Doctor Katz staggered over to the river's edge, clutching his dry bag tightly to his breast, mournfully looking downstream. "Bo, come back!" he commanded of the empty river. "I need you! We need you! Sun Valley needs you!"

"Modern literature needs you!" Wild Bill added.

Hank made a mad dash for his boat, with Katz and the others close on his heels. Maurice and his friend shouted after them, "We'll come with you. You'll need all the help you can get!" And they too bolted for their boats, followed immediately by all the other paddlers who by this time had gathered on the rocks beside Pillow Rapid.

An armada of small craft surged onto the river, paddles slicing the water into a froth, every mind focused on the certainty that they had to catch Bo, to wake him, to save him.

"There's not a second to spare," Hank shouted over his shoulder as he stroked furiously downstream. "If we don't overtake him before Lost Paddle, he'll die. Nobody can make it through that rapid alive without sneaking at least one peek. Not even Bo Rocker. Come on guys, paddle! Our grubstake's about to plug an undercut at Tumblehome!"

An Explosive Situation

But Hank and the gang didn't find Bo at Lost Paddle Rapid, or at any of the other big rapids on the river. Instead, at every major rapid they discovered paddlers milling about on the banks . . . in shock.

At Sweets Falls, where the Gauley River plummets ten feet, they found six kayaks abandoned on the left bank. A dazed bystander volunteered that the boats had belonged to an elite waterfall-running team training for the Olympics. When the Olympic hopefuls saw an open canoeist run over the waterfall backwards while apparently sound asleep, they realized they were in the wrong business, threw down their paddles in disgust, and hiked out of the canyon.

Hank and his group never caught up with Bo that day. He floated past Swiss, the first downstream town. Down to the confluence with the New River and onto the mighty Kanawha River. Caused quite a commotion, too. Seems there were dozens of reports to the authorities, many of them originating from members of a former waterfall-running team. In a fit of jealousy, the Olympic coach called the Federal Police Bureau (FPB) to say it was a crime what the unidentified paddler was doing, and that he ought to be arrested. The coach's call triggered an alert on the Coordinated Federal and Local Crime Prevention Hotline, which activated county, state and federal crime fighters from Atlanta to Cleveland. Every professional criminal east of the Mississippi, faithfully monitoring the Crime Hot Line, immediately redirected their activities to locales outside the alert area.

KZYT television in Charleston picked up on the news from their police scanners, and sent a mobile unit to cover the disturbance. They were so aggrieved to discover the turmoil was caused by nothing more significant than a sleepy open boater that they felt compelled to spice up their report. They broadcast that some paddler had taken an irresponsible stunt too far, and turned it into an unprecedentedly wanton crime spree.

As word spread, locals focused on the word "stunt." They assumed that where there's a stunt, there must be a "stunt-man," which they associated with Hollywood, which in turn evoked visions of movie production. A local radio station broadcast that Steven Spielberg was making a movie entitled: *"Deliverance II, The Ohio Acid Bath."*

Federal, state, and local law enforcement officials focused on the words "crime spree." SWAT teams from Nashville to Pittsburgh were placed on standby alert. Ever-vigilant against the prospect of civil unrest, top powers at the FPB directed its Southeast Regional Director, Hugh Sams, to personally monitor developments. Sams was in Washington, lobbying for additional crime prevention monies. He immediately prepared to leave for West Virginia.

The national media swung into action. Joan Broaddus Wright, controversial talkshow host, was also in Washington, along with a production crew, taping a special segment of the *Joan Broaddus Wright Show.* Using her influence, Joan Broaddus bumped Hugh Sams, taking his seat on the plane, leaving him fuming in the hangar. And no wonder he was fuming: the plane was a private FPB jet.

The Federal Centers for Crime Control initiated a world-wide computer search for all canoe-related crime sprees. Locating no previous crime sprees perpetrated by canoe bandits, the Center Director declared the crisis was unprecedented in human history, and there was no known method to combat such an emergency. The prudent response, according to the directive issued by the Center Director and forwarded to the Oval Office, was one of massive force. The White House security staff, alarmed to hear there was no known method to suppress canoe brigands, advised the President to respond authoritatively, in order to instill citizen confidence and avoid widespread panic. Accordingly, the President called the Governor of West Virginia and ordered immediate activation of twenty or thirty thousand jack-booted storm troopers, two regiments of Bradley Fighting Dread-naughts, and a Brigade or two of Abrams main battle tanks.

By this time locals were swarming to the river by the pickup truck load, bringing their spouses and children, cousins, mothers-in-law, uncles, maiden aunts, nephews, nieces, the dogs, even a couple of pet pigs, thinking some lucky family member might land a bit part in the new movie, or at least get to see that racy young actress, Rachael Murphy, take off her clothes.

As day turned to night, the sky was illuminated by dozens of Apache AH-64 attack helicopters, looking like giant praying mantises, bristling with crime-detection spotlights. The spotlights, their computer-controlled, laser-guided, body-heat-activated beams crisscrossing the broad river and its banks, had been acquired with a Presidential pork barrel anti-crime block grant.

Meanwhile, local residents were jamming the river banks, gawking into the night sky, staring into the spotlights, fighting to get a glimpse of Harrison Ford or Kevin Bacon or Tommy Lee Jones or whatever action hero was starring with Rachael Murphy in that fabulous new move, *The Ohio Acid Bath.* Ophthalmologists from seven states were rushed to the area to treat the tens of thousands of cases of singed corneas and fried retinas that resulted from use of the anti-crime lights. But civilian casualties are inevitable in major police anti-crime actions. Fortunately, representatives were on hand from the Federal Alliance to Adjudicate Claims from Victims of Police Excess Force. The reps handed out more than seventy-two thousand claim forms, with postage-paid return envelopes, and business cards from Washington, D.C. lawyers.

When a combined county, state, and federal anti-crime task force finally intercepted Bo, he was still asleep. State anti-crime authorities wanted to charge him with disturbing the peace by floating through a populated area at night in a polluted condition, without a state permit. But federal anti-crime authorities insisted the charge should be for disrupting the tranquility of the Republic by floating through a polluted area at night in a populated condition, without an EPA permit. When the argument between state and federal anti-crime authorities became so loud that it awoke Bo, Matt Hodges, the county Sheriff, stepped forward and demanded to see Bo's movie production permit. Bo dug around in his dry bag and came up with movie production permits for Alaska and North Carolina, but couldn't find one validated for use in West Virginia.

"Just as I suspected," Sheriff Hodges replied. "Your kind never bothers with permits. You think you can float in here in one of your fancy boats and get away with anything, just 'cause you're loaded with all that filthy Hollywood money. You think you can thumb your nose at the law and ride roughshod over the poor people of Tracer County, don't you? Violate our women, treat us all like dirt, laugh at our customs and old-fashioned values. Well, this time it ain't gonna work. You're under arrest, Mister Tinsel Town Glitzball. Nine felony counts of movie production without proper county permits."

"Nine counts?" Bo said, rubbing his burning eyes, trying to wake up. "How'd you come up with that number?"

"Oh, so you don't like my arithmetic, huh? Mister fancy-pants movie producer? Floatin' in here in the middle of the night in one of them expensive astronaut suits. Think you got the world by the tail, don't you, boy? You probably got one of them fancy college degrees, too, don't you? I bet you're thinking that my Tracer County High School diploma don't qualify me to count felony violations, ain't you?"

"Hell, Sheriff," said the director of the local Alcohol, Tobacco and Firearms Enforcement Agency (ATFEA). "Let me have him. I can stick him with at least a dozen counts of . . ." The director was looking around, desperately trying to think up a creative-sounding violation, anything to justify stealing a prisoner away from the bumbling local Sheriff. He spotted Bo's canoe. "What're them things right there, boy?" he said, pointing to the gunwales.

"Those are gunwales," Bo replied.

"Hell no, boy! Don't you get smart with me. Not them things. I'm talking about them things right there, below them gum whales."

"Pop rivets?" Bo said.

"Uh huh! I knew it! You said "pop," didn't you, boy? Was that "pop" as in bang? "Pop" as in ammo? "Pop" as in explosion? "Pop" as in illegal firearms? "Pop" as in a bomb you might be intending to plant in a federal building?"

"No," Bo replied. "It was "pop" as in rivets."

"I knew it!" the ATFEA director screamed, pumping his fists in the air like a high school cheerleader. "He's confessed! Right there I got him with, how many? let me see . . ." He turned to his cadre of junior ATFEA violations enforcers, all of whose salaries were paid by a Congressional pork barrel block grant crime prevention annually renewable appropriations bill, and yelled, "Quick, get over there and count the number of illegal explosive devices on that unlicensed torpedo boat."

A dozen federal law enforcement personnel fell over one another in a mad scramble to drop to their knees and tally the number of pop rivets on Bo's canoe. Seconds later, one head shot up over the squirming mass of bodies: "Fourteen violations, sir!"

"There! Did you hear that?" the ATFEA director screamed at Sheriff Hodges. "Fourteen FAED violations!"

Hodges interrupted him: "What the hell's a 'faded' violation?"

"Why, FAED means Firearms and Explosive Devices. This is big time, Sheriff. Fourteen violations are more'n they had on David Koresh! That's more'n they had on all the Branch Davidians put together! That man is a gun runner! A confessed explosives smuggler. And those violations are just on one side of his torpedo boat." He yelled back at the federal rivet counters: "How many sides on that boat?"

"Oh, for crying out loud," Sheriff Hodges moaned. He swaggered over toward Bo's boat, pausing along the way to take a couple of kicks at stray federal employees crawling around on their hands and knees, photographing the canoe from ground level with two-thousand-dollar Nikon cameras, paid for with a Senate anti-crime block grant. The Sheriff muttered, "Get out of my way, you useless scum." Arriving at the canoe, he bent down, best he could considering the tub of lard hanging out over his belt and all the federal agents in his way, and peered at the rivets. He straightened up and walked back over to the ATFEA director. "Them ain't nothin' but common pop rivets," he announced, scornfully. "Having' them thangs on a boat ain't no federal violation." He smiled ear to ear. "But it *is* a Tracer County violation, prosecutable under local Hardware Statute twenty-four-dash-seventeen-dash-nine-zero. That is, unless the boat's owner has a proper pop rivet import permit. Which I know he ain't got 'cause my deputies done inventoried all his belongings. So that makes, how many? fourteen plus fourteen is . . . let's see, now . . . uh . . . thirty-eight new violations on top of nine old violations which add up to . . . uh, approximately sixty-six separate violations, all felonies, and each punishable by incarceration for not less than twelve years nor more'n twenty-five or, at the discretion of the Tracer County Magistrate, death by hanging or appropriate substitute punishment, which is often a fine not to exceed several million dollars but usually of astronomical proportions nonetheless in order for the county to maintain a highway system that is constantly worn to a frazzle by an army of useless federal agents who insist on hangin' out hereabouts, drivin' their massive fleet of vehicles around at taxpayer expense, and all of which means that you . . ." He turned toward Bo. ". . . mister fancy-pants Hollywood producer, are under arrest."

Bo said, "Thirty-eight plus nine don't equal no sixty-six counts, Sheriff."

The Sheriff went arms akimbo, that huge beer gut hanging out over his belt, dangling like a Frank Lloyd Wright cantilevered living room. He stood there glowering at Bo, looking a lot like Jackie Gleason in one of those old Honeymooners episodes, except the Sheriff's eyes bulged out more, and he was bigger, uglier, fatter, and a lot more belligerent. About two hundred federal agents took several steps backward at the spectacle of the Sheriff making ready to pound a prisoner. The Sheriff snarled, "Frankly, boy, I think you're premature to be plea bargaining at this stage." He looked around at the mob of federal agents. "Why, the idiots from the federal district attorney's office ain't even arrived yet. There'll be at least a thousand of them morons, and they usually top any offer I can make. But okay, Hollywood, have it your way. I'll play your game: you add 'em up yourself. What's the correct number of felony counts?"

"Well . . ." Bo stammered. "I'm not sure, but it ain't sixty-six."

A Deputy Director (one of twelve for the state of West Virginia) of the Federal Office of Crime Statistics Accountability Bureau, clutching a laptop computer, rushed forward. She thrust the display screen in Sheriff Hodge's face. "Thirty-seven! Thirty-seven! Thirty-seven violations, Sheriff," she shrilled. "All of which will be dutifully entered in the FPB's Comprehensive State and County Crime Report Computer Compilation Summary Report. It's a veritable crime wave! On the basis of these violations alone, my office'll be funded for at least three more years! It'll take at least that long to process all the data and generate all the federally mandated reports. And then, of course, they'll be the Congressional hearings, and . . ."

Sheriff Hodges drew back his fist and threatened to belt the woman, as she dodged away from him in a panic, falling off her heels in a vain effort to avoid collision with his colossal quivering beer gut. When the Deputy Director Crime Statistician regained her balance, she was screaming something about sex-discrimination suits and aggravated assault charges, before disappearing into a throng of federal agents.

Sheriff Hodges looked at Bo and smiled. "Yep," he said. "Every movie mogul's gotta have one of them permits. At least one, preferably two or three."

A white limo pulled up at the curb and Brad Fillyaw, the federal district attorney, jumped out and came running over to the Sheriff, followed by six or seven assistant district attorneys. "Unhand that criminal!" Fillyaw said to the Sheriff. He whipped out a cellular phone. "I got a conference call right here. Number two in Justice is holding and he says this fiendish criminal . . ." He pointed at Bo. "Is our property."

Sheriff Hodges glowered at Fillyaw. "I got news for you, Sonny," he said. "I don't take orders from a pile of number two on the street, and I don't take orders from number two in Justice. Now get out of my sight!"

Fillyaw jumped back to avoid a backhand from the Sheriff. He pointed the cellular phone at Sheriff Hodges like it was a weapon. Like he was flashing a cross made of garlic at a vampire. He said, "I told you it was a conference call! I got the FPB Southeast Regional Director holding. He'd be here himself if he hadn't got bumped off his plane. He says for you to turn over the felon."

That got the Sheriff's attention.

He said to Fillyaw, "You got the Regional FPB Director on there? My ol' buddy Hugh Sams? Why didn't you say so? Can I see that thang a minute?"

He took the phone, looked it over carefully, then dropped it on the sidewalk and ground it to smithereens with the heel of his boot. He poked Fillyaw in the chest with his finger. "Next time you get Sams on the horn, you tell him Sheriff Matt Hodges done told him to kiss his number two." He patted his buttocks. "And when I say my number two, I don't mean my chief deputy. Now, get out of my sight!" He took a wild kick at Fillyaw.

Before another federal officer could interrupt, he turned to his deputies, and barked: "Clap that felon in irons and let's get outta this here quagmire of moral faggots and federal maggots."

When they pushed through the army of federal and state agents, they encountered another army: crazed movie fans intent on seeing which Hollywood star Sheriff Hodges was arresting.

"Look!" somebody in the crowd yelled. "It's Mel Gibson! They got Mel Gibson!"

"No it ain't," another excited spectator shouted. "It's River Phoenix!"

"River Phoenix is dead," shrieked a lady wearing a short blond wig and about a ton of mascara around her eyes.

"That prisoner ain't dead yet," yelled somebody else. "Although from his looks, I'd say they've beat on him with an ugly stick for a good long time. I know he's still alive, though. Why else'd they have him in handcuffs?"

"They got River Phoenix in cuffs? That's cruel! The poor guy's been dead for years and they got him all trussed up like a chicken. What'll they think of next? Before you know it, they'll be arresting Elvis."

"Where's Elvis!" a wrinkle faced old man shouted excitedly. "I saw him once at the Palace Theater in Memphis. On Beale Street! That was before he made it big. Before he got big, too."

A bag lady elbowed her way to the front of the crowd. She announced: "I saw Elvis last week, at the Krispy Kreme doughnut shop. He was doing wheelies in the parking lot. In a '57 Ford. A black and white convertible!"

Joan Broaddus Wright's television crew was scrambling to complete its satellite uplink as Joan became increasingly steamed with the delay. Joan was skinny as a rail, jumping around, looking like some character out of *The Wizard of Oz*. Her short-cropped hair was swept back, like somebody had ironed it in place and then glopped on a few handfuls of KY Jelly to make sure it stayed in place. She was flapping her arms, shouting at her producer, Frank McKay. "Get a move on! We're missing it. We're missing it!"

McKay advised her to calm down. "It's just another police beating of a handcuffed prisoner," he said. "We have archives full of prisoner beatings. We got so damned many tapes of prisoner beatings, we don't have room to store half of 'em."

"No, you tech head," Joan screamed back at him. "This is real news. Can't you tell we're in the midst of a spectacle? Can't you hear a thing the crowd's saying? They're raising the dead over there. They got Elvis! They got River Phoenix! Maybe Jerry Garcia. Who knows who else they got? They may have Janis Joplin!"

"Where's Elvis?" a lady screamed, on the verge of going into a swoon. She was a big woman, six feet or better. Her husband, or boyfriend, or supportive male friend, or good Samaritan stranger, or whatever he was, was beside her. He was a small man, about five feet tall, dressed in overalls and plow boots – no shirt – his bare shoulder dug into the woman's rib cage, steadfastly holding her up, lest she topple over and be trampled by the increasingly hysterical mob.

"The hell with dead men, I wanna see Rachael Murphy take off her clothes," announced a man in a booming voice. He was dressed in his pajamas and was calmly smoking a cigar.

"Where's Rachael Murphy?" asked a man in dirty jeans and a black leather vest, with tattoos streaming down his burly arms, dripping off his knobby fists. He was looking around this way and that, his teeth bared like a dog ready for combat, rotten incisors flashing in the street light, a wild look in his eyes, like he really did expect to see Rachael Murphy tear off her clothes and rush butt naked through the streets, the way she did in that movie, *Unleashed Fury*.

"I loved her in that TV show she had," the woman with all the Mascara shouted at one of Joan's television cameras. "What was the name of it? The one with that ever-hard guy. Or was it the die-hard guy?"

"I wanna see Roy Orbison!" a homeless man shouted. He was trying to hand-roll a cigarette, but people kept jostling against him, repeatedly sending his paper and tobacco makings flying in all directions.

"I wanna hear Roy Orbison sing!" said a lady in a red dress suit.

The mascara lady chimed in with that high-pitched, grating voice: "Roy Orbison died, you nitwits! What's wrong with all of you? What do you think this is, a parade of the dead?"

"I wanna hear Rachael Murphy sing," bellowed the man in the leather vest. "I love that hussy's voice. Come on baby, let 'er rip!" He unfastened a chrome-plated logging chain from around his waist and started swinging it wildly. "Here baby, I'll keep time for you!" he shouted. The chain was whipping through the air over his head, making a deep-throated swooshing sound. "Sing it baby. Let 'er rip!" The crowd was wisely moving back, away from the fool.

A woman who looked like a cross between Martina Navratilova and Madonna, and who was actually a disillusioned stunt kayaker and Olympic hopeful, grabbed Sheriff Hodge's arm and shouted in his ear that a former member of the mob and current police informer in the Federal Witness Protection Program, who lived in a seven hundred thousand-dollar mansion on a strip mine bench outside Bluefield, West Virginia, and who preferred to remain anonymous until a court date was set, at which time he would suddenly be called away on business to Buenos Aires, had asked her to inform the Sheriff that the arrested felon was on steroids. That accusation, coming from an impeccably reliable source, produced one short cellular phone call by the Sheriff and an onslaught of green-frocked bloodsuckers from the local Federal Anti-Crime Serology Laboratory, each determined to plunge a syringe into one of Bo's arms, or, failing to reach one of those numerically limited target objectives, into any other available appendage, several of which were recklessly utilized in the resulting melee.

Within an hour, a dozen blood samples landed on the desk of Doctor Roscoe Hinkle, Chief Federal Forensic Pathologist at the local federally-subsidized Anti-Crime Pathology Institute, for overnight analysis. Doctor Hinkle, contacted at home by the Tracer County Sheriff's Office, and reminded of his obligation under Presidential Anti-Crime Mandate CS-14-345-AQT-666 to provide overnight anti-crime serology analyses, promptly called one of his eight secretaries and assigned the task. The secretary drove to the lab, analyzed one sample, wrote one report, smoked seven cigarettes, dumped the ashes and butts into one of the unanalyzed blood samples, made eleven photocopies of the completed report, and sent all twelve reports to the Sheriff's office. The secretary completed an invoice, made eleven photocopies, addressed all twelve to the local Federal Multi-Agency Anti-Crime Services Disbursement Bureau, drove home and went back to sleep, and took the next eight days off with triple-compensation overtime hazardous duty pay.

The twelve lab reports said: "It is the considered opinion of Doctor Roscoe Hinkle that the blood is either of arachnoid origin or else somebody has been bitten severely by a black widow and needs immediate medical attention. Thank you. It is a pleasure to analyze your blood."

In the Jailhouse Now

Next morning, Hank and the gang got word that Bo was lodged in the Tracer County Jail. They talked it over and decided that springing him would be a cinch because two of their group were lawyers. Indeed, one of them was a state senator who had sponsored a half dozen or more anti-crime bills. Their game plan was to march into the jail like they owned the place and intimidate the local hayseed law enforcement officials with a nonstop barrage of polysyllabic legal nonsense. Lay down the law, in other words. And demand Bo's immediate release.

However, it didn't quite work out that way.

What happened was, when Hank and the others stalked into the constabulary, they discovered the arresting officer, Tracer County Sheriff Matt Hodges, sitting behind his desk, methodically taking down crime scene details from his brother-in-law, Luther Hinkle. Luther Hinkle was the brother of Doctor Roscoe Hinkle, head of the local Anti-Crime Pathology Institute. The same Doctor Hinkle whose secretary had rendered the decision, based on a blood sample, that Bo was a spider. Luther Hinkle, in addition to being Roscoe's brother, was also one of the rafters who had been fleeced the day before by unidentified racketeers at a big rapid on the upper Gauley River near Summersville. And it was the details of this crime scene that he was avidly relating to the Sheriff.

"I'm pretty sure that the spider man you have in the cell back there was the one in the canoe yesterday," Luther was saying to the Sheriff. "Roscoe says that spiders have an extraordinary sense of balance, 'cause they spend so much time swinging on thin strands suspended from spiderwebs."

Sheriff Hodges interrupted his paperwork for a moment and said, "Is that how Roscoe thinks he managed to stay in his canoe through all them big rapids?　Because he has an unhuman sense of balance?"

"Plus the fact spiders fear water," Luther added. "That kept him from turning over."

"I don't think fear kept him from turning over," the Sheriff said. "That ol' boy wasn't fearful of nothin' when we found him. He was passed out. Stone cold passed out."

"I know that," Luther said. "But Roscoe said he was unconsciously aware of the water around him the whole time. Even while he was passed out. That's why he didn't turn over. That, and of course the fact that he's a spider – part spider, anyhow – and therefore possessed of that unhuman sense of balance that you mentioned."

Sheriff Hodges leaned back in his chair, scrutinizing Luther. The Sheriff said, "Your brother didn't find airy trace of drugs in all them samples he analyzed?"

"Nope."

"No alcohol?"

"Nope."

"No steroids?"

"Not a one."

"No crack cocaine?"

"Nope."

"No marijuana?"

"Nope.　Just spider enzymes, loads of 'em."

"No nicotine?"

"Nope."

"That's odd," said the Sheriff. "One of them blood samples Roscoe sent back up here was full of cigarette butts. How do you explain that?"

"Didn't happen in my brother's lab. You can bet on that. He's a research scientist. His standards are beyond reproach.

If there was any contamination, it must have occurred once the samples arrived up here."

The Sheriff said, "That brother of yours could be wrong, you know. If he managed to get cigarette butts in one sample, he could have got a load of spider crap in another. I don't think there's no such thang as a man that's part spider. I'd as soon believe he's the Marlboro Man and got cigarette butts floatin' through his veins as to believe he's part spider."

"I'll remind you," Luther said indignantly, "that my brother is a bona fide criminal pathologist. He's had all the proper training. Had all them courses with the FPB. His clinical opinions have stood up in the highest courts of this land. Take my advice: don't second-guess one of his clinical opinions."

The Sheriff put down his pen and clipboard and frowned at Luther. He said, "I always wanted to be a doctor myself. And if I'd had half the advantages Roscoe's enjoyed over the years from them federal authorities, I could've been one, too. I just didn't have time to take all them correspondence courses like he did."

"Well," Luther said, "I'll admit that Roscoe's had his share of lucky breaks. More'n me and you put together, that's for sure. And I'll also admit that I've never heard of anybody being part spider. But you'll have to agree with one thing: even if the fella in that cell back there ain't a spider, he shore ain't normal like the rest of us. How could he have floated all the way down that river in a canoe if he'd a been normal?"

"You got a point there," the Sheriff admitted. He picked up his pen and looked for where he had left off on the Uniform Crime Report Form. Finding his place, he said to Luther, "Let's see now, it's your theory that our friend in the cell back there was in cahoots with the culprits on the bank who swindled you out of twenty-seven hundred dollars?"

"Uh, did I say *twenty-seven* hundred dollars?"

"Sure you did," said the Sheriff. "I got it writ down right here on my Crime Report Form. See?"

Luther glanced down at the form. He said, "Well yes, I guess you do, don't you? But you see, I meant to say *forty-seven* hundred dollars. Not twenty-seven hundred. It was Pete Holbrooks who lost twenty-seven hundred dollars to those hoodlums. And they clipped Fred Watkins for thirty-five hundred more. Those racketeers were pros, I'm telling you. They took us for every dime we had."

"That was an awful lot of money to have with you on a river," said Sheriff Hodges.

"I know it was," Luther assured him. "But you got to remember, them boys with me was my clients. Don't forget that I'm Chief Strategic Planning Officer for the upstate Unified Federal Agencies Procurement Bureau. And Pete and Fred and all them other ol' boys with me in the raft were federal contractors. And that makes them my clients. Heck, Matt, it ain't like I enjoy it, but I have to entertain them guys. It's my job. In fact, it's federally mandated. Why, once we got off the river, we was set to head on up to Charleston for a load of business entertainment. That's why I had all that money with me. It was to pay for the entertainment. And of course, them ol' boys had a lot of cash with them too, 'cause they're all federal contractors. They was carrying their travel money with them."

"Jesus," said the Sheriff, shaking his head side to side. "It sure takes a lowlife criminal to hide out on a wild river like that, waitin' to pounce on unsuspecting businessmen and rob 'em of their hard-earned money." The Sheriff paused and looked his brother-in-law in the eye. "You're sure," he said, "that you'll recognize them criminal scalawags if you ever see them again?"

Luther said, "Believe me, Sheriff, I ain't ever forgetting the faces of . . ." Luther looked up to see Hank, Wild Bill, Doctor Katz, the state senator, and six or seven of their friends walking through the door. Slowly, all the blood drained from Luther's face. He looked near as pale as Bo Rocker had the night before, after the dozen Serology Lab bloodsuckers had finished drawing his blood.

The Sad State of American Jurisprudence

Sheriff Hodges, Tracer County's staunch defender of law and order, quickly swung into action. His first act was to confiscate Doctor Katz's bulging dry bag, which the doctor was tightly clutching to his breast. Then came Wild Bill Barkley's cherished recipe and poetry notebook. He even confiscated Bo's battered coffee pot and his stash of herbal tea.

The Sheriff also confiscated Hank's kayak, because of a permit violation. "That particular model of boat requires a permit," the Sheriff informed Hank. "Otherwise, it's a matter of felony possession, plain and simple." Then the Sheriff decided to confiscate all their kayaks, and all their paddling gear as well.

When Wild Bill Barkley suggested that the Sheriff take Bo Rocker's canoe in lieu of Bill's kayak, the Sheriff laughed for five minutes before he could get his jelly-roll belly to stop shaking. The Sheriff had taken a careful look at Bo's boat the night before, or the collection of dents, pings and scrapes that Bo called a boat, and he wasn't interested in it. Not in a canoe! Certainly not one with its pop rivets missing, pop rivets that would now rest for perpetuity in a dozen or more Federal Crime Scene Evidence Collection Kits. But he did consent to confiscate Bo's gleaming new motor home, once he caught sight of it.

"I'm doing all of you a great big favor," the Sheriff told everybody. "I'm afraid that motor home you've been ridin' in is contaminated with spider venom. Now, possession of spider venom with or without intent to resale is a federal crime, a felony under the Environmental Controlled Substances Act of 1986. Under that statute, anybody that's rode inside that thang would hafta be quarantined for twelve, mebbe even fourteen years, doing hard labor. Or else cauterized with fire, whichever the violator prefers. But fortunately for all of you, ridin' around in a spider-infested motor home is only a misdemeanor here in Tracer County. We're a lot more tolerant 'round here of minor pest infestations like spiders. So I'll just charge each of you with a misdemeanor punishable by confiscation of said spider-infested property."

He paused to wipe sweat from his brow. Then wadded the dirty handkerchief and shoved it back in his hip pocket. He added, "Law enforcement is hard work."

When Sheriff Hodges learned that Fazil Katz was a doctor, he confiscated his medical kit. Confiscated his American Express Gold Card, too. (Strictly for medical purposes.) Confiscated his big oil painting of the Summersville Dam release tubes, too. Hung it on his office wall. The Sheriff said, "A doctor *and* art lover, too, huh?" He admired the painting for some time, viewing it from several angles, before summoning his chief deputy. To the deputy he said, "Call the National Gallery of Art, see if they been burglarized lately. This here painting's obviously the work of a master, and the back room of that motor home out yonder's full of others just as good as this one. This renegade ol' doctor musta stole them some place. Even doctors don't make enough money to pay for high class art like that." Then he turned to Katz and asked, "How long'd it take you to get your doctor's degree?"

"Four years at Harvard Medical School," Katz replied, haughtily. "Plus an internship at Stanford Teaching Hospital and two years of residency at the Rochester Neuropsychiatric Institute."

Luther Hinkle laughed derisively. "You must be a little slow, fella. Roscoe finished up his degree in two years. And he didn't have to go off to none of them foreign places, neither."

Sheriff Hodges said, "Yeah, but Roscoe had help from the FPB. If the FPB would've helped me, I could've earned me one of them doctor degrees, too. I got a natural talent for doctoring. Why, if . . ." He suddenly grabbed Katz's medical kit and said to a deputy, "Brang that spider man out here! It's high time he was give an official medical examination."

The Sheriff rummaged through Katz's medical kit, emitting appreciative oohhhhs and aahhhhs as he checked labels on the drug bottles. He pocketed a couple of bottles before carefully extricating the stethoscope. "Look at this," he said to Luther, in a reverential tone, holding the instrument in both hands like a newborn baby. Luther reached for the stethoscope, but the Sheriff jerked it back. "Only doctors are privileged to have these thangs," the Sheriff said, doing a fair job of mimicking Doctor Katz's haughty tone.

"Roscoe has two," said Luther. "Better ones than that."

When Bo arrived, Sheriff Hodges made him unbutton his shirt and take deep breaths while he held the stethoscope against his rib cage and listened. Then he used a tongue depressor to look down Bo's throat. He found a light in Doctor Katz's bag and used it to examine Bo's ears and nose. Checked his reflexes and tapped on his back and chest with a small rubber hammer. Then he donned the stethoscope again and listened for a long time with a look of bewilderment on his face, while all his deputies gathered around to watch the master at work. Two deputies were betting on whether Bo was human or spider. One of them kept saying, "Which is he, Sheriff? Human or spider? Human or spider? Which one, Sheriff? Human or spider?"

After a thorough examination, the Sheriff stepped back from Bo and lowered his stethoscope. He looked at Hank Menzel and said, "Okay, I want you and your friends to take Mister Spider Rocker here and get your sorry butts out of Tracer County and never come back. You understand?"

"Yes sir," Hank Menzel said, grabbing Bo's arm and shoving him toward the front door.

"Just a dadburn minute!" Luther screamed. But Hank, Bo, and the others were oblivious to his protests. They hit the front door at a full run and never looked back.

Luther wheeled around and confronted the Sheriff. "You're not gonna let them just waltz out of here, are you? After what they done?"

The Sheriff looked at him quizzically. "You got all your money back, didn't you? And a little extra to boot?"

"Well, yeah, I did, but . . ."

"And you recovered all your clients' money, too, didn't you? Plus a little extra to boot. Which I trust you'll dutifully return to its rightful owners?"

"Well, yes, I did, and of course I will, every dime, but . . ."

"And we got us a brand new motor home for fishin' trips, right?"

"Yeah, right, but . . ."

"And your half in that motor home is pretty good compensation for a delayed business trip, wouldn't you say?"

"Yes, it is, but . . ."

"And I have to uphold the law, don't I?"

"Well, yes of course you do, and I can understand lettin' most of them ol' boys off. They've paid their debt to society.

But the thing I can't abide is lettin' that spider felon off scott free."

"Well, believe it or not Luther, being a spider ain't no violation that I'm aware of. Leastwise, not in Tracer County."

"But," Luther stammered, "but what about all them felony counts of importin' pop rivets without a permit and making movies without a permit, and not to mention . . ."

"I just made up all that stuff to impress them federal agents," said the Sheriff. "That ol' boy didn't even have a camera with him. How could he have been making a movie? And you can brang in truck loads of pop rivets to Tracer County for all I care. Pop rivets are one of the few things without some kinda import tariff."

"Then what about grand theft of national art treasures," Luther pleaded, nodding toward Doctor Katz's painting. "You know them criminals must've stolen those masterpieces from some gallery or museum."

"I suspect they did," the Sheriff admitted. "But I done checked the CrimeNet, and there ain't no bulletin out on an art heist."

"Then what about all them federal charges we could sock the spider with? All that stuff about floating in polluted waters and polluting bloated waters and firearms violations and . . . and . . ."

"That was just a lot of hot air, Luther. Them idiots didn't have a thang on that ol' boy. I couldn't afford to let them fools have at the spider. Why, right now in Washington they're holding Congressional hearings on the FPB's latest rampage, when they went wild and shot up that family out in Idaho, and then tried to cover it up."

"But," Luther insisted, "they're the FPB. They can get away with anything."

"Mebbe they can," the Sheriff countered, "but we can't. How would you like to be hauled in front of a Congressional committee to answer questions about law enforcement practices in Tracer County?"

"Uh . . . uh . . ."

"That's what I thought."

"Well then," Luther stammered, "what about medical science? Do you realize how important it is for scientists to hear about the first spider-human hybrid? It's our duty to tell them. Why, we could get on David Letterman and make that spider man do stupid pet tricks. We'd be famous! I tell you, Roscoe's convinced Bo Rocker's part spider."

"I know," said the Sheriff. "And that's what concerns me."

"What do you mean?"

The Sheriff carefully folded his stethoscope. He said, "Well, I took a careful listen to that man's heartbeat, and based on what I heard, along with what I know about his blood tests, I'm afraid Roscoe just might be right."

"Jesus!" Luther shouted. "Then why'd you let him go?"

The Sheriff dropped the stethoscope back into his new medical kit. Snapped it shut. He tossed the kit on his desk and slowly looked around the constabulary, rubbing his chin and face with one hairy paw as his gaze once again stopped on his newly acquired art work. For several minutes his eyes drank in the spectacle of Summersville Dam's immense release tubes blowing water, spray, and foam a hundred thunderous feet downstream. He had been to the base of the dam and seen the tubes dozens of times, but he'd never seen it look exactly like this, never fully appreciated the relentless power of the exploding water. The Sheriff was thinking that whoever created this painting was one of planet earth's premier artists.

After a long silence, he said, "Hell, Luther, we're good friends, ain't we? Brothers-in-law, and all that? We don't hafta kid one another. I'll level with you. My becomin' a doctor is just a pipe dream, and we both know it. My future's not in medical science, and neither is yours, for that matter. I'm a lawman, and you're a successful grants administrator, and we hafta keep those facts in mind. Now, we both know what's involved in keeping law and order. Keeping the law here in Tracer County means keeping federal agents in line, mostly – keeping them from shootin' too many innocent citizens. And keeping order mostly means cleaning out the jail cells occasionally, whenever they get intolerably dirty." He paused and looked back toward the grimy cell block at the rear of the jail. "Which brangs us to your job. Which one of your clients is it that holds that new federally subsidized County Law Enforcement Facilities Anti-Crime Janitorial Services contract?"

Luther said, "You know good as I do Pete Holbrooks was awarded that plum. You approved the contract award yourself. Why? Are you saying you ain't gettin' your monthly kickback? Is that it? If that's the problem, you just let me know and I'll . . ."

"Oh, no," Sheriff Hodges said. "I ain't saying nothing like that. On the contrary, I'm eminently pleased with how the contract's being administered."

"Then what's your point?"

"My point is that Pete Holbrooks, the capable federal contractor whose staff cleans this county law enforcement facility, is one of your clients, ain't he?"

"Uh, yeah. Of course he is, but . . ."

"And this place is hard enough to keep clean as it is, wouldn't you say?"

Luther looked around at the grimy facility, and nodded in agreement. "It sure is."

The Sheriff said, "Well, if we had an ol' river spider the size of Bo Rocker living here permanently, we'd never keep all the webs cleaned out of the corners. Now, would we?"

That set Luther to thinking.

Sheriff Hodges continued, "My guess is, ol' Pete Holbrooks would actually have to hire a janitor or two to clean this place. And if that happened, the hefty kickback of a certain grants administrator that I know just might hafta be reduced, mebbe even eliminated. Did you ever think of it in that light, Luther?"

Luther was quiet for a moment. Then he said, "You got a point there, Sheriff. We shore don't wanna overload our janitorial services contractor. No sir. That would be criminal."

Cataract Creek

He had seen the VISA commercials and read the travel brochures. He had heard all the hype. Yet when he came off that ski lift the first time and looked around, it was even more spectacular than he had dreamed possible: Telluride, the crown jewel of Colorado ski resorts. And Eugene (Bo) Rocker had caught it on a perfect day: midweek with not a cloud in the sky, few skiers on the lifts, good corn snow on the slopes, and all of it set amidst a panorama of fourteen-thousand-foot Rocky Mountain peaks.

It was enough to take your breath away.

Certainly not bad for March. And not bad, either, for somebody who the day before had been in Atlanta, Georgia. Hotlanta, Bo called it, which was an apt name for the place yesterday when he left Hartsfield International. The southern colossus was already sweltering from early heat and oppressive humidity. It was a sauna.

By contrast, the Colorado high country probably had another month of good skiing in it. And with a couple of late dumps, the season could easily extend into early June.

Bo leaned over and tightened his boot buckles another notch. The tighter the fit, the better the control, as long as circulation isn't impaired. And he would need all the ski control he could muster today, for the slope that lay at his feet consisted of vertical terrain the likes of which he rarely had the chance to ski any more.

He treated himself to one last look, lowered his goggles into place, and launched down the slope, ready to savor three thousand vertical feet back to the base.

He had made less than a dozen turns when, from approximately three o'clock, a fast-forward visual blur came off a ledge and was on him before he could react, producing one of those gruesome collisions and resultant entanglements that are remembered for years. The surprise blur was another skier, who turned out to be a lady named Claudette Remey. Fortunately, neither skier was injured in the collision.

After an exchange of apologies, they struck up a conversation. And decided to make one run together. Just one.

However, the rest of the day was spent with Claudette Remey showing Eugene (Bo) Rocker her favorite runs at her favorite ski resort. The two skied with a common enthusiastic abandon.

Apres-ski

Over drinks in Telluride that evening, they discovered other common interests, including whitewater rivers. Claudette had been fascinated with whitewater since viewing films of some of Doctor Walt Blackadar's wilder exploits, including his first descent of Devil Creek Rapids on the Susitna River in Alaska. Blackadar had been a whitewater pioneer, with many first descents all over North America to his credit. The Susitna River had been so remote, and its rapids so enormous, that in order to capture his descent, much of the filming had been accomplished by helicopter.

Later in the evening, Claudette revealed that she was assistant to Jacques Povlsen, the movie director. She had been trying for some time to interest Povlsen in doing a whitewater feature film. She had shown him the Blackadar footage, and had enticed him on a few occasions to view other films containing whitewater sequences. John Boorman's movie, *Deliverance,* had intrigued him. He considered it classic cinema, but thought that its deep, dark, and moody texture was too depressing for most audiences. And he had enjoyed watching *The River Wild*, with Kevin Bacon and Meryl Streep, although he had clearly been more interested in watching Meryl than the river sequences.

All-in-all, her entreaties had received lukewarm reception until recently when Povlsen saw Rachael Murphy's new movie, *Unleashed Fury.* He had been captivated by the film's whitewater scenes, and since seeing it, he had aimed an endless stream of questions at Claudette concerning her ideas for a related project. He had even asked to see the Blackadar footage again, and quizzed her at length about how the shots had been staged. In fact, he wanted her to arrange a meeting with Blackadar, to discuss story ideas, and he seemed genuinely saddened to learn that the famous kayaker had drowned years before, while boating the Payette River in Idaho.

"I told him," Claudette confided in Bo, "that what we need is another whitewater pioneer, like Blackadar. Somebody out there on the cutting edge all by himself – or herself, as the case may be – running rivers that nobody's ever run before. Then we could base the movie on that person's life."

"That sounds like a good idea," Bo agreed.

"You ever been to Alaska?" she ventured, tentatively.

"Sure," Bo said. "Lots of times."

"Ever run the Alsek River?"

"Through Turnback Canyon? No, that's one I missed."

"Did you know," Claudette said, getting excited, "that Blackadar couldn't get anybody to run the Alsek with him? He spent almost a year trying to line up somebody – anybody – to go with him, but nobody would bite the bullet and take on what was considered at the time to be possibly the wildest river in the world." Her eyes were lighting up. She was turning herself on, talking about Blackadar's adventures.

Bo said, "I believe the Alsek was considered unrunnable at that time."

"It was," she agreed, eagerly. "But Blackadar was convinced he could do it. So he stuffed a sleeping bag, tent, and some food in his kayak and all by himself launched on Turnback Canyon. Five days later he flushed out the bottom and nobody could believe what he had accomplished."

"That's impressive," Bo admitted. "But unfortunately, Doctor Blackadar is no longer with us. It sounds like your task is to find a new superman – or superwoman, as the case may be. A new whitewater action hero."

"I know it," Claudette said, resignedly, the fire and enthusiasm slowly draining from her face. "And that's exactly what I told Jacques. He called a friend of his who knows all about whitewater, to ask for advice. Somebody named Conrad. Ever hear of him?"

Bo moaned. "Sure," he said. "Conrad publishes about a dozen magazines, including two or three on whitewater paddling. We've never met, but we've talked on the phone. I think he calls his business Conrad Communications. How does somebody of Jacques Povlsen's stature know a bonehead like Horace Conrad?"

Claudette answered, warily, "I am not sure how they met." A pause, and then, "Oh, yes I am. It comes to me now. They have some kind of joint venture, some creative new magazine they're launching. I forgot about that. Jacques is bankrolling it, I think."

"Jacques is backing a new paddling magazine?"

"Oh, no. It's not paddling. I don't know much about it, but I think it is something very avant-garde, something experimental, you know? It will be very "hush-hush," until they spring it on the world. I do know, however, that it will be published on-line." She watched for Bo's reaction to such high tech terminology. She said, "Oh, don't you know about the Internet, America Online and all that high tech computer business? I guess not. I can see in your eyes it is all strange to you, this computer language. But it is their plan, I believe, to produce the first mass-circulation cyber magazine."

"It sounds ambitious," Bo replied. "And I wish them the best of luck. But I can't help thinking that those two seem like strange bedfellows."

Claudette said, "That's strictly a judgement call, I think." She paused again, still looking at Bo, sizing him up. Then she got the conversation back on track. She said, "Conrad told Jacques that nobody's doing first descents anymore. When Jacques heard that, he became indignant. 'Why not?' he demanded to know." Claudette was mimicking Jacques' thick accent and garbled pronunciation. "He said, 'Don't the cowards knows I has to makes movies about something?' And Conrad said, 'All the wild rivers have already been run. That's why nobody's doing first descents anymore. Because there're no rivers left to run for the first time.' " She looked at Bo and tilted her head. "Is that true?"

Bo mulled it over and agreed that most rivers probably had been run, although there were still a few isolated drainage ditches remaining. "The frontier right now seems to be waterfalls," he said. "People keep running higher and higher ones. I have a friend who specializes in running waterfalls. Bill Barkley's his name. We all call him Wild Bill Barkley. He'll run anything."

"Really?" Claudette said. "Would you believe that what Jacques liked most about *Unleashed Fury* – other than Rachael Murphy running butt naked through the streets – was the waterfall scene? Remember the big waterfall that Rachael ran the raft over? The scene where the bad guy tied her into the raft by her ankles, so she'd drown if the raft capsized, and then made her oar the raft over the big drop while tied up like that? Remember that? Well, Jacques loved that scene. He must have watched it a dozen times. I think he really likes waterfalls." She stirred her drink and watched closely for Bo's reaction to her next statement. "And, of course," she said, "the bondage part helped. He's kind of into that."

"I have a friend like that."

She almost spilled the drink in her lap. And then she leaned across the table and put her hand on his. A dreamy look came into her eyes. She whispered to him, "This friend of yours enjoys bondage and discipline?" Her eyes were so dreamy, a hypnotist could have crawled into either iris and fallen asleep.

"Yeah, that too, sometimes. But waterfalls, mostly."

"What?" she said, flustered, jerking her hand away and sitting back. "I thought we were talking about . . . well . . . about . . . oh, never mind."

She was actually blushing.

Bo said, "Sometimes we have to help ol' Wild Bill whip up his courage. And then, if he appears to waver in his convictions, we tie him in his boat and shove him over the waterfall. How's that for discipline *and* bondage?"

"Oh, for heaven's sake," Claudette said, frustration showing on her pretty face. "That's really poor."

Bo let the emotional dust settle. Then said, "Was it really so bad?"

After a tense moment, she seemed to relax. "It wasn't really so bad," she admitted, and smiled at him. "It's just that you kind of caught me there."

"Kind of tangled you up, huh? Snared you, so to speak?"

"There you go again," she said, tensing up, sitting up straight in her chair. "It's hard to tell about you. I never know when you're joking. When you talked about your friend, and his preferences, I thought you were letting me know about yourself. That's how some people do it. But with you, who can tell?"

Bo said, "My heart is an open book. What do you want to know?"

"What you like, of course. The things you like to do."

"I'm fond of blackwall hitches."

"What?"

"And I've always been partial to carrick bends and figure eights."

She gave him a look of disgust, and stammered: "This has gone far enough. I think perhaps it is you – and not Mister Conrad – who is the bonehead." She started to rise, to push back from the table.

Bo took her hand. "No, wait," he said. "Don't leave. I'm trying to share my innermost thoughts with you, and I realize I'm being clumsy. It's just that I don't meet a woman every day with your interests. You see, the thing is, I have a technical mind, so when I think of bondage, I think of specific knots. I know that sounds weird, but that's how it works for me." He squeezed her hand. "Please stay."

"You're not making fun of me?"

"Not at all, I like rope tricks. I love knots. I know dozens of them; earned a merit badge in knots when I was in the scouts. I use ropes on the river all the time. In fact, ropes are a necessity for river work, did you know that? It's a knotty sport. And I'm a *River Master*. I invented z-drags – and the Steve Thomas rope trick. Ever hear of the Brackman Reverse with double belayed pulleys? I invented that one, too – or I will some day when I get around to it. There's nothing I enjoy more than harnessing a good friend for a Tyrolean lower."

"You can do Tyrolean lowers?"

"Baby, I can do inverted Tyrolean lowers with up to three z-drag intercepts."

That impressed her. He could see it in her eyes.

There was a restrained smile that flickered and then faded. Pursed lips. And then, "What is your favorite knot?"

"It depends," Bo said. "Wrist to wrist?"

"No," Claudette replied. "That's too easy. Wrist to bed-post."

"Metal or wood post?"

"Good question. Hummmm, let me see. Make it brass."

"A timber hitch is good," Bo said, "but I like a clove hitch better, and my favorite is the fisherman's bend."

Claudette licked her lips. "You do know your stuff, don't you?"

"And your favorite?" Bo asked.

"The sheet bend is nice, and I also like the sheepshank, but my favorite with a brass post? It has to be the Turk's head."

Bo leaned forward, and whispered, "A Turk's head takes forever to tie."

"That's what I like about it. There's something I do to for my partner while he's knotting me down."

Bo rolled his eyes. "I think I'd like to practice my knots with you."

"Really?"

"Really."

Claudette smiled demurely. "That would be nice. But there is a possible problem: Jacques. He is terribly jealous. If he ever learned that you and I had . . . practiced knots, he would . . . well, you understand, don't you? Jacques can be terribly vindictive."

"Jacques Povlsen," Bo said, slowly, "sounds to me like a tyrant. If he's so oppressive, why do you put up with him? Why don't you leave?"

"Oh!" she replied, with a theatric gesture, one hand going to her breast, fingers spread, like she was gasping for breath. "I could never leave Jacques. I have been with him since I was practically a child."

Bo took her trembling hands in his and looked deep into her lovely eyes. "Claudette, you're practically a child now."

She blinked those eyes, long lashes fluttering, like a damsel in a silent movie. She said, softly, "I know."

The Next Action Hero

Next day, Jacques Povlsen received a call at his office in Malibu. The call came from Horace Conrad in Atlanta, publisher of *River Probe, Drift Indicator, Wild Sierra Kamikaze Kayak Journal,* and other whitewater paddling rags. Conrad said he had been thinking more about the question Jacques had asked him earlier, the one concerning first river descents. And although Conrad reconfirmed that most first descents were a matter of history, there was, he added, a new rage on the whitewater paddling scene that might lend itself to cinematic treatment. And that was jumping waterfalls, the bigger the better. Conrad said a youngster named "Wild" Bill Barkley had emerged as the latest thing in whitewater daredevilry. Waterfalls were his specialty. Wild Bill would run anything. He was running waterfalls that nobody else would get near, accomplishing feats that the whitewater community would be talking about for years to come.

"The only problem," said Conrad, "is that the guy doesn't realize the commercial potential of what he's doing. That's the reason I didn't think of him or what he's doing when you called the other day."

Jacques, astonished by what he was hearing, replied, "But how cans he be oblivious to commercials? That is, how does you says it? Un-American?"

"He's a weird bird," Conrad admitted. "I'll give you an example: several months ago I had this idea of running an interview with him in *River Probe,* but he wouldn't even talk about doing the interview. He said he was above crass commercialism. Can you believe somebody actually said that?"

Jacques replied, "It aggrieves me to hear this."

Conrad agreed, but added, "There is one hopeful note: Wild Bill has a friend who is more amenable to commercial inducements. If you could prevail upon this friend to talk to Wild Bill, it just might be possible to . . ."

* * * * *

That single phone call cost Bo Rocker eight thousand dollars. Bo also had to promise Horace Conrad a bit part in any movie that resulted.

For Bo, however, the cost of Conrad's intercession was an investment. An investment that began paying dividends only a couple of days later, by which time Bo, with Claudette's behind-the-scenes influence, had finagled lunch with Jacques Povlsen, to be held in the open air, on the veranda overlooking the Pacific Ocean at Julio's by the Beach. Claudette was at the table also, along with a brace of her flunkies.

* * * * *

"I've seen that footage on Blackadar," Bo was saying to Povlsen. "And it's pretty good, considering where most of it was shot, on the Susitna and the Tatshenshini."

Jacques replied, in his heavy accent, "Something is wrong with these rivers? No? These is not real whitewater?"

"Oh, they're whitewater rivers all right," said Bo. "They're big, bodacious rivers with outrageous rapids. Their sheer size and volume give them enormous power. Unfortunately, all that size and power doesn't come across convincingly on screen. Most of what you see is a lot of dirty, swirling water and a tiny little boat out there in it. The boat looks insignificant, especially when the camera's located in a helicopter hovering way up in the sky. You can get approximately the same visual effect by dangling a video camera over a flushing toilet bowl. Jiggle the camera to simulate vibration from the helicopter, and Bingo! It looks about the same. The dirty, swirling water looks very similar to that in a swollen river, and the boats . . . well, surely I don't have to tell you what objects in the toilet bowl represent boats?"

"That's right," Claudette hastened to say. "You don't have to tell us."

Jacques said, "But Mister Rocker does has a point. It is not easy to has perspective when these camera is on a helicopters." He looked at Bo. "You has obviously given this matter lots of thoughts."

"Precisely," said Bo, leaning back and signaling the waiter for another champagne cocktail. He had just finished the Julio Special: pasta diablo, with tiny bits of pepper so hot it was about to send his soul to purgatory. He continued: "I has given it lots of thoughts. And I can recommend a radically improved approach. What you needs is a heavy dose of what I calls camera-in-the-face technique."

That got Jacques' attention.

"These technique you mention, "Jacques said to Bo. "It is something I has never heards before. It is called camera-in-the-face?"

"That's right," said Bo. "I know a small creek that's loaded with waterfalls, one after the other, where the water plummets down through boulder chutes. And the boulders themselves make excellent camera locations. There's no need for helicopters. No need for ultra-long- distance telephoto lenses like they had to use in *Deliverance*. No need for specially constructed camera platforms, or cameras suspended from cables, like they use in most river films. The cameras can be set up alongside the creek, so close to the paddlers that the lenses are practically poking them in the face as they come over the waterfalls. You get these wonderful facial expressions, and that's what the audience loves. People who watch this kind of stuff like to think they could get right out there and do it themselves if they really wanted to. And seeing the play of emotions on the paddlers' faces reinforces those delusions. People in the audience say to themselves, 'You see, that daredevil's human too. He's scared witless, just like I'd be if I got out there and did that stuff, which I could do if I wanted to.' That's what I mean by camera-in-the-face technique."

"These is brilliant!" Jacques declared, banging his fist on the table for emphasis, giving Bo time to knock down his sixth cocktail and order again. Another half dozen of those thimble-sized treats, Bo calculated, and he'd have the Julio fire in his belly under control. If that tactic didn't douse the flames, he'd have to order in a bulldozer crew to cut a fire line.

Jacques exclaimed, "Claudette, my lovely nymphet, where does you finds this brilliant man?"

Bo, feeling a little giddy from Jacques' compliment, or maybe a little dizzy from the deluge of champagne cocktails, or perhaps just desperate to divert his attention from the ravages of Julio's incinerator sauce, said, "She lassoed me in the old west town of Telluride. She's a lassoing lass, this one is."

Claudette gave Bo a kick under the table, and a look that could kill. "Let's just say I ran into Mister Rocker by accident," she replied coolly, giving Bo the evil eye. "On a ski slope."

Rubbing his shin and grimacing, Bo said, "And getting back to business, Jacques my boy, on the creek I'm talking about there's none of that filthy, turgid water like you get with heavy snow melt. I'm talking about crystal clear water sparkling irrepressibly in the sunlight."

Jacques was getting excited, and it showed. "I loves what you is saying! You nots only is full of new ideas, buts you also says them with such flair! And the sun sparkles on the water . . . how is it you say? Irrepressibly?"

"Yeah, that's right, Jacques. Irrepressibly. I learned that word from Wild Bill Barkley, himself. He knows tons of big words like that."

"He does?"

"Yeah, he does. He's a poet, you know?"

"He is!" Jacques had now gone well beyond containing his enthusiasm. He was bouncing up and down in his chair. A huge smile adorning his whiskered face. He turned to Claudette: "But you should have tells me these things, darling."

"Yes darling," Bo said to Claudette. "You should have tells Jacques these things. You should have tells Jacques everythings."

That comment put a grim expression on Claudette's face.

Jacques said, "These friend of yours. He is both a poet and a whitewater daredevil? That could be a useful combination of talents. My studio publicists may be able to work that angle. But tells me, can he acts at all?"

"Not a lick," Bo said flatly.

Jacques' face fell. He held up a thumb and index finger, separated by about an inch, and asked, "Not even one teeny lick?"

Bo shook his head, and then leaned back and smiled at Jacques' obvious disappointment. "But not to worry," he added confidently. "You're looking at the next Robert DeNiro. We'll let Wild Bill run the falls and help write the script, and then I'll pick up when the camera zooms in for a closeup." He gave Jacques his best side and smiled like a drunk hyena. He added, "If you like my new ideas on technique, just wait until you get a load of my acting skills. I make Marlon Brando look like a beginner. Believe me, you've never seen anything like it."

"These is almost too good to be true!" Jacques said excitedly. "And you has a location in mind?"

Bo assured him: "Not only do I has the best new undiscovered actor in the world ready to star in your next movie, not only do I has the right stunt paddler for the dangerous scenes, but I also knows the best place in the world to shoots whitewater footage."

"Of course! That is what we needs. The right place to shots this Wild Bill friend of yours! Is these place better than in *Unleashed Fury*?"

"Did you think that movie had good action footage?"

"I thought it is, how does you say? Tolerable?"

"You remember in the movie the section of river that supposedly had miles of nonstop cataracts? Well, all it really had was one dinky little waterfall. All the footage you saw in the movie was shot from different angles on the same silly little drop. And they had to run the same dumb raft over that drop time after time in order to get a few seconds of suitable footage. It took them six weeks to shoot that waterfall sequence. And you know what they did? They tied cables to stunt doubles and jerked them out of the raft at the last split second with a helicopter. Then they spliced in footage of dummies actually going over the falls. Can you believe it?"

"My friend Rachael Murphy tells me as much," said Jacques.

"You know Rachael Murphy?" Bo exclaimed.

Jacques laughed. "Knows her? She is my dear friend. And you knows what? She loves the river work! The excitement! She tells me so."

Claudette said, "Several times we considered Rachael for a whitewater project, didn't we, Jacques? But each time, before we could get around to talking with her, Jacques would get tied up with some other project. Wouldn't you, dearest?"

"Oui," Jacques said. "Always I gets tied up with something else."

"You gets tied up a lot, don't you, old boy?" Bo said, giving Jacques a conspiratorial wink. "Believes me, I can commiserates with you."

This comment resulted in a second kick from Claudette, a devastating blow to the medial collateral ligaments of Bo's left knee. The blow brought an immediate flood of nausea. For a second, Bo thought he would spray Julio's creative concoction all over the fine linen tablecloth. He was wondering how it would feel to become a human flamethrower. But the nausea subsided, replaced by throbbing knee pain.

So much for skiing at Telluride next season.

Bo belted down another champagne cocktail, and began the painful process of recovery from a major knee injury. He would need medicine, lots of it. And he knew where to get it.

He signaled the waiter and told him to bring over a pitcher of champagne cocktails.

Jacques was saying, "I does? I gets tied up too much?" He looked at Claudette with a baffled expression. "What does he means?"

"He means," Claudette said, in a studiously businesslike tone, "that you're a very busy man. That your time is always in demand from your Hollywood colleagues. And that you're often tied up with other commitments when you want to do something new and unusual. Isn't that right, Mister Rocker?"

Ignoring Claudette, Bo said, "Speaking of binding obligations, I hear that ol' Rachael Murphy loved being trussed up in the raft, that she liked the feel of the rope around her ankles, liked the way it bit into her flesh as she oared the raft."

"What!" Jacques said, almost jumping out of his chair. "Is these true? Who tells you? I does not knows these things about my dear friend Rachael. She like the bite of rope on her flesh? Tells me more!"

Claudette began laughing hysterically. "You bastard," she muttered, shaking her head. "You perverse bastard."

"Who me?" Jacques said. "Oh no, my lovely, do not blames me for whats I does not does. I merely wants to knows more about Rachael. It is idle curiosity. Nothings more. I does not knows that she . . ."

"No, no," Claudette said, pointing to Bo. "He's the bastard."

"These brilliant Bo is a bastard?" Jacques said. "Surely nots."

"Of course nots," Bo said, knocking back yet another cocktail. "I know lots of knots, but I'm nots no bastard and Claudette knows it. She knows I'm nots a bastard, but she says it anyway. Which is nots good. Although she knows I am. Good, that is. With my knots, I mean. In fact, she knows I know all the knots and she knows all the knots I know how to knot. Or something like that. Does that nots make sense?"

Jacques was dumbfounded.

Bo continued, "I wish I knew why she says these awful things about me, when there have been so many binding affections between us. I'm afraid she hates me."

"You hates these Bo Rocker?" Jacques said to Claudette. She had balled up one fist and was threatening to slug Bo. "Hummmmm," Jacques said. "I does not understands. So perhaps we should gets back to business. Now, where was we?"

Claudette said, "Mister Rocker was telling us about a place he knows with loads of waterfalls."

"Oui," Jacques said, "Or what is it these Bo call them? Nonstop cataracts?"

"Not just nonstop cataracts," Bo said. "But nonstop cataracts with ready-made camera platforms."

"And these Wild Bill, the poet who can run these nonstop cataracts? He can do these feats not in a globby raft, like in *Unleashed Fury,* but in a sleek kayak, no less? These is true, I believe?"

"You bet it's true."

"And you knows these Wild Bill, the poet and crazy paddler?"

"Knows him?" Bo roared with laughter. "Why, I taughts the guy everything he knows. And I means everything. He is my, how does you says it? Understudy?"

"Does these mean that you is authorized to negotiate on behalfs of Mister Barkley? To sign his name on dotted lines?"

"That's exactly what it means."

"These is good. And if you and I can agree on terms, when can we look at these magic river of yours that has, how does you say, nonstop cataracts?"

"When does you wants to look at it?"

Jacques laughed. He said, "Time is money, Mister Rocker. You has piqued my interest, so naturally I wants to looks at these river today. But of course, I knows that these daredevil whitewater river is always located in Alaska, or British Columbia, or Montana or some such dreadful place where you has to wait until July for the snow to melt. So the question is, when does the snow melt enough for me to gets a good look at these river?"

"This river's not in Alaska," said Bo. "And not in Montana, neither. It's in the Southland, and it's snow-free practically year 'round. Yesterday it was running at more than a thousand cubic feet per second, and that's a lot of water for a stream that's barely ten feet wide in a lot of places."

"Merciful!" Jacques said. "We must strike whiles the irons is hot." He looked at Claudette, and asked, "Does my pilot knows where these Southland is?" Claudette looked at her assistant, who looked at his assistant, who grabbed his cellular and started making calls. Jacques said, "You are these Wild Bill Barkley's agent, I am right?"

"You am right."

"And who is your agent?"

"You're looking at him," Bo replied. "The best in the business."

"That means we can negotiate on the way, I am right?"

"You am . . . On the way? On the way where?"

"On the way to these Southland, wherever these is. I presume there is landing field in these Southland for my Lear jet? These Southland is a developed country, is it not?"

Lights, Camera ... Understudy!

They landed early the next morning at the Asheville, North Carolina airport and by the time they transported all the cameras, crew, and gear to Cataract Creek, its one thousand cubic feet per second had multiplied to what looked more like a million cubic feet per second. It wasn't really a million, of course, but the creek was definitely in flood, exhibiting ten foot standing waves in its quieter stretches, holes that would have stopped the Queen Elizabeth II, and a background rumble on the order of Niagara Falls.

Jacques was absolutely ecstatic. As far as he was concerned, conditions were perfect to commence a major production. At the very least, he could capture Wild Bill Barkley jumping the creek's waterfalls and then stitch a story around this critical footage at a later date. Jacques wasted no time in sending Peter Clancy, his chief cinematographer, to scout out the creek for camera locations. Clancy, none too happy to be uprooted from his vacation in Colorado and transported with virtually no prior notice to the wilds of western North Carolina, nevertheless returned from his scouting expedition in a state of elation. In only a couple hours, he had located a dozen camera locations at the creek's biggest drops. It was exactly like Bo had promised: tons of water flushing over nonstop cataracts, with perfect camera locations all along the stream, and perfect conditions for filming the whitewater extravaganza of the decade.

"Only one thing is missing," Jacques said to Bo. "Where is these Wild Bill friend of yours? These fool who will run anything?"

And that was a very good question. Bo had last reached Wild Bill by phone at Rafter, Tennessee, where he was in training for his film debut. He was staying with an old pal named Hooter so he could spend all day paddling the water-falls on the Tellico River, and its tributary, Bald River, and then stay up all night drinking with Hooter and reciting poetry. This was Wild Bill's idea of a rigorous training program. Wild Bill had solemnly promised to be waiting at Cataract Creek when they arrived, but there was no sign of him. Breaking promises and missing appointments was nothing new for Wild Bill Barkley. Poets had a knack for such things. But missing a run down Cataract at this water level was not like him. A run down Cataract at this level was enough to inspire an epic poem – or a catatonic trance, both of which were highly prized by Wild Bill Barkley.

* * * * *

By midday the crew was ready, Peter Clancy was ready, Jacques Povlsen was ready, Claudette Remey was ready, the equipment had been checked and certified to be in good working order, and Bo Rocker, who by this time had negoti-ated a third contract, making himself the film's technical advisor in addition to Wild Bill's agent and the leading actor, was more than ready to launch his brilliant film career.

Wild Bill Barkley, however, was nowhere in sight.

* * * * *

By sundown, Jacques was getting a little testy. "These conditions is excellent," he confided in Bo. "Everything you says is true. Perfect river, perfect camera locations, perfect light. And the water has a certain, how is it you say, irre-pressible sparkle?"

"Yeah," Bo said. "It shore is purty."

"Purty?" Jacques said.

"Southland slang."

"What?"

"Never mind."

"Sometimes I thinks you is making funs of my English," Jacques said. "Claudette has warns me that you cans be, how does she says? Spiteful?"

"No, no," Bo said. "I'm not spiteful. Not at all. Why should I be spiteful?"

"You tells me," Jacques said, with an accusatory sneer.

Bo replied, "Now, if Claudette had trussed me up like a chicken and flogged me like a turkey, *then* I might feel spiteful. But of course nothing like that happened, so I couldn't possibly feel spiteful. And I'm not making funs of your English, either. That is the last things on these good green earths that I woulds ever do. Trust me." Bo sucked in his breath and looked around, like he expected to see Wild Bill saunter into camp at that moment. But there were no new arrivals. He added, "I'm just upset that Wild Bill hasn't showed. It's not like him. Something bad must have happened."

Jacques gave him a hard look. "Mister Rocker," he said, with a new, demanding tone in his voice. "Let us face the facts. We shoulds has started shooting today, when conditions was perfect. But we dids not, and now these river is dropping. Tomorrow it will drops more. Next day it mays be too low for good footage. I thinks you understands that time is money, and these venture is costing me a fortunes. Unless these mysterious Wild Bill is here first things in the morning, ready to run these nonstop cataracts, these deal is off."

"You can't call off the deal. I've got a contract! Three contracts!"

Jacques produced copies of the eighteen pages of contracts they had jointly signed and shoved them in Bo's face. "I suggest you reads these small prints, Mister Eugene (Bo) Rocker," Jacques said, pointing to the bottom paragraph of the last page in the packet. "It says right here that for nonperformance, these deal is off. I knows what it says. I tells my lawyer whats to write. I tells her to makes it says so. I tells her to writes it in plain English that even nitwits like you can read and understands. It also say I can sues you for breeches of promise, to recover all my costs."

"I believe that's breach of contract," Bo said. "Breeches are what prissy little French boys wear to school."

"What?"

"Never mind."

"You makes funs of my English again?"

"Don't get your tit in a wringer over minor semantics," Bo advised.

Jacques gritted his teeth. "I thinks the problem with breeches here is that yours has grown, how does they say? Too small? Oui, that's it. Bo Rocker's breeches is too small. And he had better watch out, lest he busts them open and something tumbles out."

Looking for Wild Bill Barkley

Claudette managed to calm the bickering pair and, in order to allay Jacques' growing concern, extracted a promise from Bo to locate Wild Bill Barkley before morning. Bo commandeered one of the film crew's rental vans and, as he headed out of camp, Claudette flagged him down. "I'm going with you," she announced, talking to him through the window. "Jacques has grown so irascible I can't stand to be around him. What did you say to him, anyway?"

"Just that I'm not a spiteful kind of guy."

"That's all you said?"

He shrugged. "That's about it." He cut the engine, and added, "But I don't think going off with me will improve his disposition. I just can't imagine that ol' Jackie boy would approve."

"Somebody has to make sure you find Wild Bill what's his name," she said, climbing in the van and slamming the door hard enough to rattle the windows. "Besides, I don't care what Jacques approves of. He's so angry he's . . ."

"Fit to be tied?"

"Heaven help us," she said, shaking her head as they drove away.

* * * * *

It was reasonable terrain until shortly past Robbinsville, where the pavement ended. Then it was dirt and gravel and a rutted goat trail up and over the main brunt of the Unaka Mountains, all the way to Rafter, where Bo learned from Hooter, the mountain recluse Bill had been staying with, that Wild Bill had suffered an accident two days earlier on Bald River. After the mishap, Wild Bill had rejected the idea of going for medical help, but when he woke up in the middle of the night in excruciating pain, he reconsidered, announcing that he was leaving to find a doctor or a shopping bag full of strong drugs, whichever came first, hopefully the latter.

Hooter had not heard from Bill since he left.

Bo started calling hospitals and at midnight located a William Henry Barkley at Brookwater Memorial, near Sweetwater, but hospital personnel would not divulge the patient's status. Bo and Claudette bid adieu to Hooter and arrived at the hospital at two o'clock in the morning.

Wild Bill was in the intensive care unit, in critical condition. His doctor had left strict orders that no information on him was to be released until next of kin were notified of his condition. Claudette pretended to be his nearest relative, but got his name wrong, calling him William Henry Browning.

Her pretense raised the charge nurse's hackles. And the nurse's officiousness upset Claudette.

Bo smoothed the nurse's feathers by slipping her fifty dollars. That immediately sweetened her disposition and produced Wild Bill's chart, revealing that the patient had dislocated his right shoulder, broken his left clavicle, and pulverized his fourth and fifth lumbar vertebrae while running a big waterfall.

The nurse said, "I hear it was a first run over Bald River Falls, up near Tellico Plains. That thing must be a hundred feet tall. Must be some kinda record."

Bo looked up from Wild Bill's chart and nodded agreement. He hadn't even considered that the nurse might know something about whitewater, and he was pleasantly surprised.

But Claudette was still very much in a snit over the way she had been treated. "That's a tremendous consolation," she said sarcastically. "Thank you so much for your heartfelt concern for my brother."

"It'll probably be his last run over any waterfall," the nurse said to both of them. "Maybe his last time in a kayak." And then she said to Claudette: "And for your information, I am sorry about your son's misfortune."

Oh boy.

Claudette made an effort to stifle her anger. A not very successful effort. She said, between clenched teeth, "I'm his sister, nurse Dolt, not his mother."

The nurse, wearing a tag on her blouse that said "S. Crawford," popped her gum again and said, "Older sister, I'd have to guess. Much older."

While Claudette was turning red and stammering unintelligibly, the nurse walked over to Bo. "Another fifty and you can look at his MRI scans."

Now that might be entertaining.

Bo looked at Claudette, however, and quickly changed his mind. "That won't be necessary," he said. "This tells me more than enough." He closed the folder and handed it back to the nurse.

"You sure?" S. Crawford asked, popping that gum again. "Those MRI pictures are something else. Compression fractures are a sight: crumbled vertebrae, gelatinous discs squirted out in all directions, bulging nerve tissue. You do enjoy seeing bulging tissue, don't you?" There was a glint in her eye that said another fifty dollars would show Bo a lot more than Wild Bill's MRI scans. Bo said, "I'm sure those pictures are something else. And to tell the truth, I'd really like to see them. Bulging tissue is one of my specialties. But right now we're in kind of a hurry. I hope you understand. You've been very helpful, though. Thank you." He took Claudette by the arm and guided her toward the door.

S. Crawford called after him, "You sure I can't be of more service to you, sir? Twenty'll get you his medication record. It'll only take a few minutes."

"Twenty?" Bo said, giving it serious thought.

Claudette said, "Twenty minutes with that slut and you'll need medication yourself."

"I'm afraid we have to leave now, nurse," Bo said. "We're kind of short on time."

"I understand," the nurse replied. "It is getting late." She glanced at her watch. "Time to put your mom to bed, I guess. Older women need their sleep."

Every muscle in Claudette's body tensed. "What did that alley cat say?"

Bo was urging Claudette toward the door, but that wasn't an easy task. She had dug in her heels. Her fists were clenched and her body was rigid. One more taunt from the nurse and it would be hopeless. Another smart remark and there would be nothing he could do to stop the fur from flying. To his immense relief he heard S. Crawford say, "Ya'll come back now, ya'll hear?"

Bo gave Claudette another push toward the door and, at the same time, looked over his shoulder at S. Crawford.

The nurse was smiling. "You guys ever hear that expression before? It's an old Southern saying. Southland slang, some people call it. It means you're welcome to come back anytime." She cocked her hip, gave Bo a petulant look. Popped her gum. She resembled the way Kathleen Turner looked in *Peggy Sue Got Married.* She looked pretty good, actually. She had just come on duty and looked fresh-scrubbed and full of energy. Or full of the devil. Whichever. Blond hair with a big curl dangling above the shoulder. Like they used to wear way back when. Decked out in her nursing whites. It was cool on the intensive care ward. She had pulled on a sweater but left it unbuttoned. She said, "You're not from around here, are you? Where're you from?"

"Kentucky," Bo said, making it up. It seemed like a neutral site.

"Uh oh, you're a Yankee," S. Crawford announced. "But a nice one." She added, "You can still come back if you wanna, even with that Yankee heritage." She paused, looked at Claudette like she had just noticed her standing there next to Bo. She started to say something to Claudette, then changed her mind. She looked back at Bo and said, "I'll take good care of your friend until you get back to see him. You can count on it." She hesitated for a moment, then said, "Mister Barkley *is* your friend, isn't he?"

"Yeah, he is."

Crawford smiled wanly. "Then you'll want to come back and see him, won't you?" She paused, then said, "See you around."

Bo and Claudette reached the door and he opened it. He hesitated long enough to look back at nurse S. Crawford. She was still watching him. He said, "I'll be back in a couple of days. To see the patient."

Nurse Crawford said, "Right. To see the patient." She smiled at him.

Claudette grabbed his collar and jerked him out the door.

On the River Again

At daybreak, Bo and Claudette arrived back on location. The gloom in Mudville when mighty Casey struck out was nothing compared to the despondency that descended upon Cataract Creek as the realization settled in that all the film crew's efforts had been for naught. Jacques announced that he had to be in Aspen the next day. He would leave immediately and send the plane back later for the film crew and equipment.

As Jacques prepared to leave, he stopped to take one last look at the creek. Instead of dropping overnight, as everybody had expected, it had risen. It was carrying a couple of thousand cfs and it was moving downstream fast. Jacques let out a deep sigh. "It's too bad," he said, making sure that Bo could hear, "that no one has balls enoughs to take these broken poet's place."

Bo looked at the creek. He had run it at high water before, but never at anything approaching this level. Even Bill Barkley wouldn't have run it this high.

With all that water, anybody in an open canoe would have a monstrous time with the creek's big drops and grabby hydraulics. But then . . . ? Was it possible? Could he do it?

He'd be rolling all day, and paddling with a boat full of water. But so what? Even if he took a couple of swims, it certainly wouldn't be the end of the world. They could edit out the unpleasant parts. And then he'd be not only the new acting sensation, but also the new *action hero*. One of those rare actors who could do his own stunt work. Chuck Norris, move it on over.

"Wait a minute," he called out to Jacques. "I'll do it. I'll take Barkley's place."

"You will does it?" Jacques said.

"I will does it," said Bo, benificently.

"You will stands in for the fool Wild Bill?"

"I'll do it, for you," Bo said. "Because I like you so much. Jackie boy, you're looking at the next action hero. Arnie Schwarzenegger's day in the sun is done."

"Splendid!" Jacques screeched. "These is splendid!"

Jacques slapped Peter Clancy on the back. "See, I tells you he will does it!" Jacques then started shouting orders left and right to Clancy and the rest of the crew, sending them scurrying in all directions. He interrupted his directorial theatrics for a moment and ran up to Bo, grabbed him by the shoulders and kissed him on both cheeks. He said, "That Clancy! He bets me fifty thousand dollar you not have the balls, but I knows better. I calls Horace Conrad after you leaves last night. He tells me you is fantastic paddler. Good as the poet, he say. Maybe better. He say you can runs the falls good as Barkley. Oui! I will makes you the new star and I will makes, how does they say it? lots of bread? from Clancy."

Bo said, "I'll do it, but first I gotta find a boat. I need to get started."

"Leaves that to me," Jacques exclaimed proudly. "Last night, when I hears you is world class paddler, I sends out for boats. I wants to be ready in case the Wild Bill is broke. I says to Peter Clancy, buy the best boats available. The best boats that is sold in these crazy Southland, as you calls it. You knows what I says to Peter? I says, 'If you buys it, Bo will come back.' Hahaha, that is what I says to Peter. Peter finds that is funny! He laughs and laughs!"

"You bought boats?"

"Oui. Peter find a place called Outdoor Emporium on the River, or something like that. They has loads of boats."

"The Nantahala Outdoor Center? The NOC?"

"Oui! These is it. The NOC. You knows these place?"

"You bet."

"These NOC sells good boats, no?"

"Oh yes, they sell the best."

"Looks what we has for you," Jacques said, grabbing Bo's elbow and leading him through a border of dense foliage to the creek's edge. "We has them already down by these river, ready to go. All lined up. We has a Perception boat. You likes the Perception? The NOC says these Perception is a very good boat. Good enough to run any wild river in the world. And the color is very nice. No?"

"It is," Bo agreed. "Fine boat, great color."

"And if you does not likes the Perception, we also has these beauty next in line. Just look at these colors! Wild, no? NOC says these boat, called a Dagger, is great whitewater boat. Maybe the best. You is familiar with these Dagger boat?"

By now Bo was getting nervous. Sweat was beading up on his forehead. "Yeah, that's a great boat, too," he said. "But, but . . ."

Jacques said, wagging his finger at Bo, "Nots to worry. I knows that an expert like you may be hards to please, so I tells Peter, 'Buy one of each, every kinds they gots.' And he dids, but he can not carry them all. He bring six. Six beautiful boats. The best whitewater boats made, says these man at

NOC. These man that Peter says act like he know whitewater a lots. You knows these man at NOC? He says he knows you a long time. Peter says he has a big beard over his whole face, like this." Jacques was holding his hands out around his face, indicating what must have been the world's biggest beard. Either that or the guy at NOC had a pumpkin for a head.

Bo was feeling weak, and sick to his stomach, his knees wobbly.

Spread out along the rocky ground were six brand new shiny kayaks, all different makes and models. Beside them, heaped in a pile, were a variety of paddles, paddling jackets, dry suits, spray skirts, helmets, and four yellow life jackets. It was a beautiful, multicolored spectacle, all this new equipment arranged on the side of the creek.

Jacques was pleased with himself. He said, "Well, what does you says, Bo Rocker?"

Bo said, "Where's the canoe?"

"Hahaha!" Jacques draped his arm around Bo's shoulders. "You makes such funny joke. But of course I knows not even a fools like you go down these river in a canoe! That would be, how does you say? Ludicrous? Hahahahahaha! Such funny joke you tells."

"Is there a C1?" Bo asked meekly. "I used to paddle a C1. Please let there be a C1."

Jacques said, "A see who?"

"I have to have a canoe," Bo stated flatly. "Or a C1."

"You is joking again? No?"

"No."

"No?"

"I don't paddle kayaks. I have to have a canoe. Decked or open, either way; I'll take either one. But it has to be a canoe."

"No canoes," Jacques said, shaking his finger in Bo's face. "Nobody want to sees a canoe go over these, how does you say, nonstop cataracts? They wants to sees a kayak. These audience demand a kayak, and you has to gives these audiences what these audience want. That is how these business work. Remember that, Bo Rocker. Now, has you pick the one of your choice? Which kayak you choose?"

Bo said, "Oh, No."

"We has no 'Oh, No' brand. Just these ones here. Pick one. Oh, oui! And one other thing, I almost forgots. My research department says Walt Blackadar always likes to wear the yellow life jacket. So wears the yellow jacket, so you can at least looks likes a great paddler."

* * * * *

Peter Clancy walked up to tell Jacques that the crew was set and ready to shoot. Bo could start whenever the mood hit him.

Bo was leaning against a sweet gum tree, moaning, trying to keep from throwing up. Each time he looked at the torrent of water churning down the narrow canyon, he'd turn a whiter shade of pale. He shoved off the tree, stumbled over to a boulder and sat down, fighting off vertigo.

"What's wrong?" Peter said. He walked around and looked at Bo's face. "Uh oh," he said. "No sleep last night, huh?" He bent over and whispered, "You stay out all night with Claudette? She can wear a man out, can't she? What'd she do, truss you up like a chicken? Don't you just hate it when she does that?" He stood up straight and raised his voice, so that Jacques could hear. "Oh well, this scene shouldn't take long. Whenever the star's ready, let's get it over with. Just pick a boat and let's go." He gave the nearest boat a nudge with his foot. "I recommend this Prijon. The colors will look great on camera. But it's your choice, really. Just pick one. Everybody's waiting."

"I need a canoe," Bo stammered.

"What?"

Jacques said, "He insist he need a canoe for this creek. He say a kayak will not works for him. But the man at NOC, he tell you he know these Bo Rocker, no? And he assure you he know the boats this Bo will love, no? And you boughts the boats he recommends, no?"

Peter said, "The guy at NOC said Bo Rocker loves kayaks, and would be thrilled to paddle any of these models."

"He did not," Bo moaned.

"Oui," said Jacques. "He says you is kayak lover; Peter tells me last night these NOC man says these things."

"I've never been in a kayak in my life," Bo groaned. "And everybody knows it. Canoes, yes; C1s, yes; but not kayaks."

"Sea whats?" said Jacques.

"A C1," Bo replied, "is a decked canoe. It looks like a kayak, but there's a world of difference. The paddler kneels, instead of sitting, and uses a single-blade paddle."

Jacques looked accusingly at his cinematographer.

Peter gave an exaggerated shrug. He said, "What does a macho river man care about boat type? Kayak? Canoe? Pirogue? Bass boat? What's the difference? Conrad said Rocker's the machoest of the macho, didn't he? And a boat's a boat to a macho man, isn't it? So let's get with it. I have places to go. The slopes at Beaver Creek are calling me."

Jacques strutted over to where Bo was slumping, bent down and got right in his face. And said, "That Peter, he has, how does you say? a way with words? A boat is a boat, right macho man? Hahahaha. I loves it. And by these way, how you like my English now? Hahahahahaha."

Peter Clancy pulled out a light meter and took a reading. "The sun's getting on up there," he announced. "It's now or never, Mister macho man. You gonna be the new action hero, or you gonna make me fifty grand by crawling in a hole and languishing in obscurity for the rest of your miserable life?"

Blades on Both Ends?

No matter how hard he tried, Bo just couldn't get the hang of using that double-bladed paddle to roll up with when he turned over, which he did often. He discovered, though, once he had the proper motivation – which was provided by dangling upside down from the kayak while blasting downstream about forty miles an hour, dodging rocks with his head – that if he jettisoned the cumbersome paddle he could execute a hand roll with little difficulty. The problem was, every time he rolled up, he was without a paddle, so he'd have to chase his discarded paddle through the next cataract, hand paddling like mad to catch up with it. No sooner would he catch up with the paddle and latch onto it than he'd flip again and have to jettison it underwater in order to hand roll once more. Then off he'd go again hand paddling after his wayward paddle. It was hard work. Especially since – in Bo's value system – the main objective was to concentrate on locating the cameras, positioned at carefully selected vantage points throughout the canyon, in order to smile in their direction as he approached. Bo was blithely ignoring the river – what little time he was upright – and merrily smiling and waving at every camera he spotted. "Hi Mom! Hi Mom! Look Ma, no paddle!"

By the time Bo flushed over a waterfall called The Tiger's Tooth, upside down and backwards while trying to complete a hand roll, Jacques knew he had a classic on his hands – a comedy. Thinking to avert a tragicomedy, Jacques waved him over before he reached the waterfall called Tyrannosaur.

Bo eddied out and waited as Jacques, Peter, and Claudette worked their way down the rocky bank toward him. As soon as Peter arrived at stream side, he trained his camera on Bo and powered it up. Bo, seeing the red light, and pretty much on autopilot by now, went into his familiar spiel, the one he'd been rehearsing all the way down the river.

"Yes float fans," Bo said into the camera. "If I look like an expert, it's because I am one. I've been paddling kayaks for a decade, continuously refining my skills. I love these things. In fact, I invented the kayak. In my basement workshop. Did I mention that?" He affectionately patted his boat with one hand, in the manner that a rider on horseback might pat his faithful steed, while surreptitiously fishing across the eddy line with his free hand, trying to snag his lost paddle as it floated past, all the while smiling into the lens.

Smiling like a hyena.

"Yes float fans, it's true," he said, almost turning over as he finally managed to spear his paddle with his off-camera hand. "A stream like Cataract Creek, where we're paddling today, is suitable only for experts. Olympic hopefuls need not apply. This creek makes the Olympic slalom course look like child's play." He paused for effect, and then waved a finger in the air for emphasis, before adding: "And whatever you do, float fans, don't try what you've seen here today at home. It could result in serious injury. And it could flood your living room, too."

Claudette said, "Bo, you're so full of it, it's running out your ears."

"Quiet Claudette," Bo admonished. "The star is on camera." He flashed an extra big smile at the lens. "Yes, float fans," he continued. "Many of my friends call me a natural born kayak paddler. Why, I've paddled a kayak so much I don't feel dressed unless I'm wearing my skirt."

Jacques interrupted him: "What is these stuffs on your face?"

Bo replied, "What stuffs?"

"I think it's the stuffs from his ears," Claudette said. "I told you he's full of it."

Peter shut off his camera. He said, "I think it's flaps of skin that he's ripped loose." He bent over to get a better look. "Probably from the dynamic full-facial he did on The Tiger's Butt."

"That's Tiger's Tooth," Bo reminded him.

"Might look like a tiger's tooth if you're upside down and backwards," Peter replied, looking upstream at the huge drop. "But from this angle . . . definitely his butt."

"Whatever," Bo said, feeling of his face. "It's minor. I just need a little makeup. Jacques, could you call the makeup crew down here please?"

"I will not calls makeup," Jacques announced, in his most assertive directorial voice. "But these is what I will calls: quits. I calls quits. That was it. Enough. It was a wrap, as they say in Hollywood."

"Good call, boss," Claudette said. "This turkey's finished."

"Wait a minute," Bo protested. "You can't stop now. The best rapid on the river, a thirty-foot plunge, is right below here."

"We know that," Peter said. "We've seen enough."

"Oui," Jacques agreed, "Quite enough. You is lucky to be alive."

"Are we sure he is alive?" Claudette said, looking at his face again.

"But you don't understand," Bo said emphatically, groping for a convincing reason to prolong shooting. "I've only been clowning around," he insisted. "Yes, that's it. It was only an act. I was making the water look tough, so the viewers would realize how serious it is. I was just putting on a show for the cameras, making it look dramatic, but now I'm ready to get down to business. Now I'm ready for the serious stuff."

"Really . . . ?" Jacques said, looking at him askance.

"Honest," Bo said. "Look, I've got a great idea. Listen to this: I'll run this next drop, Tyrannosaur, backwards while paddling with only one blade, and also while whistling Dixie at the top of my lungs. How would that be?"

"Paddling with 'only' one blade," Peter scoffed, "would be one more blade than you've managed to use up to this point."

"No, listen," Bo pleaded, seeing his future as the next action hero about to go down the proverbial toilet. "Viewers love to hear Dixie whistled on the brink of waterfalls. They do! It's a fact. A friend of mine at Nielsen told me. Dixie whistled on the brink of waterfalls always pulls in top ratings. It never fails!"

At the mention of "top ratings" Jacques Povlsen's eyes lit up like twin mountain peaks consumed in wildfire. He looked at Peter Clancy. "What does you thinks?" he asked.

Peter thought for a moment. "Well, let's see: we got a ragged, vicious-looking waterfall, lots of water, good light, a complete idiot whistling Dixie while deliberately running the drop backwards using 'only' one paddle blade. I have to admit, that's quite a media package. If he could get killed in the process, it might be lurid enough to attract Joan Broaddus Wright's attention. And if she did a show, it would produce a load of pre-release publicity, ensuring the film's box office success."

"Could we add one more element?" Claudette suggested. "It would add to the movie's sensationalism, and help attract

Joan's interest. Tie him in the boat? You know, like in *Unleashed Fury?*"

"Thanks a lot," Bo said sarcastically.

"No problem," Claudette replied.

"Sorry," Jacques said. "No rope."

"Oh, but we can improvise," said Claudette. "We can use my pantyhose. Bo would like that. Wouldn't you, Bo?"

Bo was shaking his head, vigorously. He had opened his mouth to lodge a protest, when Jacques said, "Now, these would be interesting."

Claudette added, excitedly, "It'll work, I tell you. We can write the script around that scenario. I can see it now."

Peter said, incredulously, "A screenplay about a man tied in a boat with pantyhose? That couldn't possibly work."

"Sure it could," she replied. "The story goes something like this: the man, who is a whitewater paddler, is having an affair with a beautiful young woman who adores him. But the man, fool that he is, starts flirting with a slutty nurse. An older nurse, at that. One that's not half as attractive as his lover. Needless to say, his infidelity devastates his beautiful and devoted – albeit jealous – young lover. Driven to madness, so to speak, she bashes him over the head with a rock and ties him in his kayak with the only thing available, the pantyhose she's wearing."

"Oui," Jacques said. "Rachael Murphy could plays that part to perfection. And run butt naked through the woods, too." His eyes began to sparkle. He said, "We can flys her in. I can sees it now. As Rachael takes off these pantyhose, the camera zooms in for a closeup of her fantastically sexy legs. Oui, oui, I likes these story. Better plot than *Unleashed Fury*, actually."

"And she ties him into the boat with pantyhose she's been wearing for three days," Claudette adds. "No, no, make that five days!"

"I thinks that mays be going too far," Jacques said, wrinkling up his nose.

"Oh, okay," Claudette conceded. "She uses freshly laundered pantyhose."

Now Jacques was smiling. He said, "I loves it!"

"It'll be a cinematic first," Claudette assured him.

"Oui," Jacques said. "Oui, oui, oui. He'll be trussed up like a chicken with pantyhose. These is brilliant! Could we also flog him like a turkey?"

"But of course," Claudette replied. "That's exactly what I had in mind. And sometimes these scenes require many takes, so I could stand in for Rachael in case the flogging wears her out."

"You would do that?" Jacques said, astounded. "Without a contract renegotiation?"

She looked at Bo and smiled. "This one time, yes."

Jacques was beside himself with glee. "Oui, oui, oui!" he shrieked.

"And then," Claudette continued, "just as Rachael gets him tied into his boat good and tight – using plenty of half hitch reef knots – just as he's beginning to recover from his flogging, she shoves him and his boat into the roaring river, throws his paddle after him, and yells 'You bastard! The only mistress you've ever been faithful to is your dumb river. So now you can love her forever!'"

"Claudette!" Jacques squealed, grabbing Claudette and warmly embracing her. "You is brilliant. You has saves us from a, how does you say, debacle? How coulds I ever has doubted you? I thought you has the hots for these scoundrel, Eugene (Bo) Rocker. But now I knows you was merely researching story ideas." He released Claudette and looked at Clancy. "What does you thinks of these new script, Peter?"

Clancy thought about it for a moment, a short moment, and shrugged. "What do we have to lose?"

They all looked at Bo. Then back at one another. In unison, the three of them said, "Let's do it!"

Jacques gave the command and soon the camera crew had repositioned along the precipices overlooking Tyrannosaur, the biggest, baddest, most cinematic drop in the canyon, where Cataract Creek plunges a dizzying thirty feet and crashes onto an impressively jagged ridge of rock.

The Day Bo Rocker Whistled Up
a Tyrannosaurus Rex

Somewhere a record of that wondrous descent still exists, captured for posterity by professional camera operators working from seven different angles. Every year at the Annual Conference of Sports Cinematographers, the piece is exhumed and shown, often on multiple screens simultaneously, to raucous howls of laughter, as all seven cameras zoom in for closeups of Bo Rocker's face, contorted with terror as he flushes backwards toward the brink of the waterfall, eyes big as saucers – and whiter – lips tightly puckered and trying to whistle, every brain cell riveted on the thought of old times in the land of cotton.

As his boat hangs momentarily on the brink of the precipice, Bo takes one look at the boiling decimation below, and has a sudden change of heart. With Claudette's pantyhose billowing out in the breeze, he flings his paddle over his shoulder, grabs a protruding ledge of rock, and feverishly claws his way up the Tyrannosaur's craggy back. He is tied into his kayak, however, with seemingly indestructible pantyhose, tied in with a profusion of stevedore and surgeon's knots, and even one big lover's knot. Inevitably, he finds it impossible to drag both himself and his kayak up the slippery face of the rock.

As Bo clings tenaciously to the outcropping, the cascading water sparkles irrepressibly in the sunlight. Then, at long last overwhelmed by the pounding waters, his grip weakens and he begins his slide into the terror below. As the cameras zoom in close enough to show his tonsillectomy scars, to the accompaniment provided by Tyrannosaur's thunderous background roar, the soundtrack picks up the unmistakable shriek of a natural born kayak paddler: "Aiieeeee!"

The Great
Swami Akalananda

On Tennessee's Little River, deep inside the Great Smoky Mountain National Park, lies a rapid with a most unusual name: the Silver Diner. This rapid was named for Doctor Wilford Silverman of Liverpool, a neurosurgeon. Oddly enough, the story of how Silver Diner got its name begins in Tibet.

Kimpur Hon and the
Royal Akalananda Family

Doctor Silverman, a world class alpinist in his younger days, was providing medical support for a British climbing group's first assault on Kimpur Hon, a precipice of ice and wind in the frozen Tibetan backcountry. That's when the doctor met Eugene (Bo) Rocker. Bo was working out of Lhasa at the time, scouting the upper reaches of the Brahmaputra for a possible river documentary. He heard about the climbing expedition and contracted with the climbers to provide logistical support.

While the climbers assaulted Kimpur Hon, Bo hung around base camp and assaulted the support staff with a game he called poker. A local medium lama, who called himself His

Royal Highness Swami Akalananda, fell into the habit of sitting in on Bo's poker games. During one of these all-night sessions, Bo won Kimpur Hon Mountain from the Swami.

Bo was ecstatic. He had never won a mountain. He told everybody in camp: "I beat His Majesty with a royal flush!"

Perhaps Bo would have been less exuberant if he had known that Kimpur Hon Mountain had been in the Akalananda royal family for centuries. Originally, it had been awarded to one of Swami's ancestors by a local deity in recognition of generations of faithful service. The royal family could not bring itself to admit that Swami had lost the mountain to an outsider in a game of chance. Such an admission was the equivalent of publicly proclaiming that the local deity had forsaken the royal family. And that, of course, was royal anathema. So when Swami's esteemed father, His Royal Majesty (and provincial medium-high lama) Akalananda the Elder, heard what Swami had done, he invited Bo to the palace and came at him with a jewel-encrusted royal dagger.

Fortunately, Bo knew exactly how to fend off a knife assault. Faced with the Elder's homicidal onslaught, he grabbed a ditching tool, assumed the standard combat crouch, shouted a warning to the Elder to stop where he was or face the consequences, and without the slightest hesitation, threw the ditching tool at the enraged potentate and ran for his life. At full speed Bo blasted through a wall of the castle and out into a blinding snowstorm, with Swami close on his heels.

After eluding the Elder, and patching up the myriad wounds on his body caused by running through a wall, Bo asked Swami what had come over his crazy daddy.

"All my life," Swami said, bitterly, "he has treated me with disrespect. Since I was age twelve, I have barely set foot in the palace. I have spent my youth in a succession of second-rate schools, all in the name of education. First there was Eton. Then a dump called Oxford. Then came five miserable years at the Sorbonne. Next stop was to be Harvard, but I put my foot down on that one. He might as well have sent me to Dipstick University!" With downcast eyes, Swami moaned, and added, "Not even my Father likes me."

Bo said. "If somebody forced me to do time in those dumps, I'd be thinking about getting even."

That idea brought the Swami back to life.

He said, "Yes!"

Bo said, "Yes."

Swami said, "Let's collect a sample of the royal jewels and get out of this mangy little country."

"Excellent suggestion," said Bo Rocker.

"We can bribe the palace guard."

"Pay money to steal jewels?" Bo said. "Is that how it's done? I thought you stole jewels to get money. Am I missing something here?"

"Think of it as an investment," Swami suggested. "At Oxford they taught me: 'It takes money to make money.' "

* * * * *

The captain of the palace guard wanted forty thousand American dollars to turn his back for thirty minutes. Bo told the Swami: "I can't believe your old man has forty thousand dollars worth of jewels in his palace. If he had that kind of money, he'd fix up the place. Shore up some of those crumbling walls. Some of them're about to fall down."

Swami retorted, haughtily: "At the Sorbonne I was taught not to judge a palace by its exterior walls. Instead, judge a palace by the gleaming jewels in the basement vault, stacked head-high in treasure chests made of precious mahogany and yak skin."

Bo gulped. "Chests full of precious jewels?"

"Many chests," he was assured.

"Well, if there're so many jewels laying around in that over-sized old shack, why doesn't the guard captain load up a couple of wheelbarrows for his own use?"

Swami lowered his voice, almost to a whisper, "You mean you don't know?"

"Don't know what?" Bo replied, watching Swami. Bo was having a hard time believing the transformation that was taking place. Swami's eyes had grown into great white orbs. He was crouched like a wizened old man, visibly shaking, looking nervously in all directions. Bo said, "Oh, no. Don't tell me there's some kind of curse on the jewels? Like with the curse of King Tut's tomb?"

"Worse than that," Swami whispered.

"What could be worse than that?" Bo replied.

Swami tried to answer, but couldn't. The whites of his eyes had enlarged to superhuman size. His turban was being pushed up on his head by his hair, which must have been standing straight up on his head. He said, "The Ye . . . Ye . . . Ye . . ."

Bo grabbed him and shook him until his turban fell off. He had been right. His hair was standing straight up. And he had a lot of it. Swami without his turban was quite a sight. Quite an ugly sight, actually. Bo said, "Come on man, snap out of it. What's wrong with you?"

Swami said, "The guards live in mortal fear of the palace Yeti."

Bo couldn't help it. He started laughing and couldn't stop. It was incredible, the irrational fears that people heaped upon themselves, carried with them through life, like immense loadstones around their gullible necks. Even ostensibly rational people like Swami, who had been educated in the western world, could fall into a virtual trance just thinking about their primitive superstitious beliefs.

And this wasn't the first Yeti tale Bo had heard since his arrival in Tibet. Everybody had a Yeti tale up their sleeve. Yet, he noticed, nobody had ever seen one themselves, although they all allegedly knew somebody who had.

If he thought there were really Yetis roaming around in the mountains, he'd be up there with a film crew, conducting an interview himself with the chief Yeti. That could be the big break he needed in his career, his opportunity to show the world what a talented interviewer he was. And what a dashing and intrepid explorer, as well. He might hire two film crews, to ensure that at least one camera operator captured him from his best side as he conducted the interview. Or even better, he'd get Joan Broaddus Wright to fly over and conduct an interview with him and the chief Yeti. Yeah, that would do it, that would make him an instant star. An international celebrity.

The only problem was: there were no Yetis.

Belief in Yetis, Bo knew all too well, was an ancient superstition that Swami's countrymen clung to out of ignorance, and as a comforting link to the past. The tradition had probably been invented by one of Swami's shrewd ancestors, who recognized that fear of a bogey man helped keep the peasants in line. Fear of a superhuman force embodied in Yetis kept their minds from such repellent concepts as revolution and social justice. The superstition had become so ingrained in the culture that now it was even accepted by members of the royal family, like Swami. He told Bo that the Yeti roamed the palace halls at night, looking for intruders, ever-vigilant to protect the royal family. Even palace guards were scared witless by the Yeti. It was said that the palace Yeti was so physically powerful, and so zealous to protect the royal family, that he would horribly abuse any intruder he caught.

"It is true," Swami told Bo. "One morning, when I was a child, everyone in the palace was brought to the central court to see what happens when the Yeti catches a thief. There was a man there – a palace guard – whom the Yeti had caught stealing jewels. Both the man's arms had been pulled out by their roots. It was hideous. And that wasn't all that had been pulled from his body. He also had . . ."

"Whoa," Bo said. "I don't believe I want to hear the gory details about those other missing appendages."

Swami, who by this time had recovered from his bout with demonical possession, or whatever it was that had rendered him a quivering blob of protoplasm, was growing increasingly scornful of Bo's cavalier attitude. He said, solemnly, "You, Bo Rocker, are an infidel."

"Thanks, Swami," Bo said. And then began wondering what that word meant.

"It means," Swami explained, "that you are an unbeliever."

"You got that right," Bo said proudly.

* * * * *

Late that night, they sneaked into the palace and delivered the guard captain's bounty. "Don't spend it all on one yak," Bo advised him.

After taking the money, the captain said over his shoulder, as he was walking away, "Beware the Yeti."

"Yeah, right," Bo replied.

With keys that Swami filched, they made their way into the cavernous bowels of the palace, until – several floors underground – they discovered a room stocked with more treasure than Bo thought the entire country could possibly contain.

"We'll only take enough for travel expenses," Bo said, while stuffing fistfuls of sparkling jewels into a bag made of brushed yak leather. He was glancing around the room, trying to comprehend the enormity of treasure stacked around him, wall to wall on every side of the room and piled as high, in most places, as a person could reach. Huge chests of jewels of every color under the rainbow. Gleaming trinkets of gold and sapphires and jade and diamonds. And over in the corner, what appeared to be ingots of pure gold. No wonder the country's so poor, he was thinking, all the wealth's right here in one room. While the people subsist on rancid yak butter and a pittance of barley flour, the Elder accumulates this fantastic treasure in his grungy, ill-lit basement.

And ill-lit it was. Bo was depending on Swami for light. But Swami's hands were shaking so badly that the candle lantern he was holding was sending weirdly dancing shadows against the walls of the long, deep room. Bo had topped off the first yak bag and was now stuffing a second one, concentrating on diamonds and rubies this time, shoving them into the bag by the handsful, when he first heard it. It was above him somewhere. And when he looked up, he realized the room must have had a thirty foot ceiling. Whatever it was he had heard was up there somewhere, in the cavernous darkness.

"Give me that light," he said to Swami, and hoisted it, but its glow would barely reach the rafters, ten feet over their heads, huge beams crudely hewed from logs that had probably been hauled from the Scarzi Valley hundreds of years earlier, before the forests were depleted. Bo detected some motion up there in the shadows, but couldn't make it out. Then he heard a clicking sound behind him and swiveled around to discover Swami's teeth were chattering.

"Hold this," he said impatiently, thrusting the lantern back into Swami's trembling hands. Instantly, the shadows started dancing again. "Hold it still," he said to Swami. And then they heard another sound, a different one this time, coming at them from somewhere in the back of the dark room. First a clanging noise. Then a shambling gait dragging something across the jewel-cluttered floor. Swami began screeching, a high-pitched sound like: "Aaaaaaaaiiiiiiiii!" as he shifted quickly from foot to foot, as if he were standing on a hot plate.

And then the grunting started. Back somewhere in the dark.

Bo grabbed Swami and shifted him around in an effort to cast light back in that direction, and tried to take the lantern, but Swami had locked his fingers around it in a death grip. Bo raised the lantern, with it still in Swami's hands, and caught a glimpse of it in the dim light, coming at them out of the dark moving twice as fast as anything that big should be able to move, looking for all the world like an enormous shaggy ape. Bo stumbled backwards and his hand landed on a bejeweled scepter. As the thing sprang, grunting furiously, Bo came around with the scepter, wielding it like a baseball bat. He felt it make contact, a solid thudding sound, and the thing veered off, staggering like a drunk monkey, and braced itself against a stack of treasure trunks, shaking its head and grunting.

Bo grabbed the yak bags, then grabbed Swami and dragged him out the door.

Waiting for the Cooldown

"Maybe I'm not an unbeliever after all," Bo was telling Swami. It was two days later, and they were hiding in an ice cave, on the outskirts of the Elder's kingdom.

"It was merely a palace guard," Swami assured him. "A guard who wasn't in on the bribe."

"Never saw a palace guard with body hair like that," Bo said. "And I never smelled anything quite that strong. Although, there used to be a bar bum at the Down Yonder Saloon with body odor nearly that bad. His name was Mikey."

"It was his breath," Swami said.

"I think it was his whole body," said Bo. "That Mikey was a real stinker."

"No, you infidel! I am speaking of palace guards. They are notorious for eating rancid yak liver. It gives them bad breath."

Swami was counting their loot. He said, "It's all over now, anyway. And look at our haul! A bag and a half of precious jewels."

"We could've had a bushel," Bo lamented. "If only you would've held that lantern still."

"But," Swami replied, "you said we only wanted enough for travel money." He hefted the half-filled yak bag. "On this bag alone we could travel to the far ends of the earth."

Bo said, "You wanna go first class, don't you?"

"Well of course, but . . ." The Swami got a puzzled look on his royal face. "Which reminds me, where are we going?"

"We'll find a place to settle down and meditate for a while, until the Elder cools down."

"Perhaps we can hide in the frozen interior of my country," Swami said. "That region is so cold and hostile, no one goes in there. Not even my Father's tax collectors."

That got Bo's attention.

"No tax collectors in the frozen interior, you say? That sounds like my kinda place."

Bo thought about it for a while. "But an ice cave's not very comfortable," he said, thrusting his hand into one of the yak bags, letting emeralds, diamonds, sapphires and rubies stream through his fingers. "I like the part about no tax collectors, though. That part has a definite appeal to it. But an ice cave's not exactly what I had in mind for accommodations. Unless of course, we consider that great big ice cave in Manhattan."

Swami said, "I didn't know Manhattan had ice caves."

"Sure," Bo replied. "Dozens of them. You just have to know where to look. My favorite one's called the Hyatt Regency." He paused for a moment, thinking of something else, then sprang to his feet, clutching the bulging yak bag. "Wait a minute," he said. "I know what we can do. You're big into education, right? You love earning them college degrees, right? Spent all that time at Oxford and the Sorbonne? And now you're into metaphysics? Levitation and walking on water and all that? Then what we'll do is, we'll continue your education, maybe even teach you a few new tricks, something useful, something spiritually uplifting. We'll teach you whitewater paddling!"

"Paddling of whitewater is uplifting spiritually?"

"Of course it is," Bo replied. "Just look at what it's done for me."

Swami considered that statement. And started to frown. Before he could reply, Bo said, "I'll teach you myself. Just think: instruction from the *River Master* himself. Only a member of the royal family could be so lucky. You'll love paddling whitewater. It's fun. Beats hell out of living in an ice cave."

"Wherever we go, it'll have to be far from here," lamented Swami. "My Father will put a bounty on my pitiful head. And send the Red Guard in search of me. I have stooped very low, stealing jewels from the royal treasury."

"I know the perfect place," Bo said. "The perfect place to spend a couple of million . . . I mean, the perfect place to paddle whitewater, to experience a spiritual awakening. It's called America. And you've never been there, have you? Been to Europe and studied in England, been all over the Asian subcontinent, but never been to America."

"Never wanted to go, either," said Swami.

"That's because," Bo assured him, "you've heard nothing but negatives about my country. You've heard about racism, and discrimination, and rednecks, and corrupt, jack-booted FPB agents, and crime, and the homeless living in the streets, and Ku Kluxers burning crosses, and avaricious Congressmen and perverted clergymen. But the whole country's not like that."

"It's not?"

"Of course not."

"What else is there?"

"Rivers. Loads of rivers. Rivers everywhere."

Swami was frowning. He said, "I thought they dammed all the rivers in America?"

"They missed a few," Bo said. "You're gonna love it there, Swami. We'll hit all the cultural hot spots. We'll get Doctor Silverman to go with us. That lecherous old sawbones has nothing better to do."

Susie Marlowe

Swami, Doctor Silverman, and Bo Rocker spent that spring roaming the Appalachians in a seventy-foot motor home, eating steak and caviar (except for Swami, of course, who was a vegetarian), drinking champagne, and searching for peace of mind and karmic transcendence.

In Friendsville, Maryland, they hired Susie Marlowe to drive their shuttle. Before they could put on the Youghiogheny River at Sang Run, however, Doctor Silverman had fallen in love with her. He abandoned the day's river trip to help Susie drive shuttle. Somewhere between the rapids known as Meat Cleaver and National Falls, Swami caught an eddy and told Bo that he could feel karmic transcendence in his heart. Meaning, he insisted, that at that very moment Doctor Silverman and Susie had found union.

"It concerns me greatly," Swami confessed. "This Susie is a mere child. I am concerned the doctor is taking unfair advantage of her, that he is child molesting."

"I think you'll discover," Bo assured him, "that Ms Susie Marlowe is a lot more woman than she is child, and eminently capable of taking care of herself."

"I do hope you are correct, Eugene (Bo) Rocker, for at this moment they have found union." He looked toward the sky. "Of that the great Swami is certain."

Whatever Susie and the good doctor found on that shuttle run, it cemented them into a relationship that earned her a regular spot on board their humongous road cruiser, the road cruiser that half a handful of Swami's jewels had purchased.

Searching for a Miracle
at the Down Yonder Saloon

By early May, after two months of cruising the Appalachian chain, the bond between Susie and Doctor Silverman was stronger than ever. Their relationship was the only one that hadn't grown tattered around the edges. Bo and the Swami were getting on each other's nerves. And the exchanges between Bo and the Doctor, as well as those between the Doctor and Swami, were growing increasingly acerbic. To relieve the growing tension, they made frequent stops, always at significant cultural centers, in the interest of furthering Swami's education. One rainy Saturday, they stopped at the Down Yonder Saloon in Maryville where the Swami, stricken with a malady known in the western hemisphere as home sickness, was treating his entourage to a nonstop outpouring of angst.

"Never will the Great Swami ascend his rightful throne," he complained. "For my Father has disowned me."

"Hey, Swami," suggested Doctor Silverman. "Tell your old man you made a mistake and now you're sorry. Tell him Bo Rocker led you astray. Tell him you've suffered enough already, spending all this time in a motor home with Bo. Blast it man, two months in close confinement with Bo Rocker amounts to cruel and unusual punishment by any reckoning, even by the bloody primitive illiterate standards of your society. Tell your old man all that, and he'll forgive you."

"You don't understand," Swami said, wringing his hands. "In a fit of anger my Father officially banished me from the province. Even if he wanted to, he couldn't retract his holy royal decree. A medium-high lama potentate cannot go back on his word. To do so would alienate the people, who believe the lama's decree is the same as the word of Buddha. And his Chinese friends wouldn't like it either. They might rescind his tax authority. No, I am banished forever. Now, I'm a miserable reprobate like Bo Rocker, with no place to call home. It would take an act of Buddha to reinstate me."

The despondent Swami was buying pitchers of beer for anyone who'd listen to his woes. And a lot of redneck bar bums were suddenly sympathetic. A dozen or more of them were congregated around his table, swilling beer and moaning in commiseration upon hearing each new travail that Swami recounted.

"Poor ol' Swami; poor ol' thing," declared one of the more eloquent bums, a fellow named Mikey, a short, wiry redneck with florid face, an unquenchable thirst, and industrial strength body odor. "His Daddy's plumb mean to the Swami, because of what that ol' Boat Wrecker's done. Won his daddy's favorite mountain in a poker game, he did. And wouldn't give it back!" Mikey stared down the table at "Boat Wrecker," giving him a healthy dose of the evil eye. "What's a poor ol' Swami to do?"

Bo ignored Mikey's malevolent stare, and said, "Listen Swami. As much as I enjoy living off the royal coffers, I'm sick and tired of hearing you moan about paradise lost. If you really want to go back to that backwards, disease-infested province, then we'll get you back. You say the Elder would be satisfied with an act of Buddha? Then let's give him one. What Burmese dialect does Buddha speak in your province?"

"What do you mean?" asked the Swami, reluctantly taking interest.

"You said it'd take an act of Buddha to return you to the good graces of the Elder without alienating his loyal subjects, right? Well, what kind of holy miracle would the loyal subjects accept? We don't have too many lamas in this country, but over in Charlotte, just a few miles from here, I have holy friends who can pull off virtually any miracle. They don't know squat when it comes to Burmese, but maybe I can teach them a few syllables, enough to make a miracle happen. And for such services, they would charge only a few crumbs from the royal family coffers. A mere handful of sapphires would probably placate them."

"You have friends who are emissaries of Buddha?"

"Sure," Bo said. "A whole gang of 'em over in Charlotte. They even got their own television show. That's how I met them, actually, through that television show. At the end of every broadcast, they'd invite people to come up from the audience and be healed. I figured it might give me the exposure I needed to break into the big time, so every night I'd show up in the audience with a different affliction, with a broken leg, or a body cast, or something like that. Sometimes I'd pretend to have lost my memory, or my speech, or my hearing. And they'd heal me. The one I liked best was the time I dressed up like an old man on crutches, pretending to have a calcified sacroiliac. Then, when they healed me, I did cartwheels across the stage. The audience went wild. I thought a talent scout would call for sure after that performance. But my phone never did ring. Can you believe that?"

Doctor Silverman was rolling his eyes. He said, "Didn't they get wise to you, coming back time after time?"

"Sure they did. But the show's producers knew talent when they saw it. Soon as I'd come in the door, no matter what disguise I'd be wearing, they'd run over and tag me for a stage appearance. They'd say the same thing every time: 'This poor ol' thang is lookin' mighty afflicted. He's in need of a good layin' on of hands.' But you know what? I'm not sure Hollywood talent scouts watch that particular television show. They never did call me up for an audition."

Silverman was holding his stomach, laughing.

Bo said, "Laugh if you want to, but those television evangelists make a load of money." That got the doctor's attention. He leaned forward and raised one eyebrow, Sil-
ʌn's way of saying, 'Tell me more'. Bo continued, "Why,
ʌl' preacher boys lives in a mansion dang near as

big as the Elder's palace. He even has an air-conditioned dog house!"

"You are friends with holy men?" Swami asked. "An infidel like you? What're these holy men called? Is your friend with the big house an American Panchen Lama? Or a Dalai Lama?"

Bo was thinking fast. "Why . . . why . . . they're . . . they're from Charlotte, so naturally they're known as . . . charlatans. Yeah, that's it! Charlatan lamas. What else would they be called?" He wagged his finger at Swami. "You'd have known that yourself, if you were a real scholar, like you claim."

"Oh, but Bo Rocker, you do not understand. Cheap television tricks and self-appointed holy men will not work in my country. There is no television in my province! And lamas are the people's representative of Buddha, ordained by Buddha. Only a truly fabulous event that only Buddha himself could produce will redeem me: a miracle, a true miracle, nothing less."

"Ordained by Buddha! My foot! Your old man was appointed medium-high lama and province tax collector by the Chinese delegation from Szechwan. And he holds office only through the presence of an armed Chinese regiment. He's thrown in with those rotten swine and you know it. All he does is extort yak cheese from peasants. The common people'd string him up in a minute without the Red Guard standing at his back. He's at most one-tenth lama and at least nine-tenths robber baron."

"You do not understand the intricate structure of Tibetan culture, Bo Rocker. You are the classic manifestation of the ugly American: stupid, self-centered, ungrateful, and above all, an infidel. What you don't realize is that Buddha instructed the Chinese saviors to appoint my Father as medium-high lama."

"And Buddha told the Chinese to drive the legitimate Dalai Lama out of Tibet, forcing him to flee for his life to Kathmandu?"

"You, Bo Rocker, are imposing simplistic western concepts onto a complex geopolitical societal structure that you don't understand. My Father is the provincial medium lama. His word is the word of Buddha – as well as that of his Chinese friends. And because of you, he banished me from the holy kingdom. Only Buddha can restore me. But that would require a miracle. A real miracle."

"A real miracle, huh? Well then, what if, say, a train ran over you, but you survived. Would that qualify as a real miracle?"

"No. My people have never seen a train. The mountains are too high. Rail lines go only so far as Nepal. It would have to be something natural."

"Suppose you fell off a mountain and survived, dropped about a thousand feet and then walked away unscathed?"

"That might qualify," said Swami, "but only if accompanied by a pronouncement from Buddha that He had recognized my past sins and selected to spare my sinful soul from a mountaintop tragedy, in order for me to return home and beseech my Father's forgiveness. Yes, that might work, Bo Rocker – if it really happened. But there's something about my country that infidels like you don't understand. When summoned before the Supreme Council, a person is unable to lie. When faced with testifying in the Holy Chambers, even an inveterate liar like you would speak only the truth."

"Me? Tell the truth? Baloney!"

"Not crushed cow flesh! The truth. The truth! It's true, ˜˜ɑ Bo Rocker. It is the truth: every person testifying ˜ ˜nreme Council must drink a cup of truth juice beforehand. Afterwards, they are incapable of lying. It would be the same with me. I could speak only the truth."

"Hey!" interrupted Susie Marlowe, the mercurial young lass from rural Pennsylvania. "That sounds a lot like the relationship I have with my Juvenile Court probation officer. I always tell him the truth. I never lie."

"You have a probation officer?" gasped Doctor Silverman. "A Juvenile Court probation officer?"

"Didn't I tell you?"

Doctor Silverman was too busy choking on his tongue to answer.

"I thought I told you," she said. "Anyway, the Juvenile Court assigned him . . ."

"Juvenile Court!" the Doctor sputtered. "You're under age?"

"Why, Lord yes, honey, I'm only seventeen. So when I was released, I had to have a probation officer."

The good Doctor was not looking healthy. "Why were you in detention in the first place?"

Susie said, "They picked me up on a vagrancy charge. It's nothing to worry about, just a misdemeanor. And my probation officer's real sweet. I confide everything in him."

The Doctor swallowed hard. "Everything?"

"Everything," she said, smiling sweetly.

Doctor Silverman said, "When you say everything, I know you mean everything. But you don't really mean every little thing?"

"Yes sir, everything. I tell my probation officer 'bout everything I do. But it's okay. He's real understanding."

Doctor Silverman started to topple from his chair. Swami grabbed him and propped him back upright.

"Don't worry 'bout a thing, Doctor Silverman," Susie said. "I spoke to him already 'bout you and he ran a background check. He told me except for that slew of malpractice suits that's outstandin' against you, your record's not in too bad a shape. Course he did mention a stack of citations for drunk jaywalking, and that one conviction for embezzling seventy thousand pounds from the Royal Climbing Society. But he said as far as he could tell, walking around drunk wasn't all that uncommon in England, and kind of expected of doctors. And he said the embezzlement conviction was reduced to time served and six months probation when you promised to pay back the money you stole. So, as far as he's concerned, if you stay out of trouble here in the states and don't fornicate with no minors or nothing like that, then he probably won't arrest you."

Doctor Silverman broke out in a cold sweat.

"Not unless, that is," Susie continued, "the immigration authorities find out that you entered this country on a bogus passport that Mister Eugene (Bo) Rocker got for you."

That Susie. She really had a way with words.

Doctor Silverman ripped a pitcher of beer from Mikey's grasp, turned it up and chugged its contents.

Bo leaned across the table and said to Susie. "Other than the false accusation about forging passports, what else did your probation officer's background check reveal about me?"

"Not a thing," Susie said cheerily.

And then she reconsidered. "Oh, wait," she said. "Now I remember, there were a couple of items. Something about an international jewel heist? You know anything about that, Mister Rocker?"

"Obviously a case of mistaken identity."

"Oh, yes, and there was another item about assaulting a palace guard. I believe it was assault with intent to maim and incapacitate. Is that the way you remember it, Mister Rocker?"

"That thing wasn't a palace guard," Bo said. "It was a Yeti. And it attacked me. It tried to take my jewels. I acted in self-defense. Just ask Swami, he'll tell you."

"Uh huh, yeah," Susie said, with more than a little scorn in her voice. "I'll be sure to report your version to my probation officer."

"Listen Swami," Bo said, turning away from Susie and shifting mental gears. "Let's get serious. Suppose – just suppose now – you could truthfully say that you dropped a thousand feet down the side of a mountain and survived without injury? Suppose you could say that on the way down the mountainside you floated on a protective fluid, encased in a shell that protected you from the rocks you hit on your descent? When you struck an outcropping rock, you merely glanced off unharmed, thanks to the miraculous protective shield. Suppose that upon landing unharmed at the base of the mountain, a man dressed in white flowing robes appeared, telling you that Buddha wanted you to go back to your home country? Suppose the man in robes told you to go home and beseech the forgiveness of Daddy Swami and your countrymen?"

"Yes, yes! Bo Rocker. You describe a genuine miracle. However, I cannot survive a thousand-foot plummet from a mountain. No mortal can. As great as I am – and I remind you, infidel Bo Rocker, I am the great, pure and holy Swami Akalananda, educated at the Sorbonne in France, and Oxford in Great Britain – a lama, clean of mind and master of the ancient art of levitation, including self-levitation and walking on water. As great as I am, nevertheless, I am mortal. And as great as my capacity is for alcohol consumption, even as great as my love is for downtrodden humanity, even I cannot survive such a great fall. And even I cannot summon a messenger from Buddha for my own selfish purposes."

Bo rocked back in his chair. "Leave it to me Swami. Trust me on this one."

"You can make this miracle happen?"

Bo said, "Only a few miles from here, the Little River drops more than a thousand feet down the side of the Great Smoky Mountains. As much rain as we've had around here lately, it's probably dropping down the mountainside pretty fast. Getting on it will be about like falling off a cliff. I have no doubt that if you go up and float down it tomorrow in your boat, a messenger from Buddha, wearing a great flowing white robe, will greet you at the takeout."

Swami came out of his chair, eyes blaring with passion. He said, "Bo Rocker, Bo Rocker! You can do this for the Great Swami?"

"Absolutely, Humble One. And all I ask in return is what little's left in that yak bag of yours and a few acres – a couple of thousand will do – up in the north sector, on the Tsinghai border in the forbidden T'ang-Ku-La Mountains, where no one wants to live anyway. Up where the wolf packs roam and the grand lama tax collectors are afraid to tread. What do you say, Swami? Is it a deal?"

"It's a deal, Eugene (Bo) Rocker. That land's worthless up there, and the few inhabitants live like mongrel dogs. Perfect place for an infidel like you. I knew that somehow you'd get me out of this mess. You have the potential for greatness, Bo Rocker. It's not your fault you were born a barbaric infidel and find it hard to change your ways." He commenced waving his arms excitedly. "Bartenders!" he called. "More alcoholic beverages over here. Provide them in your largest containers to every man and woman of crimson neck! And a double serving for Doctor Silverman. For some reason, he's looking terribly pale."

White Sheets, Red Necks
and a Leap of Faith

In his jubilation, Swami didn't notice as Bo Rocker whispered to Susie. "Didn't you tell me your daddy's big with the Klan?"

"Why, Lord yes honey," she said proudly. "My daddy's Ground Lizard of Flea Katch #14 in Sperry County, Pennsylvania. You can't get much more bigger'n that with the Klan without bustin' plumb out of your pants."

"Then I suppose you've been shopping many times for linen bed sheets?"

She shook her head. "Actually, daddy prefers polyester-cotton blends. They last through more lynchin's and they're fire retardant. Fire retardation can be real important on a cold night 'round a burning cross. Sometimes you have to scrooch up real close to the flame to stay warm."

"Right," Bo acknowledged. "And you look like a native born scroocher." He reached in his pocket and pulled out a thick wad of bills, peeled off a fifty and handed it to her. "Do you think you can find a great big ol' white sheet that would look just like a robe if I draped it over my head and around my shoulders?"

"Bo Rocker, you scoundrel! I know what you're up to, and I'm not lettin' you trick the poor Swami."

"Oh, yeah?" Bo said, leaning forward and lowering his voice. "Perhaps you and I can come to an understanding. You see, your probation officer isn't the only one with computer access. I did a little background checking of my own, and unless you get your nubile butt out there and find me a suitable sheet, I'll feel compelled to relieve Doctor Silverman's apoplexy by telling him what I found in the FPB National Crime Files. He'll be interested to learn that you're really twenty-four years old, and working as an FPB informer. And by the way, there're a lot of entries on your rap sheet, but vagrancy isn't one of them." He paused to let it sink in. "Now, what do you say to that?"

Susie pushed back from the table and stood up. She really did look about seventeen, or even younger. Part of it was the way she dressed and comported herself, like an addled child. But part of it had to be in her genes. Susie Marlowe was the proverbial woman-child, especially when you took note of her skin, so soft and creamy that it obviously had never felt the harsh glare of direct sunlight. And she was wearing an outfit that amply displayed her epidermal assets, a skimpy halter top and cutoffs that were about as cut off as cutoffs could be cut off. She gave her halter a tug and gave Bo a hateful look. "I say yes *sir*," she said, snatching the fifty from his hand.

"Oh, and one other thing," Bo said. "Try and not sleep on the sheet before you get it back here, okay?"

"Oh, you're such a romantic." She grabbed Silverman's hand. "Come on Doctor, we have shopping to do."

Lunch Stop at the Silver Diner

Next morning they drove into the Smoky Mountains and put on the Little River near Elkmont Campground. The river was nearing flood stage.

Despite the high water, all went well until Swami tried to run a waterfall called "the Sinks" in his canoe. He sank like a rock.

That's when Swami – obsessed with Bo's idea of him floating down the mountain inside a protective "shield" – decided that canoes (which otherwise were his preferred river craft) were an abomination, because they permitted water to penetrate his holy shield and contaminate the vessel of his sanctified body. He decided that a kayak was more in keeping with his holy principles, but Doctor Silverman was paddling the only kayak, and he objected to giving it to Swami. However, because Swami's jewels had paid for all their boats in the first place, the potentate eventually persuaded the surgeon to relinquish his kayak. Doctor Silverman settled himself, unhappily, into Swami's open canoe.

A rapid or two downstream, Doctor Silverman, struggling with the unfamiliar boat, missed an eddy. He flushed sideways into a rocky rapid and overturned. As he flipped, his foot was snared by a loop of rope that the Swami had affixed to one of the boat's thwarts for secret holy purposes. The overturned boat broached across a narrow chute and Doctor Silverman, his foot firmly secured in the loop, was trapped. The force of the current prevented him from reaching upstream to free his entrapped foot. Fortunately, he had managed to hold onto his paddle. Using the paddle, he probed for river bottom, luckily found it, and propped his weight on the paddle sufficiently to elevate his head above water. After gulping a few breaths of Smoky Mountain air, he screeched, "Help, help! Bo! Help! Swami! Help!"

A Difference of Opinion

Bo and Swami eddied out, ditched their boats, and scurried along the rocky bank to within fifteen feet of the trapped surgeon. But the fifteen feet were filled with a jet of fast water.

"What do we do, *River Master*?" Swami asked, anxiously.

Bo said, "What we do is, we use some of that walking on water talent that you've been bragging about for months. What we do is: you walk your great Swami self out there and rescue that old sawbones before he goes under for the count."

"I really can walk on water," Swami replied. "But only on calm water."

"Calm water my elbow," Bo said. "Water's water. And it's your fault the old sawbones was in an unfamiliar boat, and got himself into trouble. And it's your loop that his foot's caught in. So walk out there right now and retrieve that old fool, before he drowns."

"You're an infidel, Eugene (Bo) Rocker," Swami said, with utter conviction. "Levitation and water walking are gifts from Buddha, and will not work in the presence of an infidel. Get out there and save him yourself."

Bo said, "You pompous twit, get on out there!"

As their argument escalated into the realm of unprintable epithets, matters were deteriorating fast for Doctor Silverman. Only by tremendous exertion and repeated feats of balance did he manage to teeter atop his paddle. He was heard to mutter, "Hurry, you scum buckets . . . glub, glub, glub." Then, weakened by his exertions and the icy mountain water – not to mention a lifetime of swilling enormous quantities of gin and sherry – Doctor Silverman's strength ebbed and he sank into the froth.

"Go save him, you bonehead!" Bo screamed, shoving Swami toward the water. "He's your responsibility."

"I must meditate on this matter," said Swami. "I'm not sure I can find it in my heart to forgive a swine like you of such insults." He shoved Bo toward the water. "You go save him yourself, almighty infidel!"

Suddenly, a blur whistled past them. It was Susie Marlowe. She had been shuttling the motor home along the parallel road when she saw Doctor Silverman's predicament. Abandoning the seventy-foot motor home in the middle of the road, she had scurried down the embankment and, at a full run, dove for Doctor Silverman. She came up, took a few strokes, and, clutching onto a midstream rock with one arm, fished in the froth with her free hand until she located the surgeon. By the thin hair on his head she hoisted him above the surface. With his head above water, desperately gasping for air, Doctor Silverman looked around and spotted Bo and the Swami. "My foot's trapped," he screamed. "Cut me loose, you perambulating pods of far eastern filth!"

"It's your loop of rope that's entangled him; you go get him!" Bo shouted, as he shoved Swami toward the water.

Swami turned toward the stream and shouted, "Stop it! Stop it, Silver Doctor, you British swine! Stop teasing the poor Swami. Such tricks did your grandfather play on Ghandi."

"Go get him, you fake!" Bo screamed as he grabbed Swami and dragged him toward the river. "He's not teasing. He's about to become trout food because you were too cowardly to paddle your own boat."

The Swami's face contorted with rage. Being of a royal family, no one had ever spoken to him with such directness, and frankly, he didn't quite know how he should react or what he should do. But of one thing he was certain: he was not willingly going out into that jetstream of water. Swami concluded it was time to take the offensive and outmaneuver his enemy. Without warning, he delivered a guju blow to Bo's neck.

It made a smacking sound. "Take that, you jerk!"

Bo, caught by surprise, crumpled to his knees. "Curse you!" he muttered, grappling on the river bank for a rock of exactly the right proportions. Finding it, and clutching it tightly, he brought it up with all his strength into the Swami's groin.

"Oooooooohhhhhhhh!" moaned Swami. "You've shattered the royal jewels. Beelzebub is your brother! May the fleas of a thousand yaks infest your armpits."

"Scum buckets! Nothing but scum buckets!" Doctor Silverman howled, as Swami and Bo locked into combat and rolled over the rocks, flailing and thrashing at one another.

Enter Ken Bob
Smoky Mountain White Knight

At that moment, Ken Bob Phillips was inching along in the backed-up traffic on Tennessee 73 through the Smoky Mountains, with his sweetheart Mary Sue Swafford, wedged in close by his manly side, both of them sitting proud in a bright red Chevrolet pickup truck. Ken Bob loved that truck, almost as much as he loved Mary Sue. He worked hard at the tire store for his monthly truck payment. But it was worth it. Driving that Chevrolet truck made Ken Bob feel like a rock.

Ken Bob was peering ahead, wondering what could have possessed anybody to abandon a fancy new motor home in the middle of the road, a motor home which he correctly estimated was worth about sixteen years of his tire store take home pay. The abandoned motor home was causing an horrific traffic jam, giving Mary Sue plenty of time to look over the embankment and observe the sorry plight of Doctor Silverman and Susie Marlowe.

"Oh no," Mary Sue whined in her inimitable nasal delivery. She grabbed Ken Bob's arm, her red nails digging into his flesh. "Look yonder, honey. Down in the river. That poor man's caught and 'bout to drown while them two wrestle on the bank. Help that poor man, honey!"

Tires screeching, horns wailing, tourists' ire rising – it didn't matter. Mary Sue had spoken. And Ken Bob responded. He halted the pickup beside the motor home – thereby tying up all traffic on the serpentine road – and stormed down the river bank yelling like Tarzan, sending small trees, two unsuspecting black bears, and a half dozen modest-sized boulders flying in various directions. He leapt across the water, landed on the broached boat, pulled a genuine Roy Rogers pen knife from the pocket of his Levis, sliced the rope holding Doctor Silverman's ankle, and watched him and Susie flush into an eddy. Not content with this mere lifesaving effort, Ken Bob slipped into the frigid water, lifted the pinned boat from the rock that held it, dumped the boat, and shoved it downstream into the eddy from which Susie and a bedraggled Doctor Silverman were crawling. Then, splashing through the powerful water, immersed to his armpits, Ken Bob returned to bankside. He squished back up the bank toward the reward which he knew Mary Sue surely would bestow upon him, delaying only long enough to deliver several quick kicks to Bo and the Swami.

"Get up from thar!" Ken Bob ordered. "And get your butts headed back home, 'fore I tell your daddies what mischief you've done."

Dazed and confused from the kicks, Bo and Swami disentangled and sat up. "Who was that?" Bo asked, his head still stinging from the impact of Ken Bob's boot.

"That was the Panchen Lama," Swami replied, in hushed tones. "I prayed for Him to rescue the old sawbones, and he heard my prayer. And did you hear what he said to us before he left? He commanded me to return to my beloved homeland. In fact, he said if I didn't return, my Father would be angry. It's a miracle, that's what it is, a miracle. Now I can return and beseech my Father's forgiveness." He looked at Bo, scowled, and added. "You're lucky He didn't turn you into a pillar of salt, or a pile of yak dung."

That Great American Farce
Known as the Connubial Institution

Three days after what came to be known locally as "the Little River Miracle," Doctor Wilford Silverman and Susan Christine Marlowe committed to the universal farce known as the connubial institution. It was a gala affair.

Susie's daddy, Marvin "Rock" Marlowe, accompanied by his motorcycle gang, rode down from Pennsylvania on Harleys to give away the bride. Rock was employed as a Federal Police Bureau (FPB) informant.   He had worked for them about twenty years. He was in his early forties, but looked to be about twenty-five. With all the kickbacks he received, he was looking forward to early retirement.

* * * * *

After an epic post-nuptial celebration at the Down Yonder Saloon, attended by rednecks from as far away as Wilkes-Barre, the newlyweds departed for England.

* * * * *

When the wedding party ended, Rock and his gang roared out into the woods and burned a big cross.

Bridge Dancers

Norman Knight was Associate Professor of Ergonomic Adaptation Mechanics at Dipstick University in Nashville when, along with a university colleague, two doctors from Knoxville, and other carefully selected companions from Nashville, Oak Ridge, Chattanooga and Birmingham, he went paddling for the first time in the Obed watershed, located on the Cumberland Plateau near Crossville, Tennessee. It was an era when paddlers had only begun exploring the many mysterious canyons of this labyrinthine system.

Canyons of the Obed

The Obed canyons at that time were unknown, and intimidating. Although most of the system had been paddled, and descriptions of some sections published, the reliability of information about the system was questionable. Accounts from early paddlers agreed on only a few points, paramount among them:

> The Obed was a confusing river system, containing many different runs, and access points were difficult to locate.

> Some trips were through canyons hundreds of feet deep, with sheer sandstone walls.

> Streambeds contained undercut rock hazards.

151

Local residents often were hostile toward outsiders, and were especially fond of vandalizing parked cars at river access points.

Carefully Laid Plans

Norman's group consisted of experienced paddlers, but only one of them had ever ventured into the Obed system. They painstakingly researched the endeavor; talking with every person they knew who had paddled anywhere in the watershed; scrutinizing topo maps for hours on end; examining county road maps; debating endlessly as only the assuredly overeducated can, holding semi-formal interviews with paddlers who expressed an interest in participating in the expedition.

Finally, they selected 11 paddlers. Malcolm B. Cradwell, trip organizer and Distinguished Professor of Pontification at DSU, characterized the group as "balanced," consisting of several premier paddlers of the era and a supporting cast assembled "to ensure a composite of talent, motivational resiliency, and spiritual strength sufficient to overcome all obstacles."

They would paddle seven miles, from Waltman Ford to Lilly Bridge on Clear Creek, a tributary of the Obed River. Distinguished Professor Cradwell, an astute judge of human character, selected the legendary Eustis Frambole to lead the trip. Eustis was the best paddler in Tennessee, and maybe in the Southeast, so skilled that he often astounded his mates by standing up in his canoe, hopping onto the gunwales and paddling downstream while perched, bird-like, in the most unlikely positions.

The professor also selected Tom Hardin, Les Cranston, Willie Buckner, and Gene Tomkins because of their paddling experience (and because Willie had paddled in the Obed system), two Nashville doctors to ensure ample medical knowledge, and a nurse, Cynthia Pardue, in case the wise men, upon completing a diagnosis, should feel compelled to yell, as they so often did in their daily practices, "Nurse!" Roger Morton was included partly because he was a fair paddler but mostly because he was a fiery, fast-voiced attorney fully capable, the good professor thought, of intimidating any backwoods yahoo in an eyeball-to-eyeball confrontation.

Norman Knight was last to make the professor's cut list. Actually, the good professor protested against addition of Knight but after two weekends of argument relented when Willie Buckner threatened to abandon the expedition and the legendary Eustis Frambole conceded that Knight, because of his training in ergonomic adaptation mechanics (the scientific study of how people get themselves into and out of tight situations), was experienced at helping extricate boats and bodies from undercuts.

Where is Lilly Bridge?

After much difficulty in locating the putin and takeout, and heated arguments among Professor Cradwell, Eustis, Willie, and Les about whether the access road to Lilly Bridge was passable, they finally gathered courage to pitch into the canyon, down a serpentine, badly rutted goat-path of a road. After an exciting descent they reached Lilly Bridge, the takeout, to discover a parked car.

The car caused Eustis to pitch into a fit of paranoia. Convinced that it belonged to a gang of local hoodlums who had heard about their great adventure and were lurking about in the woods and along the cliffs towering hundreds of feet above, Eustis dashed to his vehicle yelling insults to the unseen brigands, pulled out a 9mm Luger, racked the slide, and strode agitatedly back and forth across the bridge, boasting loudly of how many rounds it contained and imploring any and all rapscallions with intent of pillaging parked shuttle cars to emerge now and meet a real man. After several minutes of this display, Professor Cradwell arrived at a plausible alternative explanation for the car.

"Perhaps it belongs to another group of paddlers," suggested the recipient of the American Psychopathic Association's Distinguished Research Award. "It's their takeout car. They've heard of our brilliant plan to run Clear Creek down to here, and they're trying to run it first, to steal our thunder." The professor's hypothesis gained credence when Eustis checked the car's license plate and confirmed that it was registered in Nashville.

Interrupting a mad scramble to jam into the shuttle car, Willie Buckner offered a third explanation. "Could it be," suggested Willie, "a shuttle car for someone running Lower Clear Creek through the canyon? Downstream of here? I've heard that a group called the Dickson Decked Boaters have been running from here to Nemo for the last couple of years."

"That's preposterous," Professor Cradwell shouted out the window of the shuttle car.

Eustis chimed in, "The canyon's never been run. Besides, I've hiked downstream from here for almost a mile and there're waterfalls and rock entrapments down there that no one could survive. Take it from me, pal, Clear Creek Canyon below here is unrunnable."

So much for that theory.

On the River

By the time they reached the putin it was noon. Another heated debate ensued over whether it was better to eat lunch at the putin or stop later on the river. Or skip lunch entirely and devote their limited time to paddling. They finally launched with empty stomachs into a palpable nervous haze upon water which they thought, but wouldn't admit, too high. Hours later, in the midst of encroaching Cumberland nightfall, having been delayed by a dozen swims, a too lengthy mid-afternoon lunch stop, two pinned boats, and several heated arguments, they rounded a bend that brought into view the newly completed Lilly Bridge, glowing new-concrete white against the ever-darkening backdrop provided by the towering walls of downstream Clear Creek Canyon.

Professor Cradwell's day had been rough. He had taken two long swims, suffered an entourage of what he considered idiots, and now was faced with encroaching darkness while still on the river. "At least," he thought, "a bunch of mavericks from Nashville didn't beat me to the river." The more he reflected upon the day and how it promised to enhance his stature in paddling circles, the more exultant he became. He could envision himself pontificating for months to come following club meetings, and during impromptu gatherings at the Dipstick Club, about how he and his friend the legendary Eustis Frambole, and notwithstanding the ineptitude of nine others with whom he would never deign to paddle again, had managed to negotiate one of the last great stretches of unexplored wild river in eastern America.

In truth, by today's standards the run which the intrepid group braved that day is a mild Class II with a single Class III at the takeout, running underneath Lilly Bridge. But at that time, to that group, in strange surroundings, pinched by imminent darkness, Lilly Rapid was Class IV and thundering under and past the bridge into the sinister and unboatable Clear Creek Canyon.

Eustis and the professor conferred in the pool above Lilly Rapid and decided to lead the group into a river-left eddy behind a large rock midway through the approach. From there they would reconnoiter with scant remaining light from the rocky bank on river left. It was a sensible plan, formulated by sensible and intelligent people accustomed to making decisions in a rationally structured world.

But something happened. Something went wrong, very wrong; something with long-lasting consequences. Although they were here by choice – urban dwellers in a primal setting – and aware that the courage to renounce television addiction and substitute canyons of the Obed in its place entailed acceptance of associated risks; although they had read *Deliverance*; although they thirsted for adventure and alleviation of the stultifying monotony of their daily routines, none of them could have predicted what was about to unfold.

Dreaded Local Miscreants

As legendary Eustis slipped into the safety of the river-left eddy midway through the approach and the other paddlers, buoyed by his seemingly effortless success, headed downstream to join him, several rough figures appeared on Lilly Bridge. Three men and one woman with strong and confident movements, accoutered in hats and beards and long hair and denim and garb that marked them as dreaded local miscreants. Images of a haunting scene from James Dickey's story on the Cahulawassee flashed through the cranial interstices of the paddlers on the creek. They were not beginners. But they were nevertheless new to this game. And they were soft. They were not prepared for what was about to happen and as they peered downstream through the gathering gloom, they knew it. They knew it well.

Everyone looked to Eustis as he grabbed the steel army surplus ammo box lashed to his center thwart, popped it open, reached inside and squished a triple-decker Moon Pie. In horror he realized his trusty 9mm Luger was stashed in a shuttle car left at the take-out bridge.

Eustis yelled, "Let's get to the cars!" In a desperate frenzy of strokes he powered across the eddy line, peeled out into the current and flushed downstream. Astonishingly, as if in unison with Eustis, one of the bridge figures bounded in a single powerful, catlike movement onto the concrete parapet overhanging the river and strutted back and forth on the narrow platform with the abandon of an animal in the wild or a corporate weekend pimp caught on a dance floor in the pincers of a brain warping chemical agent, or both.

Eustis Frambole successfully negotiated the maelstrom of the main rapid, and still tossing and bobbing in the tempest of the washout, looked upward at the bridge and its ominous dancer. Only one thing was in legendary Eustis' mind: his Luger. Above all else he feared that the dancer had broken into the shuttle cars at the bridge and discovered his deadly possession.

Thunderbolts from the Bridge

As Eustis approached the bridge, the dancer stopped his demonic prance, reached behind as if to grasp some object or gain momentum, and in an exaggerated motion swirled wildly around in a flurry of foot action, any single misstep of which would have pitched him off the bridge railing into the froth below, executed a 360-degree flamboyant turn that culminated in a throwing motion toward the trip leader, as if he were Zeus delivering a thunderbolt. Eustis jerked his body, attempting to dodge some faintly seen object, radically shifted his weight and fell out of his boat.

In the upstream eddy, panic ensued. For no one, ever, had witnessed Eustis Frambole in the water. White-haired Tom Hardin gasped audibly and whined in a nasal tone, "They've hit poor Eustis with his own gun. Beamed him with it from the bridge!" as he paddled into the current and headed downstream, followed by Gene, Cynthia, Roger, and an unidentified swimming doctor who overturned while attempting to peel out into the current, screaming the whole while, "Help. Help! God, help me! Mercy!"

The bridge dancer, meanwhile, seemed possessed, prancing and dancing and strutting and hurling thunderbolts, or some objects, with unerring accuracy.   Paddler after paddler overturned dodging, or anticipating, the menacing objects hurled from above.

The little academic cogs in his little academic brain had never whirred faster as Norman's time came to approach the demonic dancer. His years of ergonomic theory suddenly paid dividends as he scanned the current differentials of the rapid and spotted a micro eddy on river left barely upstream of the bridge. Deftly catching the eddy, he looked up to witness a sight he was never to forget.

Raven Hair

A young, slender woman dressed in denim bounded onto the parapet near the dancer, caught her balance with arms outstretched as if walking a log, and commenced to dance with the wild man, her long raven-black hair streaming behind and around her, and them, as they stopped and embraced. Falling apart, hands entwined, they began an old-time rock-and-roll dance routine with her pirouetting along the parapet gracefully, elegantly, daringly, bounding in reckless long sweeping unrehearsed movements. As they cavorted together, Willie Buckner floated past Norman and under the bridge, seemingly unnoticed by the tenders above.

Norman was unable to take his eyes from the mesmerizing figures above. Never had his scientifically trained, ergonomically sensitive eyes witnessed such utterly reckless behavior. He was frightened out of his wits by what was happening yet drawn inexorably, ineffably, to the scene above.

But not for long. His reverie was broken by a bloodcurdling scream from none other than Distinguished Professor Malcolm B. Cradwell, his face flushed red. Cradwell paused only momentarily, as he furiously stroked toward the bridge of no return, to scream at Norman: "Come on, you cowardly bastard! They're going to kill us all. It's Aintry revisited!"

Norman looked back to the swirling couple, almost directly overhead. The wild man gestured to the woman as if presenting her with center stage. She whirled about and pointed down at the renowned professor with a grand, exaggerated theatric movement, which Norman recognized as the same thunderbolt which sank the earlier boats. The professor catapulted from his boat as if struck by lightning, whereupon the wild man above launched into yet another frenzied dance along the parapet, laughing and howling and seeming at any second destined to misstep and hurtle into the rapid below.

Suddenly the woman broke step, stopped, shook back her long, black streaming hair, and stared down at Norman, who was transfixed. Pushing up the unfastened sleeves of her denim jacket she placed arms akimbo and turned directly toward Norman, placing her feet well apart on the narrow parapet to ensure solid footing.

Even in the waning light, at the odd and strained angle afforded by craning his neck and peering upward from a none too commodious makeshift eddy, Norman was awed by her unadorned beauty. She was catching her breath from the dancing. Norman could see her chest heave with each breath, her denim jacket hanging open, a plaid shirt within, partly unbuttoned at the top, beads of sweat forming on her forehead. Although paralyzed with fear, Norman could not take his eyes off her. He was obsessed with two thoughts, one purely self-preservationist in nature and the other due to years of scientific training. His first thought was that he might escape by falling out of his boat into the current and swimming under the bridge as deep beneath the surface as possible, perhaps shedding his life jacket in the process. His second notion was purely professional and illustrates how individuals under conditions of life-threatening stress revert to familiar thoughts and comfortable cognitive routines. As mentioned earlier, Norman was Associate Professor of Ergonomic Adaptation Mechanics, the science of getting people into and out of tight situations. Norman was fascinated, from a purely scientific point of view, with how this creature perched on the bridge parapet above him could get into and out of her jeans, tight fitting as they were.

Suddenly her face broke into a wide, friendly smile. Joined now by the wild man who slipped an arm around her waist, she waved and motioned as if to say: "Come on up."

As they disappeared from the parapet, Norman began to shake. With fear. With rage. With humiliation. With lust. With almost every emotion he knew. Coming at him all at once.

He looked downstream and saw a stranger on the bank with a throw rope pulling a very wet bespectacled swimmer from the drink. The swimmer was Professor Cradwell. Other wet hulks littered the banks, some with boats, some without.

Night Comes to the Cumberlands

Totally confused, Norman paddled to the rocky bank, falling from his boat and grabbing a small tree, stumbling and slipping through the stubble field to the low cliff of broken rocks that led upwards to the bridge. He was no more sure of his motives than of what hidden reserves of inner strength and fury propelled him along as he clawed, exhausted, to the top of the embankment and heaved himself onto Lilly Bridge. Standing there, fists and teeth clenched, realizing he was going to strangle anyone within reach, he was immensely relieved to discover the bridge deserted, the only sounds the roar of the rapid below, the screeching of Malcolm B. Cradwell as he needlessly shouted confusing directions, and the eerie echo far downstream, in the darkness of Clear Creek Canyon, of real rapids.

Norman walked across the long bridge, dazed and disoriented, buffeted by a sudden chill November wind, staring up at the awesome cliffs overhanging this narrow ribbon of deserted concrete. He thought of a book he had read years earlier, *Night Comes to the Cumberlands.* He reached the spot where the couple had danced to discover no trace, no record, no proof they had ever been there. No proof at all that they had been anything more than confused figments of his own imagination. He felt a strange emptiness, a primordial longing that confused and enraged his scientific sensibilities and which with great logico-deductive rationalization he barely managed to push back into the unconscious miasma. Suddenly he wished he were a dog, to sniff the parapet and confirm, quasi-scientifically, that they had been at this very spot, and that she had danced on that narrow railing.

With a shift in the wind he heard a motor grinding on the far cliff and turned to see headlights as a van and a car slowly rounded a curve, then disappeared back into the folds of the canyon, inching toward the rim hundreds of feet above, laden heavily with boats. Even in the semi-darkness he saw that the van was yellow; the first yellow van he had ever seen. And then he knew that Willie had been right. They really were paddlers who had put in here early this morning and taken out somewhere far downstream. They had paddled the unboatable canyon, through the rock entrapments and over the waterfalls. And then danced like demons on a bridge railing.

An Obed Authority

As Norman played the event over and over in his mind he realized that Willie was the only one who had paddled past without a thunderbolt hurled his way. A week later he invited Willie out for drinks after work and confronted him. Willie denied knowing the bridge dancers, but it mattered little.

While most of the group never returned to the Cumberland Plateau, Norman was hooked. He returned again and again to the Obed and all its tributaries. Before long he was an authority on the system. He fell in love with it. And with *her* memory. On every trip he watched for her, at every access point, along the rivers and creeks, on the myriad shuttles, even on the long drives to and from the watershed. But the only place he ever glimpsed her was in his dreams. He would awake in the middle of the night from troubled sleep with her image almost palpable. Once he was convinced she had been there with him, in the room, in his bed. He could almost feel her muscular softness, smell her streaming raven black hair. Often he would return to Lilly Bridge, usually alone, especially at sundown, that loneliest time, longing to rediscover the strange couple and get to know them, or her, anyway. But they were never there.

Why should they be?

Birth

of a

Renegade

A year later, on a cold November day with a great deal more water in the stream, Norman and Willie Buckner and three kayak paddlers made their first descent of Clear Creek Canyon, the section that Eustis and Professor Cradwell considered unrunnable. Just above confluence of Clear Creek and the Obed River, near the bottom of a long rockgarden, one of the kayakers edged too close to a river-left undercut rock. The kayak washed sideways into the undercut and Robert Friendly, the paddler, was trapped inside his boat. The other paddlers caught eddies and threw ropes to the victim, but they couldn't free him. Their every effort only seemed to complicate the pin. The situation was exacerbated by the sheer canyon wall that ran along the left side of the stream, preventing access to the entrapped paddler from that side. As everyone watched, the forceful current began folding the kayak, with the frantic paddler trapped inside it. Although Friendly's head was above water, the situation became undeniably desperate as the paddler panicked, commenced flailing desperately, and eventually lost his paddle.

Panic spread to Norman and Willie as they realized the hapless paddler was going to drown unless someone, somehow, could reach him and pull both him and his kayak upstream against the force of the current. Willie looked to Norman, the expert on tight situation extrication procedures.

Norman said, "Well, I guess we could . . ."

The Rescuer

Suddenly from around the upstream bend two C1 paddlers appeared in the rapid, but only one continued through to the bottom. Notwithstanding the dire circumstances with the trapped kayak paddler, all eyes momentarily shifted upstream to the remaining C1 because, although there were no eddies, it came to a standstill in the fast current. Norman and Willie especially, as they were accustomed to stroking with single blade paddles, watched incredulously as the C1 paddler maintained his position in the fast current by alternately back-stroking in the standard on-side fashion and then smoothly swinging the blade across the bow, twisting the torso and wrists into a seemingly impossible contortion, accomplishing a precisely measured offside back-stroke. Even the trapped paddler briefly interrupted his panicky gyrations to look upstream and admire the display of paddling legerdemain.

Most noticeable of all was the C1 paddler's style: every stroke, both sides, precisely measured and velvet smooth; not a single wasted motion. Norman thought the paddler was buying time until he could read the rapid and find the best route, until he realized that the trapped boater was not really blocking the rapid, and it wasn't all that technical a rapid anyway, and the other C1 boater had continued through without a hitch. Perhaps, Norman thought, he's waiting for other companions, possibly less skilled and probably unfamiliar with the river, to appear from around the upstream bend to see him establish the preferred route through the bottom of the rapid.

As Norman was to realize later, the paddler had paused in midstream to size up the situation, to determine if the entrapment would self-correct itself through benign application of force of current and frenzied movement of the entrapped, or if his intervention was required. One thing was obvious to the C1 boater. If intervention was necessary, it had to be accomplished from upstream. Pulling the paddler or boat from downstream would only force the boat deeper into the undercut and compound the entrapment.

The Rescue

As Norman and the others watched, the C1 paddler subtly exerted more force on his on-side backstrokes. His boat turned slightly in the current, with stern angled toward river left. Norman thought at first that he'd lost control and would flush sideways into the rocky bottom of the rapid, then realized he had deliberately set a back ferry toward a spot just upstream of the entrapment. Increasing the boat angle as he neared the cliff, he drove the C1 backwards into an eddy which he seemed to manufacture for the occasion, crawled from his boat with a rope and snaked his way up and across the face of the rock outcropping within fifteen feet of the trapped boater. Here he secured the rope to a scraggly pine and belayed himself to within inches of the kayaker's hapless form. Bracing himself against the rock and somehow finding purchase for one foot, he placed his other foot on the trapped boater's shoulder, took the boater's arm in one hand, and pushed. In one motion the kayak pivoted and twisted. The paddler screamed in agony as the sudden motion dislocated his shoulder. As the boat twisted, it forcefully popped free of the crevice, throwing the paddler, still encased securely in his would-be coffin, into the care of waiting boaters.

Without a word to anyone the C1 paddler scrambled back up and across the face of the cliff, untied and recoiled his rope, reentered his C1 and headed downstream. As he passed the group, he looked at Willie, smiled, and said, "Willie, you know this water's too technical for kayaks."

At that instant Norman recognized him as one of the bridge dancers.

"Who's that with him, Willie?" asked Norman excitedly as they watched the two C1 paddlers head downstream.

"I'm not sure who she is," replied Willie.

"She? Did you say *she*? You mean, that was a woman with him? The first paddler to come through the rapid was a woman?"

"Sure looked feminine to me. Didn't you think so?"

"I didn't notice," Norman said, "but I think my prayers may have been answered."

"Say what?"

"Never mind. But Willie, who's the guy? Who is that man? Who is he?"

"That," said Willie, "was Eugene (Bo) Rocker."

The Grateful Victim

Norman and Willie ferried across Clear Creek to check on Robert Friendly. Willie removed the injured man's helmet and life jacket. Gingerly, he stripped off his paddling jacket and neoprene vest, getting him positioned for a shoulder reduction procedure. His skin was so pallid that at first Norman thought it was the result of immersion in the cold water. Then he saw his wan complexion, faded blue eyes and blond hair – hair so blond it was almost white. Robert Friendly was practically an albino. Willie told him he was lucky, considering how close to death he'd brushed, that he was still alive.

Friendly was in tears and obvious pain, complaining that the powerful brute had separated his shoulder while wrenching him from the undercut. "The inconsiderate bastard," he sobbed uncontrollably, wiping snot on the back of his hand. "I had almost worked myself free. And then he climbed up on the cliff and jumped on me like a damn big monkey. I'll sue him for all he's worth. I'll get him. My daddy's a Criminal Court judge and that scum bucket's going to jail."

Willie stopped his ministrations and slowly rose to his feet. He said, "Come to think of it, maybe you'd better set your own shoulder." He turned around and walked off.

Suddenly a plan crystallized for Norman: a very neat, tidy, parsimonious, virtually scientific plan. It went like this: two bridge dancers minus one bridge dancer sent to prison for assault leaves one bridge dancer without a dancing partner. "You're right," he said to Friendly. "He had no right saving you. He should rot in jail for the rest of his miserable life for such a deed. I'll chase him down for you. Bring him to justice."

The other two kayakers with Friendly exchanged questioning glances. Then one of them, a theology student at Dipstick University in Nashville, said, "You'll really chase him down? You'd do that for Robert?"

"Yeah, sure. Why not?" said Norman, thinking of how the dancer's partner had looked a year earlier, cavorting along the bridge railing.

The third kayaker was a thin kid about fourteen or fifteen years old, with big black eyes and dark curls poking out from under his helmet. The helmet, which was somebody's castoff hockey equipment, had been painted a hideous off-pink color, and had "Ricky Batson" stenciled in bold black lettering across its left side. In small letters, centered beneath Ricky Batson, were the words: *"The Great."* Ricky chimed in: "He certainly had no right breaking Robert's shoulder. That much's for sure. If you're willing to help, I'm sure our dad won't forget your kindness."

"Your dad? You two are brothers?" Years of rigorous scientific training had made Norman a keen observer. One glance told him Ricky's and Robert's gene pools had absolutely nothing in common. Not the first chromosome.

"I'm adopted," Ricky said, with downcast eyes.

"You catch that brute," Robert Friendly blubbered through his tears, "and you can be sure our daddy won't forget you."

Norman said, "Of course. After all, it was assault, wasn't it? And whether you guys realize it or not, that guy has a history of assaulting people on this river."

"He looks the type, like a chronic offender," Ricky Batson said bitterly, through clenched teeth. He was blaring his eyes and curling his lips like an alarmed animal about to attack. Norman thought it was a most unusual emotional display. Then, as suddenly as they had appeared, all Ricky's emotions seemed to subside. His expression returned to normal. He said, "We'll put him in prison where he belongs, if . . ." He turned his big eyes on Norman. "If you can bring him in."

Norman felt an inexplicable chill run up his spine. There was something about Ricky Batson that his scientific mind couldn't quite grasp.

The theology student added, "We'll stay here and comfort Robert. God bless you, Doctor Knight, for your help. And may godspeed your efforts to bring that merciless bastard to justice."

Looking for Bridge Dancers

Norman headed downstream in a frenzy, in hot pursuit of
the dancers. But he couldn't catch sight of them, and would
have despaired of ever seeing them again, except that he was
accompanied by a vision that spurred him on, a vision of a
raven hair beauty dancing on a Lilly Bridge parapet.

At Nemo Bridge, the takeout, Norman arrived in time to
see the dancers entering the yellow van, with their boats
already secured atop. As the lithe young woman, dressed now
in skin-tight faded denim, started to climb into the van,
Norman yelled and caught her attention. She looked around,
puzzled at first, then spotted him approaching from upstream.
She smiled warmly, removed her watch cap and waved to him
with it in her hand, then shrugged her shoulders and climbed
in, her golden tresses almost as yellow as the van.

Hank Menzel's Boring Drive

Hank was rolling toward Knoxville at a high rate of speed, coming in from the east on I-81. His big Suburban was comfortably settled into its long distance lope, with the engine humming and a soft whine coming from the lug tires.

On long, solitary drives like this, Hank would often find himself thinking back to the old days, to the wild times. When he hung around with Eugene (Bo) Rocker. But nobody had seen ol' Bo lately. He had been laying low since that Nashville judge had issued warrants for his arrest, something to do with an attempted murder on a Clear Creek river trip.

Last time Hank had seen him, Bo was two steps ahead of the law. Bo had come by Hank's house to tell him he was leaving the country and to ask Hank if he wanted to go with him, to some desolate location in the Himalayas that Bo swore was so remote they'd never find him.

Bo had been spinning some wild story about having a Gulf-stream V standing by at the airport, waiting for him, and how he couldn't stay long. He was telling Hank about how he planned to make a documentary on some river with a name that Hank couldn't even pronounce, and about a climbing expedition somewhere in Tibet that he might hook up with. And would Hank go with him? It would be the time of their lives; it would be a blast. After the documentary was released, they would both be stars. They would entitle it: *The Outlaws of Brahmaputra Gorge*.

There was, to be sure, a certain zany seat-of-the-pants appeal to Bo's suggestion, but on closer analysis the whole idea was too radical for Hank: a mad dash for the airport; a twenty-two-hour plane ride; a new way of life.

And of course, there were the charges against Bo. Not that Hank believed them. Not for a minute. But still, making a run with a wanted man was a risky proposition.

He simply couldn't wrap his mind around changes of that magnitude. Instead, he shook Bo's hand and wished him luck and drove him to the airport and watched his plane lift off the runway and disappear into the night sky.

He had spent a good part of the following year wondering what had happened to Bo. And then, recently, he read in the paper that the charges against him had been dropped, that some Dipstick University professor in Nashville had come forward and confessed that the charges had been without basis in the first place. That news had cheered Hank, and he looked forward to seeing Bo again. No doubt, he'd be showing up again. Popping up unannounced, like he always did.

* * * * *

All this was running through Hank's head.

As he sat at the wheel of his big Suburban, listening to a K-town country station on the radio and, between songs, hearing the sonorous drone of lug tires against the super slab.

Blasting down the Interstate, toward Knoxville.

* * * * *

He was midway through K-Town when he noticed the cutoff to Maryville. And that reminded him of the Down Yonder Saloon. Which reminded him again of Bo Rocker. Because the Down Yonder had always been one of Bo's favorite watering holes. It was just a dive. But it was an interesting place, nonetheless. Never could tell who you'd run into there.

Hank whipped across four lanes and took the Alcoa Highway exit. And headed for Maryville.

For old time's sake.

* * * * *

Hank Menzel stepped up on the porch of The Down Yonder Saloon, and heard the planking creak beneath his weight. It was a dilapidated old building; not a place he visited often. But it had always been one of Bo Rocker's favorite watering holes, and Hank missed his drinking buddy. He would have one drink for old times' sake, and then roll on down the road.

As he was pushing open the saloon's front door, he heard the unmistakable sound of a chair splintering over somebody's head. And that sound brought back a cascade of memories. Then came the sound of shattering glass and the cacophony of voices calling encouragement to the crowd favorite.

Hank stepped through the doorway and found himself watching the most vicious fist fight he had ever beheld. Two men, one of whom he thought he recognized, were going at it with a vengeance.

Once he got a good look at the combatants, he mumbled to himself, "Tell me it ain't true."

* * * * *

He heard a voice at elbow level. "Welcome to ringside; my name's Mikey." Hank glanced down and saw a bristle-bearded bar fly, a full pitcher of beer cradled in his left arm, who could have put antlers on his head and passed for Rudolph the red-nosed reindeer.

The little man reeked like a toxic waste dump.

The bum made an expansive gesture with his free hand. "Welcome to the spectacular Down Yonder Ruummbbllc Palace," he said, with obvious pride in his surroundings. "On the bill tonight are two of the finest barroom brawlers in the western hemisphere, a dirty fightin' Boat Wrecker and a Tibetan Swami!"

"Oh my word," Hank muttered, after watching the fight for a few minutes. "What set those two at one another's throat?"

The word "throat" sent Mikey's hand flying to his own, probably to make sure it was still there. Satisfied it was, he put his pitcher of beer to his lips and began chugging its golden contents. After half a pitcher had disappeared, Hank thought it best to stop him. He said, "Whoa there, little buddy. You don't wanna bust a gut."

Reluctantly, Mikey lowered the pitcher and looked up at Hank. He resembled a little terrier that had just taken a drink of water. The amber brew was dripping out of his beard stubble, off his chin and down the front of his shirt. He was looking up at Hank, expectantly, so Hank reached down and patted him on the head. "Good boy," Hank said. "Save the rest for later."

Mikey went: "Buuuuuuuurrrrrrrrppppppp!"

"Oh, God," Hank muttered, holding his breath and trying to move away from Mikey, through the crowd of excited fight fans.

But Mikey was tugging on Hank's shirttail. When Hank turned back around to see what the little man wanted, Mikey launched into an explanation. The fight had started, according to him, when mean ol' Judas Boat Wrecker swaddled himself in a polyester-cotton sheet and told the Swami he was a messenger sent from Buddha, sent to tell Swami that he should surrender all his jewels to his dear and trusted friend, the Boat Wrecker, so he could invest them in a Hollywood movie.

"They been at it for some time now," Mikey continued. "We're all bettin' on Judas Boat Wrecker." His voice, almost as deep and resonant as Hank's, was emanating from a decrepit five foot two frame. The man looked like his voice would be a squeak, at best, yet every time he opened his mouth it was boom time. It was boom time out in the middle of the bar, too, where Bo and the Swami were pummeling one another.

"It's their second ruummbblle of the day," proclaimed Mikey, like some Vegas ring announcer, a stentorian voice hidden away somewhere inside the little squirt of a man. "Round one took place a couple of days ago up near the Sinks, and Silver Doctor said it ended in a draw. But that sorry ol' Judas Boat Wrecker'll win this time, 'cause he fights the dirtyest."

Out in the arena, Swami had Bo in a hammerlock and was pounding him with a chair leg.

"Looks like the other guy's holding his own," Hank observed.

"True," said Mikey. "But poor Swami don't have the treachery of that Judas Boat Wrecker. Just watch. You'll see what I mean."

Bo reached down and grabbed one of Swami's ankles and commenced wrenching it violently. Swami lost his balance and they both crashed to the floor, Bo on top.

"See what I mean?" Mikey said, looking concerned.

"What'd you say his name was?" Hank asked.

Mikey's eyes lit up and his voice boomed out: "In the polyester-cotton white robe, standing six foot two and weighing in at one hundred eighty-seven pounds, hailing from only God knows where, with an undefeated record against Tibetan Yetis, we have . . . Judas Boat Wrecker!"

"No," Hank said, "the other one."

"And in the beige turban, weighing in at . . ."

"Just his name, please," Hank said.

"That's Swami Akalananda," Mikey said proudly. He turned up the pitcher of beer and drained the rest of it down his scrawny neck.

Hank said, "Swami Akala who?"

* * * * *

"We love Swami," Mikey explained. "He buys beer for everybody." Mikey winced sympathetically when Bo almost succeeded in clawing out the Swami's left eye, and, undoubtedly realizing the crassness of his motive for loving Swami, added, "And the Swami's a holy man, too. That's very important. People 'round here don't hold for no godlessness. We love him 'cause he's a holy man, too."

Bo, astraddle the Swami's back, had him face down on the grungy barroom floor. He was busy grinding Swami's face into the splintered plank flooring when Hank decided it had gone on long enough. He lifted Bo up by the scruff of his neck and when Swami recovered his feet and came charging at Bo with a beer bottle, Hank caught him by his neck too and hoisted him up in the air and shook some sense back into him. The Swami, unable to breathe in Hank Menzel's iron grip, quickly saw the error of his ways and ceased his struggle. Soon as Hank deposited him back on the floor, the Swami caught his breath and launched into a heavily accented diatribe that Hank couldn't understand.

Hank asked Mikey, "What'd he say?"

"He said free beer to all men and women of crimson neck!"

The bartender, who had been standing by with a sawed-off baseball bat in case things turned ugly, heard Mikey's translation, tossed his bat in the air, and scurried back behind the bar. He grabbed a half dozen cold pitchers and lined them up under his keg spouts, then began spilling rich, golden beer into the waiting receptacles. "I love that Swami," he said over his shoulder. "He's a holy man."

Bo said to Hank, "Did you bring your video camera? Did you get any of that fight on film? It was an incredible scene. We could sell it in Hollywood. They could use it in an Indiana Jones epic. We could make a fortune. It would make me a star, too. Everybody says I look like Harrison Ford. What do you think, Hank?" He struck his best photographic pose, with his chin jutted out like Kirk Douglas. "Do I look like Harrison Ford? Or maybe like Tom Cruise?" His nose was bleeding profusely where Swami had bashed him with a table leg. Both eyes had been gouged, and Swami's claw marks stretched down the left side of his face. In his present condition, he looked a lot more like Frankenstein, risen from the dead, than Harrison Ford.

Hank rolled his eyes and moaned. Bo Rocker would never change, he decided. He directed Bo to one end of a long table, and placed Swami at the other end, sternly admonishing them to stay in their places, and then joined the other bar bums in their determined quest to drink all the beer Swami could buy. After a couple dozen pitchers had disappeared, Bo and the Swami stopped snarling at one another, shook hands and made up, and pledged eternal friendship.

* * * * *

Sitting around the table with Bo, Swami, and Mikey and his friends, guzzling pitchers of beer, Hank was caught up in a euphoria he hadn't felt in years. It was just like old times, with the booze flowing and Bo in high gear, telling wild and crazy stories about chests full of jewels, living in ice caves, walking on water, a doctor with his foot caught in a stirrup, some old potentate trying to stab Bo with a dagger, a heavenly messenger kicking Swami in the head, somebody falling down a thousand-foot mountainside, an underage chick burning crosses in the woods late at night. On and on. One weird story after another. Each story a little more outrageous than the one before. It was just like Bo: wild and crazy and totally unbelievable. Making it up as he went. And everybody around the table, joining in, insisting it was all true. Hooting with glee and howling with laughter. The bartender at a full run, delivering pitchers of beer by the armful to the score of miscreants clustered around the table. Swami passing out fifties to grasping bar bums, like he was feeding cabbage to rabbits.

Hank knew it was all craziness and nonsense. The kind of stuff Bo's famous for. But nonsense or not, it was still fun, listening to Bo spin his yarns. Undeniably fun. All of it. Even knowing, as he did, that it was mostly a pack of lies.

A Doctor Silverman, whom Mikey and the other bar bums called the Silver Doctor, dropped in to say goodbye to Bo and the Swami. The doctor had just been married, and he was accompanied not only by his pert young wife, but also by most of the wedding party, including an entire motorcycle gang from somewhere in Pennsylvania. Hank took one look at the blushing bride and his eyes about fell out and rolled around on the table. She was too young, way too young. Couldn't have been a day over fifteen. But he guessed it was okay. Her daddy, whose name was Rock and who was leader of the motorcycle gang, had given her away. Rock looked to be about twenty-five or thirty.

The doctor and his bride were leaving next day for England and their honeymoon, and they couldn't lollygag. They drank about a pitcher and a half apiece, pulled a few splinters out of Swami's face with a pair of pliers that Rock carried in his right boot, hugged and kissed everybody around the table, and left.

Bo and Swami started talking about how great a place Tibet was, and within minutes they, too, had decided it was time to do some traveling. Before Hank knew what had happened, he was caught up in Bo and Swami's enthusiasm for going to Tibet. Three days later, he had signed over his hardware store to his son-in-law, given away all his kayaks, and climbed aboard a chartered Gulfstream V with Bo Rocker and a Swami whose strange name he never could pronounce.

* * * * *

On the plane, Bo was saying to Hank, "Well, you gave away all your kayaks, didn't you?"

"Sure I did," Hank replied, "but they were old and scratched and about wore out. All of 'em together wasn't worth more'n a few hundred dollars. That motor home, on the other hand, must've been worth a hundred grand."

"More like two hundred," Bo replied.

"And you gave it to somebody you never even met?"

"I met him once," Bo said. "Kind of."

"Where?"

"On the river."

"Which river?"

"Just a river."

"What'd he do? Save your life? That why you gave him a two-hundred-thousand dollar motor home?"

"Naw," Bo said. "Nothing like that."

Hank was having a hard time accepting it. He was shaking that big head of his. Passing his thick fingers through his curly locks. He said, "What was that ol' boy's name, anyway?"

Bo said, "Ken Bob Phillips. Works at a tire store down in Maynardsville."

* * * * *

Bo Rocker didn't stay long in Tibet. He received a summons to Tinsel Town – something about an on-again, off-again movie project. Hank asked him to stay, but Bo said the summons concerned the ". . . ties that bind. Or is that 'Bindings that tie'? Or possibly . . ." Bo let it trail off and looked at big Hank, who only shrugged. Hank didn't know what the summons was about.

Bo said, "Ah, hell. It's about being trussed up like a chicken and flogged like a turkey, but if it's what I gotta do, then it's what I gotta do." After a short conference with Swami, Bo was back on the Gulfstream V, winging his way toward his Hollywood destiny.

Hank Menzel, on the other hand, found a home in Tibet. The Elder presented Hank to his court as an emissary from heaven who had returned the prodigal son to his rightful place on the throne. The Elder's court considered Hank's daunting physical size and never challenged the story. Some people say Hank's still over there, working as the Elder's bodyguard, and in his spare time running waterfalls on the headwaters of the Salween and Brahmaputra. They say his regular paddling partner is a big hairy guy that used to work as a palace guard.

* * * * *

Bar bums in Maryville still talk about the far eastern holy man who once prowled local establishments, accompanied by the Devil's Advocate, otherwise known as Judas Boat Wrecker. And they also talk about the holy man's other friends, the healing man and his child-woman, and her father and his disciples, who built crosses in the woods late at night and set them afire, while wearing white robes and peaked hoods.

* * * * *

Each day, bar bums faithfully attend opening ceremonies at the Down Yonder Saloon, where they meditate on how the holy man turned their thirst into bottomless pitchers of beer. And they recount the litany of horrors that the holy man told them he had endured on his pilgrimage to a heathen land, especially about Judas Boat Rocker tempting him daily to renounce his birthright and live a wanton life of debauchery, in a suburb of hell called Tinsel Town.

* * * * *

And every day, on street corners throughout the Southland, bums doggedly solicit money for a lamasery of their own, convinced that if they build it, the dynamic duo will return — to take them to a land of ice caves and holy mountains, and bottomless pitchers of frozen Margaritas.

Piney Tavern

"Look at that place, would you?"

I didn't have much choice. He had already slowed the van to a crawl and now he was pulling over on the shoulder of the road to get a better look. As we came to a halt, the right front tire rolled onto an empty beer bottle. The bottle disintegrated under the tire with a muffled "pop-crunch."

"It's a beauty; an absolute classic." His tone was hushed, almost reverential. "This's maybe the purest example I've ever seen. I didn't know you could still find 'em in pristine condition like that. Bet you a dollar it ain't changed a lick in thirty years. That place oughta be in a museum, you know? The American Museum of Hillbilly History. No, even better than that, it oughta be in the movies."

I kept waiting for him to twist it around into some absurd joke, but as far as I could tell, he was serious. He just sat there staring – awe struck, with this misty, faraway look in his eyes. I checked the place again to make sure I hadn't missed something. But no, I hadn't. It was a ramshackle, dilapidated old building – probably a converted chicken house – sitting back among the scraggly pines there in the bend of Clarence Darrow Drive.

For the life of me, I couldn't see anything special about the place. I'd seen a thousand others just like it. They used to be all over the Southland. Mangy looking places stuck back on

181

throwaway parcels of land, usually up against some ugly red cutbank, often alongside a river, like this one, and always with kudzu growing like jungle fungus in every direction. The nearby river, I surmised, made for convenient disposal of Saturday night garbage – or Sunday morning corpses.

When I was growing up, my family called them beer joints. And although the sign out front proclaimed this one to be a tavern, it was nevertheless a beer joint – plain and simple and in the best southern hillbilly redneck tradition. One of those places where a belligerent, smelly old drunk with cirrhosis of the liver hangs over your shoulder and blows his fetid breath in your face, the old fool blathering endlessly about how Hank Williams stopped by once, slugged down half a case of beer, vomited in the floor, staggered over to the corner table – that one right there by the juke box – and wrote Cold, Cold Heart. On the back of a coaster, by God.

That kind of place.

Bo started in again, speaking in this dreamy monotone that I never knew was inside him, "It shore is purty; plumb beautiful. I'll bet Hank Williams passed out in that bar."

Give me a break.

"It's true, boy," Bo insisted. "Ol' Hank used to tool through these hills in that big ol' Cadillac of his – hiding out from Audrey, his wife, 'cause they just couldn't get along – and he'd stop off in all these little out-of-the-way places. Places just like that one right there. Hank'd get drunk as a hoot owl and raise holy hell. Wrote most of his songs in places just like that. And, you know something? They love him in those places. Sometimes, they'll have a big portrait of Hank up over the bar. And at closing time, or at some other special time of the day, they'll all stand at attention and salute his picture. Or a picture of George Jones. Either one will do. They tend to be pretty much interchangeable."

Now Bo had me looking at the beer joint, wondering.

"You know how old Hank was when he died?"

"Died?" I said, surprised. "I thought he was still living up in Nashville. They're always playing his songs up there."

"And why not?" Bo retorted. "He only wrote the best songs ever recorded. Classics, all of 'em: *Your Cheatin' Heart; Cold, Cold Heart; I'm So Lonesome I Could Cry; Mansion on the Hill; I Saw the Light; Jambalaya; Hey Good Lookin', Kaw-Liga.* The list just goes on and on. You remember the song, *Kaw-Liga?* Well, it's a love song, a serious love song. People used to listen to that thing, when it first came out, and break down in tears. That's how good it is. Yet it's a love song about a wooden Indian. Can you imagine trying to write a love song about a cigar store Indian? It takes talent to pull that off. Talent, and a whole lot of time in places like that one there."

"Uh, Bo?" I said, ostentatiously looking at my watch, trying to convey that we were wasting precious time making small talk about a dead country music artist. But Bo was on a roll. Knowing that I wasn't about to ask how old Hank was when he croaked, he volunteered the information: "Twenty-nine. That's how old he was."

"You're kidding?" I said. "That old? Jim Morrison was what? Sixteen?"

Bo was looking at me with mock astonishment. Or I thought it was mock, until he said sharply, "Have you no respect for nothing?" He grabbed the steering wheel and started to drive back on the road, and then stopped again. He looked at me, and I realized I must have hit a nerve. He said, in his sternest voice, "Hank really was only twenty-nine when he died. And yet he produced all those songs. He was a great man; the greatest songwriter of all time." With that off his chest, he took a deep breath. "And he drew much of his inspiration," he continued, "from places like that one right there." He was pointing to the beer joint. He added, "It shore is a beauty. It's really something."

It was something, all right, its windows adorned with the usual collection of garish red, yellow and blue neon beer signs, and its facade an amalgamation of split logs and tar paper patches. Over the front door, propped up against the roof by four cinder blocks, was a big hand-painted sign – blood red lettering against a starkly white background – announcing that the establishment's name was 'Piney Tavern' and that the coldest beer in Henshaw County was to be found inside.

Bo was saying, "I might be able to use a location like that in one of my movies."

That was too much. Bo was always talking about the movies he was making, but I had never seen a finished product. Not one. And I told him as much.

He looked at me with a wounded expression. "They made fun of Frank Capra, too."

"Who made fun of Frank Capra?"

He didn't bother answering. Instead, he added, "And Steven Spielberg. They made fun of him, too."

It was more than I could take. "Yeah, yeah," I said. "And Federico Fellini. They made fun of him, too, right? Not to mention Godard and Hitchcock and Orson Welles and John Boorman and Jacques Povlsen and all the other great ones. "They" made fun of them all. And you're right up there with them, right? Same talent level, same cinematic genius. And now here I am, unappreciative clod, uncomprehending dimwit, making fun of the great Eugene (Bo) Rocker. Well, Bo, there's just one problem. You're always talking about making movies, but I've never seen one of them. Have you scheduled your first theatric release?"

"It won't be long now."

"Yeah, right."

He gave me a disdainful look. "Povlsen and I are working on a classic adventure film, called *The Outlaws of Cataract Creek*." He quickly wheeled around and looked back toward the tavern. "And we might just use that place for a barroom scene. It would add a certain authenticity."

No doubt about the authentic part.

Bo was staring at the place, mesmerized. I nudged his elbow and got his attention.

"We'd better be going," I reminded him. "We've never been on this river before. It took more than an hour to find the takeout and we have only a vague notion of how to get to the putin. We haven't the foggiest idea of what the river's like, and there's just the two of us so we'll have to run cautiously, which will take extra time, and we also have to . . ."

"It don't matter what's on the river," Bo announced, looking at me like I was a fool for having suggested otherwise. "Long as there's water. And we know there's plenty of water 'cause that's the river right there, right across the road from Piney Tavern, and there's a ton of water in it. We'll come out right here, right by the Tavern. So what's to worry about?"

Bo logic.

* * * * *

He fired up the van and eased back on the road. But he was creeping along, still looking at the place. "You can tell it's a fine establishment by the clientele."

"I don't see any clientele," I said. "Everybody's inside."

"That's exactly what I mean. It's a loyal clientele. Here it is ten o'clock in the morning and they already got, how many would you say? a dozen cars out front?"

They were pickups, actually, rusted and battered pickup trucks already congregated, this early in the day, in the beer joint's pot-holed dirt parking lot. But Bo was right about the number. At least a dozen pickups, and not a one of them less than ten years old, some twice that age. Not a single one with a decent coat of paint. There were more dented fenders and banged up tail gates and scraped doors and cracked windshields in that one parking lot than in most medium-sized junkyards.

Without even trying, I began to form a distinct mental picture of Piney Tavern's loyal clientele. Ne'er-do-well good ol' boys with a penchant for solving problems with their fists. Hard workers when they worked, which wasn't often because they preferred to hang out in beer joints and drink all day. It was a handy way to dodge child support payments. Not too well educated, and definitely not overly tolerant of what they considered deviant life styles. Which would include anybody from outside the county, if not from outside the local community. I met some of these good ol' boy types when I was growing up. A guy down the street was a member of the club. When he wasn't beating up on his wife or kids, he liked to hang out at a place at the foot of the hill called the Midway. The place was notorious. And so were its habitués. Unsuspecting outsiders who innocently sauntered through the Midway's front door often got beat to a pulp. They always blamed locals for picking on them. But that really wasn't the case. If no outsiders were available, the locals would beat on each other. Those ol' boys just plain liked to fight. And after they'd beat hell out of one another, they loved to sit around and whine about all the bad luck in their lives.

The heartbeat of America.

* * * * *

Bo Rocker has this way about him, this approach to life: he never does anything in moderation. It's not that he's hell bent on self-destruction; it's just that he never learned any other way of doing things. There's no switch on his control panel that says, 'Slow: Proceed With Caution'. All his control buttons are variations of 'Fast Forward: Go For It'. With Bo, it's either all-out, full-tilt boogie — or nothing. So it was perfectly natural that when he finally got his eye full of Piney Tavern, he floored the accelerator. Practically stood on the damn thing. And we went roaring down the narrow, crooked road way too fast in his big F-250 Ford van. I was screaming at the fool to let off the gas but by then we'd already come to the sign that says: "Maximum Safe Speed 20 MPH." Half way through the curve, we went into a four-wheel drift and all the significant events of my life, all two or three of them, began to flash before my eyes. Next thing I knew, there it was: shiny as a new penny. A bright blue, sparkling-clean, brand new, straight-off-the-showroom floor sport utility vehicle — a SUV, the kind with a name that reminds you of a restless prairie dog.

I won't say they were parked in the middle of the road. They had made a halfhearted effort to pull over on the shoulder. Except there wasn't much of a shoulder, and not wanting to get the new Yupmobile too close to the edge, they had just kind of stopped in the road. Not that it made much difference what part of the road they were occupying, because at that moment it all belonged to Bo. When they came into view — both of them standing out in front of the Range Rover with a map spread out on its hood, two boats on racks atop it — we were drifting around the curve sideways, Bo gunning the engine like Mario Andretti, a collision imminent, estimated time of impact about two seconds and closing fast.

It's strange the things you fixate on at a moment like that. Here we were, careening toward disaster, Bo at the helm and me cringing in the passenger seat, trying to coax myself into a bloodcurdling scream. I should have been bracing for the impact. Or saying my prayers. Or fingering a rosary. Or something. But all I could do was helplessly moan and stare at the faces of the two guys we were about to annihilate.

If they'd been real quick, they could have made a dash for it. But even if they had, there wasn't much place to dash. The road was about twenty feet wide. On one side was a shallow ditch backed up by a steep bank. Too steep to climb. On the other side, the road pitched straight off a bluff into the Piney River.

The two dudes froze. Just stood there watching us skid toward them. Staring at us, slack-jawed. Not even wanting to comprehend what was about to happen to them, what their grisly remains would look like after the gruesome thud of impact.

And then Bo hit the brakes. Locked them. Stood on them with both feet and did a war dance. And commenced wrenching the steering wheel like a madman, back and forth, like he was determined to rip it from its shaft. When the van started spinning, I lost sight of the doomed faces. And gained renewed appreciation for just how steep the bank was across the road, as we plowed toward it. Then the bank disappeared, replaced by a bird's-eye view of the Piney River. And then, as we continued the spin, in frighteningly quick succession: the dudes again, and the bank, a stretch of road leading back to the tavern, the shiny blue Range Rover, thick green kudzu, the river, the dudes, kudzu, the Range Rover, the bank. Then I got kind of dizzy from all the spinning, and the world turned into a confusing blur and the blue smoke and sound of screaming tires welled up from the road and enveloped my senses.

And then, silence.

As we finally came to a halt, still in the road, all I can remember is that Bo turned loose of the wheel, leaned back, and said, "I wonder if ol' Hank did it this a way?"

I hadn't the slightest idea of what he meant, and wasn't about to ask. I opened my door and stumbled out. My legs were so weak I had to lean against the van. For a minute, I thought I might find myself down on hands and knees, staring at the road surface, or collapsing on it. Fortunately, the acrid smell of burnt rubber and evaporated brake linings revived me. That, and the sound of approaching footsteps.

I looked up and saw the two dudes that I thought we must surely have massacred, strolling up nonchalantly. And a hundred feet down the road sat their shiny Range Rover, unscathed. Bo had miraculously missed the dudes, their car, the bank, most of the kudzu, and the Piney River, and somehow wrestled the big van to a safe halt.

I was speechless. But not Bo. At that moment I heard him open his door on the other side of the van. Then the door slammed shut and I heard Bo's voice, booming loud and clear, "Hi, I'm Bo Rocker, the *River Master*. I noticed you guys had boats on your old Jeep, so I thought I'd stop and say howdy. What're you paddling today?"

"Cool driving, river man," the ugly one said. "And that's not a Jeep back there. That's a Range Rover, man." He snatched off his shades so we could take a gander at what was undoubtedly the ugliest face in creation. He said to Bo, "I'm Horace Conrad and this here's Vince Follett. We're running the Piney Canyon today, and we had stopped to double-check the gradient figures." He paused for a minute and got this real funny look on his face, like he was trying to remember if he'd put the garbage out before leaving home that morning. He said, pointing his shades at Bo, "Say, you're not *the* Bo Rocker are you?"

"I am if you're *the* Horace Conrad, publisher of *Drift Indicator* Magazine."

Conrad smiled. Which was a pleasant change because he wasn't quite as ugly when he was smiling. "I publish a number of fine magazines," he said proudly, "including *River Probe* and *Drift Indicator,* the two that a man of your interests would know. Of course, you're most familiar with *Drift Indicator* because of that special feature we ran on you a couple of years ago. And what a splendid feature it was!" He clasped his hands and rolled his eyes toward the sky. The man was practically drooling. "I still remember all those glorious photographs of you on Overflow Creek and the Green Narrows. Remember those? Some of the most remarkable photographs I have ever published." Bo was avidly nodding his head. Conrad continued, "Did you know that article, along with its cover photo of you, brought in more mail than any other piece in *Drift Indicator's* history? And it was ninety percent positive mail, too."

"Yeah," Bo said, getting into it. "Bill Barkley wrote that piece. Did a pretty good job, too, as I remember. Only cut out one or two of my quotes. If he'd left them in, the mail would've been one hundred percent positive."

"Wild Bill did write that piece, didn't he?" Conrad replied, rubbing his chin thoughtfully. "Yes, indeed. How is he doing, by the way? I heard he was injured recently. Something about a waterfall?"

"He's on the mend," Bo assured him. "He complains of a backache occasionally, but otherwise, he's coming along fine."

"That is good," said Conrad. "And your project with Povlsen? Is it back on? I heard it was canceled. Something about a script impasse?"

"It was nothing," Bo said, with a dismissive gesture. "There was a scene about trussing and flogging that had to be cut, that's all."

"A scene about what?"

"It was nothing," Bo said again, a little testily this time. "A dude was supposed to be conked over the head, trussed up like a chicken, and flogged like a turkey. I thought it was creatively objectionable, and insisted that the scene be cut. At first Jacques resisted, but he came around. Everything's back on track now."

"Is that what it was about?" Conrad replied. "Those Hollywood prima donnas can get in a snit over the slightest little thing."

"Jacques calmed down when he received the yak bag."

"The what?"

"A friend of mine – from Tibet – decided to invest in the movie. He sent his investment in a yak bag, and it was enough to ensure me a say in the film's creative direction. Jacques thought the yak bag was a nice touch. Especially when its contents assayed at a cool seven million dollars."

Conrad's eyebrows shot up. "That's major capital!"

Bo buffed his nails on his vest, and replied casually: "Major productions require major infusions of capital. Elementary economics, Mister Conrad."

Conrad said, "So that's what you're doing here. You're on location, aren't you? Shooting the next whitewater classic with Jacques Povlsen." He paused, and looked over at me. I could barely believe my ears, and the surprise must have been showing on my face. Bo Rocker was really making a movie with Jacques Povlsen? Conrad continued, in an upbeat tone.

"Oh, yes, I can see it now: Eugene (Bo) Rocker, destined for greatness. Move it on over, Brad Pitt. Look out John Travolta! Make room for the biggest star of all." He whispered something to Follett, who made a mad dash for the Range Rover. Conrad turned back to Bo. "Incidentally," he said, "I hope you haven't forgotten that without my assistance in setting up the meeting with Povlsen, you would never have had this opportunity in the first place?"

"I haven't forgotten."

"That is good," said Conrad. "Because when new talents are poised on the brink of stardom, sometimes they have a way of letting important matters slip their minds. Now, that wouldn't happen with you, would it?"

"I haven't forgotten," he repeated.

"That's good. And I sincerely hope you also haven't forgotten that . . ."

"I promised you a part in the movie? No, I haven't forgotten. I'm sure there's a part for you somewhere. I'll come up with something."

Conrad forced a laugh. "Of course you will." He held up both hands, forming an imaginary frame, and looked at Bo through the frame, tilting it slightly this way and that, to get him into focus. He said, "Collaborating with Jacques Povlsen, huh? Man, oh man, Mister Bo Rocker's star is rising fast. With Povlsen's genius for making action films, you could have a colossal hit on your hands." He casually glanced at Bo's van, "Say, Jacques isn't in the van with you today, is he, so that I might discuss the matter of my role with him?"

Bo shook his head, and said he wasn't sure that speaking to Jacques would advance his cause anyway. He said he had already mentioned the possibility of casting Conrad in a minor role and it had caused Jacques to burst out laughing.

"Jeezzzzzz," Conrad said, making a tight fist to emphasize his displeasure. "That's the reaction I always get from Jacques when I try to discuss my acting career. I don't understand it."

Follett came running back with cameras hanging all over him. Cameras with telephoto lenses, cameras with normal lenses, cameras with wide-angle lenses, cameras with super wide angle fisheye lenses. He had cameras with strobes, cameras with motor drives, cameras with reel attachments, cameras with zippers up the side and tattoos on the bottom. He had one boxy camera with Haselblad in shiny raised letters on one side and down its other side somebody had scrawled in blue magic marker: "Mama, You're The Most." He selected a bulky job with the Nikon name plastered all over it, pointed it at Bo, and hit the motor drive button. *Whirrrr-snip-whirrrr-snip-whirrrr-snip-whirrrr-snip-whirrrr-snip.* Four exposures every second. Four exposures every second of Bo Rocker preening and smiling, glorying in the attention.

When Follett had run off a couple hundred frames, Conrad said, "Is Jacques' assistant, Claudette Remey around? Perhaps she could write me into the script."

"Claudette Remey!" Follett lowered his camera. His eyes were bugging out as he said, "Did you see that Joan Broaddus Wright special on her and Jacques Povlsen a couple of months back? I'd like to have an assistant like her. She's *only* the foxiest chick in Hollywood! I'd do anything to get a photo op with her. And I do mean anything."

Bo stopped posing long enough to say, "Actually, Claudette is no longer scripting this movie."

Follett said, "No? That's too bad. She's so talented, so beautiful."

"She's a nice lady," Bo said. "No denying it. But frankly, she looks a lot better than she writes. Her script had this bizarre ending that didn't make much sense to me. Her story line got all knotted up, so we brought in Wild Bill Barkley to untangle some of the kinks. He's writing some new scenes as well, some creative stuff, maybe a few fast-paced barroom action scenes." He looked at Conrad. "That's where we may be able to work you in. With Wild Bill's mastery of the written word, he can surely add a bit role that's tailored specifically to your unique talents. We'll start shooting again, just as soon as Bill gets the script straightened out." Bo frowned at Follett, and said, "Speaking of shooting; you out of film there, bud?"

"No sir, Mister Rocker!" He brought the big Nikon back into play: *Whirrr-snip-whirrrr-snip-whirrrr-snip-whirrrr-snip-whirrrr-snip.*

Four exposures every second.

Bo Rocker immortalized. Again.

* * * * *

At first I was impressed with meeting Horace Conrad. After all, he did publish two or three paddling magazines. And he knew important people, like Jacques Povlsen, the famous movie producer. But the man quickly got on my nerves. He kept blabbering about Piney Tavern, which he described as the cultural oasis of the Tennessee Valley, which made no sense whatsoever when any fool could see it was nothing but a run-down beer joint. And then there was the way he looked and talked. He had a dozen gold chains around his neck, which struck me as kind of odd for a whitewater paddler, and a diamond on his pinkie the size of an acorn. And he had this gaunt face, with sunken eyes and thinning hair and pock-marked skin, and he was forever running on about this or that, mostly nonsense as far as I could tell, using outrageous Hollywood babble. He was just really weird.

"That's the way they all are," Bo explained, as we headed back to drop the Range Rover at the takeout, where we had left my truck earlier. He continued, "Never met anybody in the publishing industry that wasn't a bit weird. Comes with the territory. And Conrad, he's worse than most because he hangs out with those boneheads from Hollywood." Bo glanced over at me as he drove, perhaps sensing my discontent with letting Conrad and the photographer join our river trip. He added, "And you did say we needed more paddlers." Which was true enough. "And you have to admit, Follett seems like a nice guy." He did. A good ol' boy from down in Georgia, somewhere around Macon. Friendly fellow, with this great big smile. And he had all those cameras, any one of which was sufficient to qualify him for the Eugene (Bo) Rocker river trip of his choice.

So we loaded all the boats, people, and gear onto and into Bo's van and headed up the side of the Cumberland Escarpment, looking for the putin. It was like driving up a mountain. My ears started popping half way up, and Bo swore his nose was about to bleed, from the change in atmospheric pressure. It was quite an experience, driving up on top of the plateau and then looking over its edge back down into the valley, more than a thousand feet below, and knowing that with a little luck – and some half-diligent map work – we would find a little wildcat of a creek up here that would slingshot us back down to the valley floor, through steep and narrow and bony creek corridors, and dump us out into flatwater, somewhere in the vicinity of Piney Tavern.

We stopped for Bo and Conrad to look at maps, and instead of finding the best route to the putin, they got into a heated argument, something about promises made and not kept. Follett and I got out of the van and let them go at it. We climbed a little knoll and looked across the Tennessee Valley.

In the distance was Watts Bar Nuclear Reactor, with its ominous reactor shields rising like sinister cancer growths from the lush green valley floor. An eerie sight.

"You been working with Conrad long?" I asked.

"He's published some of my work before," Follett replied. "But I never met him until yesterday. He called and told me to come on up, take him down the Piney. He wants to do a feature on it."

"You've run it before?"

"Twice."

"What's it like?"

He smiled, the big Follett smile, eyes sparkling, "Piece of cake."

In the background, Rocker and Conrad were going at it like there was no tomorrow.

* * * * *

After a few minutes at the putin, unloading boats and rigging for launch, everybody was ready – except Bo. His center thwart was broken almost in half. To buttress the crippled thwart, he was trying to duct-tape a hickory limb to it. His repair tactic looked unorthodox, but I had seen him use it before, and it would work if he could get the stick of hickory wood taped down securely. Bo had this thing about old boats: he never liked to let them go. He would run a boat until its bottom fell out, or until it absolutely came apart at the seams, or both. Usually both. He liked well-trained boats, boats with lots of experience. He'd always say that once you had a boat properly trained, once you'd run it down most every river in the country at least four or five times, then it would remember where all the eddies were located and it would know how to jump in the eddies to avoid undercut rocks. According to Bo, the last thing you ever wanted was to abandon a loyal, well-trained boat for some shiny new model that didn't know the difference between an eddy and an undercut.

Bo logic.

Conrad, annoyed with the delay, came over. He looked at Bo's boat and snickered. Gave it a rather unkind nudge with his foot, and declared, "What dumpster did you salvage that from?" He laughed and walked off, and I started having a premonition that something bad was going to happen to him. I looked at Bo's boat again and had to pretty much agree with Conrad's assessment. The old rig was kind of beat up, kind of battered around the thwarts and bilges. Kind of battered along the gunwales and deck plates, too. In fact, the hull was pretty much pulverized. The only thing holding it together was duct tape. But it was Bo's boat. A gift from none other than His Royal Majesty Swami Akalananda.

And everybody knows: you don't pick on Bo Rocker's boat.

Everybody, that is, with the possible exception of Horace Conrad.

I edged up to Bo and asked if he was still sure that we did the right thing by inviting Conrad to come along. Bo glanced over at Conrad. "Are you kidding?" he said. He raised his voice, just enough for Conrad to hear him. "Look at him standing over there. You ever seen anybody that ugly? With him along, the rest of us look like princes." Bo took another look at Conrad, then shook his head and whistled under his breath. He said, "I'm feeling handsomer by the minute."

I said, "It's not too late, you know? I think that Follett dude's okay, but Conrad's a loser. Magazine publisher or not, we should dump him right here. Tell him to get lost. It's our trip."

"No way," Bo said. He explained that from all he'd heard, Conrad was probably a pretty good big water paddler, but he was likely to be miserably inept on tight, technical streams. And from everything we knew about the Piney, it promised to be Tennessee technical to the nth degree. "With any luck at all," Bo said, "the old fool'll drown downstream somewhere and we'll be rid of him."

More Bo logic.

* * * * *

The first time the famous publisher pinned his shiny new kayak, Bo caught the eddy below the rock that had snagged him, and as Conrad struggled valiantly to free himself, Bo, instead of offering a helping hand, offered instead a never ending stream of insults concerning Conrad's lack of paddling skill. Bo asked if his boat was stuck on the rock, or if it was merely his boat's glossy shine that was causing the problem.

By Conrad's third or fourth pin, Bo was shamelessly ridiculing his predicament, laughing at the preposterous idea of a magazine publisher thinking he could actually paddle whitewater, asking him how much he'd pay for a well-trained boat, one like Bo's. Eventually, the *River Master* had enjoyed enough payback, and thereafter occupied himself with hamming it up for Follett the lens master – leaving me to shepherd the great man of letters safely down the river.

Even with all of Conrad's pins and swims, we somehow managed to sluice almost a thousand vertical feet down the side of the Cumberland Plateau, splashing down in late afternoon a few yards upstream of Piney Tavern, cultural oasis of the Tennessee Valley. I had had a pretty good day on the river, and Bo and Follett had had the time of their lives, doing what they loved most: Bo posing and Follett wearing out his camera shutters. Conrad, of course, was another matter. He had pinned about seven or eight times, a couple of them fairly serious affairs, and had taken four brutal swims. By the time we reached the takeout, Conrad wasn't speaking to anybody, me included, although I'd spent most of my day saving his miserable butt. To make matters worse, Bo walked up to him at the takeout and asked if he'd had a good day on the river, then laughed in his face and asked if his shiny new Jeep hung up on speed bumps as badly as his shiny new boat pinned on river rocks.

As we were loading boats in palpable silent tension, Bo said, "I don't think Conrad can take a joke at all, do you?"

We got our boats strapped down and Bo made a beeline for the ice chest in the back of my truck. He tore open the lid, practically ripping off the hinges in the process, and only then did we realize that in the excitement of running a new river, we had neglected to transfer any beer into this chest. Up on top of the plateau, in Bo's van, sitting at the putin, was a 72-quart Gott cooler packed to overflowing with icy cold Bass Ales. And here at the takeout were the two thirstiest river rats in the history of paddlesport, both of them with ice up to their armpits, fishing desperately for cold beer in an ice chest containing nothing but a few stray sodas and one ruptured package of sliced bologna.

Until that day, I had never seen Bo Rocker cry.

But there he stood, with this pathetic look on his face, staring incredulously at a can of Diet Red Berry Soda that he'd fished out of the icy sludge, with these big crocodile tears welling up in his eyes and about to spill down his cheeks. He was cringing at the thought of having to drink that artificially sweetened belly wash for brats. I was about to console the guy, to slap him on the back and assure him that in forty-five minutes – an hour at the outside – we would be back atop the plateau, dry and comfortable in his van, sitting pretty, guzzling dark rich amber nectar of paddling gurus.

But right then, before I could even open my mouth to console Bo, we heard that magic sound. That unmistakable metallic-liquid *"ker-pop-fizzzzz"* sound of somebody opening a can of cold beer.

We wheeled around and there it was, the source of the sound, parked right there by the river in the shade of a big hickory tree: Conrad's shiny blue Range Rover. He had opened up its back door and slid his big, bright, red and white ice chest right up to the door opening. And that ice chest was brimming full of beer. Yuppie brand beer from Mexico to be sure, but beer nonetheless. He tilted back the can he had opened and I could hear the beer glug-glugging down his scrawny throat as his Adam's apple hitched up and down, and that sound just about killed me. He finished off the beer and let out this heinous slurping burp and crumpled the can and threw it on the ground at our feet.

"Love that stuff," he declared, eyeing us. "Where's yours?"

I looked at Bo but he wasn't looking back. He was fixated on that red ice chest in the back of Conrad's Range Rover. He licked out his tongue, never taking his eyes off the chest. He would have been drooling if there's been any moisture left in his mouth. But there wasn't. We might as well have been two vaqueros, just blown in off the pampas, with a twelve-day case of the dry mouth.

"Thank you, I believe I will," Bo said, edging toward Conrad's chest, his hand outstretched for an imaginary can of brew that Conrad wasn't about to offer.

Conrad slammed down the chest's lid. "Don't even think about it," he admonished sternly. "This is my private stash: the publisher's special reserve."

"Why thank you, I don't mind if I do," Bo said, reaching for the chest lid.

"No way," Conrad said, blocking the ice chest with his body. "Buy your own beer, hotshot movie star. Or better yet, let Jacques Povlsen buy it for you."

"Since you insist," Bo said. "I will have one. But only one."

Bo sidestepped and made a desperate lunge for the ice chest, but Conrad was quick, surprisingly quick for a publisher. He caught Bo's face and pushed him back. Then he shoved the ice chest into the Range Rover, slammed its back door, and shouted, "Get in Vince, we're out of here! This barbarian's lost all control."

Before I could even maneuver around for a flank attack, Conrad and Follett had ducked into the Range Rover, locked the doors and fired it up and roared off, leaving Bo and me in a cloud of dust. High and dry, so to speak.

"I told you he was no good," Bo said, scrubbing Conrad's palm print off his face with a dusty wetsuit sleeve. "That man is undoubtedly the biggest, most selfish lout in the whole world. Somebody like that ought to be shot with yak manure and hanged for stinking. I hope he's nabbed for DUI on his way home. See if I ever waste my time saving his life again. Next time he gets pinned on a rock, I'll let him drown. You wonder how somebody like that could be a publisher. He hardly knows his ABC's. The rudiments of grammar are almost as alien to him as the basic principles of courtesy and human decency. He's a moral derelict. Turpitude is his middle name." He stopped to catch his breath.

Amidst Bo's outpouring of virulence, we were forlornly watching the shiny Range Rover round the bend downriver and disappear from our view, when Conrad suddenly slammed on his brakes, skidded to a stop, and started backing up.

"He's had a change of heart!" Bo said. "I knew he couldn't drive off and leave us in this pitiful condition, way out here in the boonies with no beer. He's not really a moral derelict, he just seems that way sometimes. He can't help that he's weird – he's a publisher. Comes with the territory."

Stopping the Range Rover about fifty feet down the road, Conrad cranked down his window, stuck out his ugly head, and yelled, "Hey, I got an idea. Why don't you boys stop at the little tavern down the road and have a cold drink? They really like your kind in there. Tell the bouncer Conrad sent you!"

When the Range Rover disappeared around the bend we could still hear Conrad's laughter, echoing up the river corridor.

Piney Tavern Here We Come

Bo Rocker, of course, thought it was a capital idea, stopping by Piney Tavern to soak a few cold ones. I finally convinced him that we should stop only long enough to buy some beer to go, enough to last until we got back to his van: a couple of six-packs.

I pulled into the Piney Tavern parking lot, among the haphazard array of battered pickup trucks, which by now had multiplied in number to at least two dozen, and switched off the ignition of my truck. Bo looked at me and said, "Well, big boy, you ready?"

"Ready for what?"

"For the adventure of your life?"

"Picking up a six-pack of beer at a seedy beer joint is going to be the adventure of my life? I don't think so."

Bo got out and hitched up his grungy wet suit. As I walked up beside him, he said, "Something tells me this is gonna be a most excellent adventure."

An Invitation to "Git!"

We discovered that Piney Tavern's front door had no doorknobs – at least not on the outside. You could walk up to the door and knock on it, but you couldn't open it – not from the outside. To get in, you had to be admitted.

Bo didn't just knock, he hammered – with both fists – until the door eventually cracked open about an inch, far enough for us to see a wad of tobacco with a bulging, hairy jaw wrapped around it. The door opened a little wider and we could make out some creature looking at us with beady little eyes. Suddenly the creature spewed a vile stream of tobacco juice in our direction, and grunted, "Git!"

Which sounded to me like good advice.

But Bo Rocker wasn't in a gitin' mood.

"It speaks English," Bo said, as the door slammed in our face. "Never saw one before that speaks English."

"Let's get out of here," I suggested.

"Get outta here? Are you nuts? This's obviously the gathering place for the social elite of that little town down the road. What's it called? Scopes City?"

"Do you think for one minute that the social elite would have a trained gorilla for a doorman? I don't think so, my friend. Especially not a barefoot gorilla wearing overalls and chewing a wad of tobacco the size of a baseball."

Bo gave me one of those looks. One of those condescending looks that world travelers reserve for provincials. One of those looks that intellectual sophisticates bestow on simpletons. "That wasn't a gorilla," he said solemnly. "Gorillas can't speak English."

"That was English?"

"Of course it was," Bo replied.

"Then maybe it was an orangutan?"

"No way, man," he said. "That was a Yeti. I know 'cause I saw one in Tibet. The Swami's family keeps one in the castle, to guard the royal jewels. He's a mean son-of-a-bitch, too. Won't let nobody get near them jewels."

"This one isn't exactly friendly," I reminded him. "He almost smashed my face with that door."

"The Yeti didn't mean nothing personal by it," Bo said. "Slamming that door in our face is just what the Yeti's been trained to do. That's the social elite's way of being snooty to outsiders." He thought for a moment. Then he said, "Man, oh man! An English-speaking Yeti. This has real potential. I've gotta get inside this place, study that critter's habits, see how it thinks."

Bo went over to a window and wouldn't quit banging on it until some woman finally raised the blind and opened the window and sold him a six pack of Bass Ale. We sat in my truck in the Piney Tavern parking lot as it got dark and drank the ale and talked about Yetis, watching with interest whenever customers left the establishment. We were especially enthralled by the elite quartet that staggered over to where we were parked and proceeded to educate us regarding the intricate nuances of local profanity. After a couple of minutes, Bo stuck his head out the window and thanked them profusely for their erudite etymological edification, and particularly for repeatedly clarifying our maternal pedigree. Then he bestowed upon their appreciative ears a few choice Tibetan Yeti syllables. That seemed to mollify them for a few minutes. Until they thought of yet another way to convey some more of that ingrained southern hospitality that socially elite rednecks are so abundantly endowed with at birth. Without even being asked, they lined up and took turns washing the dusty hubcaps on my truck. A big lanky fellow with eyes that looked like red glowing coals tried to wash the windshield, but his hose wasn't quite long enough.

Did a tolerably good job on the hood, though.

I was so grateful for the big guy's efforts, I thought I might cry with joy.

That adorable quartet eventually staggered off into the dark, and we sat for a while longer, polishing off the ale and enjoying the spectacle of those emerging from the establishment. I finished my second Bass Ale about the time Bo finished his fourth. He rummaged around in the ice chest for a while, looking for another ale, then resignedly settled back and watched the tavern's front door with an intent expression on his face. I heard him mutter something that sounded like, "Next time."

"Next time what?"

He said, "Next time, I'm getting inside that social club right there." He nodded toward Piney Tavern. "Mark my words, I'm getting inside there, so I can mix with the social elite."

* * * * *

Truth is, I didn't mark his words. I was thinking about the incredible river trip we had made that day. I was thinking about Horace Conrad, and how I'd spent half the day pulling the old fool off rocks, and about the weird scene at the takeout. How he wouldn't even share a beer with me or Bo after I'd saved his life half a dozen times. And then his backing up and telling us to come to this place. Why had he done that? Of course, Bo had laughed at him on the river. But so what? Bo laughs at everybody on every river. Inappropriate levity, after all, is the prerogative of expertise. The best, in other words, can laugh any time they please. And at whomever they please. They can get away with a lot more than the rest of us can. And when it comes to whitewater, Bo is just about the best; the best I ever paddled with, at any rate. Truth is, I was thinking about a lot of things as I fired up the engine and slowly pulled out onto the road. I was thinking about a lot of things, but I wasn't paying much attention at all to Bo.

And I should have been. I should have marked his words.

Inside Piney Tavern

Monday the rains began, and every day at work that week I'd call all the river gauges, checking levels. Piney River doesn't have a gauge, or not a telemetric gauge. So I'd get a reading from the Emory at Oakdale gauge and a reading from the Tellico gauge, and one from the Little River in the Smokies and one from Town Creek in Alabama. Then I'd attempt to triangulate all the readings and estimate what volume the Piney would be carrying. Any way I'd calculate it, the water was rising fast. On Thursday the rains continued unabated, and every river in the region was getting on up there.

Bo and I drove up Friday night, separately, and met at the Piney River takeout. Arriving late, we slept in his van. We slept late the next morning, too, hoping the rain might stop. After we woke up and ate breakfast, and it was still raining, we passed the time in conversation. Bo had learned a few things about Horace Conrad, which he shared with me, including the interesting fact that Conrad's ex-wife worked as a barmaid at Piney Tavern. Conrad's wife had walked out on him a couple of years earlier, and it had crushed him. He couldn't accept the fact that she had left him for another man. "That's what he was doing up here last week," Bo said, "spying on his ex-wife. My sources say he spies on her everywhere she goes, constantly sending her messages, pleading with her to come back to him. The poor woman moved all the way up here, thinking nobody in his right mind would follow her from Atlanta all this way back into the boonies. But sure enough, Conrad spends every weekend up here, trying to get a glimpse of her. Of course, he pretended to us that he was up here to run the river, or to land a bit part in my movie, but he was really up here to see her."

It sounded to me like a no-win situation. I said, "Why can't he just break it off?"

"Something to do with Frieda, I guess. That's his ex-wife's name, Frieda. They say she's something else. A real looker. A pretty good dancer, too, I hear. Works down at Piney Tavern."

* * * * *

Finally, about noon, the downpour ended and we ran shuttle, with some difficulty, over mud-rutted roads. We left Bo's van at the takeout this time, and made darn certain that it was well stocked with icy cold Bass Ale.

It was about 2 pm by the time we put on, and near dark when we finished the run, but the trip was an absolute flush. When we came off the river, we were still luxuriating in the afterglow of an extended adrenalin rush. We loaded boats in semi-darkness and headed back to the putin, to pick up my truck, happy as two Down Yonder bar bums at the sight of Swami Akalananda with a fistful of fifties.

I was basking in a warm afterglow that promised to sustain me at least until I could do it again tomorrow, when Bo, before I could stop him and practically before I even realized what he was doing, wheeled into Piney Tavern's parking lot, slammed on the brakes, jumped out and commenced hammering and kicking on the front door, demanding entry. I scrambled out and grabbed him by the arm and was dragging him toward the van when the tavern's front door swung open and the same vile wad of tobacco appeared, the same one we had seen a week earlier, surrounded by the same surly jaw. This time I could see that the jaw was affixed to a face, which was part of an enormous hairy head, which rested on an unnaturally short neck and the brawniest set of shirtless shoulders I've ever seen, and the whole concatenation, including two sinewy arms dangling from soiled work overalls and reaching almost to the ground, took one barefoot step outside the door and stared malevolently into Rocker's face.

And then the Yeti – or whatever it was – said, "I thought I told you to git?"

"Unbelievable!" Bo shrieked ecstatically. "This varmint even has the rudiments of grammar and syntax. I think we've discovered the missing link. It's been right here all along, right under our noses, right here on the outskirts of Scopes City."

That's when I saw the muscles knot in those elongated arms and the fire commence to burn inside the beady little eyes sunk deep but close together in the sloped-back head that carried the gob of tobacco in its protruding jaw. That's also when I forgot all about pride and self-respect and constitutional rights and polite but insistent self-expression and all that crap you read about in self-help best sellers – and got ready to bolt down Clarence Darrow Drive faster than even a Yeti can run.

Bo, of course, wasn't getting ready to run. He hooked his thumbs inside his wetsuit vest and said, "Yep, I believe you did tell us to git . . ." And then he sucked in his gut and puffed out his chest and actually managed to strut without taking a step. "You said to git, all right, but that was before you knew that I was a famous movie star."

The hulk blocking the door looked stupidly from Bo to me and back to Bo, and finally said, "It was?"

"Yeah," Bo replied. "It was. But now that you know who I am, you're gonna invite us in."

Gradually some of the hate and belligerency drained from the critter's face, replaced by a look of puzzlement. The critter said, "How do I know you're a famous movie star?" The thing looked over at me, and then over my shoulder at Bo's highly conspicuous van, with two brightly colored boats loaded atop its racks. "You could be a liar," it said, "or worse yet, one of Conrad's friends."

Bo looked over his shoulder at me and winked before answering. He puffed out his chest again and rocked back on his heels. Hooked his thumbs in his vest and wiggled his fingers in the air. "You'll believe I'm a star when I tell you how I broke into the movies. It's all in who you know. You see, my daddy was . . ." Interrupting now to look over his shoulder at me and wink again, before continuing. ". . . Hank Williams' limousine driver."

That was all it took.

The thing in front of us stepped back and motioned us inside. I took a tentative step forward and peered into the dimly-lit hovel, and was greeted by billowing tobacco smoke. Or some kind of smoke. I could see something moving in the half-dark of the place's interior, and I heard somebody giggle. In the background, mixed with hoots and shouts and guffaws and the clinking of glasses and bottles, I could make out George Jones' voice, wailing about some dude that stopped loving her today.

"Come on," Bo said, strutting past the Yeti. "Follow me before the dummy changes his mind – if he has one."

I had one foot over the threshold when I heard a bass voice say, "Oh, my. That second one's really cute."

That's when I did an about-face and set a new land speed record getting back to the van. I jumped in and locked the doors and reached for the ignition, only to discover that Bo had taken the keys.

Horace Conrad had been right about him all along: he was totally out of control.

When I calmed down from my conniption fit, I had no alternative. I hunkered down, out of sight.

And waited

And wished.

Wished that I had not squandered my youth in such trivial pursuits as higher education and clean living. Wished that I had learned useful social skills, like how to hot-wire Ford vans, so I could drive off and leave that worthless Bo Rocker stranded, in there with the Yeti and all those adorable social elites. I thought about getting out and searching through the parking lot for a car with its key in the ignition. There were certainly plenty of cars – or trucks, rather – in the lot, even more than the week before. The lot was jam-packed. Down at one end, backed partly under the spreading oak trees, almost out of my sight, was a row of five or six moving vans. I had no idea why they were parked down there.

There must have been a million pickup trucks in the lot, too, along with six or eight shiny new cargo vans that I hadn't noticed the week before. One of them surely had a key in the ignition. I gave it a lot of thought, and at one point, even slid from the van's seat and ambled over toward the vans, trying to see if anybody was down that way, in the shadows, watching them. And then I got scared, my heart thumping like galloping horses' hooves on soft earth. Facing grand theft auto charges was not my idea of a fun time. I turned around and headed back toward the van, and when I did, out of the corner of my eye, I thought I could read something on the side of the nearest van. It looked like *"Povlsen Enterprises."* But it couldn't have been. Not here, not in the Piney Tavern parking lot. I crawled back inside the van and settled back to wait for Bo to return.

According to Bo

Several hours later, Bo emerged from Piney Tavern, staggered over to the van and gleefully commenced washing the right front hub cap. That chore accomplished, and undoubtedly to demonstrate that he'd successfully absorbed the full repertoire of elite redneck social skills, he devoted several minutes, while hanging onto the rear view mirror for balance, to commenting on my mother's lineage. He finally crawled into the van and told me that if I'd drive pell-mell for the Down Yonder Saloon in Maryville, he'd tell me what had transpired inside Piney Tavern.

I never did get the story completely straight – and indeed I suspect there was no completely straight story, considering the condition of its source. So the following account perhaps should not be taken too literally, especially the part about the dismemberment. Bo's speech was pretty garbled, but from what I could piece together, the proceedings inside Piney Tavern had something to do with a Hollywood film crew doing a movie about "Intergalactic Smooth Dude" who drifts from one planetary constellation to the next in search of the ultimate whitewater river. The scene they were filming supposedly takes place in a bar near SwirlerDown, probably the most famous whitewater river in the universe, on a planet called Mystery Move. Smooth Dude was the centerpiece of the scene, brandishing a laser paddle that hummed like an electrified hornet's nest. Smooth Dude said the paddle was possessed of a "force" that protected him from recirculating hydraulics and abominable undercut rocks.

In the scene, a gang of derelicts on Mystery Move had caught Smooth Dude trying to launch his boat on the Holy Corkscrew, the section of SwirlerDown where the river flushes into an uninterrupted vertical spiral, plummeting straight down for seventeen miles. The derelicts escorted Smooth Dude to the bar, where he was informed that he would have to drink his weight in Bass Ale or be put to death. To their surprise, Smooth Dude promptly drank his weight in Bass Ale. And then ordered another round.

The movie director, Jacques Povlsen, had overrun his budget and was cutting costs by casting regular Piney Tavern customers as the ruffians who were hanging out on Mystery Move. They were supposed to be members of a roving pan-galactic motorcycle gang, real freaky creatures – mutants and what not from out-of-the-way planets and other galaxies. In most cases, the Piney Tavern regulars required little or no makeup, which saved on production costs.

Bo said, "That Povlsen is shrewd. He knew these elite locals are such natural actors that they don't need makeup to look freaky. Especially that clan from down around the nuclear power plant. The one at Watts Bar? I'm telling you, man, some of them stand-ins from down that way are plumb weird looking. They're weird actin' too. One boy kept grabbing Smooth Dude by his skinny butt and telling him what a great figure he had. Smooth Dude got so fed up that the next time the boy reached out to grab him, he swung around with that buzzing canoe paddle and lopped the boy's arm slap off. Whacked it right off, just like that, and it plopped onto the table and then slid greasy-like onto the floor, with blood and bone and tendons and everything hanging out of it and smearing all over the top of the table and down the table leg and all over the place. And with the cameras running the whole time. And with Jacques screaming 'Cut! Print it! It's a take!'

"It was so gruesome that at first I suspected it was all part of the playacting, that they'd just faked cutting off the boy's arm. But then Claudette Remey, who is Povlsen's assistant, started screeching at Jacques, threatening to sic the Yeti on Smooth Dude because she wasn't paid to clean up appendages and stuff like that from off the floor. 'Not in my contract,' she said. And Jacques, he's no dummy. He didn't want his leading actor tangling with that Yeti. And he was pretty happy by that point, pleased with himself that the cameras had all been running and that he'd captured the dismemberment on film. He kept slapping Smooth Dude on the back and babbling something about 'brilliant improvisation, better than anything Marlon ever did.' So Jacques promised Claudette a raise and a major role in his next action adventure if she'd just shut up, which she did, promptly.

"Meanwhile, the boy with his arm cut off crawled under a table and was moaning like he'd die or something, but nobody except his friends from down around the nuclear power plant was paying him much attention. His friends kept hollering at him, 'Hey boy! Don't worry, it'll grow back!' Every time they'd holler that at him, he'd try to stick his arm back on, but it wouldn't stay on and every time he tried and it didn't work he'd moan louder. And finally Claudette told him that it wasn't in her contract that she had to listen to his shrieking and moaning and that if he didn't shut up, she'd sic the Yeti on him. And that was all he needed, I guess, 'cause he shut up right away. Jacques bought the boy a drink and then paid for him a six pack to go and that seemed to mollify him. I guess Jacques was feeling sorry for him 'cause he was so ugly. The makeup artists must have worked overtime to make him look that hideous.

When we came to the nuclear facility at Watts Bar Dam, Bo said, "That ol' boy's friends live around here somewhere. They said his arm would grow back. They seemed pretty sure it would. You ever hear of that happening?"

"No," I said. "I can't say as I have."

"Me neither."

Bo was quiet for several miles. I looked over to see if he'd nodded off. But he hadn't. "You know," he said, "it might have been better if Smooth Dude had cut off the boy's head instead of his arm. He was plumb hideous looking. Dang near as ugly as ol' Conrad"

Bo thought about it for a long time as we drove along. Suddenly he sat bolt upright. "You don't suppose," he said excitedly, "that could've been ol' Conrad in there tonight, do you? Could Povlsen have broken down and given him a bit part? And then the makeup crew plastered on so much makeup that I didn't recognize him?"

I looked over at Bo and we both said, at the same time, "Not!"

It was miles later, with the bright lights of the Down Yonder Saloon looming ahead, before it occurred to me to ask, "Who was it playing the part of Smooth Dude, the guy with the chain saw canoe paddle? Some big-name Hollywood star?"

Bo didn't answer. And the silent treatment only intensified my curiosity. I prodded him with a few names. "Was it Tom Cruise? I can just see him whacking off somebody's arm with a canoe paddle. Did you see *Interview with the Vampire?* Wasn't it him who bit off a rat's head in that movie, and then drank the rat's blood? Somebody that'd bite off a rat's head would whack off an old boy's arm without thinking twice about it."

No response from Bo.

"Was it Brad Pint? Did you see *The Seven Deadly Sins*? A bad guy in that movie cut off Brad's wife's head and shipped it to him in a box. Can you believe they make movies about stuff like that? That was more gruesome than whacking off somebody's arm." Bo didn't seem to care.

"How 'bout Gene Hackman? Was it him? He plays a convincing bad guy. Or Ed Harris; he'd be good in that role. No, no, wait. I know: it was Chuck Norris, wasn't it? Or . . . who's that guy who actually looks mean enough to rip off somebody's arm? What's his name? Steven Seagal? Is that who it was! It was him, wasn't it? Steven Seagal! I'd like to meet him. From a safe distance."

Bo shook his head.

"Let's see, then. Who could it be? They wouldn't have some unknown in an important role like that. Let's see . . . It must have been . . ." I looked over at Bo. "Come on, man, give me a hint, who was it?"

Bo rubbed the stubble on his chin, thinking it over. "I'm not sure," he finally admitted, "but whoever it was had a lot of talent."

* * * * *

It was a long time before I ever went back to Piney Tavern.

Bo, of course, became a regular. He'd always wanted to be a member of the social elite.

Jennifer

Lemke

When changes in atmospheric pressure occur more rapidly than the body can adjust, excessive pressure can build up inside the head, producing unpleasant side effects. These effects can include harmless "popping" of the ears and, in more extreme cases, nosebleeds. Some people experience these symptoms on mountainous roads. It happened to Eugene (Bo) Rocker once, as he was negotiating the Piney River shuttle road. He promptly used his nosebleed as an excuse not to paddle that day.

Some of his companions were amazed that Bo would let a mere nosebleed keep him off the river, but what they didn't realize was that all during that particularly wet spring, every time Bo ran the Piney River, he'd stop afterwards at Piney Tavern, a little beer joint located near the takeout, and carouse with the locals. On the day of the shuttle-induced nosebleed, Bo delivered everybody to the putin and then sped back to the seedy bar to woo Frieda Thompkins, a barmaid and exotic dancer, with whom in the course of his visits that spring he had become, shall we say, close friends.

Upon completing their river run that day, his boating buddies anticipated dropping by Piney Tavern to find Bo.

They were looking forward to tipping a few drinks and celebrating having survived the Piney River, before continuing on their way. However, at the conclusion of their river trip, they didn't have to go to the bar to find Bo. They discovered him staggering around the takeout in a daze, his nose still bleeding profusely. He was a mess, with a couple of teeth missing, lumps and bruises about his head and ears, and clothes tattered and disheveled.

Bo told his boating buddies that he never recovered from the morning nosebleed, lost so much blood that he became dizzy, and eventually fell off a bar stool, crashing to the floor on his face. Months afterward he sheepishly confessed the truth: that Frieda's husband (who worked as a barefoot bouncer at the tavern) dropped in unexpectedly, observed his wife and Bo in an ill-timed embrace, and proceeded to pound him viciously in the general vicinity of his cranium.

* * * * *

"It was only a Platonic embrace," Bo insisted. "I was showing her how the ol' ugly boy had been grabbing Smooth Dude's butt when the accidental dismemberment occurred. You remember when that happened, don't you?"

"I remember you telling me about it, but I didn't see it. I was waiting out in the van, if you'll recall."

"Oh yeah," Bo said. "I remember that, now that you mention it. You do have a knack for missing out on the real fun, don't you? How is it you always manage that?"

"I also have a knack for keeping all my natural teeth, which is more than I can say for some people I know."

We were sitting at a table in Pete's Corner Bar and Grill in Hillsborough Village on the edge of Nashville. A young waitress named Jennifer, with whom Bo had been flirting, and who for some unknown reason had started calling him "BoBo," came over and set a platter of steaming french fries and a plate with two double-patty cheeseburgers on the table in front of us. Bo said to me, "You sure you don't want something?" and I shook my head. The french fry platter was the size of a wheelbarrow. It must have held a good portion of Idaho's annual potato production.

Jennifer, who apparently had overheard my last remark, said, "You don't have all your teeth, BoBo?" She was leaning over and looking at Bo's mouth. "Oh, poor little boy, how'd you lose those teeth? Come on, open up, let me see." Her dumb-looking Pete's Corner Bar and Grill waitress hat almost fell off, but she caught it, got it repositioned, and continued her pseudo dental exam.

"Hey, hot thing," Bo said, picking up one of the greasy cheeseburgers. "I'm not missing any essential parts. I got everything it'll take to satisfy you."

"Whoa!" she said, straightening up. "I love a man with a load of self-confidence." Bo devoured half the burger in one bite. She added, "*And* a man with a big appetite. It takes a big appetite to satisfy me."

Bo just about choked on his cheeseburger, but before he could offer a reply, Jennifer spun around and sashayed back over to the serving counter. Bo was watching her back side, taking it in. "That is one hot chili pepper," he said. "I believe she loves me."

"I believe she's married," I said. "You don't want more of those complications, do you?"

"What makes you think that sweet young thing's married?"

"The wedding band on her left hand. Those things are a dead giveaway."

"No," he said emphatically. "I didn't notice any ring."

"You didn't look," I said.

"But she's been giving me the come-on," he protested. "Calling me "BoBo" and flirting around. And you heard her talking about how she loves a man with a big appetite."

"That big appetite she loves is her three hundred pound husband." I pointed at Bo's plate. "He sucks burgers that size through a straw. He's a sumo wrestler, on the team at Dipstick University. They brought him over here and gave him a full ride scholarship just to wrestle for them. Since he married Jennifer, the school officials're having a hard time controlling him. He's insanely jealous of her. Pounds hell out of every man she looks at."

Bo was chewing on the last bite of the first burger, and he was having some trouble forcing it down. He swallowed with a big "uullppp" and followed it with half a Bass Ale. "You're making that up," he announced calmly.

"Yes about the sumo wrestler; no about the ring. But regardless, you should check things like ring fingers before you start flirting."

"I check things."

Right now he was checking the french fries, shoving them in with one hand and using the other to hoist cheeseburger number two into position. I felt sorry for the cow.

I said, "Did you check Frieda's ring finger before you made your move on her?"

That stopped him.

Bo dropped the burger back onto the plate and motioned for Jennifer to hurry over with more Bass Ale. He held his empty ale bottle up to the light and peered through it. He said, "I don't think these things really hold twelve ounces, do you?"

"You didn't answer my question."

"Yeah," he said, frowning, slouching over his platter, staring at the table top. "I knew she was married. But I didn't know she was married to the Yeti." He carefully set his empty ale bottle on the table between us. Then he suddenly looked at me and sat up straight. "Wait a minute," he said, accusingly. "You're moralizing to me, aren't you? Doing that head game crap you love so much. That story about the sumo wrestler was one of them Wild Bill Barkley devices, wasn't it? It was, what's he call it? an allegory? Yeah, that's it; that's what he calls it. It was an allegory wasn't it? Well, I got news for you, good ol' ex-buddy of mine, I don't put up with that kind of crap from friends. Not from you, not from Wild Bill Barkley, not from any of you overeducated buffoons. Just because you got a PhD, you think you know everything and you think you can lord it over me. Well, I know a couple of things too. You can just take that kind of crap and stuff it. You hear me?"

"It wasn't an allegory, Bo."

"It wasn't?"

"It was a simple parable."

"It was?"

"Yeah."

"Honest?"

"Honest."

He frowned intently, scrutinizing me. Then smiled. "Oh, well, why didn't you say so? That's different."

Suddenly his appetite returned. He grabbed the second burger and attacked it with gusto, just as Jennifer arrived at the table with three fresh Bass Ales. She set one in front of me and two in front of Bo. "Brought you an extra, BoBo," she said. "Thought a man with an appetite like yours'd want at least a couple of these little things."

"I believe you can read my mind," Bo said, around the edges of a massive mouthful of hamburger.

"You better know I can," she said, and turned to leave.

Bo put down his burger and said after her, "Hey, how's that husband of yours doing? The sumo guy?"

"What?" She stopped and turned around.

"Your husband's a sumo wrestler, ain't he?"

She made an effort at a smile. "My husband is a graduate student at Dipstick University, in the psychology department."

"He's a mind wrestler?"

"Is this some kind of joke?"

"Does he weigh three hundred pounds?"

"Oh, I get it. This *is* a joke. You know Harold, don't you?"

Bo said, "Harold?"

"My husband. Harold. The fledgling psychologist. And no, he doesn't weigh three hundred pounds; he barely weighs a hundred. He's all skin and bone. Is that it? Because he's such a shrimp you're calling him a sumo wrestler. Is that the joke?"

"Yeah, that's it. Funny, huh? Hahaha."

Jennifer was looking thoroughly puzzled and not a little irritated. She said, "Actually, it's not a very funny joke. Is there something I missed?"

"It's a parable," Bo said. "Now do you get it?"

"Oh," she said, her expression changing. "It is? A real parable?"

"Absolutely," Bo assured her. "A PhD special."

"Oh, God," she said, her face now registering alarm. "I just realized it. You're a professor, aren't you? Let me see . . . No, not Divinity. Let's see . . . a Classics professor, right?"

"English Literature," Bo said.

"I should have known it the moment you walked in here." She slapped her forehead. "The ale was a dead giveaway. You're Doctor . . . Doctor . . ."

"Doctor Rocker. Doctor Eugene (Bo) Rocker. Harvard PhD. Postdoctoral studies at Yale." Jennifer was about to faint. Bo added, for good measure, "And post-post doctoral studies at the Sorbonne with Swami Akalananda. That's His Royal Majesty Swami Akalananda, by the way, levitation master. Oh, and also at Oxford with Sir Wilford Silverman. And did I mention Bill Barkley? We've collaborated on several papers and a dozen poems. Bill has trouble with his rhyme-structure, and he's plagued by over-dependence on iambic pentameter, so I help him out occasionally."

He has trouble walking, too, I was thinking, since he crushed all those vertebrae on Bald River Falls.

"I've heard of him," Jennifer said. She appeared to be awe-struck. "He's a famous poet, isn't he? He's the one they held that symposium on at Dipstick last month, isn't he?"

Bo Rocker, self-appointed PhD and consort of famous poets, sagely nodded his head, not having the slightest idea that anybody had ever held anything on Wild Bill other than a gun.

Jennifer was hesitantly edging up close to the table, staring at Bo like he was some kind of deity. She said, "You know all these important people and here I've been calling you "BoBo" and kidding around with you. And you let me get away with it. Why didn't you tell me you were a professor? Oh God. And I bet you know Harold's advisor, Doctor Cradwell, don't you? Doctor Malcolm Cradwell?"

The name Malcolm Cradwell almost propelled Bo out of his chair.

Jennifer said, "I knew it!"

"Doctor Cradwell and I go back a long way," Bo said, telling the truth for a change. "He and I have had some real adventures."

Real adventures was an understatement. In fact, the day he met Malcolm Cradwell was burned indelibly in Bo Rocker's mind. It had been at Lilly Bridge on Clear Creek, in the Obed/Emory watershed. Nor would Bo ever forget the day on the same creek, about a year later, when he rescued some goofball by the name of Robert Friendly. Robert had been pinned in his kayak, in an undercut, when Bo happened along and saved his life. Robert and his brother, Ricky Batson, had told their daddy, a Nashville Criminal Court judge, that Bo had jumped on Robert and deliberately broken his shoulder. Their false allegations led to criminal charges and other legal repercussions. All of which had eventually been dismissed, but not before Bo was forced to spend a fortune in legal fees. And not before the judge, Ricky Batson, and an avid Malcolm Cradwell, had joined in a campaign to smear Bo's reputation.

Bo said, "Malcolm's a famous canoeist. I suppose you know that?"

"Oh yes," Jennifer replied. "He badgers Harold incessantly to go off with him to one of those wild whitewater rivers, but Harold doesn't want to go."

"He's right to resist."

"He is? Oh, I'm glad to hear you say that! Harold's been so worried that his failure to go on one of those trips may have jeopardized his career."

Bo, winging it now, said, "Oh yes, Harold *is* having trouble with that one course isn't he?"

"Trouble's not the word for what he's having," Jennifer admitted. "*Misery* is what he's having with that course. He's driving me mad. I don't think I can stand it much longer. Do all graduate students live such miserable lives? My manager's getting an MBA, and his professors have him running around like a chicken with its head cut off. And poor Harold, he tries hard, but he just can't seem to do anything that pleases Doctor Cradwell. And Doctor Cradwell is such a stickler about that one course, because it's his baby, his favorite. He wrote the book on that one."

"That would be the psychopathology course, wouldn't it?" Bo said.

Jennifer nodded. She was getting upset, her face flushed. Looking a little down in the dumps.

"Yeah," Bo mused, almost to himself. "If anybody knows the ins and outs of psychopathology, it's Malcolm Cradwell." Then he seemed to shift gears, like Bo can do sometimes. In an upbeat, but nonetheless properly professorial, voice, he said, "Look, I hate to see you distressed like this. I may be able to offer some assistance."

"Maybe put in a good word for Harold?"

Bo nodded his professorial head. "And even better than that, maybe I could offer a few tips on how to handle Cradwell, tips that you could subtly – without divulging your source, of course – pass on to Harold?"

There was a new glimmer of hope in Jennifer's eyes. "I can't tell you how grateful I would be," she said to Bo.

Bo replied, "What time do you get off? Maybe we could hold a private tutorial, at about . . ."

I'm not sure what got into me, but without even thinking about it, I reached over the table, taking care not to brush against the remains of the greasy cheeseburger, and grabbed Bo's arm. Shook on it until I got his attention. "Okay," I said. "I *will* moralize to you: you've gone too far this time. You're taking unfair advantage of this young woman. Stop lying to her and tell her the truth, that you're not really a professor and that there's nothing you can do to help Harold." I stood up. "I have to go to the restroom now. Tell her. For once in your life do the decent thing and tell the truth. Tell her while I'm gone." Bo was sitting there speechless, looking shocked and dismayed. I brushed past the waitress and couldn't help but notice the vulnerable, hurt look in her eyes. I said, "Look, this is none of my business, but if you really want to help Harold, tell him to help himself. Tell him to get out from under that psychopath Cradwell's thumb. Tell him to take command of his own life. Tell him to get out of that creepy department he's in and do something meaningful with his life. And if he won't listen to you, then help yourself by telling Harold to take a hike."

* * * * *

I piddled around in the restroom for several extra minutes. Washed my hands twice. Splashed water in my face. Paced the floor. Combed my hair several times. Made sure my shirt was tucked in neatly. Turned sideways and checked on my incipient beer gut in the mirror. Sucked it in and tried to hold it. Then let it out. It wasn't so bad. Not half as big as Bo's.

For a brief moment I even wished that I still smoked. Anything to waste a minute or two, give Bo a chance to cool down. Or even better, to leave, which is probably, I concluded, what he would do, royally angered at yours truly for interfering with his womanizing. Armed with this conviction, that Bo was by now long gone, I ambled back out.

I was surprised to discover him still at the table. I thought he would have stormed out in a huff, furious that I would have had the unmitigated temerity to interfere in his affairs. I looked around for Jennifer, the waitress, but she was nowhere in sight. Probably in the ladies room crying her eyes out, I concluded. Bo could be a real cur sometimes. At least I had stopped him in his tracks this once. I walked back over to the table and sat down, expecting to catch some heavy flak from Professor Doctor Rocker.

"Where were we?" Bo said. "Talking about Frieda's husband?"

That surprised me. It took me a moment to realize that he was trying to smooth the transition back to our original topic of conversation; but then I got with the program and said, "Yes, you were telling me that he's a Yeti."

"He *is* a Yeti."

"There's no such thing as a Yeti."

"You've seen him. You think he's human?"

"I wouldn't go that far," I agreed. "I have to admit, I've never seen anything quite like him."

"Well, I have," Bo said authoritatively, with more than a hint of professorial arrogance. He was slipping easily into the routine. World's authority on every topic under the sun. Hear ye, hear ye, Doctor Bo Rocker, professor of ethnology, about to hold court. Bo said, or rather, pontificated: "I've seen his kind in Tibet. They call them Yetis over there. The Tibetans domesticate them and train them as bodyguards, or as palace guards."

"And you think Frieda's husband is a Yeti?"

"Convinced of it. Just consider how he looks. You've seen him. There's nothing else in the world looks like that. The Tibetans call them abominable snowmen, and I think they got the name down pretty good. They're big and hairy and ugly and smelly and mean. Most of all mean. That meanness is in their blood. They're back fighters. Alphonse jumped me from behind, you know? Otherwise, with all the marital arts I know, he wouldn't have stood a chance."

"Alphonse?"

"Frieda's husband."

"His name is Alphonse? A Yeti named Alphonse?"

"Oh, that's not his real name, of course. That's just what Frieda calls him. She always wanted to meet a romantic man from New Orleans, but she never did, so she pretends Alphonse is from the French Quarter."

"New Orleans, Tibet; they're practically the same."

"Hey, don't be misaligning Frieda. She may not be too sharp on her geography, but that's a minor deficiency, and she has plenty of compensating assets."

"I'll bet she does. And the word's maligning, professor, not misaligning."

"I know that. I was just testing you, seeing if you were paying attention. Us professors do that a lot, with our slower students."

"From what I saw of you that day on the Piney, Alphonse must have done a little testing himself, on one of his slower students. As I recall, your head looked like he had administered a pop quiz that you flunked with flying colors, mostly blacks and blues, but with some gangrenous greens and putrid purples thrown in for good measure."

"Back off, man!" Bo said testily. "The Yeti sneaked up and jumped me from behind. That's the only way he could get me. Otherwise, I'd have laid him out cold."

Right. Bo the kung fu master. The spirit of Bruce Lee incarnate. Professor Doctor kung fu master Bo Rocker, vanquisher of dirty back-fighting Yetis.

"Look," I said. "One thing has always puzzled me. You and Frieda were inside the bar, right? And you locked the doors from the inside? And then you got busy doing . . . your thing – whatever it was you were doing with her. And while this was going on, somehow her husband sneaks in and jumps you, right? Well, what I've never understood, is how he managed to surprise you. Didn't you hear him coming? Didn't he have to break down the door to get in? Or did he have a key?"

Bo knocked back his last Bass Ale and then started waving and yelling for the manager to bring another. The manager, pressed into serving tables when Jennifer inexplicably disappeared, was sweating up a storm. He was wearing a white shirt with the sleeves rolled up to just below his elbows, a red striped tie loosened at the neck, and managerial black pants and shoes. His name tag said he was "Freddie," and Freddie was balding at age thirty. Around his waist Freddie sported a roll of fat, what some men call a "doughnut," and others call "love handles," that jiggled and bounced with his every step. He delivered Bo's ale and while clearing away some of the empties from the table, made the serious mistake of implying that we were drinking excessively.

Bo snapped at him, "What'd you say?"

"I said," he replied, employing his ultimate snotty-nosed delivery, " 'You're putting away quite a few of those. Would you like me to bring them out by the six-pack?' "

The look Bo gave the guy told me that at any second a certain soft-pink manager named Freddie was about to discover the thrill of having a Bass Ale bottle shoved down his throat. Or maybe shoved up some other orifice.

But Bo surprised me. He leaned back in his chair and said to the manager, "That's an excellent suggestion. I hereby authorize immediate implementation of your recommendation."

"What?"

Bo said, tapping the table top in front of him. "Right here, Freddie boy. Line the first six frosty bottles down the edge of the table. Put them right here."

Freddie's eyes showed a flash of anger. "Sir," he said, "When I suggested . . ."

Bo said, "Look here Freddie, I've just arrived in Nashville, and I'll be the first to admit that perhaps I don't fully understand the management practices of some of our local business establishments, but I'm Doctor Eugene (Bo) Rocker, the new Eustis Frambole Professor of Management Sciences at Dipstick University, and when I give an order to a waiter, I expect it to be fulfilled promptly unless there's a compelling reason for noncompliance. And since the recommendation for six-pack delivery originated with you, I expect to see the recommendation implemented by you or by a designated member of your staff in a forthright and courteous manner. Do I make myself entirely clear?"

"I'll be right back," Freddie said.

Bo rocked back in his chair and cackled. "It's good being a professor," he assured me.

Freddie reappeared at Bo's elbow, along with a kitchen helper he had pressed into table service, and the two of them busily arranged six cold frosty bottles of Bass Ale along the edge of our table. When the arrangement was completed, Freddie stood back and said, "Would there be anything else, Doctor Rocker?"

Bo replied, "I'll signal when we need a refill."

"Thank you, sir," said Freddie, hustling away, every step sending his doughnut into a paroxysm of jiggles.

I said to Bo, "Nice touch there, professor. The guy was hinting that maybe we're drinking too much, and you browbeat him into bringing them out six at a time. Not bad. Not bad at all."

"Such is the power of higher education," Bo said. He added, "But of course you, of all people, realize that Dipstick University doesn't hand over the Eustis Frambole Chaired Professorship to just any bozo that falls off the turnip wagon? I was selected from among a field of more than two hundred – no, make that four hundred – candidates, including the finest management scholars and entrepreneurial impresarios in the world."

"Oh, brother," I said.

Bo smiled and thought about it for a moment. He said, "You would never have done something like that would you?

Ordering six drinks at a time, I mean? For you, that would have been, what? socially awkward?"

"That was just about the ultimate in gaucherie," I admitted.

"That wasn't a compliment was it?"

"No."

Bo said, "I didn't think so. I won't even ask you what that dirty word means." He gestured to the row of frosty bottles and said, "Have one."

I took the nearest bottle and knocked back about half of it, straight from the bottle. Cold rich malty taste.

"Nectar of the river gurus," Bo said, laughing. "Compliments of that old fool, Eustis Frambole." We clinked bottles and Bo proposed a toast. "Let the good times roll," he suggested.

And that seemed like a splendid idea. We both knocked back what was left in our bottles and reached for fresh ones. No use letting them get warm just sitting there. Not with ol' Freddie waiting in the wings, anxious to bring another round.

"Now where was I?" Bo said. "Oh, yes. I remember. You wanted to know if Alphonse had a key to let himself in? Well, he didn't. Piney management doesn't entrust keys to Yetis. And I knew that, so I thought I was being super careful. I made sure it was just me and Frieda inside before I locked the door. Then I rechecked all the booths and behind the bar and in the office and the storage room and the walk-in cooler and out in the big dance hall and even down in the cellar, and nobody was in there but me and Frieda, locked up safe and snug. So naturally I thought it was clear sailing."

"This sounds like a detective story, Bo. If Alphonse wasn't in the bar anywhere, and he didn't have a key, then how'd he surprise you?"

"I'm pretty sure he jumped down out of the rafters."

"He was hiding up in the rafters?"

"Not exactly hiding. I think he lives up there somewhere. He has a nest, I guess, or maybe he hangs by his tail. I don't think many people outside Tibet know a great deal about Yeti behavior. I mean, most people don't even believe they exist."

Bo stopped until I could absorb the details of his story. Or begin to absorb them. As freakish as it all sounded, I knew better than to reject it out of hand. I had seen that bouncer at Piney Tavern with my own eyes and while I couldn't swear he was a Yeti, I wouldn't testify that he was human, either. I can tell you one thing, though. Under no circumstances would I tangle with a bouncer that looked like him.

Bo must have read my mind. He said, "You ever wrestled one of them things?"

"A bouncer? Heck no, I know better'n that."

"No, no, I mean wrestled with a Yeti?"

"No, not one of them, either. Pretty strong, huh?"

"Strong? Man, we're talking industrial strength here. And bare strength ain't the half of it, neither. Main thing is, he fights dirty. Jumped me from behind and clobbered me with a club or something. Then he starts choking me. And it went downhill from there. Got kinda violent before it was over. I think it might've been the end of me, except for what Frieda did."

"She really came through for you, huh?"

"She's a scrapper, that one. Plenty of spunk. But don't get me wrong, she's not mean-spirited or anything like that. Deep down, she's about the sweetest woman on the face of the earth. Although she is kind of kinky – I will admit that. And I have to admit this, too: sometimes I wonder about her taste in men, present company excepted, of course."

"Was she really married to Conrad? You think that's why he was hanging out up there that time we saw him?"

"Affirmative on both questions."

"And the judge really granted her a divorce on the grounds that having to look at Conrad's face every morning was cruel and unusual punishment?"

"Well, that's what I heard."

Somehow, I couldn't help but wonder if Ms Sweetheart of the Piney Tavern hadn't pulled the wool over Bo's eyes. A woman who would marry Conrad and a Yeti couldn't exactly be all sweetness and light. I said, "You sure she's not just manipulating both of you? You *and* Alphonse? Or maybe all three of you, including Conrad? Playing you off one against the other, just to get whatever it is she's after?"

Bo squirmed just enough to let me know I'd hit on something. I pressed the issue. "There *is* something she's after, isn't there? Is it possible Frieda knew all along that the Yeti was hiding up in the rafters? Maybe watching you the whole time? Did that ever occur to you?"

He said, "Well, I did say she's a little bit kinky, didn't I?"

"Kinky? Yeah, I'd say so, marrying a Yeti!"

Bo rolled his eyes, as if to say 'Earth to Mister Naivete. Come in Mister Naivete. Please be advised: you are living in the last gasp seconds of the Twentieth Century; things have changed; you need to get with it.' He said, "That's not the kind of kinky I'm talking about."

"Uh oh," I said. "She's not into that bizarre bondage and discipline stuff, is she? Whips and handcuffs and ropes and all that spooky business? I've heard that some people actually enjoy being trussed up like a chicken and flogged like a turkey. Can you believe it?"

Bo looked at me like I was a lost cause. "You know me better'n that," he said. "Do I look like a man that'd get involved with a woman who's into that routine?" He shook his finger in my face, and repeated, "Never, never, never, never!"

"I'm glad to hear it," I confessed. "That stuff is sick." But now he had me really wondering. I said, "What is Frieda's brand of kink? Masochism?"

Bo leaned back and regarded me; sizing me up to see if I could take the shock. And I was kind of halfway hoping that he'd go easy on me. Maybe tell me some harmlessly titillating lie about how Frieda liked to have the soles of her feet tickled with an ostrich feather. Something like that. But no, protected I wasn't to be. Bo said, "Frieda loves three-way."

I grabbed the arms of my chair and held on. "She's into ménage à trois? That's her thing?"

"Exactly."

"She likes to keep two guys around? One of them a Yeti? Or worse yet, Conrad?"

"Now, don't get the wrong notion about her," Bo advised. "She's not some strumpet. And certainly not some pervert. It's me she really loves. After all, she saved me from Alphonse."

"How'd she do that?"

"She got him off me."

"She pulled that brute off you? She must be pretty hefty herself to have managed that. Is she a sumo wrestler?"

"Frieda ain't no sumo wrestler. No, man, not at all. She's a looker, a real looker, with a beautiful face and out-of-this-world figure. I wouldn't say she's petite, she's too tall to say that. She's tall and slender and three-fourths legs. Long, slender, perfectly proportioned legs. With skin that's like satin and this long black mane that tumbles down her back, and her eyes are like . . ." I guess the skepticism showed on my face, because he stopped for a moment, and then said, "You ain't believing this, are you?"

"Well," I admitted. "I've seen that bouncer friend of yours, that Yeti or whatever he is, and he's enormous. If this Frieda is so sweet and delicate, how'd she manage to pull that thing off you?"

"She didn't have to physically pull him off. She used her head. She outsmarted him. She waved a banana in his face."

"There's no way I believe that! You're saying Frieda waved a banana in her husband's face and he stopped pounding you?"

"She waved a banana in his face to get his attention, and then tossed the banana into the corner. Over by the stand-up cardboard likeness of George Jones? The one they use for target practice Saturday nights?"

I had to remind him again: "I've never been inside that place, Bo. I don't know what they use for target practice on Saturday night."

"Oh, yeah. I keep forgetting that. Anyway, the Yeti leapt up off me and made for the banana, grunting like an ape. He was so worked up, he knocked poor ol' George for a loop." Bo paused and rubbed his cheek, probably remembering the lumps that Alphonse left there. He thought for a while and then came back to the drama at the tavern. "But anyway," he said, "I took full advantage of the break in action. I got to my feet and made for the door. Frieda came running after me, begging me to stay, saying Alphonse wasn't so bad once you got to know him, that I just needed to give him a chance to warm up to me. 'Alphonse likes you a lot more than he ever liked Conrad,' she shouted. But I never slowed down. I got out of there. Never looked back, neither. Not once."

I was about ready to fall in the floor.

And it wasn't from the Bass Ale. At least, I didn't think it was from the booze. I said, "You mean to tell me that Frieda, the Yeti, and Horace Conrad were getting it on?"

"Until Alphonse got fed up with Conrad. Alphonse claimed that it was cruel and unusual treatment, making a Yeti look at somebody ugly as Conrad. He was about to file a complaint with the Circuit Court. And Frieda, knowing there was a legal precedent for Alphonse's complaint, ran Conrad off to placate Alphonse. But then I came along and naturally she fell in love with me, and was ready to run off Alphonse."

"I thought you said she wanted both you and Alphonse for a ménage à trois?"

"Well, I did say she was a little kinky, didn't I? I guess she thought if Alphonse saw me and her together there in the bar, then he'd come down and join in the fun. I did notice that day that she kept getting louder and louder. I realize now that she must have been trying to attract Alphonse's attention. Every time I'd show her how the ol' ugly boy grabbed Smooth Dude's butt, she'd let out a shriek that could've raised the dead. The way I figure it, Alphonse fell asleep up there in his nest. Then, when he woke up and heard Frieda hootin' and moanin', he thought I was attacking her. And then, you know the rest of the story."

"Oh, Jesus."

Bo said, "Anyway, you'll be glad to know – even as fond as I am of that girl – I didn't stop running. I never looked back. I ran all the way to the takeout and hid in the woods."

My head was reeling. I stood up and said to Bo, "Look, that is about the wildest story I've ever heard. I think it's made me a little woozy. I need to go splash some cold water in my face. I'll be back in a minute."

"Sure thing," Bo said cheerily. He looked at his watch, and added, "Take your time. I'll take care of the tab, and when you get back, we should be about ready to leave."

* * * * *

The cold water therapy worked. I felt a lot better as I made my way back to the table. Bo's story was wild and crazy and – for somebody like me who leads a decidedly traditional lifestyle – kind of shocking, but after a few splashes of cold water, and a minute alone to think it over, I realized it probably contained a core element of truth, surrounded by a healthy dose of embellishment. That was Bo's way. He exaggerates things. I think he lives out a lot of his fantasies through his stories, fantasizing about exotically beautiful women with kinky sexual predilections. The ménage à trois part I didn't believe at all. Not for a minute. It was pure fantasy. But harmless fantasy. Let him delude himself with visions of exotic sexual liaisons. What could it hurt?

On the other hand, the way he had treated Jennifer, the girl who had been waiting our table earlier, had really bothered me. I thought he was taking unfair advantage of her by pretending to be a professor, and I just didn't like it. She was too young and too vulnerable. That's why I stepped in and said what I did. And although she had obviously been hurt by the whole thing – so hurt she had left work without her manager's permission – I was convinced that the pain she was feeling was less than what she would have felt if I had said nothing.

And frankly, I was gratified at how Bo had reacted when I spoke my mind. He could have gotten nasty and told me to keep my nose out of his day-to-day philandering. But he hadn't reacted like that at all. He had accepted my rebuke with commendable equanimity. I didn't know exactly what he had said to the waitress after I left the table, but obviously when she realized what a fool she had been about to make of herself, she chose to leave, probably to regain her composure. It was the right thing to do. Her manager, being the jerk that he was, would chew her out when she returned, but they would eventually smooth it over. And in the end she would be a little bit older and a whole lot wiser.

I was feeling good, thinking about how well things had turned out versus how disastrously the evening could have ended. When I arrived back at the table, Bo had already made Freddie happy by paying the bill in full and awarding him a fifty-dollar gratuity. The MBA-in-training was at the table, avidly genuflecting. Bo was telling him, "I had no idea you were in the MBA program, Freddie. But I'm certainly not surprised, given the professional management practices I have observed in the operation of this fine establishment. I earnestly hope that we may have the mutual pleasure of working together at some point in your professional development. And if not, that you will at least refer your other professors to me for what I assure you will be a splendidly positive summation of your impeccable managerial talents." Bo paused to bestow a benevolently professorial smile upon the groveling graduate student. "See you around the management school," Professor Rocker added, and dismissed the lackey with a wave of his hand.

Bo had definitely taken a liking to the role of university professor, and I had to admit, he'd probably make a good one, although that certainly wouldn't have been my judgment only a few years earlier. A few years earlier, he would have slam-dunked that smart-mouth manager without giving it a second thought. Or literally stuffed a bottle down his throat. An empty bottle, to be sure; he wouldn't have wasted a full one. But today, a kinder, gentler Bo Rocker merely manipulated him like the fool he was. And set him up for an even bigger fall the first time Freddie bragged to his major professor about his close personal relationship with Doctor Eugene (Bo) Rocker, the Eustis Frambole Professor of Management at Dipstick University. Yes, Bo was mellowing out some at long last, and I was happy to see it.

With the command of interpersonal tactics and manipulative skills that he had demonstrated today, it wouldn't be long before he'd be able to land himself an academic sinecure at some elite institution of higher education, if that was what he wanted. Maybe even at venerable Dipstick University. Then he could selflessly devote himself to teaching others through example, like all great professors.

Like Norman Knight and Malcolm Cradwell.

Bo would enjoy rubbing elbows with cronies like that.

I sat down at the table and said, "How much do I owe you on the tab?"

"My treat," he said.

"Then I guess we're about ready to go?" I said, standing up to leave.

Bo didn't move. He looked up at me and said, "I thought maybe we could talk for a few minutes. That okay with you?" I said that would be fine and sat back down. He said, "You feeling okay now? That cold water therapy get your head back on straight?"

"As a matter of fact, I feel pretty good. And a lot of it is thanks to you. You see, in a way I kind of stuck my nose in your business a while ago, and I probably shouldn't have."

"You mean with Jennifer?" I nodded and he said, "That's kind of what I wanted to talk to you about."

Uh oh. I felt my heart rate jump by a factor of about eleven. Here it comes. He's been holding it back, saving Freddie's bottle for me, and now he's ready to pull the cork, dump the load, let me have it. Full frontal assault. Bottle down the throat, if I'm lucky.

I said, "You're mad about me interfering in your affairs, aren't you? Well, I hope you can understand that I just had to say what I did."

"Oh, I understand," Bo said. "And I'm not mad about it at all. On the contrary, I respect you for what you did."

"You do?"

"You spoke from your heart, and it had great impact."

"It did?"

"Especially on Jennifer. She'd been wanting to tell Harold to get off his butt and stop whining about everything in his life and to stand up to that freaky Cradwell and to take control of his life, and your heartfelt honesty inspired her. She went home to tell Harold she's had enough. She's leaving him."

"You're making this up," I gasped. But something told me he wasn't.

"What you said had a big impact on me, too," Bo confessed. "It made me realize how selfish I can be. How I can get carried away sometimes and say anything – whatever it takes – anything at all to make a woman notice me, to . . . well, let's face it, to get into her pants. I felt so damn rotten, being called on the carpet like that right in front of Jennifer, that I broke down and told her everything: the truth, the whole truth, and nothing but the truth. I confessed to her that I wasn't a professor, or a PhD, or anything like that. I told her I was a full-time river rat with a couple of part-time businesses on the side, bringing in just enough money to support my vices. I told her I was a no-good scoundrel and that I had just broken off a torrid relationship with a married woman who had invited me to share in a three-way relationship with her husband, who was a Yeti. And that I had even given the proposition serious consideration, until I got a good look at the Yeti."

Bo continued, "I guess your honesty and then my outpouring was contagious because Jennifer confessed she had longed for a ménage à trois herself, but her stick-in-the-mud husband nixed the idea every time she brought it up, but now here she was discussing it with one of the two most honest and forthright men she had ever met in her entire life and the more she thought about it the more she liked the idea and did she think you would be interested in the two of us sharing her and naturally I said that I thought you would be absolutely delighted, and then she . . ."

"Stop right there," I said. "I was only in the restroom a few minutes. Five or ten at the most. How could all this have transpired?"

"It didn't take long. Pivotal life events rarely do. Just like that," he snapped his fingers, "and it was a done deal. She was out the door, on her way to say goodbye to Harold and pack her bags."

I stood up, but Bo didn't budge. "Let's get out of here right now," I said. "Right now, before she returns."

Bo said, "Can't."

"Why can't we?"

"Van's gone. I let her drive it. She doesn't have a car. Has to share one with Harold, and that pig insists on taking it every day. Why don't you sit back down? She'll be back any minute. Then we can hightail it out of here."

I was getting dizzy again. I thought about bolting for the door, just to get out of the place, to get away from Bo. I thought it would be refreshing to run straight out into the street, stopping traffic so I'd have plenty of witnesses, shouting at the top of my lungs, "I don't know any nitwit named Bo Rocker! Never heard of him!"

Bo said, "You ever see anything like that girl? Can you believe her face? It's perfectly radiant. She's the next Ingrid Bergman. I can cast her in *Outlaws*. She'll be perfect."

"I thought *Outlaws* was finished?"

"There've been a few problems," he said, with a pained expression. "Remember me telling you about some guy losing his arm during filming? Well, he filed a lawsuit, seeking damages, and the film can't be released while litigation is pending. So, while we're waiting for things to be worked out, we're gonna re-shoot a few of the scenes. The love scenes. Jennifer'll be perfect. Bill Barkley wrote one of the scenes. It's about a ménage à trois."

I couldn't believe my ears. I absolutely could not believe what I was hearing.

Bo was staring at me. He said, "You seem to have an emotional reaction every time ménage à trois is mentioned. You really like that idea, don't you?"

"No."

"Oh, sure you do. I can tell. Jennifer likes it too. I think it's gonna work out great for the three of us."

I said, "I thought she was a nice, innocent girl, putting her husband through graduate school."

"She was, until she met us: the world's two most honest men. What is it they say in the philosophy department? 'Money corrupts, and power corrupts even more, but honesty is the absolute corrupter.' I think that's the way it goes. If not, that's how it oughta go." He folded his hands, put them behind his head and leaned back in his chair. "You know," he said, "I like this honesty approach. It has a lot of potential. I should have tried it years ago."

Jennifer came in the front door and walked straight up to our table. I won't say she was as radiant as Ingrid Bergman walking into Rick's Place, in *Casablanca*, but she looked good, no doubt about it. She had changed clothes. The Pete's Corner Bar and Grill hat was gone. Teva sandals stood in for the black pumps. In place of the standard-issue waitress skirt and blouse were a pair of snug-fitting jeans and a black turtleneck with a single-strand gold chain around her neck. The black looked good with her short-cropped blonde hair. I wondered if somehow the short hair symbolized her new declaration of independence, if the shorn locks were symbolic of the dead weight named Harold that she had jettisoned from her life.

She said, "Hi guys. Hope I didn't keep you waiting. But I had to pack a few things. My bag's in the van and I'm ready anytime you are."

Bo said, "You look terrific. And that's the honest truth."

That made her smile. She said, "Thank you." And for a split second, I was so lost in her smile that I thought we might actually be in Rick's Place. The light was playing off her face in a soft metallic glow, the complexion perfect, the eyes sparkling.

There was an aura of serenity with her now, that had been missing earlier. And an unmistakable maturity. This was no grown-up girl, as I had thought earlier; this was a woman. A woman who, for better or for worse, had decided to make profound changes in her life. For her sake I hoped it wasn't going to be a matter of trading old shackles for new ones. But who was I to judge? I was beginning to realize she needed my protective attitude about as much as she needed her old waitress job. She glanced over at the serving counter, at the manager, who was scowling at her, waved her pinkie at him and said, "Hi Freddie, bye Freddie."

Cool as could be.

Bo stood up to leave and I sat down. Bo said, "What's the matter?"

"There's something I gotta do." I motioned for Freddie, who dashed over practically at a run, eager, I'm sure, to find out what we were plotting with his premier waitress. He said, "Something for you, sir?"

I tapped the table in front of me, "I'll have Bass Ale right here."

Freddie said, with that unctuous manner of his, "That will be one Bass Ale, sir?"

"That will be six Bass Ales, Freddie boy, lined up along this edge of the table." I indicated where I wanted the bottles placed. "And make damn sure they're frosty cold."

Freddie looked surprised. He glanced over at Doctor Rocker, but the esteemed Eustis Frambole Professor of Management merely shrugged. "That will be six frosty cold bottles of Bass Ale," Freddie said. "Coming right up, sir."

Before he could leave, I tapped the opposite side of the table, and said, "And along this edge . . ."

The Kindly
Sheriff

"My paddling's come a long way in the past few months," Jennifer was telling Bo, "but there's something about this creek that makes me nervous. I guess it's because I've heard so much about it, so many stories. I've even heard you say this one's like grabbing a tiger by the tail. Are you sure I'm ready to paddle something like this?"

Bo looked over at her and smiled reassuringly. But then his eyes darted back to the road, which was a good idea because they were in his van, barreling down the rain-slicked side of the Cumberland escarpment, on Route 68 south of Crossville, heading for the Piney River. The road was steep and curvy, and it was raining like it was April in Tennessee, which it was. Bo was behind the wheel, driving entirely too fast for conditions.

Bo said, "You'll be fine. We'll see to it, won't we Norman?" Bo glanced in his rear view mirror at the figure behind them, sitting in the van's third captain's chair, looking out the big touring window at what some maps still label as the Great Valley of the Tennessee. Only today the great valley wasn't much in evidence. Rain was sheeting down, whipped by the wind, stinging into the side of the van with a million staccato metallic impact sounds.

Norman heard Bo's voice, turned from his window, and saw Jennifer looking at him, imploringly. He smiled at her and said, "We'll keep an eye on you. That we will."

Jennifer Lemke had met Norman Knight only the evening before, at a local paddling club's annual whitewater camp, as fifty paddlers had huddled underneath a makeshift tarp, raptly listening as Bo Rocker described the thrills of running Piney River at high water. Last night, all fifty of the attentive listeners had vowed to run the river today, but a dozen had overslept this morning and another dozen had missed departure time and the way Bo was driving, he would lose another dozen or more on the way to the putin.

Jennifer looked at Norman and wondered about him, about what he was thinking, sitting there raptly staring out his window. She wondered how he and Bo had met. It had been on some river. Bo had told her as much, but that's about all he would say. She sensed that at one time there had been bad blood between the two men, but she doubted if she would ever learn the details. Bo didn't talk much about himself, and he practically never discussed his past.

Other people sure did, though. She had been paddling and tooling around with Bo for almost a year, and they were forever meeting people from his past. Every river they paddled, they would run into somebody who knew him, or used to know him, or who had heard so much about him that they thought they knew him. Some of the people she met disliked Bo, and didn't mind saying as much. And it was said that a few people actually hated him, held him accountable for wrongs, real or imagined, and would, given the opportunity, take their revenge by whatever means available. But a lot of others seemed to really like him. And she had noticed that everybody had definite opinions about him. When it came to Bo Rocker, nobody was neutral. And everybody also had some story to tell about something that Eugene (Bo) Rocker had done. Most of these accounts she considered to be outrageously far-fetched.

In Friendsville, she met a man named Katz who claimed to be a gynecologist. Doctor Katz also claimed to have once seen Bo Rocker float the entire Gauley River asleep. She didn't believe that story. She wasn't convinced Katz was a real doctor, either, especially after he offered her a free pelvic exam.

She had told Bo about meeting a strange doctor named Katz who had offered her a free examination in his tent, and Bo replied that perhaps she should have accepted his offer.

That had hurt.

"Really?" she replied, feeling terribly wronged that the man in her life could be so callous. It was true that she and Bo had originally planned a ménage à trois, but that had never worked out. Her relationship with Bo had been strictly monogamous, and that was how she intended to keep it.

"Why not?" Bo replied. "After all, Katz is one of the best psychiatrists in the country. You might have gained some valuable insight."

"He's a psychiatrist?"

"Sure," Bo replied. "Allegedly one of the best in the country. Has an office out in Monterey. He's in such demand that new patients – whom he calls clients – have to get on a waiting list. Perhaps you should have given it a shot. He might have gone straight to the core of your disaffections."

"I don't think it was my disaffections he wanted to examine," Jennifer said, and let the matter drop.

* * * * *

Katz's story about Bo's escapade on the Gauley wasn't atypical of other things she heard about him from time to time. And just when she would come to the point of not believing any more of the stories, she would meet somebody of unassailable integrity, like the famous poet Bill Barkley, who with complete sincerity would claim that Bo had once master-minded an international jewel heist that still had Interpol stumped. And then there was the story everybody told about how he loved to wrestle with Yetis, about how he would travel to the far corners of the globe for an opportunity to engage a Yeti in close combat. Or the yarn about him standing on a bridge and throwing imaginary thunderbolts, causing every paddler passing under the bridge to overturn. And the stories of his violent nature, about the time he deliberately ripped a helpless paddler's shoulder out of its socket. And the tales about barroom brawls: story on top of story about him brawl-ing with every roughneck miscreant he encountered in every seedy watering hole up and down the Appalachian chain. One story had him actually cutting a man's arm off with a samurai sword. And the freaky people he was said to consort with: bar bums in Maryville, burnt out surgeons from England, a Swami who could walk on water and levitate beer kegs, even a state legislator.

All the stories were about crazy stuff like that. No wonder she believed so little of what she heard.

Jennifer glanced back at Norman again, and couldn't help but wonder about him, about what episode from Bo's past he was from. He wasn't one of the loonies like Katz. She could tell that. There was something about him that Jennifer Lemke liked. A certain coolness and calmness in his manner, yet an intensity that burned just beneath the surface. A controlled melancholy that set him apart. And then there were those times last night in the campground, when she could feel someone's eyes burning into her. And each time she turned around, Norman would be standing off to the side, looking at her. And he wasn't just looking. Jennifer knew how it felt to have a man look at her. Lots of men looked at her. Norman was doing more than just looking.

He was watching.

Yet it wasn't a spooky kind of being watched. It was more like he had recognized her from sometime in the past, and was trying to remember the circumstances. But she knew that wasn't possible. She had never seen him until last night at the campground.

Just before she and Bo had turned in, she said, "Where did you meet Norman?"

He gave her a funny look and thought about it for a minute, then stared off into space and said, "Norman got me into a great deal of trouble once. And then he got me out of it. But even so, I don't exactly trust him. And I'd advise you not to, either. Do you know what I mean?"

She knew she couldn't wait to talk to Norman, to see what this was all about.

Bo added, with a deep sigh, "Oh, I didn't mean that. He's okay, I guess." He was silent for a moment, and then added, "It's time we buried the hatchet, anyway. I asked him if he'd like to paddle with us tomorrow. He's a fair paddler, I've heard. He's probably paddled on the Cumberland Plateau more than anybody alive."

Jennifer put her hand on Bo's shoulder and said, "That's what everybody says about you."

* * * * *

"What do you think, Mister Rocker?" Charlie Crenshaw asked. "I reckon you must've paddled this stretch more'n anybody. That water look too high to put on?"

"It's a mite low," Bo replied, giving Charlie a taste of the *River Master*'s proverbial understatement. "But there should be enough water for us to scrape down it." In truth, the river was a veritable flush, promising to rise soon into the vicinity of flood stage. Bo looked up at the gray sky which had, after three days, finally stopped pouring rain, although there was still a mist in the air.

They were standing on the takeout bridge, on Deep Rut Road, on the outskirts of Scopes City. When they left the campground an hour earlier, on top of the Plateau, Bo's van had been followed by five boat-laden cars. One of the five, driven by Charlie Crenshaw, had made it to the takeout behind Bo. The other vehicles had turned back or gone astray. Charlie's car and Bo's van were parked in a small gravel pullout about fifty yards from the bridge on river right. Bo and Charlie talked it over and agreed to wait five minutes to see if anybody else showed up.

Charlie had one other paddler with him, a kayaker named Ricky Batson, who had been striving all morning to set a new world's record for obnoxiousness. Ricky had his motor mouth in overdrive and wouldn't give it a rest. After a couple of minutes, Bo said to him, "I wouldn't be talking so loud, if I were you."

Ricky jumped back, like he had a tightly wound spring up his butt, and glowered at Bo. "You telling me to shut up?"

"Just advising you not to talk so loud." Bo lowered his voice, as if sharing a confidence, "You see, there used to be this ol' Yeti named Alphonse, worked down at Piney Tavern? He worked as the night bouncer and slept most of the day. He hid out somewhere up in the tavern's loft. I think he hung by his tail from a rafter. Or maybe he had a nest up there, I'm not sure which. But anyway, he had this wife named Frieda – good looking girl, too – and he had a real nasty disposition whenever somebody woke him up." Bo drew himself to his full height and looked at Ricky. He added, "And that's about all Alphonse had going for him: Frieda and a mean spirit."

Ricky took several quickstep hitches, like maybe his internal steel coil had slipped a couple of notches. He was kind of lightweight and wiry and when he moved he just somehow came off the ground and jumped to wherever he wanted to be next. He closed one eye and peered at Bo. "So what does all this monkey business have to do with me?" he said.

"Nothing, I hope," Bo replied. "But I hear that Frieda ran off with a beer salesman from Chattanooga and that made Alphonse even more irritable. It got to where nobody could stand him, he was so ill-tempered. They finally had to fire him, 'cause he kept beating up all the Piney Tavern customers, thinking they all looked like beer salesmen. Now, I can't swear to it, but from what I've been told, that ol' Yeti didn't have no place to go once they threw him out, so he came up here and took up residence under this bridge where we're standing. And unless he's changed his habits – which I doubt, because in my experience Yetis ain't too flexible – then I'd guess that at this very moment Alphonse is somewhere under this old wood bridge, just a few feet below us, curled up sound asleep – probably dreaming about Frieda."

Ricky got right up in Bo's face and said, "What does all that crap have to do with me?"

"I'm just trying to tell you, as politely as I know how," Bo replied, "that if you wake up Alphonse, it's strictly between you and him. Don't expect me to come to your rescue."

Ricky said, loudly, "You think I need your help to handle some homeless bum that sleeps under a bridge?"

Bo regarded Ricky solemnly. "I realize," Bo said, "that a man like you ain't afraid of nothing that winks, stinks, or blinks. But I also know this: you ain't never seen nothing like Alphonse. And if you know what's good for you . . ."

Ricky laughed in his face. He laughed loudly and arrogantly. He said, "I've heard a lot about you, Bo Rocker. None of it's been good, except that you're supposed to be some kind of ace paddler. Which I seriously doubt."

"Whoa, bro," Charlie Crenshaw advised in a low, soft voice, which was Charlie's habitual manner of speech. "That wasn't called for. Mister Rocker is just advising us there may be a bad-tempered Yeti sleeping under the bridge here. That's plenty reason for me to keep my voice down. In fact, I'd do it out of consideration for any poor homeless person trying to get some sleep."

Ricky laughed again. Derisively.

Bo shrugged his shoulders and started walking back toward the van, where he could see Norman and Jennifer standing, engaged in conversation.

"Hey!" Ricky shouted. "Don't turn your back on me when I'm talking."

That stopped Bo in his tracks. He turned slowly around, wearing a frown.

"I don't believe you ought to have said that," Charlie observed, upon catching sight of the look on Bo's face.

Ricky shouted at Bo, "I've been told you were crazy. Now I've seen it for myself. There ain't no such thing as Yetis. Takes a crazy man to say there is. You should be locked up, in a looney house!"

"You definitely shouldn't be saying things like that," Charlie advised.

"You know Robert Friendly?" Ricky screamed at Bo.

"Him *and* his daddy," Bo calmly replied.

"They both say you're crazy!"

"Consider the source: perverts like that'll say anything."

"You bastard!" Ricky bellowed. "Judge Friendly and Robert are my best friends! They're family!" Ricky had his fists balled tightly and he was doing a little hip-hop as he shouted, probably thinking he was a young Muhammad Ali, about to pop it to a lumbering Sonny Lipton. His erratic movements were causing the rickety old bridge to shake and vibrate. From somewhere, there came a muffled grunt. Two grunts, actually, in quick succession, grunts such as large animals make when their slumber is disturbed. Ricky's eyes were bugging from his head, his lips contorting wildly. He screamed at Bo, "You don't remember me, do you? I was there! I saw you do it! You broke Robert's shoulder, and neither him nor his daddy's forgiven you!"

Bo commenced glancing around nervously, and backing away from Ricky. Charlie was backing away, too, looking around, trying to locate the primal sound. Ricky, who was shouting incoherently at Bo, had heard nothing. Now Ricky was literally jumping up and down on the bridge, causing its old infrastructure to tremble, shouting at the top of his lungs. He had met the mighty Bo Rocker, called his bluff, and literally frightened him into retreat. This single, tremendous act of courage would make Ricky Batson king of Paddlers' Hill. Undisputed top dog. The big ape in town. What tales he could tell Robert and the Judge! How he had sent Bo Rocker packing, with his tail between his legs! Sent him scurrying madly for the safety of his van.

No use stopping now. Time for Ricky to press his advantage. He hop-dashed to the far end of the bridge, like a bounding retriever, picked up a rock the size of a grapefruit and used it to clang vigorously on a metal sign, affixed to the bridge, that said, "Limit: 2 Ton Per Axle."

Bo and Charlie had reached the opposite end of the bridge. Bo stopped and shouted, "Don't do that!" But his warning only served to intensify Ricky's determined flailing of the unfortunate sign.

"What's the fool doin' that for?" Charlie Crenshaw gasped.

Ricky Batson had heard all the bad stories about Bo Rocker. And now he was getting even on behalf of Judge and Robert Friendly. Bo Rocker was the metal sign, or what was left of it, and Ricky Batson was the avenging angel. He was administering an unmerciful beating to the Bo sign. Giving the sign what Bo Rocker deserved.

From beneath the bridge, the agitated grunts had risen to a crescendo. Finally hearing them, Ricky screamed at Rocker, "I'll show you, I'll show you! You coward! Your scummy friends don't scare me." He wheeled around and in three short jumps reached the bridge railing. In a quick motion he vaulted over the railing and down the embankment.

"Don't go down there, you idiot!" Bo shouted. He looked at Charlie and Charlie looked at him, as if to say, "Well, you just gonna stand there? or what?"

Both of them broke for the other end of the bridge, where Ricky had disappeared. They had taken two steps when a bloodcurdling scream emanated from beneath the bridge.

That stopped them, cold in their tracks. They looked at each another again for a clue as to what they should do. "That guy a friend of yours?" Bo asked.

"I never saw him before this morning, when he hitched a ride from whitewater camp. I thought he was *your* friend."

"*My* friend?" Bo said.

They looked at one another again, as if to find inspiration for what to do next. Then came another agonized flurry of grunts and screams from under the bridge. Without another word passing between them, they simultaneously turned and bolted toward the van, screaming as they ran for Jennifer and Norman to jump inside and get ready to lock the doors behind them.

* * * * *

Bo was driving again. The four of them (Bo, Jennifer, Norman, and Charlie) were in the van, heading south toward the cutoff for the Piney River putin. Jennifer and Norman, as had been the case for most of the morning, were deeply engrossed in a private conversation.

Charlie Crenshaw was saying to Bo, "I reckon we did our civic duty, don't you Mister Rocker? We reported the incident, and the Sheriff was satisfied we did the right thing. He said we had no legal obligation to follow that fool under the bridge to see what happened to him."

They had stopped at the Sheriff's office on their way through town to report Ricky Batson's disappearance. Charlie was still a little vexed at himself for not having played the hero, for not having dashed under the bridge to help Ricky Batson with whatever it was that he had encountered under there. The Sheriff, however, told him it wasn't his fault if his friend had disregarded their advice and run under the bridge.

"Why, there could be anything under an ol' bridge like that," Sheriff Comer had attested. "Wild varmints have been known to den up in places like that. Bears and painters and hyenas and who knows what all might be back under there. Maybe even a wolverine, you never can tell. Heck, I don't blame you for not going after him. I wouldn't go myself without proper backup." He grinned, patted his monstrosity of a sidearm, and said, "That would be Colt .357 backup, if you know what I mean?"

The Sheriff's advice had made Charlie feel better. But his conscience was still nagging at him. "Is it possible there was a Yeti under there?" he asked the Sheriff.

"A what?"

"A Yeti. You know, like the one that used to bounce at Piney Tavern?"

The Sheriff scratched his head. "Well," he replied, "I know they have high turnover in them bouncer positions up at that ol' beer joint, but for the life of me, I can't recollect nobody named Yeti working up there." He thought about it for a couple more minutes and then said, "I guess it is possible that some ol' derelict from that beer joint was holed up under the bridge, sleeping off a bad drunk. But even so, I kind of doubt an ol' drunk would have harmed your friend."

"Acquaintance," said Bo. "He was our acquaintance. Not our friend. None of us ever met him before this morning."

"That's another thing," said the Sheriff. "You hardly know this Ricky Batson. You don't really know what he's like, what kind of person he is. For all you know, he could be the world's biggest practical joker. Why, right now he could be up under that bridge, laughing his head off. This may be his idea of a practical joke."

"Couldn't you just go up there and look around, Sheriff?" Jennifer pleaded.

Sheriff Comer looked at the pretty young woman talking to him and swallowed hard. It was the kind of request that a big, bold Sheriff couldn't ignore. He said, "Well, all right, little lady. I guess I could go on up there and look around for that ol' boy."

"It might pay off handsomely for you," Norman suggested. "I understand he has influential friends up in Nashville, powerful judges and such."

That got the Sheriff's attention. His eyebrows shot up. For some reason, he looked to Bo for an explanation. "That missing boy the governor's son, or something?"

Bo explained to the Sheriff, "I'm not positive about this, but I think Mister Batson is in some way connected to Criminal Court Judge Thad Friendly."

"Catfish Friendly?" the Sheriff said. He sat back in his chair and relaxed. "I'll tell you what I'll do, boys . . ." He looked at Jennifer and tipped an imaginary hat, "And you too, ma'am." He checked his watch and pulled out his duty roster and scanned it. "I got two deputies scheduled to come on in about three hours. When they get here, I'll send them up to that bridge to look around." He looked back at Jennifer, at her imploring eyes. "Oh, all right Missy. I'll go with them to make sure they do a thorough job."

* * * * *

And that's the way they had left it, in the capable hands of Sheriff Comer. There wasn't much else they could do, short of going back to the bridge and looking for Ricky Batson themselves, and nobody was much interested in that option. And so they had decided to go ahead and run the river.

And now they were coming up fast on the turnoff, so Bo slammed the gear stick into third and popped the clutch and the big rig's drive train emitted a high-pitched whine and the chassis began to tremble. When his speed had dropped to about fifty, he yanked the gear stick down to second and whipped the van sideways into the turn, popping the clutch and accelerating at the same time. It was a Bo turn, with the van hop-jumping sideways like a branded maverick.

Before them loomed the Cumberland escarpment.

Jennifer broke off her exchange with Norman, gave her lap belt an extra tug, and said to Bo, "I think you should have gone under the bridge to check on him."

"You do?" Bo replied.

"It would have been the decent thing," she said. "There's no telling what was under that bridge."

"All the more reason for not going," Bo said.

Charlie added, "You heard what the Sheriff said. We had no obligation to risk our necks for that fool. Mister Rocker told him not to go under there. He told him in no uncertain terms there might be a Yeti hiding under that bridge. Some Yeti that used to work at Piney Tavern. That right, Mister Rocker?"

Bo nodded.

"Did you know that Yeti, Mister Rocker?" Charlie asked.

"Not personally," Bo said. "But I've heard tell he's a rough customer."

Charlie said, "He used to bounce at Piney Tavern, didn't he, Mister Rocker? Boy, oh boy. That Piney Tavern must be some kind of place."

"Oh, it sure is," Bo said.

"I'd love to see it," Charlie added.

"You never been there!" Bo exclaimed.

"No," said Charlie. "I heard it was a private club, for members only."

"Would you like to check it out sometime?" Bo said.

"You mean, you're a member?"

Bo smiled, "A lifetime member, no less. I highly recommend the tavern; it's the social oasis of the Tennessee Valley. It has everything a discriminating customer could want: world class service, a prestigious clientele, live entertainment. You name it, it's got it."

Jennifer said, "From the stories I've heard, Bo Rocker's been the entertainment on several occasions."

Bo ignored her. He said to Charlie, "It's kind of a famous place. They shot part of a movie in there, did you know that?"

"Heck no, Mister Rocker!"

"Well, they did. They shot part of *The Outlaws of Cataract Creek* right inside Piney Tavern. You ever see that movie, Charlie?"

"No sir, Mister Rocker, can't say as I have."

"Then you missed a classic. That footage from Piney Tavern has been hailed for its authenticity. Part of the scene shows this ol' boy from down at Watts Bar getting his arm whacked off with a sword. Any number of doctors have told me that scene is the most realistic simulation of an amputation they've ever seen. One doctor told me that for a while they were using that footage to train new surgeons at Harvard Medical School."

"Why'd they stop using it, Mister Rocker?"

"Well, the film was so popular that every time they showed it, general surgery residents and psychiatric interns would fight over who got to sit in the front row seats. Those young doctors are soft, I guess. They were busting up their hands in those fist fights."

Charlie was getting excited. He said, "That's the first I ever heard of *The Outlaws of Cataract Creek*, but I'll be sure and rent it for tomorrow night."

"Well," Bo admitted, hesitantly. "It's not available for commercial viewing. Not yet, anyway. There's a big lawsuit that's still pending, so distribution is limited to nonprofit educational institutions until that suit is settled. Now, if you'd like to enroll at Harvard Medical School . . . ?"

"I'll pass on that one, Mister Rocker," Charlie replied, "but I sure would like to see the inside of Piney Tavern, if that's possible."

"Tell you what," Bo said. "We'll drop in for a visit when we get off the river."

"That's one place," Jennifer said emphatically, "that I'm not going in."

"Well, maybe you could just wait outside with Norman," Bo replied, sarcastically.

Jennifer swiveled around and looked at Norman. "Maybe I could," she said.

Bo was saying to Charlie, "We get off early enough, we may be able to get seats for the Saturday George Jones Dedication Exercise. It's like nothing you've ever seen. They bring out a cardboard likeness of George and stand it up in the corner. Really looks like him too, that hair all slicked back, the sparkle in his eye, life size, playing his guitar and smiling just like a possum. If you didn't know better, with the jukebox wailing in the background, you'd think the ol' Possum himself was right there in Piney Tavern. Then everybody gets out their sidearm, and on the count of three . . ."

Jennifer said, "Oh, for heaven's sake!"

"I'd love to see it," Charlie said. He was beside himself with excitement.

Bo pulled up to the intersection at the base of the escarpment and stopped. He leaned forward and peered through the windshield at the formidable cliff in front of them. "Oh boy," he said, cinching up his seat belt. "I just hope I don't get a nosebleed this time."

* * * * *

It was Charlie Crenshaw's first trip down the Piney, a river he'd heard about for years but hesitated to paddle because of its reputation. But now he was headed down its bony corridor with Bo Rocker, the *River Master* himself, the man who was said to know the stream better than all the rest of the world put together. Because he had heard so much about it, Charlie intended to get as much footage as possible with his new miniature-format video camera, a version so compact that it tucked neatly inside his kayak cockpit. Charlie wanted to get some footage of Bo Rocker so he could show it to all his friends and prove he'd been paddling with him. Everybody had heard of Bo Rocker, but some of the newer paddlers didn't believe he was for real. Some of them thought he was more legend than real, kind of a riparian Paul Bunyan. Heck, it wasn't every day that a fellow like Charlie got to paddle with a legend.

Charlie was a little hesitant at first to bring out the camera and aim it at Bo. He thought Bo might be camera shy. But boy was he in for a surprise. From the moment Charlie popped his spray skirt and produced the camera, a major change seemed to come over Bo. He ignored Jennifer and Norman, and devoted all his time to staging sequences for Charlie to film. Soon they had developed a rhythm: as soon as Bo briefed him on what to expect downstream, Charlie would run on through the rapid, catch an eddy, and then shoot the others as they came through. By the time they reached Signal Falls, in the hoariest section of Piney River's hair water, Bo was really hamming it up for the camera. He ran the swirling, swerving approach to the waterfall standing up in his canoe, and to everybody's utter amazement, continued to stand as he catapulted over the drop, twirling his paddle overhead.

At the base of the waterfall, Bo paddled up to Charlie and made a suggestion, "I've noticed you're trying to shoot everybody as they come through the rapids, and that's a tough assignment. A better tactic would be to concentrate on one person: me. Jennifer and Norman just aren't as photogenic as I am. Keep that camera trained on me. If you'll get lots of footage of me, I'll pay you a hundred bucks for the video tape when we reach the takeout."

"A hundred bucks?"

"Make that two hundred. *And* I'll get you front row seats for today's George Jones Dedication Exercise at Piney Tavern."

Charlie's mouth dropped open.

"And," Bo added with a flourish, "Drinks are on me."

Charlie was stunned. Getting to paddle with and video somebody famous like Bo Rocker had been more good fortune than he could believe. And now he had the opportunity to see inside Piney Tavern, a guest of lifetime member Eugene (Bo) Rocker. And front row seats at the dedication exercise, and all the drinks he could pour down. And all of it for free. Plus two hundred bucks for his video tape. It was a heck of an offer. But, there was no denying he enjoyed taping Jennifer Lemke when she came through the rapids, too. And when they had stopped to scout that one waterfall, it had been a colossal treat taping her when she got in and out of her boat. There was something about the way she moved that made watching her a pleasure. Something about that girl made Charlie long to point a camera in her direction. He said, "Well, I just don't know, Mister Rocker, I just don't feel right about not . . ."

"Now," Bo said, ignoring Charlie's protests. "Scoot right over to that eddy where Norman and Jennifer are sitting, and get that camera ready. I'll show you something you've never seen before. I'll guarantee it."

Charlie paddled over to the eddy with Norman and Jennifer. When he arrived, he was wearing a pained expression, and Jennifer said, "What's wrong, Charlie?"

"Nothing."

"Oh, but something's wrong. You've been happy as a little puppy ever since we put in, and now all of a sudden your chin's hanging down on you chest. Bo said something nasty to you, didn't he?"

Charlie hung his head. Jennifer edged up beside him and put her arm across his shoulders. "What'd he say, Charlie?"

"Well, I really do respect Mister Rocker and I want to do what he wants, but I just don't think it's right . . ."

"What did he ask you to do?"

"He wants me to keep the camera trained exclusively on him all the time and not video you at all, and . . ." Jennifer dropped her arm from around his shoulder. She was sitting in her boat with a stunned expression on her face, like she was in another world. Charlie stammered, "But, I'll tell him that I'll do whatever I want to do, and . . ."

She came out of it with an abrupt shake of her head. She reached over and put a slender finger across Charlie's lips, and made him stop talking. She said softly, "Do what he wants, Charlie."

Charlie was watching her lips move when she spoke. What an incredible sight.

"No, I don't think . . ."

She looked him straight in the eye, and said, "Don't argue. Do what he wants."

Charlie could think of only one thing: how he had to train the camera straight on her and get a closeup of that face, of those lovely eyes, of . . .

Bo was yelling from over at the base of the waterfall, "You ready, Charlie?"

Charlie hoisted the camera and glanced at Jennifer, wishing he had the courage to ignore Bo and train the camera on her, where it belonged.

But Bo kept shouting, and when Charlie looked over, he saw Bo quickly paddle to the far edge of the falls and deliberately turn over, then roll up in less than an instant. "Not bad," Charlie commented under his breath, and switched on his camera. And then he couldn't believe what Bo did next. He flipped and rolled again, except this time he didn't stop at the top of his roll. He merely stayed in his tuck and flipped again, and again, and again. Flip-roll, flip-roll, flip-roll . . . almost faster than the eye could see, he executed fifteen or twenty crisp barrel rolls across the base of the falls.

"I don't believe it," Charlie said. "This guy is everything he's cracked up to be."

"And more," Norman commented, drily.

Bo was yelling again, "Now get this, Charlie." He paddled straight into the falls and let its backwash grab his boat and pull it under the pounding froth. Only this time he couldn't – or didn't – roll. The boat just stayed under the falls, upside-down, absorbing a tremendous beating.

Charlie lowered the camera. "He's stuck! He can't get out. We gotta help him."

"He's not stuck," Norman said calmly. "He's just show-boating."

"But," Charlie protested, "he can't breathe under water. He's been in there a long time."

"He can stay in there all day if he takes a notion," Norman explained. "He just tucks forward and breathes from his air pocket. It's one of the advantages of paddling a canoe. When he gets ready, he'll roll up."

Charlie was getting his camera back in action when Bo half-rolled his boat on the edge of the pounding falls and, from under his boat, waved to them, then let his boat succumb to the pounding water and sink back into the backwash.

"That guy must be the best paddler in the entire world," Charlie was saying. "Heck, this video's probably worth two hundred bucks."

"That what he offered you for it?" Norman asked.

Charlie nodded.

"Then it's worth four hundred," Norman observed. "Minimum."

Jennifer said, "Eight, easily. No, wait, I have a better idea. Demand a thousand – which he'll eagerly pay – and then give him a blank tape."

Norman clapped his hands, threw back his head and laughed uproariously. At that moment, Bo popped out from under the falls, rolled up, and paddled over to their eddy. His boat was half full of water and he was paddle bailing as he advised them of the next rapid downstream. "It's called NoMistake, and it's a doozy. Get that camera ready, Charlie!"

Bo Rocker, Media Star

When they reached NoMistake, they stopped and scouted . . . and gawked . . . and scouted some more.

Even Bo.

"Well, well," Bo said at last, as they gazed at the awesome spectacle: a hundred yards of unprincipled maelstrom, crashing and churning into, under, and around undercut boulders in a mad swerve to river left, crashing through a sieve-looking rock arrangement only to explode into a massive log jam. "I'm not crazy enough to run that thing," he said, "but if we mope around here any longer, we'll miss the daily George Jones Dedication Exercise at Piney Tavern. Here's what I'll do."

Bo got everybody up on a big river left boulder and explained what was about to ensue. Pointing to the top of the rapid, forty yards upstream, he said, "I'll sneak around that first big jumble of rocks up there, take the drop into the megahole, back ferry left, and then catch this big eddy right here in front of us." The big eddy he was pointing to was a spot that, upon close inspection, might pass for a barely distinguishable current differential. "Now Charlie," Bo said, grabbing him by his shoulders and maneuvering him into position. "I want you to stand right here. That way, you can shoot me as I appear from behind that big rock and drop into the hole. From here, it'll look just like I was running into the main part of the rapid. That way, I'll tell everybody I ran No-Mistake at this water level and have the video to prove it. Remember, two hundred and fifty bucks for that video tape."

Bo swaggered off toward his boat and Jennifer said, solemnly, almost sadly, "Something comes over that man when he gets in front of a camera."

Charlie called after him, "I wish you wouldn't try it, Mister Rocker. This looks like one bad mother of a rapid."

Bo stopped suddenly, flinging out both arms in wild, barely controlled gesticulations. "I know!" he said, as excited as a cash-rich kid in a discount candy store. "We'll make a movie. The whitewater movie to top all whitewater movies. A movie that'll put Jacques Povlsen to shame. It'll be even more famous than *The Outlaws of Cataract Creek*. Now Charlie, get set and don't miss a stroke of the scintillating action you're about to see. You're going to be famous, Charlie, my dear friend. You're going to be the most famous sports cinematographer in America!"

"I'm worried, Ms Lemke," Charlie said. He carefully laid aside his camera and picked up his throw bag. "This is a mighty mean rapid."

Bo made his way upstream and climbed into his canoe, adjusted his position in the boat several times, and then peeled out into the pulsating current. The water took hold of the canoe quickly and decisively. As Bo made the big drop into the monstrous hole, he took on a boat load of water, and had to struggle to escape the hydraulic's grip. And then began the painful but mandatory back ferry in heavy water.

A back ferry through heavy whitewater in a solo open canoe is never easy. When a boat is loaded with water, it's almost impossible. But no one told Bo. With alternating flurries of back strokes and cross-boat reverse back strokes, his skill and plain gut determination brought the over-laden canoe across the turbulent water. Against unfathomable power, Bo managed to ferry within striking distance of the target micro eddy, situated a mere twenty feet upstream of a row of partially submerged boulders which marked the point of no return in NoMistake. The smile that had adorned his face only seconds earlier as he dropped into the upstream hole had long since metamorphosed into a determined grimace.

Norman and the others watched transfixed as Bo Rocker back ferried a canoe loaded with water across the Class IV top of a Class VI rapid. And they rooted for him, knowing he was pulling off a feat that very few others in the world could manage, yet realizing even as the act unfolded that he would puff and brag about it for days to come and even exaggerate and embellish the account by claiming he ran the rapid while the rest of them stood by, afflicted with vertigo and apoplexy.

Charlie tossed aside his throw bag and picked up his video camera. "I guess I'd better get this on tape, or I won't be the greatest sports cinematographer in America, whatever that means." He raised the camera and said, "Come on, Mister Rocker, bring it on home!"

In a daring maneuver, so unexpected that Charlie lowered his camera in order to get a better look, Bo interrupted his orderly back ferry. Leaning way out and backward, harness-ing some tiny current differential only a desperate man would have noticed, he threw his strength into a left side reverse quarter sweep and produced a dramatic 180 degree slingshot turn aided and abetted by hundreds of pounds of water shifting from bow to stern.

Mirabiledictu!

His bow was within five feet of the micro eddy and with furious paddling Bo propelled the boat into the safe haven even as his companions stood slack-jawed, unbelieving. Bo's eyes scanned the group and stopped on Charlie, who stood there mouth agape and video camera dangling by its carry strap.

It dawned on everybody simultaneously. So absorbed had Charlie been, so absorbed had they all been by the display of mesmerizing Bo Rocker river magic, that not a person had aimed a single camera toward the maestro. Bo, of course, was enraged, turning various colors of red, green and blue. Slamming down his paddle, shaking with rage, he screamed at Charlie, the man who moments before had been his nearest and dearest friend: "You nitwit excuse for a perambulating afterbirth! Where's my video? Where's my video?"

Jennifer said to Charlie, "You see what I mean? Something comes over him."

Engrossed in an emotional state approaching a full-scale conniption fit, Bo screamed menacingly and shook his knobby fist toward Charlie, unaware that his boat was slowly but inexorably slipping from the safety of the micro eddy. The hundreds of pounds of water behind him, downstream of him, downhill of him, but still inside his canoe, sucked backwards into the current, into the decided tilt at the top of which he was perched so precariously.

Suddenly realizing his perilous circumstances, Bo dropped his epithets, grabbed his paddle, and commenced stroking desperately. Try as he might, however, those needless gallons inside his boat would not be coerced back upstream into the micro eddy. He was sucked, backwards, into the labyrinth of NoMistake with no option but to try and ride it out. He hit the first rock and his boat whipped around ninety degrees, placing his strong paddling side downstream.

Bo luck.

Leveraging this advantage, he leaned out downstream, over the fulcrum rock, enabling the current to pop the boat free and into a lateral sluice. He used the split second respite to fullest advantage, twisting around and surveying the best-shot course through the sieve downstream.

The Chilling Sound
of Metal Meshing with ABS

The boat jerked, like it had hit something solid in the raging turbulence, and then stopped broadside in the current. Bo seemed unconcerned. He leaned downstream again and seemed to expect the boat to swivel, completing his turn. By now his scan of downstream conditions, a perusal of precious few seconds, was complete. He had plotted his best-chance route through the churning cauldron that lay before him. He leaned up, out, and into one of those classic high brace positions that require body torque so exaggerated they can be accomplished without risk of shoulder dislocation only in the freedom of open canoe.

Charlie gasped, "Mister Rocker's gonna make it. He's gonna pull it off!" Belatedly, he raised his video camera and pressed the record button.

But "making it" was not to be the story line for this video.

It happened fast, in a matter of seconds. The boat did not swivel around the obstruction, as Bo expected. Instead, it wrapped. In four or five seconds it crumpled like paper and collapsed into a horseshoe shape, with Bo still in it, still hanging out over the downstream gunwale, paddle dangling over the obstructing rock into the mad froth below. Even with the roar and din of the awesome rapid the chilling sound of meshing metal and ABS filled the air. As Bo climbed over the downstream gunwale, the bilges and thwarts merged – where his legs had been seconds before.

The crumpled canoe and the rock upon which it was plastered formed a partial water break, with white froth blowing over and by the wreckage with hurricane fury. Bo dangled from the downstream gunwale, body flapping in the fury like a sock in a storm, head occasionally breaking surface to bellow, "Damn a wore out old boat! Damn a wore out old boat!"

Dangling there, one hand grappling into the canoe, the other in a life-grip on the thwart, his companions at first feared his hand was trapped, perhaps crushed between the thwart and the bilge, held tight by thousands of pounds of pressure. But soon they realized he was fishing desperately inside the boat's carcass for his dry box, squashed as it was between seat thwarts and canoe bottom.

As he dangled and grappled, a rescue effort brought help to a boulder within fifteen feet of the wreckage. Norman and Jennifer positioned themselves and threw Bo a rope, but he wouldn't take it.

"Take the rope, Bo, it's your best chance," Norman coaxed. "Even you will have a hard time slithering through the logjam at the bottom of this rapid."

"Got to get the dry box," Bo blubbered. "My Rolex's in it!"

"His what's in it?" Charlie asked.

"His watch's in it," Norman replied.

"Mister Rocker's hanging on out there for his watch?" Charlie said. "I'll be darned. I never knew anybody to love his watch more'n his own life. That watch must keep really good time."

"I think it has an alarm on it," Jennifer said, disdainfully. "An alarm that announces starting time for the George Jones Dedication Exercise, that big ceremony they hold every day at the Great Valley of the Tennessee's premier social club and cultural oasis, otherwise known as Piney Tavern."

The Miraculous Metaphysical Tuna Transformation

Charlie interrupted his taping long enough to crawl atop the same boulder with Jennifer and Norman. He made a point of sitting close to Jennifer, and noted with satisfaction that she made no effort to move away. For Charlie, it was the thrill of a lifetime. From his new video vantage spot, he aimed his camera and commenced recording the random undulations of the flapping figure out in the water. Each time the current surged, it caught Bo's body and swept it upward to a near-horizontal position, transforming him into a comical, hapless, aquarian superman flying upstream against the roaring current.

"This little camera may not be worth a Rolex," Charlie leaned over and said to Jennifer, "but something tells me it'll pay for itself before the day's over."

"Look at him out there," yelled Norman, above the din of the rapid. "If he hangs on much longer, he'd better think seriously about sprouting gills. Look, Charlie, look. Look at his face! I think he's entered stage two of the miraculous tuna transformation!"

Out in the river, Bo was having no luck in trying to free the dry box. Despite his determined efforts, the box was wedged securely between rock and seat thwarts. He was about ready to give up when he noticed Charlie sitting there, capturing

every detail of his wretched circumstances. "Stop it, damn
you," he screamed as yet another surge of white fury blew over
the boat and swept his body upward to a point almost parallel
with the streamblow. As if to deliberately agitate him,
Norman removed his still camera from its dry bag and also
commenced shooting.

Click, click, click. "I don't think anybody's ever filmed the
transcendent tuna transformation," Norman giggled. "That
would be a scientific coup of major proportions. If we get this
down on both video and 35mm we may win the Nobel prize!"
Click, click. "At least a Pulitzer Prize in photography!" *Click,
click, click.*

"I don't think you need that alarm watch anyway, Bo!"
Jennifer shouted encouragingly. She checked the speed of the
current, which was approaching Mach I. "Once you turn loose
of that gunwale, you'll be floating past the tavern in two
minutes, maximum. Be sure to wave at the Possum as you go
by!"

* * * * *

Bo finally relented, accepted the rope, and abandoned both
his gold Rolex and his boat to the froth. He floated the
remaining distance to the takeout scrunched uncomfortably
between Norman's saddle and bow flotation bag. Before they
reached the takeout, Charlie's video cassette had netted him
an offer of fifteen hundred bucks. But on advice from Jennifer,
he was holding out for more. A lot more.

When they reached the takeout at Deep Rut Road, they
were greeted by Sheriff Comer.

* * * * *

"What did I tell you?" he said to them. "Didn't I say there was no cause for alarm?" The Sheriff pointed over to the bridge, where a couple of deputies were flanking Ricky Batson and a big gorilla of a guy dressed in overalls. The gorilla was barefoot, with arms the size of utility poles, his knuckles practically dragging the ground. Sheriff Comer continued, "As you can see, it's exactly as I suspected. Them two ol' boys didn't have no fight under that bridge like you thought. Why, they're real good friends from what I can tell." The Sheriff yelled to his deputies: "Bring 'em over here, boys."

One glance at the big gorilla told Bo it was Alphonse, looking as hairy and ugly as ever. As the deputies escorted them over, Alphonse had a brawny arm wrapped snugly around his newfound friend, Ricky Batson. Ricky was having a little trouble walking, if not breathing, and seemed to be in a daze.

The Sheriff spoke sternly to Ricky, "I hope you're pleased with yourself, boy. These people have been worried sick about you. Especially this nice young lady, Miss Lemke." Whenever Sheriff Comer mentioned Jennifer's name, his voice would soften noticeably. He touched the brim of his hat to Jennifer before turning back to Ricky. "They spent half the morning down at my office filing missing person reports, like you was somebody worth looking for. And you up here the whole time frolicking with Alphonse, having a big ol' time way back under that bridge. Now, go ahead, tell these people you're okay, so they can stop fretting over you."

Ricky raised his hand, as if to make a point, and started to say something, but Alphonse tightened his arm around his rib cage, causing Ricky to roll his eyes back and make a gurgling sound. Alphonse said, "Me like, me like," and kissed Ricky on the cheek.

"Oh, that's gross and disgusting," the Sheriff said scornfully, making a dreadful face, "but entirely constitutional – or so I've been informed." He took Bo aside and started to say something to him, and then stopped and began idly digging in the dirt with the toe of his cowboy boot. Bo knew he was thinking carefully about what he was going to say. He wanted to get it just right. He finally stopped his digging, and said in a whisper, "I understand now why you made a point about that ol' Batson boy being an acquaintance, and not a friend. At least we know now why he run off like he did and crawled under that bridge. I guess he sensed there was one of his kind under there. They say them kind can always tell their own." Sheriff Comer rolled his eyes. He added, "They used to call it 'Coming out of the closet.' I guess now they'll start calling it 'Crawling under the bridge.' " He paused for a moment, probably to read Bo's reaction, and then added, "I'd love to run 'em both in for about ten or twenty years, but I reckon you must know that what them two's been doing under there is perfectly legal far as I can tell. Unless, that is, you think there's been some element of force or coercion?" He tilted that big head and looked at Bo, waiting for his answer.

Bo took a long, hard look at Ricky and Alphonse, and rendered an opinion to the Sheriff: "Looks to me like two consenting adults."

The Sheriff nodded, and started to walk away. Just then, Ricky said something that caught his attention. It sounded like, "Bjork, bjork." Between bjorks, he was lolling his tongue out about six inches.

The Sheriff straightened. "What'd he say?"

"I think it was something about knowing an influential judge in Nashville," Bo replied.

The Sheriff said, in an exceedingly scornful tone, "An influential judge's butt!"

"Yeah, he probably knows that, too," Bo agreed.

Alphonse squeezed Ricky again and said, "Me like, me like!"

"Oh, for Christ sake!" Sheriff Comer said, snatching off his hat and angrily slapping Ricky up the side of his head with it. He ordered his deputies to usher Ricky and Alphonse back under the bridge before any locals drove by and were offended by their behavior. The Sheriff took Bo aside again, and whispered, "They may have the legal right to do that stuff, but they ain't gonna do it out in public, not in my county." He leaned in close to Bo. "And whatever you do," he said, in an ultra-hushed conspiratorial tone, "don't let on to that nice Miss Lemke what them two's been doing back under that bridge. You hear me?"

Bo nodded. "Right, Sheriff."

They all watched as Alphonse led Ricky back down to the bridge. A few seconds after they disappeared into the shadows, Ricky came staggering back out, unsteady on his feet, the whites of his eyes showing prominently. Suddenly a hairy arm snaked out of the shadows, wrapped itself around him, and jerked him back under the bridge. The Sheriff laughed contemptuously. "Them two shore are playful, ain't they?"

Jennifer said, "Can't you do something for him, Sheriff? I'm not sure he wants to be back under there with that thing."

"Well, Miss Lemke, I could lock him up, I guess. If that's what you want. He did destroy county property when he banged up that poor ol' sign there on the bridge." Jennifer glanced over at the dilapidated sign and shook her head, and the Sheriff seemed willing to forget about the damage. He turned to the others. "Everybody have a good day on the river?"

Norman said, "Well, we did lose a boat up . . ."

"We had a great day," Bo said. "No problems. No sir, nobody in this group had any problems."

The Sheriff looked at them suspiciously. "Lost a boat, had a great day. Uh huh, I see." He glared at Bo and Norman for a long moment, waiting for one of them to break down and confess what really happened upstream. But nobody said a word. And then his gaze chanced to fall again on Jennifer. His blustery expression softened. "Well, at least you didn't get this pretty little lady injured up there on that crazy ol' river. If you'd a done something dumb like that, I'd be forced to run you in for a couple of life sentences." He touched his hat brim to Jennifer again and smiled. Then got back to business, looking serious. "You folks be careful on that ol' river, you hear? I don't want a have to hike into that ol' canyon with an arm load of grappling hooks, fishing for one of your bodies. You hear?"

They heard.

Sheriff Comer, having made his point, flashed that big election-time grin of his, and added, "And have a nice day." He deferentially tipped his hat to Jennifer and walked away with his two deputies.

* * * * *

They watched the county cruiser disappear from sight around the downstream bend in the road. Bo said, "And now, boys and girls," his voice and countenance shifting to an upbeat tenor, "we have more pleasant matters at hand. Because at this time, it's my pleasure to invite everybody down to Piney Tavern. Drinks are on me."

"Right on," Charlie said.

"No way," Jennifer said, with an unmistakable edge in her voice. She looked at Charlie. "I need your car keys."

Charlie said, "My keys?"

"You have a lot of negotiating to do with Mister Rocker, don't you?" Charlie patted his video camera, which was clutched securely in the crook of his arm, and smiled his agreement.

Jennifer continued, "Do you suppose after you finish your negotiating, you could hitch a ride back to camp with Bo? You'll find your car there when you arrive."

"But where are you going?" asked Bo.

She looked at Norman, who had been close by her side all day. Now he slipped an arm around her waist and she snuggled close to him. She said, "I've been talking today with Norman, and . . ."

"I've been noticing that," Bo said, glaring at them.

Norman added, "And I've told Jennifer all about the Ergonomic Adaptation Mechanics program at the University."

"And there's an opening in the program," Jennifer added. "And Doctor Knight thinks he can get me admitted."

"Are you out of your ever-loving mind?" Bo said. "You'd actually go back to Dipstick University? You know the kind of people up there! Remember Harold? Remember Professor Cradwell? Remember Freddie? Just take a look at Norman here. This is what you wanna be like? Like him? Like Norman? A burned out listless old fart at age thirty-five? You're gonna be content to hobnob with people like Norman for the rest of your life? Go to their little tea parties? Play bridge with them? Discuss politics?"

Usually a cool customer, Jennifer wasn't taking kindly to Bo's harangue. She had fire in her eyes and color in her cheeks as she retorted, "And what would you have me do? Be content to follow you from river to river? I want more out of life than that. I want to make something of myself. I want to go places and see things and meet important people and accomplish things, not just flush down flooded river canyons."

"I can't believe it," Bo stammered. "I took you places. I showed you things. I introduced you to people. A lot of people. Important people, influential people."

"Look, Bo," she said, easing off some. "I'm not saying it hasn't been fun; it has, in a lot of ways. And I did meet people. And we did go places. I'm not denying that. Those weeks in Santiago were great, and Montreal was fun too. So was Tahiti."

Bo tried to comment, but she wouldn't let him get a word in edgewise. She added, "And that trip to Monterey was a special treat. Especially staying at Pebble Beach and eating at that little restaurant in Carmel that I liked so much, and driving down US1 to Big Sur, and seeing the place where Henry Miller lived. And I had a large time in Bangkok and Sidney and Melbourne too, I won't deny that. But a girl has to think about her future. Surely you can understand. And besides, I deserve a shot at a doctorate. I'm smarter than Harold ever was, and he was doing okay until he wouldn't do things Professor Cradwell's way. So if he could almost make it, I'm sure I can go all the way. This is a great opportunity for me, Bo. It's a chance for me to make it on my own, to prove to myself and to the world that I can amount to something, without hanging onto some man's coattail. I know that deep down you understand. You're really a sweet and understanding man, despite yourself. And I love you, but this is the way it has to be."

For once in his life Bo was speechless. Jennifer tiptoed up and kissed him on his chin, then stepped back and looked at Charlie. She said, "So, Charlie, if I may have your keys?"

"Don't give them to her," Bo commanded.

Norman opened his camera and removed the roll of film. He showed it to Charlie, "I'll add this little item to your negotiating chips."

Bo reached for the film canister, "Give me that!"

Charlie grabbed the film, pocketed it, and then tossed his car keys to Jennifer.

"Thanks, Charlie," Jennifer said, grabbing the keys. "I won't forget this." She kissed him on the forehead. "I love you, too, Charlie, although I only met you yesterday."

"You do?" he said.

"I do, and I won't forget this favor. I promise."

"I'll do a favor for you anytime, Ms Lemke."

Jennifer smiled. "I may just hold you to that, fella. And speaking of favors, here's one for you: I know plenty of people who'd pay a small fortune to own a video of Bo Rocker wrapping his canoe around a rock in the Piney River. One of those people is Horace Conrad. He publishes a whole string of paddling magazines, like *River Probe* and *Drift Indicator*. I bet he'd devote an entire issue to that video and roll of film. I suspect his *opening* offer would be fifteen to twenty thousand."

She looked at the forlorn and dejected figure standing beside Charlie. "Goodbye, Bo," she said.

"You can't run off with the shuttle car," Bo said, on the verge of tears. "How will I get back to the putin? All my cold beer's up there."

"Get one of your dear friends at the tavern to take you," Jennifer recommended. "Maybe George Jones? Or even better, the one called Frieda. You remember Frieda, don't you, Bo? Frieda's a real special friend of yours, isn't she? She's the one that really sets your gonads to fluttering, isn't she? Get her to drive you back to the putin."

With that last salvo, Jennifer and Norman got in the car and drove off, leaving Bo and Charlie standing in the gravel pullover by the bridge. Bo said to Charlie, "Some more friend you are, aiding and abetting a lizard like Norman Knight! Helping him to steal the woman I love. The *only* woman I've ever *really* loved."

"I'm sorry, Mister Rocker," Charlie said. He hung his head in shame and commenced digging in the gravel with his toe, giving a reasonably fair imitation of Sheriff Comer's technique.

"Oh well," said Bo, "it's not your fault. But tell me something, will you? What did I do to turn her against me like that?"

Charlie meekly looked down at the video camera he was holding. He said, "Oh, heck, Mister Rocker, you know how women are."

Bo said, "I do?"

* * * * *

Bo wore his smelly wetsuit and booties down to Piney Tavern, where his apparel never so much as drew a second glance. He borrowed a Ruger .44 magnum from Billy Joe Holbrooks and won the dedication exercise grand prize, a case of ice cold Bass Ale, by blowing the Possum's head clean off with one cylinder of 200 grain hollow points.

But even a case of his favorite brew couldn't cheer him up for long. Bo was slipping into a grand funk, thinking of how Jennifer had left him for a lowlife university professor. If she had run off with somebody useful, like a truck driver, it would have been painful enough. Or an insurance salesman, or even some derelict surgeon. But a university professor? The woman was cold.

Bo was feeling really down in the dumps when Bubba Suttles, Piney Tavern's assistant director of promotional events, slapped him on the back and congratulated him on his sharpshooting. Bo replied, "Well, you know the old saying, 'Lucky at blowing George's head off, unlucky at love.'"

Bubba's zit-pocked face twisted into a quasi-hostile, quizzical expression, which it held for a long, uncomfortable moment, before suddenly erupting into laughter. He slapped Bo on the back hard enough to give him whiplash, smiled through snaggle teeth, and proclaimed, "Hell professor, I keep forgettin' you got one of them PFD degrees. You oughta know them educated sayin's go right over Bubba's head."

Bubba helped himself to one of Bo's Bass Ales, tipped it back and sucked down twelve ounces of rich amber velvet in record time. He dropped the empty back in the box and belched loud enough to wake George Jones' bullet-riddled and decapitated cardboard corpse. He said, "But speaking of love – which is one subject ol' Bubba knows a few things about – would it interest you to learn that a mighty good looking woman was in here this afternoon looking for you?"

"Who?" said Bo. "Hot Lips Remey, from Hollywood?"

Bubba was shaking his head. "Naw, not her. This gal was even better looking than Hot Lips. This was maybe the best looking woman I've ever seen. I couldn't figure why she was looking for you. But she said she spotted a van parked out at some crick crossing way up yonder on the ridge and thought it might be yours."

Bo was getting worked up. "Well come on, Bubba," he implored. "Enough of this suspense. Who was she? Was it Frieda!"

"No, no, not her. This girl might've looked even better than Frieda, if that's possible." Bubba was frowning, rubbing the stubble on his chin, trying to think of the name she had given him.

"Was it Betsy?"

Bubba shook his head. "No, not Betsy. I ain't seen her in months. This gal was dressed up like she was goin' somewhere. You know what I mean? Spike heels and all. And she had real sexy legs and that long raven black hair streaming down her back. And this look about her, like by God, she was on a mission and she meant business."

"Barbi? Was it Barbi? Please say it was Barbi."

"No, that's not it either." He frowned again and then gave up. "Heck, ol' Bubba can't remember names. You oughta know that."

Bo was about to collapse. He was in agony. "Oh, Christ, Bubba. Then what did she say? What did she want with me?"

"Oh!" Bubba said. "That I remember. "She said she had unfinished business with you."

Bo said, "Uh oh."

"That's what she said, all right. Something about you not finishing something that you started with her up on the Gauley River."

"Would you remember the name," Bo said, slowly and carefully, "if you heard it again?" Bubba was nodding. Bo said, "Could it possibly have been something like A . . ."

"That's it!" Bubba said, excitedly. "Amy!"

Bo's spirits were on the rebound. "Where's she now?"

Bubba shrugged, and helped himself to another Bass Ale. "How should I know?"

Bo slumped, hung his head. Deep, dark depression creeping in.

"She really meant something to you, huh?"

"Amy's the *only* woman," Bo confessed, "that I ever loved. I mean, *really* loved."

Bubba knocked back about half the ale, wiped the dribble off his chin with the back of his hand, and said, "Uh huh, I see. Well then, in that case, you'll be interested to know that she'll be stopping back in later tonight to see if that really was your van parked out up there by the crick."

Bo grabbed Bubba by the straps of his overalls, started shaking him violently, and said, "When? When? When!"

"Take it easy, Bo," Bubba said. He set his drink down and rummaged through his pockets, finally locating his watch. "If she keeps her word, she'll be here in about . . . let's see what time it is now . . . big hand on the twelve, little hand on the six . . . oh, I'd say in about half an hour."

Bo, feeling a surge of euphoria, thrust another Bass Ale in Bubba's big paws and then ran over and yanked Charlie off his barstool. He dragged him over to a corner table and sat him down. Bo said, "We have a lot of negotiating to do, pal, and not much time to do it in. Now, I want that video tape and that roll of film, and I don't mean maybe. Name your price."

* * * * *

As part of the deal, Bo made Charlie pledge that he would never disclose how much he received for that video tape and roll of film. Charlie agreed to Bo's demand on one condition: that Jennifer Lemke had to approve Bo's final offer. Although the amount of money that changed hands is a mystery, it is known that from that day onward, Charlie was always in a position to make loans to his close friends.

* * * * *

Jennifer Lemke and Norman Knight were the hottest gossip item at Dipstick University – for about two months. Until she grew so bored with the vapidity of graduate school that she couldn't take it any longer. She also got fed up with Norman constantly asking about her real hair color.

* * * * *

Using money she borrowed from Charlie Crenshaw, Jennifer bought half ownership in Pete's Corner Bar and Grill in Hillsborough Village. Before long, Jennifer was sole owner. In a moment of flippancy, she changed the restaurant's name to Freddie's Place. She put up a big sign, hand-painted, with blood red letters against a white background. Like the sign that used to be on the roof of Piney Tavern. And the name caught on. So did the sign. She franchised the concept, the whole package, based on a combination of her own ideas and a little restaurant she had once visited with Bo Rocker in Carmel. There are now one hundred eighty-seven Freddie's Places throughout the Southeast, and one in Monterey – for old time's sake. Jennifer's net worth is . . . well, a lot. And most everybody agrees Jennifer Lemke is a capable business-woman. Notwithstanding missing out on that Dipstick degree.

* * * * *

Norman Knight spends a lot of time roaming the Cumberland Plateau, especially up around Lilly Bridge on Clear Creek. They say he makes solitary excursions through the Obed canyons. By moonlight, some say. Looking for somebody. Or some thing. Or some memory. Or maybe just a special feeling that he once held, for one brief moment, before it slipped away.

Like water under the bridge of time.

Two Years Later:
Somewhere in Idaho

The pilot banked the helicopter into a wide turn, giving his passengers an unimpeded look straight down into the canyon of the upper Deadwood River. Thousands of feet below, water was alternately crashing through mile-long rapids, and disappearing into horrendous logjams. Shortly upstream of the biggest rapid on the river, several rafts could be seen tediously making their way through the obstructions.

"Holy of holies," Amy was saying, as she took her eyes from the sight below and quickly flipped through the thick river guidebook she had open on her lap. "They rate the river Class V in here, and that's when it's free of logjams." She looked again at the swirling, sucking water. "What kind of place is that? And who are those people down there?"

Bo said, "It's a film crew. You remember when Jacques Povlsen, the famous producer, died last year?"

Amy thought for a moment, and then replied: "The guy in Malibu who died while having sex? The one they found trussed up like a chicken?"

Bo grimaced. "Yeah, that's the one."

Amy looked back at the river. "Sure," she said. "I saw all the lurid details on the Joan Broaddus Wright Show. But what's that have to do with the people down there?"

"The people who took over his production company," Bo explained, "are old friends of mine. And they're down there on the river. I figure they're having all kinds of problems right about now. If I show up and offer to lend a hand, they'll be so grateful they just might give me a role in the movie they're making."

Amy said, "You're kidding? We came all the way out here for a walk-on audition? Or in this case, a float-on audition?"

"What's wrong with that?"

"Bo, will you never learn? You don't just show up out of the blue and land a spot in a major motion picture. It just doesn't happen that way."

Bo looked a little flustered. "Well," he said, "it *could* happen. It's worth a shot."

* * * * *

After a backbreaking three-hour portage, the film crew finally had all their gear at the bottom of the big rapid. They were set up on the rocks, on river right, cameras aimed upstream, ready to record the action. Only now, the stunt kayakers were refusing to do their part. Mark Wilson, leader of the group, was solemnly shaking his head. "Too risky," he was saying. "It's just too risky. The water is too high. I didn't sign onto this venture to lose my life."

Claudette Remey was in a rage. She was shouting at Mark, "Now it's too risky? You didn't think it was too risky when you accepted my money in Boise. Did you? Oh, no. In Boise, Mark Wilson was an expert kayaker who swaggered around like a gorilla with balls of steel the size of grapefruit.

But now that you're here on the river, what happens? I'll tell you what happens. Those big grapefruit have shriveled down to the size of two little peas, haven't they?"

Mark was squirming, nervously glancing sidelong at his kayak buddies, trying to think of something to say, hoping to God she wouldn't bring up what happened last night, when she and her looney partner trussed him up like a chicken and wouldn't let him loose for hours, threatening him with whips and riding crops if he didn't do better today on the river. He was trying to think of some way to distract her attention, but Claudette wasn't waiting. She laid into him again, "What's with you and your friends? Are you macho men, or pansies? Get your butts in your kayaks and let's make a movie!"

Mark didn't budge, and neither did any of his friends. After sulking a few minutes, he walked over to the edge of the river and pointed upstream. "That is what's with me," he said to Claudette. "That would be a Class V rapid, maybe a VI, without any logjams in it. But just look at it! It's full of logs."

"Dodge them, you idiot," Claudette said.

"Dodge them? Are you kidding? That first drop up there is almost ten feet, into the worst hole I've ever seen. That hole is gonna eat anything that goes in it. And then, the hole washes out into a logjam that stretches almost all the way across the river. To miss that first logjam would require an incredible move. And then, it all starts over. More holes, more drops, two more logjams, and other individual logs stuck in the rapid everywhere you look. That's not a rapid out there, that's a liquid forest."

"Look! Look!"

It was Claudette's partner in cinema verite, Peter Clancy, pointing upstream. He ran over to Claudette. "Look, on the horizon line. It's a helmet."

And so it was. One of the kayakers had screwed up his courage and decided to tackle the rapid. Or so Claudette thought, until she counted the stunt kayakers. All of them, all six, were standing in a tight huddle, pointing upstream at the unidentified boater.

Clancy was saying, "Who the hell is it?"

"Never mind who it is," Claudette said. "Get those cameras ready!"

* * * * *

At the top of the massive rapid, the *River Master* himself had caught the last possible eddy, in the lee of a log jammed between underwater rocks. The log was actually an entire tree, a ponderosa pine, which broke through the river's surface at a forty-five degree angle and jutted upstream, serving as a forbidding sentinel.

Amy was a hundred feet upriver, in another small eddy, watching Bo like a hawk, to see which way he moved when he left the eddy. Thirty feet downstream of him, the river boiled over a steep drop and exploded. From his vantage point, he couldn't see the bottom of the drop. He braced against the log, which was trembling with the force of the current, and raised himself as far above the water as he could, peering downstream, and caught sight, a hundred yards down on the right bank, of what he needed to see: *cameras!*

* * * * *

"Get ready!" Claudette shouted to her camera operators.

Amidst a flurry of strokes, they observed the paddler appear on the lip of the churning drop and, seemingly, pause there for a split second, reading downstream conditions, before plunging over, paddle lofted high.

"It's a dumb canoe!" one of the stunt kayakers was shouting. "Get it outta there! That ain't canoe water. Only kayaks can run water like that."

Claudette was shrieking. Yelling. Excitedly jumping up and down. She screamed, "Come on down! Come on down!"

The boat completely disappeared in the maw of the first drop. And then shot skyward like a banana rocket. It plopped down with an enormous splash, turned over, rolled up.

And then the paddler made a move that nobody on the bank had ever witnessed, executing a barrel-roll ferry that propelled his boat halfway across the river, upstream of the biggest logjam. At the conclusion of the ferry, the paddler took the next drop backwards, disappeared for a moment, popped to the surface upside down, rolled up in a flash, and deliberately dove into a recirculating hydraulic in the middle of the rapid.

Peter Clancy dropped to his knees, hands clasped into fists, raising them to heaven. "We have our star! We have our star! Action footage at last! Who is that man?"

Claudette Remey looked at the kayakers. "You're fired," she shouted. She was gesticulating wildly. "Get out of my sight, you ball-less wonders!"

Clancy was screaming again, "Look, look, look!"

Upstream, a red kayak sailed over the introductory drop, disappeared, and then rolled up, perilously close to the first logjam. Backstroking past the obstruction, the paddler deftly executed a one-eighty turn and took the next drop with impunity. The kayak turned again, now facing upstream, and eased backward into the midstream hydraulic. As the kayak came into the hole from upstream, the canoe paddler backed out, pivoted his boat, and made an impossible move between the remaining two logjams, exiting the worst of the rapid on the far side of the river. Glimpsing a row of cameras strewn along the river right bank, the paddler stashed his paddle under his front flotation bag and commenced waving and smiling at the lenses. He was concentrating so hard on the cameras that he forgot where he was, flushed into the big rapid's Class IV outwash, and quickly disappeared around the bend downstream, still smiling and waving.

Clancy was yelling to him, "Come back! Come back! Where ya going?"

Claudette was screaming at the camera operators, and pointing frantically toward the kayak paddler. "Forget the canoe," she shouted, "and shoot this one. This one! Shoot this one!" She was madly beckoning for the kayak paddler to come over to river right, where the film crew was congregated. When Amy paddled over, Claudette and Peter Clancy rushed down to the water's edge.

Clancy was out of breath from the short scramble down the rocky bank, sucking air, from too many days at the Beaver Creek Lodge, too many days at Laguna Beach. He looked at Amy and gasped: "She's a woman!" He turned to Claudette, grabbed her arm and pointed at Amy. "She's a woman," he said again.

Claudette growled at him, "You just now recognizing that? You oaf."

Amy was laughing. Claudette joined in. Both of them laughing at Peter Clancy. Amy tugged at her helmet, and got it off finally. She had her hair in a long braid, and it plopped down on her left shoulder, very long and shiny, where it uncurled, and snaked down her chest over the life jacket she was wearing.

Claudette clapped her hands together. "Yes," she said. Raising her hands now in a gesture of victory. "Yes, you are the one. The next star. The next action hero. Look at her, Peter. Look at that face. Have you ever seen such a face? The complexion is perfect, the eyes, the high cheekbones, the full, sexy lips. Oh God, the lips! It is a perfect face, no? But yes, it is. And a perfect braid, too." She leaned over, stroked the braid. Took it in her hand and stroked it again. And looked over her shoulder at Peter Clancy. "Have you ever seen such a braid?" Clancy was pulling his own scraggly piglet over his shoulder, looking at it with a pained expression.

Claudette turned her attention back to Amy. "I'm Claudette Remey, and this is Peter Clancy, of Remey-Clancy Enterprises. As you can see . . . " She gestured to the camera crew. " . . . we are making a movie. What we need is a great paddler who is photogenic, and you certainly fill the bill. If you can act a little, too, that would be a bonus." She paused to take another look at Amy, forming an estimate of her hidden assets. She said, "I'm betting you have everything it takes. I can give you a screen test right here on the bank. You got nothing to lose. What do you say?"

Amy hooked her thumb downstream. "That guy's a better paddler than I am. He taught me everything I know. And he's been trying to break into the movies for years. Why don't you talk to him?"

"Who was that wild man?" Peter asked.

Amy said, "That was Eugene (Bo) Rocker. Some people say he's the best there ever was."

"Yes," Claudette replied icily. "We know Mister Rocker."

"He said you were old friends."

Claudette replied: "But for some reason I seem to remember him by another name. What was it, now? Oh, yes, I believe it was 'Bonehead.' "

Peter was rubbing his piglet, and looking covetously at Amy's long dark braid.

"Men," Claudette added, while giving Peter a deprecati. glance, "are not reliable. When you need them most, they run out on you. We once tried to work with Mister Bonehead. We thought we could make him into the next Walt Blackadar, but we were wrong. He was uncooperative. And unreliable. And undependable. Like all men. But that is water under the bridge. And besides, it's time Hollywood found a believable female action hero. And you babe, could be the lucky girl. What's your name?"

"Amy."

"Amy what?"

"Amy Reynolds."

"Change that to Amy Cascade," Peter said. "It's perfect." He raised his hands, forming that imaginary grand marquee in the sky. "I can see it now, your name up in lights: 'Amy Cascade: Female Action Star. Amy Cascade: femme fatale nonpareil.' "

Claudette said, "Crawl out of that boat, Amy Cascade, and let's talk."

Amy shook her head, and looked downstream for Bo. He was nowhere in sight. She said, "Thanks a lot Ms Remey, and you too, Mister Clancy, but acting's not my bag."

Claudette said, "But how do you know acting's not your bag? Have you seriously thought about it?"

And to that question, Amy had to admit that she'd never given it any thought, one way or the other. But it really didn't matter at this point; she had to go. Bo was waiting, somewhere downstream.

She donned her helmet, tucked in her magnificent braid, bid them adieu against their repeated protests, and prepared to peel out into the surging current.

Claudette said, "Think about it, Ms Cascade. If you change your mind, let's talk. I can make you a star!"

* * * * *

A hundred feet downstream, an eddy appeared behind a rock near the river right bank, and Amy dove for it, without understanding why. It was a small eddy, and she had to paddle to stay in it. With each stroke, her boat would surge and buck with the power of the water, and she would wonder anew why she had stopped in the eddy.

She looked over her shoulder and still couldn't spot Bo anywhere downstream. She knew he was around the bend somewhere, waiting, probably concerned by now that something had happened to her. Looking upriver, she could see cameras, a half dozen of them, all pointed at her. She couldn't help but smile. All those cameras. All that film. How would it feel to actually see yourself, smiling of course, on a silver screen forty feet high? When you really think about it, it's enough to blow your mind. No wonder the Hollywood stars all get bloated egos.

And now Claudette Remey and Peter Clancy were climbing atop a boulder and waving to her. Peter Clancy was blowing kisses and motioning for her to come back.

And somewhere inside her head, in some corner of her brain that she never even knew existed, a thought formed and wouldn't go away. And the thought was so appealing, she had to give it expression, to say it aloud, to hear the words roll off her tongue, to savor the delicious residue on her lips: "Amy Cascade, action hero . . . movie star!"

Yes, she thought, as she darted for the river right bank. *Yes!*